NAME OF
THE DEVIL

ALSO BY ANDREW MAYNE

ANGEL KILLER

BOURBON
STREET
BOOKS

An Imprint of HarperCollinsPublishers

NAME OF THE DEVIL

A JESSICA BLACKWOOD NOVEL

ANDREW MAYNE

BOURBON STREET BOOKS

NAME OF THE DEVIL. Copyright © 2015 by Andrew Mayne. All rights reserved. Printed in the United States of America. No part of this book may be used or reproduced in any manner whatsoever without written permission except in the case of brief quotations embodied in critical articles and reviews. For information address HarperCollins Publishers, 195 Broadway, New York, NY 10007.

HarperCollins books may be purchased for educational, business, or sales promotional use. For information please e-mail the Special Markets Department at SPsales@ harpercollins.com.

FIRST EDITION

Library of Congress Cataloging-in-Publication Data

Mayne, Andrew, 1973–

Name of the Devil : a Jessica Blackwood novel / Andrew Mayne. — First edition.

pages ; cm

ISBN 978-0-06-234889-0 (pbk. : alk. paper) — ISBN 978-0-06-234890-6 (ebook)

I. Title.

PS3613.A962N36 2015

813'.6—dc23

2015004791

15 16 17 18 19   OV/RRD   10 9 8 7 6 5 4 3 2 1

To my parents, James and Patricia

What the eyes sees, the ear hears, and the mind believes.

HARRY HOUDINI

NAME OF

THE DEVIL

"You know what you have to do," said the distant voice at the other end of the phone.

Sheriff Jessup nodded. Moonlight glinted off the cars parked in front of the small church: the Alsops' rusted Jeep, Bear McKnight's new pickup truck, Reverend Curtis's Cadillac that had been a bequest from Elena Partridge when she passed. All of them were here.

He was here.

Jessup was a powerful man. Six-foot-three, weighing close to three hundred pounds, he was more muscle than fat. The teenagers and wise-asses in town gave him a wide berth. His handcuffs usually stayed on his belt. One grip of his iron fingers on your collar and you knew you were up against a force of nature.

The occasional fool who tried to outrun the sheriff found out the former high school football player who could sprint with the best of the track team hadn't lost much speed with age.

Jessup walked up the stone steps to the church and entered the doorway. Adam Alsop turned in the pew where he was sitting next to his wife and watched with confusion as Jessup bolted the door shut.

"Carson?" asked Adam, calling the sheriff by his first name.

Natalie Alsop, with her gray hair pulled back in a bun and the same tired eyes as everyone else, froze when she saw the ferocity of the sheriff's expression.

Reverend Curtis and Bear McKnight were huddled at the lectern turning the pages of the church's oversized Bible.

"Christ," McKnight said as he saw the sheriff.

Jessup walked first toward the Alsops. Adam was paralyzed with panic as the sheriff clenched his neck, thick fingers stabbing into his throat. His wife tried pulling at Jessup's thickly corded arm, but was backhanded so hard her head cracked against the wooden pew, knocking her out cold.

McKnight ran toward Jessup to intervene. His heavy footsteps were the only other sound in the hall besides the gurgling noise coming from Adam Alsop's mouth as he tried to breathe.

Reverend Curtis hurried to the back of the church, toward the fire exit he'd reluctantly installed after the fire marshal had demanded it. His frantic hands pulled at the crossbar. The door wouldn't open. Something was blocking it from the outside.

Curtis turned back as Sheriff Jessup grabbed McKnight by the arms and bit into his shoulder, tearing away a mouthful of flesh. Even more shocking than the savage act was the cold dispassionate look in the sheriff's eyes. It was the lifeless stare of a great white shark on the hunt. A predator that didn't see another life, only something to be eaten.

McKnight screamed and dropped, falling next to Adam's body. He tried to cover the wound with his hand, but the blood kept pumping relentlessly through his fingers until the cold, tingling sensation of consciousness fading overcame him.

Jessup kicked him aside and strode down the aisle dividing the pews. His boots left prints in the growing puddle of blood. Shreds of McKnight's shoulder muscles and skin still hung from his mouth, his face misted with arterial spray.

"Carson . . . Carson," pleaded the reverend. "I can help you. I can help you rid yourself of this . . . this thing." He fell onto his knees, hands grasped over his head in prayer.

Sheriff Jessup looked down. "Rid me of the thing? Rid me?"

His vacant expression broke for a moment. He grabbed the reverend by the back of the jacket and pulled him to his feet. "I am the cleansing fire! I'm the one ridding you of the evil!" Spittle flew from his mouth, a sputtering teakettle on the verge of exploding.

Reverend Curtis futilely kicked and punched. In an act of desperation he clawed at the large man's cheek. But the deep gouges didn't even faze Carson Jessup.

Jessup punched back, breaking the smaller man's nose. He pounded again and again until the entire bridge collapsed, sharp fragments of bone embedded into his raw fist like pieces of coral.

The reverend fell to the ground in a bloody heap. The whistling sound of his breath through what was left of his nose faded.

Sheriff Jessup pulled the phone from his pocket. "It's done."

The phone had been dead for days, yet the sheriff heard a voice tell him, "Good, my son."

He closed his eyes and waited for the fire to cleanse away the wickedness and evil.

On his knees, he folded his hands and thanked the guiding archangel for showing him a clear path. He thanked the Lord for the strength to do His bidding. He thanked God for bringing this long nightmare to an end.

WHEN THE EXPLOSION ripped through the church, a sleep-deprived grad student at the Seismology Lab at the University of West Virginia jerked upright in his chair, spilling his coffee as his computer sounded an alarm. His first reaction to the sudden spike was that there had been a plane crash, or a meteor strike.

The residents of rural Hawkton ran outside to see the source of the explosion and were horrified to see the huge ball of flame rise from the direction of the old church, a bright orange plume against a plum-colored evening sky. Some felt it was an end to

the darkness that had enveloped the town. Others suspected that
the darkness had only just begun.

A CONTINENT AWAY, Father Carmichael sat lost in thought
as he studied a nineteenth-century letter from a cavalry officer
serving in Napoleon's North African campaign. The officer had
found an inscription assumed to have been archaic Hebrew. The
location of the inscription, Carmichael deduced, was now lost,
very likely under a parking lot or apartment building. He turned
the page, and as the paper disturbed the stale air of his basement
reading room he noticed the smell of cigarette smoke.

Carmichael looked up and saw a man perched in the corner,
watching him. Behind the orange glow of the man's cigarette
was a tan face worn with wrinkles, and intense, piercing eyes.
Gray hair at his temples blended into blue-black. Dressed in a
dark suit, suitable for a Brussels banker, he was clearly not a visiting priest. He had the presence of someone who cared little about
smoke alarms or the effect the smoke had on old books.

How the man had been able to find him down here in the
labyrinth was a feat unto itself. Carmichael liked the old reading room below the Biblioteca Nazionale Centrale di Firenze in
Florence, Italy, because it wasn't on any map.

He felt himself a kindred spirit of the man who had founded
it some three hundred years prior. Antonio Magliabechi lived
and breathed words. He was reputed to have read every one of
his forty thousand books and been able to recall them in great
detail, yet he paid so little attention to worldly matters that his
threadbare clothes would fall apart on his body.

It was through this lens of history that French Lieutenant
Chambliss was speaking to Carmichael, after a fact. The library's
surroundings gave him a different context to examine these letters. Touching them was like stepping into the past.

Like his hero, Carmichael could be entirely oblivious to the world beyond the page. He'd no idea when the man had entered the room, but attributed the apparition to his mindlessness and not any stealthy intent on the man's behalf.

"You're the Mandean scholar," the man stated in English.

Carmichael had written some papers on the language and belief system of the ancient Gnostics of the Middle East. While he didn't consider himself an expert, he wasn't going to argue with his strange visitor. "Yes. I guess."

The man nodded. He reached his hand inside his jacket and pulled out an envelope and placed it on Carmichael's table. His raised eyebrow indicated Carmichael should look inside.

Carmichael slid the photograph out of the envelope. His cheeks flushed. Bottle-blond hair, a mischievous smile; he recognized the girl immediately. She was a friend of his cousin. A girl he'd met a few months ago in Austria. Carmichael had been drinking heavily that day. The innocent flirtation had turned into something more . . .

Shame wracked his guilt-trained mind. He'd confessed a week later, after much anguish. Not to his usual confessor, but to a priest in a small parish near San Marino. He didn't fear divine wrath as much as he did the long ears of the Vatican.

"I . . ." Carmichael began, not sure where the words would lead him.

The man in the corner raised a finger and wiped away the words with a gesture. His large hand reached out and landed on the photograph, concealing it from view as he slipped it back into his pocket and away from Carmichael's conscience.

There was something symbolic about the gesture. Carmichael vaguely understood there was to be no more discussion on the matter of the girl. He waited.

"Discretion can be a virtue," the man said.

Carmichael nodded.

"You have mine, and I would like yours."

"Of course." Carmichael's knee began to shake under the table.

The man reached into his other jacket pocket and removed a portable cassette recorder. He set it on the table next to Carmichael's pad of paper and pencil.

"I need the words," said the man. "Just the words. After the words, you're to forget about this. Understood?"

"Yes . . ." Carmichael said, hesitantly.

The man's stare lingered, turning Carmichael's acquiescence into a verbal contract.

Carmichael pressed the play button and held the speaker to his ear. The voice seemed half asleep, or in a trance. The words at first sounded like Hebrew, but they weren't. This language shared a common ancestral tongue, but had diverged a thousand years before; the closest version still spoken would be Syriac. This was different. This was a version of Aramaic—the language spoken by the Jews in Jerusalem in Jesus's time.

Understanding spoken Aramaic is a challenge because there are no living native speakers. The closest approximation comes from analyzing Syriac, Hebrew dialects and a few other variations. There are maybe a hundred people in the world who could speak conversationally in Aramaic. While computer translation allows anyone to read the words, comprehension is a different matter. Something told Carmichael that the man in his reading room preferred a more thoughtful interpretation.

Carmichael's nervous fingers fumbled with the machine as he replayed the tape to check his phonetic transcription. He had understood the words on the first pass, but wanted to be absolutely certain. He was also distracted by the speaker.

The man took the sheet of paper from Carmichael, quietly read the translation, then pocketed it along with the cassette recorder. He straightened the creases in his slacks and stood. "This never happened," he said flatly.

There was something about the man that implied there would be no choice but to agree.

Carmichael waited for the man to leave. After his footsteps faded down the miles of bookshelves, the young priest leaned back in his chair and stared at the ceiling and breathed for the first time in what felt like an eternity.

The Austrian girl, Anya, was the furthest thing from his thoughts. The words on the tape recorder echoed through his mind as clearly as they had when he first heard them.

I am the one who walks in darkness. I am the one who is fallen.

THESE WERE NOT the words of a disciple of God. These were declarations of evil. These were the proclamations of a demon in a religious text. This was the voice of Lucifer, or another fallen angel.

But by themselves, the words weren't anything extraordinary. Not in this day and age. He'd recently watched his nephew, Pietro, play a video game featuring an antagonist who spoke in a demonic style. Carmichael only had to turn on the radio to hear a thousand sung phrases like that, or watch them uttered on television. This was different.

Context was everything.

The speaker on the tape had used an almost forgotten tongue, and he was also someone Carmichael knew—a man that, to Carmichael's knowledge, could not speak Aramaic, Syriac or even Hebrew.

Anyone could have memorized the words. But they had no business coming out of the mouth of a man of the cloth.

Least of all the mouth of the Vicar of Christ, the Bishop of Rome, His Holiness the Pope.

FEAR

I REMEMBER THE FIRST time I experienced fear. Not a child's fear of a scary noise outside the window or an unexpected face. Real fear, the fear a young girl feels when she sees the faces of adults around her as they realize that they are no longer in control—even though they're telling her that things are going to be okay, she can see the lie in their eyes and hear the hesitation in their voices.

The old black Buick didn't scare me, not at first. I was seven and had been told countless times to look out for creepers and other weirdos. As a kid, though, this was an abstract threat, like germs or mortgages. The car was just a car following me.

I was careful, and smart enough to know this wasn't a good thing, but I wasn't *fearful*. I didn't know what it meant. The fear came later.

By this time, Dad and I had moved back into Grandfather's house and I was going to a small private school on the edge of Beverly Hills. I knew it had been a rough year for Dad, but somehow he found the money to send me there. In the evenings he'd be in the workshop, making magic tricks and collectibles to sell through ads in magic magazines. Grandfather, who prided himself on making his keep as a performer and not by selling his secrets, looked down upon this, but he kept his sarcastic comments to a minimum. He knew Dad was trying his best for my sake.

At seven I was already articulate enough for people to assume I was eleven or twelve. Letting me walk home by myself in my school skirt and Nintendo backpack didn't seem like a bad idea to my dad. Far be it for seven-year-old me to tell him otherwise.

While the other kids were being picked up in Mercedes or minivans driven by nannies, I walked away up the hill toward the sprawling house where we lived.

A mansion that would have looked like a haunted house on a studio back lot if Grandfather hadn't made sure to keep it well-coated in paint, it was set back on a path that wound through overgrown trees and bushes, which took an army of gardeners to tame.

Grandfather cultivated a certain degree of theatricality to impress reporters and other guests. Although overrun was fine, dilapidated was not. The former implied he was an eccentric who wanted his privacy, but the latter suggested he was on the edge of financial despair.

With its pointed spires and steepled roof, the mansion was more medieval Disney than tony Beverly Hills. It was built by one of the first Hollywood studio heads, who had been heavily influenced by the fairytale stories of his native Germany.

I was only blocks away from school when I heard the car's brakes squeal as it came to a stop. With tinted windows almost rolled up, the interior was dark. I saw blue cigar smoke wafting from the small gap between the top of the window and door, then turned back to my walk.

I liked the peace and quiet of my neighborhood. Each front yard seemed like a private diorama built for my own amusement. I almost never saw anyone on the sidewalk or on their lawns. At least not a gardener. I stopped from time to time to stare through the bars, or gaps in the hedges, at some of the more lavish landscapes.

My favorite had a small curved koi pond with a bridge. The

brightly colored fish liked to gather at one end, near a fountain pouring from a cement waterfall, and huddle like a rainbow tied in a knot. Occasionally one would thrash and break the surface, forcing them to line up again in a new pattern. I hadn't yet been to Japan then, but I imagined that this must be what it was like there.

At the end of the block I turned the corner. Walking under the shade of the trees, I passed the house with the large female sphinx surrounded by a circular driveway. Every now and then a heavyset man would be out washing a Rolls-Royce, and he would wave to me as I passed. I'd wave back and continue home.

He wasn't there that day. But the Buick was. It was when the car made another turn shortly after me that I got a little suspicious.

Lots of people drove through the area hoping to see a famous resident, as if they expected Paul Newman to be out mowing his lawn. The funny thing is that it was almost impossible to tell the vacant houses from the ones that were lived-in. If people went outside, it was almost always in their backyards.

The low rumble of the car engine was making me anxious so I picked up my pace, but tried not to make it too obvious. Eyes forward, I listened carefully. I was all set to run if I heard a door open. In class they'd told us the tricks a pervert might use: that he was lost, that he knew our parents. (I had retorts to all of them. Logic told me the best response would be to just get away.)

At random, I picked a back alley that ran between the big avenues fronting the houses. This was a side road the garbage men took, or where the 'help' would unload groceries. Hardly anyone else ever used it.

I didn't have to look back to know the Buick had followed me. The sound of the engine echoed down the back fences along the alley.

In my still-innocent mind, I thought of a million reasons why someone could be following me. Maybe it was a friend of Dad's or Grandfather's who was lost. It didn't matter.

At the end of one lot a long hedge ran perpendicular from the street to the avenue in front. The wall of the neighboring mansion was only a foot away, forming a dark, narrow corridor. I was certain rats, raccoons and other nasty creatures used it as an expressway to the trashcans. But it didn't matter. I ducked into the passage and ran toward the other end.

Behind me, the Buick's brakes let out a high-pitched noise as the car rolled to a stop. I could feel the eyes of the driver looking at me from behind the tinted glass. I didn't turn back. I sprinted toward the keyhole of light at the end of the path. A twig, sticking out like a skeletal finger, scraped my cheek. My blouse and skirt were covered with dry leaves.

I kept going until I reached the road that led to our block.

I slipped through the bars of the huge wrought-iron gates at the end of our driveway and clambered up it to safety.

Out of sight and no longer a threat in my mind, the Buick became just one adventure among others in that particular day. It was just one more anecdote, like when Hayley Siegel announced to our class that her sister had got her period the day before. None of us knew what it meant, but it seemed like a big deal when she said it. From the entryway, I heard voices in the back kitchen and found Grandfather and Dad sitting around the large wooden table, looking at sketches for a new illusion Grandfather wanted to add to the show.

"Hey, kiddo," said my dad, not looking up.

"Looks like you rolled your way home," Grandfather remarked before crossing out something on the sheet of paper.

I poured myself a glass of milk, then scooped in some chocolate powder. Being careful to not hit the spoon against the side of the glass and get myself shushed for overzealous mixing, or a quip from Grandfather about ruining a martini that I didn't understand, I stirred as quietly as possible before placing the spoon

NAME OF THE DEVIL

in the sink to be washed alongside the glass when I'd finished.

I peered between their hunched shoulders and kept as quiet as I could. They tolerated my presence as long as I avoided interrupting. If I was in a curious mood, that could be only seconds.

Dad traced a line across the page and gave me a quick glance. "Uncle Darius will be coming over tonight."

I hadn't seen Uncle Darius in ages. More lighthearted than either Dad or Grandfather, I always liked having him around the house. Although referred seemingly behind my back, and to his face, as a "fuck-up" by Grandfather, he seemed pretty okay to me. He was fun.

Remembering the kind of thing he should ask as a Dad: "How was school?"

"Hayley Siegel's sister got her period," I replied nonchalantly.

Dad's face grew red. Grandfather let out a chuckle. "Heck of a school you're sending her to."

I knew I'd said something funny, but I didn't get it. Trying to change the conversation, I said, between quiet slurps, "An old black car followed me all the way home. I tried to ditch it in the alley, but it kept following."

Grandfather jerked around to face me. His words came out slowly, as if he were giving me stage directions. "What kind of car?"

I knew the names of dozens of cars from watching Grandfather's mentalism act. I'd even made my own little mnemonic to remember them. My finger made the shape of a shield. "A Buick, I think?"

Dad looked to Grandfather, his eyes wide and his mouth slack. That was the moment I saw it. That was the moment I knew fear.

They knew something I didn't, and that knowledge scared them. My hand grew numb, and the chocolate milk spilled to the floor.

2

BLACK BUICKS AND the novelty of fear were a distant memory to me by the time I visited the Hawkton Hellmouth. By now, fear—usually not mine, but more often my own than I liked—had become a constant element of my work. Hellmouth. The word sticks in my mind. This was how one hyperbolic news site described the scene of the explosion when the first aerial footage became available. It caught on from there. Being here in person, I decide it's a perfectly suitable name.

There's a gaping hole in the earth where the little church once sat. Nervous couples were married there. Crying babies baptized. Worshippers found solace in prayer. Now all those memories have disappeared into a huge maw screaming at the sky.

Splinters of wood litter the surrounding farmland and are even lodged in the branches of the trees. It's as if a toothpick house has been smashed under the heel of an angry giant.

The pilot brings the helicopter higher so that the technician controlling the mounted camera and laser-ranging system can get a different point of view. I can see the screen over his shoulder; the program plotting away thousands of dots to build a 3-D map forensics will use later on to decipher what happened.

It seems farcical to think that all this destruction can be captured into data points and emailed around like cat photos. The devastation, the emotion, the passion behind what

NAME OF THE DEVIL

happened—reduced to digital bits. But that's what a detective does. We see everything as numbered lists. Dispassionate, objective, we have to turn off our emotions and focus on the facts. Truth hides in little details. My instructor at the Academy told us the first thing we have to do at a crime scene is to forget everything we've been told about what happened—focus on the atoms.

"Any sign of our victims?" asks Vonda Mitchum, the lead investigator from the local Bureau office, over the radio.

"Negative," replies Agent Knoll from the seat next to me.

"Try going lower," Mitchum commands, before clicking off our channel.

"That's helpful," grumbles Knoll as he presses his binoculars against the window. Muscular, compact, with a head like a prizefighter, he's as frustrated as me with how the search is progressing.

Five hours in and we don't have any bodies. Traces of blood were found on a few of the planks; that's it on the victims so far. Inside the search perimeter is a truck with blown-out windows that belonged to a man named Bear McKnight. Wedged into the side of the truck is Mr. and Mrs. Alsop's Jeep, also with shattered glass. Reverend Curtis's Cadillac is flipped over entirely, like a belly-up turtle in the mud.

There are four missing persons and a potential fifth. Hawkton's sheriff, Carson Jessup, is nowhere to be found. The nervous deputy can't confirm if the sheriff had cause to go out to the church last night, but his SUV was found parked a half-mile away on a dirt back road.

"You got your map data?" I ask the young technician leaning over his plotting computer.

"I think we got enough," he replies.

"Mind if we take this on a wider search pattern?" I call to the pilot.

"Not much point," says the pilot, Bilson, a sunburned man who was flying for the Bureau while I was in middle school. "We ran the numbers. This is the outer limit of the radius. The debris field ends fifty yards back in."

"I know. I understand the physics. Still . . ." I gaze out the window. Bits of the church's white planks stick out of the brown grass and dull dirt like cat's teeth. "But the physics isn't telling us where the bodies are."

"We got another hour of fuel," says Bilson. "Fine by me." He turns the stick to the left and brings us into a turn. Knoll and I use our binoculars to scan the trees and fields again, hoping to find some sign of whoever was in the church.

We don't want them to be dead. In a perfect world, we'd find them sitting on the porch of a farmhouse drinking beer and smiling up at us, eager to tell the story of how they narrowly escaped death.

This isn't that world. We know there's at least one body, or at least part of a body, to be found. Maybe three or four more, if all the missing were in the church.

Explosions can do different things to the human form. Stand one way, and even a small yield can rip off a limb. Positioned in another, an explosion that could knock down a brick wall might just leave you with only an earache and a mild friction burn.

But bodies usually don't just vaporize. There's nearly always something left. Whether in pieces that have to be picked up with tweezers or ones that can fit into a body bag, our victims are somewhere.

The ground search is going slowly. Every square inch has to be covered in a pattern that gets exponentially larger the farther away you move from the blast. Below me, men and women in blue and yellow clean-suits comb the area for clues. Igniters, bomb components, anything that points to what happened. Even a paperclip can tell a story. They look like astronauts on an alien planet searching for signs of life.

At first glance, the blast looks like a gas explosion. The trouble is that the church wasn't hooked up to a gas line, and it didn't have a tank. Laboratory analysis of the wreckage will give us a clearer picture. Traces of whatever caused the explosion are likely to have squeezed into the wood and fabric of the church. The charred debris can be chemically analyzed to reveal what outside substances were absorbed in the reaction.

The clues are here—at least the clues to what happened physically. But they don't explain how or why.

We have an explosion, but no victims. Just traces. Something tells me there's more to this than just a bomb or a gas explosion.

"Robin 2, why are you going out of the flight pattern?" demands Mitchum on the radio, like a scolding teacher.

"We've decided to extend the search radius," I reply.

"Under whose authority, Agent Blackwood?"

Knoll lowers his binoculars and raises his eyebrows. He mouths the words, "Now you did it."

"Occam's."

Vonda Mitchum is the lead investigator, but not our supervisor. We are assisting because it's crucial to get as much information as possible in the first forty-eight hours. While the helicopter is certainly under her control, treating Knoll and me like underlings is a step beyond what is appropriate.

I decide to cut her a little slack. Obviously she's under pressure. "I apologize for the deviation. I wanted to get another angle and see if there was anything outside the radius."

"The radius is a radius for a reason. Unless you don't believe in physics, or think the victims walked out of there," replies Mitchum.

"I don't think they walked . . ." I ignore her sarcasm.

"You think this looks familiar?" she says, almost as a challenge.

This is her case, and it could be a big one. She's afraid I'm going to take it away from her by tying it into my previous major investigation. The last time I was involved in murder on such a spectacular scale, the perpetrator had been a man who liked to make his crimes look like impossibilities.

"No. I just think if you can't find something where you expect to, you might want to look elsewhere."

"You're wasting resources, Blackwood. Have the pilot return to the LZ."

"Hold up," says Knoll. He points out his window to a pale object in a tree.

I train my binoculars on where he's indicating. Something, or someone, is entangled in the branches. I see what looks like bare skin wrapped in foliage.

"Can you zoom in on that?" I ask the technician in the front seat.

He aims the high-powered camera at the tree and brings it into focus on his laptop screen. There's a vague outline of what could be a body.

We all feel that sick sensation in the pit of our stomach. What hope we had for a happy ending is gone.

"Looks like our first victim," I grimly reply. There's a flicker of guilt through my conscience as I confirm the bad news. Until now, we could still hold on to that version of reality in which they are sitting on that porch, waving at us. Now it's gone. "Send that to Mitchum, and don't forget to include the GPS coordinates."

"Do you have to rub things in?" asks Knoll.

"I don't mean to."

At least, I don't think I do.

3

BEAR MCKNIGHT'S NAKED body is dangling upside down from the upper branches of the elm tree, almost thirty feet in the air. A deep gouge in his shoulder has bled out onto the ground below. His eyes are wide open, gazing at heaven above. Across his chest are smears of blood. They remind me of a child's finger painting.

Special Agent Vonda Mitchum stands outside of the hastily erected perimeter and directs the photographer. Her blond hair tucked under her FBI cap, she taps away on her tablet as Knoll and I approach.

"Who spotted him?" asks Mitchum.

I point my thumb at Knoll. "Eagle-eyes over here."

"Good work, Knoll." She nods to him, then turns back to her screen.

"Blackwood was the one who said we should look over here," replies Knoll.

I give him a sharp look. All that matters is that we found our first victim because we extended the search perimeter. I don't need him rubbing my defiance in Mitchum's face.

"I'm asking our physicist why he got the blast radius wrong," says Mitchum. "We would have figured it out eventually."

"They didn't get it wrong," I reply, hesitantly, unsure if I should bite back my words. "There's no other debris around here. Just this poor bastard."

Mitchum puts away her tablet. "You're saying he was placed here?"

"I'm saying he's here. The debris isn't. Somehow he got here outside of the blast zone." I point to where the chunk was taken from his neck. "He may have survived the blast, but I doubt he climbed up here without his carotid artery."

Mitchum shrugs and calls into her radio for the bucket truck we're using to pick debris out of the trees. In the field just beyond, two techs have finally managed to get the aerial drone working so it can take over for the helicopter. Knoll and I search the earth around the tree for clues.

"Any bets that we're going to find the other four bodies at equidistant points from the blast and each other?" whispers Knoll.

"It's not him," I say sharply, hoping he's wrong.

"He's in jail . . . but he has friends."

"He's not Voldemort," I retort. "He has a name."

"The Warlock," says Knoll.

"No. Heywood."

"That's an alias."

"It's a man's name. Not some super-villain title from a comic book. He's in jail in Texas awaiting trial. You know this because since we caught him, we've spent more time in depositions than actually solving crimes," I reply tersely. "This has nothing to do with him."

"I never said it did."

"You implied the other bodies might form a pentagram, insinuating he was involved."

Knoll holds up his hands. "All I suggested was a pentagram."

I roll my eyes. "And I guess the logical conclusion you're suggesting is that Ozzy Osbourne did it?"

Knoll lets out a sigh. "Wouldn't this search be easier for you if you did it from your broom?"

"I'm armed," I growl

"So am . . ." Knoll reflexively reaches for his holster to make sure I haven't pickpocketed his gun. I've only done that to him once or twice, but that was enough. He finds it on his hip and shakes his head. "And you wonder why you don't have many friends."

I give him a half smile and keep walking as I think about what he just said. It's a joke between colleagues, but it stings because it has the worst possible element of a burn: a kernel of truth.

We come to a stop in front of a large elm tree, similar to the one in which Knoll spotted McKnight. The first branch is about five feet off the ground. At the base of the branch there's a moist crack, as if someone recently put weight on it and then let up when it began to break.

Knoll sees this and whistles to one of the agents holding the tape and sticks we use to rope off areas for close-up inspection. We pen the tree around the outside the radius of its furthest branches.

"Vantage point?" asks Knoll.

I shake my head. "I think whoever placed McKnight in the tree may have taken a first attempt here. When the branch started to break, he tried over there."

Knoll nods. "Carried or pulled?"

"I couldn't guess. The autopsy will show us markings suggesting one or the other. Infrared can spot internal bruising under the skin."

"What if they come up empty?"

"I'll worry about that when it happens. Or rather, Mitchum will." It's her case, after all.

We duck as the drone flies overhead. It weaves through the trees at high speed and vanishes into the woods. Inside a control trailer sitting on the side of the road, a technician watches the live feed from its camera for the other victims. It's a morbid video game.

An hour later, three more bodies have been found: Those of the Alsops and Reverend Curtis. Sheriff Jessup is still a no-show. I don't let on to Knoll how relieved I am that the bodies were not found in anything that looks like an intentionally symmetrical pattern; I can tell he has been watching my reaction out of the corner of his eye. The tension releases from my neck muscles the moment we're certain of that. We don't need a replay of what happened before. There are already enough loose ends.

Like McKnight, our other victims are found upside down and naked in the trees. After Mitchum vanishes to inspect the other victims, Knoll and I hop into the bucket to look at McKnight up close.

From the ground it's hard to see anything other than his pale skin, crusted blood covering his body and part of his face. Up close, we can see scratch marks and bruises: The signs of struggle.

The worst part is the lingering scent of melted body hair. Burns on his skin prove that he's been close to an intense source of heat, most likely an explosion. Bits of fabric are singed into his skin, suggesting he'd been clothed when the church ignited.

"At least we know they weren't nudists," replies Knoll, eyeing a scrap of denim welded to McKnight's left thigh.

Something about the blood smears on McKnight's chest is odd. They appear haphazard at first, the kind of marks someone might make in a state of shock when they repeatedly touch their body. As I stare at them, though, they seem intentional. But there's no obvious pattern. I take a photo to look at later.

Knoll nudges me, then points to the man's forehead. There's a smear of ash above McKnight's nose, almost obscured by blood.

I radio Mitchum. "Which victim are you looking at?"

"Mrs. Alsop."

"Is there ash on her forehead?"

"Blackwood, is this a joke? There was an explosion. Of course there's ash."

I push my head past the protective bars of the lift to get a closer look at McKnight's face. The whole bucket arm begins to sway in the breeze. Knoll grabs the rail and groans.

I push the talk button on my radio, "On the forehead. It's hard to see on McKnight because of the blood from the scalp. But it looks like there's ash under the blood. Like a cross. Does Mrs. Alsop have the same marking?"

"Hold on," says Mitchum. There's a long pause. "Affirmative. But they were in a church, after all."

"They're not Catholics, and this wasn't Ash Wednesday. This is the kind of thing someone does to ward off evil spirits."

"You're saying they were afraid of something evil happening?" Mitchum is dubious.

"I'm saying they were afraid, and obviously something very bad did happen."

Mitchum doesn't respond.

I put my radio back in its holster and look again at McKnight's chest. There's something deliberate about the bloody daubs there. On my phone, I pull up the image and flip it to how it would look right-side up. It still doesn't ring any bells.

Knoll watches over my shoulder. "Think it's something?"

"Maybe. Either way, it doesn't look random."

"It could have happened when he was moved."

"Yeah. I don't know." I notice McKnight's left index finger is covered in blood. "Check this out," I say, pointing.

"He used his own blood to write the symbol? All right, maybe it does mean something."

"But what? Hold on." I sit on the edge of the rail and lean back, my feet tucked behind the lower guard. A ground technician stares up at me as I dangle over the edge of the lift.

"You're a goddamn circus ape," exclaims Knoll as he grabs my ankles.

Upside down, staring up at the sky, I see the world as a dying

Bear McKnight did. If he wanted to write on his chest to tell us something, he would go from left to right. I pull myself back into the lift, to Knoll's relief, and take out my phone. Using the rotate button, I spin the image two more times. When the lines are going in the correct direction, it starts looking like something familiar. A runny, bloody mess, but one I latch on to. I remember from school that the letter "A" is supposed to be a sideways ox or something. An aleph. One way it's an "A," another and it's an animal. This isn't an ox, though.

"Is there a Hebrew keyboard on these phones?" I ask. The aleph is still a widely used symbol in Hebrew. Before Knoll can answer, I find it hidden in the settings menu. I look for the closest match to the symbols on his chest, and type them into a search engine. Of course, the results are all in Hebrew and make no sense to me. Well, duh. I'm not sure what I was expecting.

"Check the image search," offers Knoll.

I pull up the first image associated with the letters, and a ghoulish face stares back at me.

The letters spell out a word.

לְזָאזֵע

The name of a demon.

4

"So your theory is that these people were killed by a demon?" Vonda Mitchum looks up from the image I just showed her and turns to Knoll as if I'm invisible.

"No," I insist, ignoring her slight. "I'm saying McKnight traced this on his chest, in his own blood, before he died."

"It looks like gibberish to me." She points to the upside-down body.

"That's because it's upside-down Hebrew letters, which are of course written right to left."

"Turn it another way and I'm sure you'll find a different random match." She hands the phone back to me.

"In what? Klingon?"

"I think it's random," she says. "You're trying to make something fit."

"If it was the name of the 1986 NBA Championship team, I'd still think it's relevant," I reply.

"You're not pinning this on Larry Bird," interjects Knoll, trying to diffuse the tension.

"Men," Mitchum and I say at the same time. She cracks a smile. The awkwardness between us is broken briefly.

The spontaneous moment changes my mood. "Listen, I know it's nutty. I know it's out of left field. But these people were in a church, and maybe they were performing some kind of ceremony. I think it's worth noting."

"Noted."

I raise an eyebrow.

"Agent Blackwood, I'll put it in my case notes. All right?" It's her way of making a compromise.

"And the broken branch?"

"I'll see what I can do." She forces a smile and walks back to the forensic technicians working on the tree where Mrs. Alsop was found.

Although she was found like McKnight, there are no symbols on Mrs. Alsop. Knoll stands back and studies her outstretched hands.

"Know what it looks like?"

"Upside-down crucifixion. Isn't that what they did to you when you were a really, really awful person?"

Knoll checks his watch. "It's what my wife is going to do to me if I don't get back before the kids head to school in the morning."

"You're leaving tonight?" I ask.

"While you were obsessing over that image, they released us. I got a desk full of kidnappings to look over. You got work too."

"Yeah. I know."

"Leave it to Mitchum. She doesn't make the same leaps as you. But she's methodical. You need a ride?"

"I'll catch one tomorrow in the van. I want to watch the debrief tonight."

Knoll rolls his eyes. "Leave some work for the rest of us."

THREE HOURS LATER, after grabbing a tuna sandwich at a convenience store and switching blouses in the bathroom, I'm sitting in the back row of the county civic auditorium as Mitchum lays out what we've learned so far to a roomful of local law enforcement and agents from the West Virginia Bureau of Investigation, ATF, local FBI, as well as the remaining stragglers from DC and Quantico, like me.

She's a confident speaker. A bit monotonous, perhaps to cover up a fear of not being taken seriously, but still authoritative. "We believe the time of the blast was around ten at night. The damage initially looks similar to that caused by a gas explosion. The blast pushed out all parts of the structure equally. Although no tank or pipeline has been found, it could well be the case that there's a gas cylinder we haven't found, sitting in a field somewhere, that went ballistic.

"We've found four victims so far. Their vehicles were parked outside of the church. Some of them show burns and other postmortem trauma indicating proximity to the blast. It's still unclear if they were inside or outside the church when it happened.

"Preliminary cause of death for all the victims seem to be the explosion, although there are anomalous signs of trauma that make this suspect. We're awaiting autopsy results.

"While it's too early to say whether this was accidental or intentional, much less infer a motive, the presence of Sheriff Jessup's vehicle nearby does suggest there might be something to look into. In the last eighteen months there have been two explosive-related attacks on local law enforcement nationwide. We're looking into the possibility that Jessup may have been the intended target here. WVBI is going through court records and cross-referencing them with possible suspects.

"Again, let me emphasize this could still be an accidental explosion. We expect more information tomorrow when we get the preliminary autopsy report. I've emailed you a document detailing all of the evidence we've accumulated so far."

As Mitchum takes a question from a WVBI agent about jurisdiction, I pull up the evidence log on my laptop. For expediency's sake, she's indexed inclusions by agent name.

I find mine and see my photograph of the symbol on McKnight's chest. There's no mention of the other tree and its broken branch.

I pull up Knoll's notes. There's nothing there either, but I give her the benefit of the doubt. The information is still very recent and there hasn't been a chance to catalog everything.

However, on the crime-scene map where numbers cross-reference specific locations with what was found there, McKnight's tree is clearly annotated—but not the other tree. She left it out intentionally.

The tree with the broken branch could be crucial. We have no idea what happened, let alone what's important and what isn't. Leaving it out as an oversight is sloppiness. Leaving it out to spite me is incompetence.

I wait for Mitchum to call the briefing to a close, then approach her at the lectern. She's going through a binder with a local case supervisor.

"Agent Mitchum?"

"Yes, Blackwood," she replies without looking up.

"The damaged branch Knoll and I found. I don't see that in the evidence log."

"It's a large forest, Blackwood. We don't have the ability to cover every fallen leaf or disturbed bird's nest."

I ignore her tone. "I understand that. But everyone in this room knows this wasn't an accident. The body placement rules that out."

"We can't assume anything."

"There could be something else critical there, like fibers."

"The tree isn't going away," she replies.

It feels pointless to mention to her that any evidence could deteriorate, or get carried away by wildlife. The potential for crime-scene contamination alone already makes admissibility a challenge.

She gives me another of her forced smiles. "I included your devil theory."

There's something behind her statement that I don't trust. According to this entire preliminary report, my one contribution was saying the bloody smears on McKnight's chest kind of, *sort of*, look like the name of a demon in Hebrew. No mention of my pushing to extend the search parameter. No mention of that possible first tree and what it might mean.

Vonda Mitchum is writing me off as a crackpot. In the final report, I'll literally be chasing ghosts.

I walk away before I say something that will get me in trouble. Field FBI agents take their jobs seriously and don't like interlopers telling them how to do things, any more than anyone else would. And I get it. Being from FBI headquarters doesn't necessarily make you more of an expert than someone who has spent twenty years in the field. In fact, some would argue that being so close to bureaucracy can make you ignorant of the real world.

I don't blame Mitchum for being suspicious of an outsider's motives. I do blame her for trying to excise me from the report for the sole purpose of making me look bad.

In the parking lot I take a deep breath of twilight air and try to calm myself. Mitchum has a million things to worry about. There's no agenda, I reassure myself. Although I suspect she's trying to make this her career case at my expense.

I don't care about a pat on the back. Just ask Knoll about the Warlock case. I made the key breaks, but I insisted he get the credit for his direction. All I want is to get the bad guys. It's why I became a cop. It's not for the paperwork, or the paper commendations. It's to make the world right.

A raindrop falls on my crossed arms. I watch the water soak into the fabric of my jacket. Another falls.

It's going to rain.

It's going to rain, and whatever evidence that may be on that tree could be washed away.

It's dark. It's cold. The other agents and cops are running to their cars to get home or back to their hotels.

The one coworker I'd trust to follow me on a stupid quest has just gone home.

I groan.

I'm going to have to do this alone.

5

THUNDERCLOUDS RUMBLE OVERHEAD as I hop out of a borrowed motor pool car and run across the meadow to the line of trees where we found McKnight. His body and the tree limb he was found on were removed hours ago. A solitary work light and generator keep vigil over the plastic-covered tree, which looks like some kind of alien artifact. The crime scene that isn't a crime scene, according to Mitchum, is a few hundred feet away in the shadows. My feet slip in the wet grass as I try to beat the downpour, and I almost land on my ass.

My tree is somewhere in the woods, but there's enough glow in the sky to find it. I try to put on my clean-suit as I run so I don't contaminate the scene. If I do find anything, I don't want some forensic tech pulling one of my long black hairs out of an evidence bag.

I reach the base of the tree and slip my feet into the booties that are supposed to keep me from tracking in outside dirt. The second-lowest branch, the one that isn't broken, is a few inches higher. I leap for it, and muscles I haven't used since high school gym start to ache. Yoga didn't prepare me for this.

Somehow, I pull myself onto the second branch and steady myself against the trunk in a crouch. My slick slippers want to glide right off the wet surface. They aren't meant for climbing.

I feel like a damn space monkey.

My theory is that whoever put McKnight's body in the tree tried this one first. Maybe even getting all the way to the top before realizing this tree wasn't going to work.

If they abandoned this tree, they might not have cared as much about tidying up after themselves. It's a leap. A diligent criminal would check for prints, fibers, and any other clues. Fortunately, most of them aren't that smart.

Rain trickles down through the leaves. I pull my flashlight from my pocket and place it in my mouth so I can hold on for dear life with both hands. Besides the pain, I don't think I could handle the professional embarrassment if someone found me unconscious from a fall.

The first thing I look for is drops of blood on the branches and leaves. A big guy like McKnight might not have gone down without a struggle. Our killer could have been bleeding from his own wound and not had the time to bandage it, or use a towel to clean the path he took up here.

My light casts a glowing cone in the rain. Nothing jumps out at me. I climb up to the next branch and focus my attention on the path our bad guy would have likely taken to carry McKnight, or to haul him up with a rope.

I spot another broken branch by my elbow. At least I know now that our climber made it higher than the first limb. I lean in to have a closer look.

My phone rings.

Now? When you're a cop, you don't get the luxury of pushing all your calls until later.

I unzip my clean-suit and pull the phone out, fumbling to keep my grasp on the tree and not let go of my light as I move it from my mouth to my free hand. "Hello?"

"Jessica?" replies a familiar voice.

"Grandfather?" This is a surprise. We haven't talked in a long time. Things in my family are awkward. I spoke to him and my father briefly a few months ago, when I was in the hospital, but I had been too busy to deal with the drama of their presence.

"Are you busy?" he asks.

The ground twenty feet below begs for closer contact, the wind makes secret plans with the rain to send me flying and a branch is getting very fresh with my ass. "A little . . ."

"I'm going to be in your neck of the woods in a few days. I'd like to talk."

My neck of the woods . . .

There's something about his voice. Grandfather is an imposing man. He has the elocution of a classically trained Shakespearean actor with the stage presence to match. But now I detect a trace of vulnerability. Vulnerability and that old bastard are two things that never go together. "Is everything all right?"

"Nothing that can't wait until we talk in person."

"Okay. Let me know when you're in town and we'll do lunch."

"Very good . . . Jessica, I love you."

I don't think I've heard my grandfather ever say that to an adult my entire life. Is something wrong? Or is he just getting old? Sentimental?

Sentimental? No. It has to be the scotch.

This isn't the time to reflect. I clumsily try to push my phone back into my pocket, forgetting that it's under the clean-suit, and miss. The glowing screen falls from the sky like a meteor.

"Damn it!"

I make a vain effort to grab the phone in midair and slide forward. One foot slips off the tree limb and I find myself hanging from a branch with one hand, like the world's worst motivational poster.

"Nice," I scold myself.

I've been hung upside down in straitjackets. Pushed off bridges in packing cases. Suspended by invisible wires. This is just one more stupid stunt.

I switch hands and move the flashlight back to my mouth. My phone stares up at me from the ground. Magically still functional after the fall, it could die from water damage at any moment.

Hand over hand, I pull myself back to relative safety. That's when I see it.

Dull orange. Just the faintest hint of a tread.

Not on a branch. This is on the trunk.

Someone tried to pull him or herself up and put a foot here to gain purchase. Flexing the heel of the shoe is probably what released the mud caked in the treads of the sole.

Red drips trail from the pattern as it melts away. Raindrops are dissolving the print. A clue is vanishing before my eyes.

I told Mitchum to pay attention to this tree. But there's no victory lap if I have nothing to show.

I can't take a photo because my camera is in the car and my phone is on the ground. So I reach into the clean-suit to dig inside my pocket, and pull out a gas receipt and plastic bag. Well, I'm half prepared. Using the receipt as a blotter, I push it down over the tread to get an impression and then slide it into the evidence pouch.

I scrape some more mud from the print into another pouch before wrapping the trunk with the sheet of plastic wrap I saved from my sandwich.

Back on planet earth, my phone goes off again. It makes a garbled sound as water splashes over the speaker.

Pelting raindrops shoot at me almost horizontally, telling me to get out of the tree. I scurry down and pick up the phone before it kicks over to voicemail.

"How's it going?" asks Knoll.

"Wet and painful." I crook the phone in my shoulder and rub my sore hands.

This catches him off guard. "Um . . . Yeah, so you hear the latest?"

"The *latest* latest? I've been up a tree."

"Ah, got it." My wet-and-painful comment finally making sense to him. "We'll talk about that later."

Thunder pounds in the distance. I cling to the trunk of the tree.

"What's that sound?" asks Knoll.

"Weather. What'd you hear?" I struggle to push my hair back to its tie. Wet strands cling to my face in defiance.

"McKnight's shoulder wound? Someone took a munch out of his neck."

"He was bitten?"

"Downright chowed-on."

"Yikes. Human?"

"Oh, yeah. It gets better."

"How better?"

"Dental match."

"Who?"

"Well it isn't your prime suspect, Beelzebub."

"Who?" I repeat.

"Sheriff Jessup."

"Christ."

"The still-missing, as in might-be-on-the-run, Sheriff Jessup. He's our main suspect right now. It looks like we have a murder."

"Lord." A shiver runs down my back.

"You read the bio on that guy?"

"Briefly."

"He's a tough son-of-a-bitch. I pity the poor fools running around those woods with our three-hundred-pound, flesh-eating, redneck zombie on the loose."

"Yeah . . . fools," I reply, glancing over my shoulder into the blackness of the forest. I reflexively pat my pistol under my clean-suit.

"So, Blackwood, where did you say you were?"

INSECURITY

THE FALL THE Buick followed me home was already a time of stress. As big as the old mansion was, and as few of us as there were, every room seemed filled with sharp words and arguments over something I couldn't quite wrap my seven-year-old mind around.

There had been talk of a winter tour since the spring. Grandfather had wanted to rent out a string of the bigger halls on the East Coast, spending more on advertising than he'd ever done before. Rather than present the show as some kind of nostalgic tribute to his glory days, he saw it as a comeback. New illusions, new sets and costumes, this was going to be a show about the future. He'd even hired an illustrator of sci-fi movie posters to create a grand one for the production.

Standing in the center of the poster in his floor-length cloak, Grandfather looked like a cross between Obi-Wan Kenobi and a classical magician of yesteryear. Laser beams illuminated the sky as cards flew over his head like spaceships. There were hundreds of details in the image referencing the acts. I loved how the artist interpreted illusions, translating the box for the sawing-a-woman-in-half effect into a woman floating in midair, her two halves divided by a vast gulf.

It promised to be an amazing production, even if Grandfather's ideas about science fiction were a bit dated. The magic was going to be like nothing ever seen before. Both Dad and Uncle Darius had worked all summer to create some spectacular effects. They contracted a Star Trek set designer to give the production a slick, Hollywood look.

There was even to be a part for me. I was to play a robot space princess who would be teleported with a laser beam. The act involved me crawling through a piece of conduit that looked too small for a hamster, let alone a human child.

I'd had lots of practice going unseen and hiding in small spaces, and not just for the shows. The mansion had actually been a speakeasy, back in the days of Prohibition. Despite its bad plumbing and rotten wood, Grandfather had bought it because of its secret passages and hidden rooms. You could travel from one end of the house to the other entirely through its warren of corridors. The secret gambling room and cellar became Grandfather's workspaces, but I found other nooks and crannies I'm not even sure he knew about. There were slim hallways that wrapped around the guest rooms, and above the kitchen there was an attic-like space. The floor was still covered with dozens of rotting mats, as if it were a kind of bunk area. Probing around with my flashlight one afternoon, I discovered newspapers that looked Chinese and some gold sequins stuck between the floor planks and the beams. Shards of broken bottles were lodged into the corners.

My childish imagination conjured up explanations for these odd artifacts. I sort of knew from old movies that a speakeasy was like a cowboy saloon, and I assumed the sequins were from the clothes of the girls who danced and flashed their legs doing the cancan. The newspaper, I decided, was there because one of them was saving up to take a trip to China and was teaching herself to read Chinese.

The truth, which I found out later, was a lot sadder. Our house had also been a brothel. The girls in the attic were brought out when customers came to drink, and sent back up there when they weren't working.

THE HIDDEN CONDUITS were a source of amusement for me at first, but I soon learned they could serve another purpose. Back then, my biggest concern in the world was uncertainty. I could be happily enrolled in school one week and then packed onto a cruise to Australia the next, all because Grandfather got a booking and needed Dad to come along, which meant me too.

Grandfather always had plans. Some came to fruition but others did not, as talk of a tour could vaporize if he didn't line up enough bookings. These endeavors were generally kept from me until they began to take definite shape and the first checks arrived. All too often, that meant a day's notice to pack my little suitcase.

When I was in school, I enjoyed the regularity of studying and did better than most of the other students. Even though I was off having adventures around the world they'd envy, all I could dream about was being in class and not having so much uncertainty.

A few months before the Buick followed me, while prowling the corridors I heard Grandfather and Dad discussing a project they hadn't yet mentioned to me. I sat still behind the other side of the plaster wall and listened. They spoke for an hour about the logistics: how many trucks they'd need, how many stagehands, which theaters were the best, whether to spend money on television or just radio ads. The conversation ended with no decisions about anything, but simply overhearing it had made me feel calm. Just knowing that it was in the works, that details were being worked out, that I could participate in some way, even covertly, provided comfort.

I made it a habit, then, to listen whenever I could. In my world it was the one way I could gain some idea of what to expect.

Tours and trips would live and die in those conversations, but being part of it gave me some sense of calm.

THE EVENING OF the day the Buick followed me home, I pretended to go straight to bed after dinner and then rushed into the passages so I could listen as Grandfather and Dad talked. I'd already noticed that the talk of the "Beyond" tour, his sci-fi comeback, had stopped. Something told me that poster was all we'd ever see of it.

"Is it Brutani?" asked Dad in the library.

I could hear Grandfather's feet shuffling across the old wooden floor. "One of his guys drove a Buick. I saw him sitting in the parking lot a few times when we went to speak to him at the restaurant."

"Bodyguard?"

"Or something . . . Damn!"

"I'm sorry, Dad," my father said quietly.

"You damn fool. I don't know why I listened to you." It was always painful to hear him talk to my dad like that.

"It could be nothing."

"Bullshit. That's not how these guys work," snarled Grandfather.

"You don't think . . ."

"This was a threat. Goddamn it! He wants it all back."

I tried to put the bits and pieces together, but I couldn't understand what it was all about.

Dad pleaded, "We don't have it. Most of it is sitting in the warehouse. I tried explaining this to him when that ice show got booked over us and we lost most of our dates. It'd just have to be next year."

"Guys like him don't think that way. You tell Brutani something is going to happen, damn it, it has to happen."

"Why can't he understand? It's not like we wasted the money," replied Dad.

"You don't see, do you?" My grandfather had lots of different ways to make you feel stupid by pointing to something that's supposed to be obvious.

"See what?"

Grandfather said something inaudible under his breath. "Brutani is small-time. He came out here to invest in the pictures and be a big shot. He wanted in on what we were doing because it excited him. But at the end of the day, it's not his money. It's his father's."

"What are you saying?"

"He's putting the squeeze on us because he's afraid of his old man."

"We can't just let him threaten us! And the business with Jessica? That crossed the line. We should go to the police."

The business with me? Was this was about the Buick?

"That's a horrible idea," interjected Uncle Darius, who must have just walked into the room.

"We'll make sure you're not here when they come over," replied my father, getting in a dig about my uncle's arrest record.

"There's a quick wit," Darius shot back. "You don't call the cops when you borrow money from the mob and they want it repaid."

"I didn't borrow money from the mob," snapped my father.

"You let the son of a major mobster invest money in the show. It's the same thing."

"What happens if we call the cops? What can Brutani do?"

"It's not what Brutani does, brother, it's what the low-rent guy fresh out of the can and desperate to go back in that Brutani paid off can do. They hit you sideways. Sending that car to follow to Jessica, that was dirty. Real dirty."

"So what do we do?" asked Dad.

"Talk to someone who's connected, so we can get to his father."

There's a long pause. "Not her," grumbled Grandfather. "God, not that bitch. I almost called her a cunt on live television. She won't help us."

"Yes, she will," said Darius.

"Why is that?" asked Grandfather.

"She'll want you to owe her. She'll want a favor."

"I can't do that. I've got my integrity."

"Well, in that case," said Darius, "I hope you and your integrity are happy here. Because I'm going to take Jessica with me and relocate somewhere under another name."

I'd never heard my uncle look out for me like that.

"Bullshit!" shouted Dad.

"You don't solve this, just watch me. That kid is all that matters. This is your fuck-up, not hers. Swallow your enormous egos and let's fix this."

"I hate that woman," Grandfather growled.

For a fleeting second I thought he meant me.

"Yeah, well be sure to add an extra degree of spit and polish. You need to charm her," explained Darius.

"I'd rather seduce a cobra."

6

Dʀ. Jᴇғғᴇʀʏ Aɪʟᴇs, who—as head of the DOJ task force I work on—is my de facto boss, shakes his head. I feel like I've just been called into the principal's office, albeit over Skype. Even in the safety of my motel room a state away, his gaze penetrates. A former Naval officer, a computer scientist-turned-black box hedge fund manager, the first African American to win the Japan Prize for mathematics, a MacArthur Fellow and rumored presidential golf buddy, he is probably the most intimidating person I know.

He looks at my cracked phone screen as I wave it in front of my laptop camera. "You fell out of a tree?"

"No. My phone did. I made it out fine. Mostly. You get the samples I sent with the van?"

He reaches across his desk and holds up the plastic bags I'd asked the returning Quantico crew to bring back. "You almost broke your neck for this?"

"It's from the Hawkton crime scene."

"Why is this here? Shouldn't this go through the local West Virginia channels?"

"Well . . . Mitchum. She doesn't think this is important."

Ailes lifts the bagged mud samples up to the light and looks at them. "So you went out and collected this yourself?"

"I put a piece of plastic over the rest of the print so it wouldn't all erode away."

"Are you going to bring this to her?"

"Well . . ." I hesitate. I'm not sure how to get into the frosty relationship I have with Mitchum.

Ailes raises an eyebrow.

I continue. "I know you've been working on that new biome lab project . . ."

"It's a pilot study. We don't even have a test case yet for admissibility. Whatever we find in here," he points to the bags, "may not even be usable in court. We have other labs here that can try to backtrace the content of the dirt. We've got an excellent database for that."

"And they're backed up for several weeks. This could be important."

"So, why aren't you taking this to Mitchum? It's her case." Ailes is being patient with me. Another boss would chew me out for going around the lead agent.

I try to find the right words. "It's not a priority for her."

"You kids aren't playing well together?"

"No. I'm trying. She's just very . . . difficult."

"Are you sure it's all her?"

The words singe. "*Me*? I've done nothing but try to help her."

"Blackwood, what may seem like polite and appropriate behavior to you may come off differently to others."

"What's that supposed to mean?"

"You're a celebrity around here. The Warlock case was all you. Of the most high-profile FBI manhunts in the past decade, you're the one face the public remembers. While a lot of younger agents look up to you, some are bound to resent you."

"This? Again? What for? I just did my job," I protest, although I know his assessment harbors some truth. Part of me still thinks that pointing out the absurdity of something will make it go away.

"Of course. Imagine what it's like for Ms. Mitchum every time someone finds out she's an FBI agent. Who do you think the topic shifts to? You have a very big shadow, especially among your female colleagues."

"I was only helping. Ask Knoll."

"I'm sure you were. But did you stick strictly to her instructions, or did you take 'initiative'?"

Our mutual respect is based in part on being straightforward with each other and admitting the truth. "I told the helicopter pilot to extend the search radius. It's how we found the first victim."

"And you wonder why she doesn't get along with you?"

"I saved us hours, maybe days!"

"It's her case. You're there just on the ground as support and you make the big breakthrough. What do you think is going through her mind?"

Sure, I thought she was acting a little bitchy and that ruffled me. But I was just trying to help! "I don't want her case," I insist. "I'm not trying to show her up. I leave the pissing matches to the boys."

Ailes shakes the dirt at the camera. "Really?"

"I just want to get the bad guy."

"The sheriff?"

"Look at the tread on the print. I checked the report. It's not the sheriff's footwear. At least, it doesn't match what he was last seen wearing. And I've been up the tree. There's no way he climbed up there carrying someone. He's built like a linebacker."

Ailes pages through a file. "So how did his teeth marks end up on the victim's body?"

"I'm not saying he didn't kill those people. There's just more to this. Have they even announced he's a suspect?"

"Not yet. They want some more lab tests."

"On what? They got dental. Did they just think it was some kind of weird coincidence his bite mark was on the corpse?"

"They just want to make sure it wasn't planted with plaster casts swiped from a dentist. This is, after all, their sheriff. Given the other circumstances, keep in mind it's West Virginia gun country. Nobody wants to start a cannibal cop panic. We'll have people shooting at mailmen."

I hadn't thought of the larger implications. "Christ. This is a PR disaster waiting to happen."

"Mitchum is being methodical. She's a good agent. Her forensic work is excellent." Ailes pulls up something on his laptop. "She's got one of the best records in the agency for admissibility. Her stuff doesn't get thrown out of court."

"Yeah, because she only goes for the low-hanging fruit. Wow, that metaphor was more spot on than I realized." My trip up the tree is still fresh in my mind, as are the sores on my palms.

Ailes shakes his head. "Have you slept at all since your trip up the tree?"

"Define sleep . . ."

"We've got every law enforcement agent in three states looking for the sheriff. Mitchum is building her case while the manhunt tries to find the suspect. You have time to sleep unless you want to go out there and look for him yourself."

I'd been up all night trying to sort things out. I'd hurried back to the Hawkton Ops Center to get the samples back to DC and Quantico. Then went over everything I could on Jessup, and looked through Hawkton arrest records. "No. It's just that there's something else we're not seeing. This footprint for instance."

"Which could have been from a hunter trying to get a good spot."

"Or a sixth person. And then there's the writing on McKnight's chest."

"He was a Kabbalist, among other things," replies Ailes.

"Really? Him? That wasn't in the report." I'd have never connected a backwoods hillbilly to something bored Beverly Hills

housewives are into. It does match with the personality type fascinated by the paranormal. Did McKnight fear this was coming?

Ailes gives me a rare grin. "That's because Mitchum wasn't on
the phone this morning with the CEO of a certain online book-
seller, looking up his book purchases."

That man and his connections. "And how is that admissible?"

"We can subpoena it later if it's valuable. You just have to know
when you're bending the rules as opposed to momentarily side-
stepping them. Handing me this sample and asking me to use
a hundred-million-dollar laboratory to do a test that Mitchum
doesn't have access to isn't playing fair."

"And calling up one of your billionaire buddies to peek into a
customer account is?"

"The deceased don't have privacy rights. I got a little curious
when you decided to stay in West Virginia."

More like worried. "It's not a contest between me and Mitchum.
If I find anything useful, I'll pass it on to her. And she can ignore it
at her discretion . . ."

"Why the urgency?" persists Ailes.

"The missing man isn't our absentee sheriff," I reply.

"The evidence will tell us in time."

"In time. That's the thing." I try to put the words together.
"What would Chisholm say over at behavioral analysis? On one
hand this looks like a crime of passion. On the other, it's highly
organized. We still don't even know how the church exploded."
I think for a moment. "There's a methodology here. You know?
This feels like a revenge killing."

"The sheriff taking revenge?" asks Ailes. "For what?"

I shake my head reflexively. "No. I mean, I don't have that part.
But either way, people who go out and settle an old score tend to
keep going. First the wacko wants to kill his boss. Then it's his
ex-girlfriend, and soon he's killing the guy in front of him who
won't step on the gas fast enough.

"If . . . and I know, it's a big 'if,' if there's a sixth man, then this might not be the only crime we're looking at. The whole thing feels like the start of something." Ailes tilts his head to the side. "Don't look at me like that. I'm not trying to turn this into another flaming body in the cemetery."

"Are you sure?" Ailes is distracted for a moment as he checks his phone.

"Yes. I don't even think it's a copycat. Those people were at the church that night for a reason. Forget McKnight's deathbed incrimination of some Judaic demon, even with that Kabbalah connection. They had ash on their heads. Crosses. They were afraid. And now they're dead. Whoever killed them did it in a meaningful way. And we still don't even know how it happened."

"All right. You made your case. I'll see what we can do with your sample, but it'll take me a while. Come home, get some actual rest."

"I will. But then I think I'm going to take a trip into Hawkton."

"Mitchum's turf?"

"Just to follow up on something."

"What?"

"Someone. The deputy."

"You think he's your tree climber? He had a pretty solid alibi."

"Yeah. But maybe he can tell me what everyone was so frightened about, and why they gathered at the church."

"I'm sure he's been questioned to death."

"But were they the right questions? If Mitchum won't even acknowledge what was on Bear McKnight's chest, I can't imagine she'd ask the deputy the kinds of questions I'm thinking of."

"About the sheriff?"

"About evil."

7

DEPUTY BALDWIN IS a scared man. Holed up in his house behind the wire fence, he refuses to speak to me. His fifteen-year-old daughter who gave her name as Kris, green eyed and filled with teenage skepticism of all things adult, walks across the overgrown yard to tell me her daddy ain't coming out.

The house is surrounded by crooked oak trees, rusted cars and rows of what look like solar panels waiting to be put on roofs. The building itself is neatly kept. Two brand-new chairs sit on the empty porch. It has the look of a home where the wife takes care of everything inside, while the husband neglects everything outside.

The girl approaches the fence, staring down at her phone and texting. She's beyond bored with running interference between the visiting investigators and their questions for her dad. "He says he's got nothing more to say."

"Okay. What do you have to say?" I ask.

She looks up at me with a serious expression. Just as her body is outgrowing the summer's jean shorts and halter top, her mind is forming its own opinions on matters around here. "I think everyone has gone bug crazy."

There's only a hint of West Virginia in her voice, despite the slang; her diction sounds more like that of a girl on a CW drama than of some hick who never stepped more than a mile outside of town.

"Crazy?"

"Everyone is hiding away and saying prayers and stuff. Not much point. That didn't do much for Reverend Curtis and those folks. The news is just as bad. People calling Hawkton a 'hell-mouth.' Stupid." The last words roll off her tongue with contempt. I spot a flash of gold near the tip.

"People are confused and scared because of what happened at the church."

"No reason to act like this." Kris tilts her head toward the house. The breeze catches one of her long blond hairs. Her nose points back down to her phone as she texts away, "You the FBI woman on the news a while back?"

"Yes," I concede. There's no point in denying it.

A smile spreads across her face. "Daddy said you were a witch." It's a joke to her.

"I've been called worse."

"I asked him if you flew around on a broom and cast spells. That made him angry." She looks up at me. "He's got an engineering degree. See the solar panels? He's got a side business putting them on folks' houses. He's not stupid."

"He's scared of what happened to his friends," I explain.

"That's for sure. He's sitting there right now, watching us, with his shotgun. He's got it on him all the time now."

"What do you think he's afraid of? Sheriff Jessup?"

"Why do you say that?" Her eyes flash up at mine.

The lab report isn't public knowledge yet, and I'm not sure how much information has made it through the grapevine to Baldwin and his daughter. "Just a question, since he's missing."

She leans over the fence and lowers her voice. "He won't say it, but I know he's watching out for the sheriff. They ain't found him yet, have they?"

I shake my head.

Kris's eyes scan the trees. "The sheriff is a good man. Daddy looks up to him. When the business wasn't doing so good, he gave him the deputy job."

"So why is your daddy afraid of him?"

Kris narrows her eyes. "Lately stuff has been *happening* around here. Before the church exploded. A lot of it involving the sheriff."

"Stuff? What kind?" There's something about the way she says this that tells me this is more than small-town gossip.

"Little things. Dead cats and birds showing up in front of the sheriff station. Jessup was complaining nothing worked. His cell phone getting all static. Daddy said there would be calls at the station where no one was on the other line. They can trace that kind of thing, but the calls were coming from phone numbers that were disconnected. Weird stuff." She shrugs.

"You don't seem too fazed by all this."

"Ain't got nothing to do with me. Something bad is going to happen, it's going to happen. Might be a prank. Someone having some fun. People get crazy out here."

A little girl comes running from around the back of the house and across the yard. Kris turns to her. "Go back, Becky."

The girl crosses her arms and looks up at Kris. "I'm bored in there. Daddy won't let me watch the TV and I can't find the iPad." She reaches up and grabs her big sister's hand. Wearing dirty socks and a T-shirt that stretches to her knees, she's got the same blond hair and green eyes as Kris. "You the witch Daddy talked about?"

"I'm an FBI agent. A cop, like your father."

"He says you're into devilcraft." It's more a question than an accusation.

Kris sighs. "Ain't no such thing as witches. She look like a witch to you? Daddy is just drunk and talking out of his butt." She rolls her eyes. "He only gets all churchy when he's scared and been drinking. If he really thought that about you, he wouldn't let us come out here and talk to you."

"When did the weird stuff start happening?"

Kris makes a face. "Hawkton's always had weird things." She points to a flat-topped mountain peak along the eastern ridge at the edge of the city limits. "Lightning Peak gets hit a dozen times a year. We have lots of strange lights. Plenty of haunted houses. A teacher said a while back there was a poltergeist. We got one of them hills where your car goes up when it's in neutral. Indian temples. Lots of odd stuff. They should do a show out here."

"But when did the weird stuff start with the sheriff?"

"A few months back. That's when I heard about it. The same time I think the Alsops found their dogs dead, strangled, I think. And Bear McKnight said he saw weird tracks around his house."

Every town has its folktales and mysteries. But this seems a little excessive. "Tracks? What kind?"

"Hooves. *Devil* hooves, they said," she replies with a grin.

"You think that's stupid?"

She shrugs again. "Wild pigs, more like it. Grown-ups get so retarded when they can't understand what's going on." She caresses her little sister's head. "What do you think, Becky?"

"I don't like it when Daddy is scared."

"Where's your mamma?" I ask.

"Inside," replies Becky. "She and Gram-Gram are praying."

Kris rolls her eyes. "Next they'll be asking Black Nick for one of his twig evil catchers."

"Black Nick? Who is that?"

"You ain't heard of Black Nick?" asks Kris.

Becky points to Lightning Peak. "He lives up there."

"Nick is a medicine man," explains Kris. "Lives in a shack in the hills. Older folks go to him for potions and stuff when they don't like what their doctor says. They say he knows the old magic. Whatever."

"He's crazy," adds Becky. "Smells like a raccoon."

"Be nice. You don't want him hexing you," scolds Kris. "He'll turn you into a chicken and Momma will fry you up."

Becky's eyes widen. She releases her sister's hand and runs back to the house.

Kris shakes her head. "When I was a kid we'd tell stories about Crazy Black Nick. How he'd come for you if you misbehaved. How he had piles of bones by his shack. It's stupid. He's just an old man."

I admire Kris's skepticism. She reminds me of myself as a teenager. I always thought adults were a bit ridiculous.

"Do a lot of people take him seriously?"

Kris points to gray twigs, bundled together with twine, that are nailed to the front of the house. Buttons and pieces of foil are threaded through the bindings. It vaguely looks like a person—made by crows. "See that? Daddy got that from Black Nick."

"What's it for? To keep evil out?"

"I reckon. Smells like dog piss to me." She thumbs away on her phone.

"Can I give you my number in case your daddy wants to talk?"

"Sure. He won't, though."

"Just in case. And could you tell me how to find Black Nick?"

Kris lowers her phone and stares at me. "Sure you want to go up there?"

"I thought you said he's harmless?"

She points to the forest cloaking the peak. Her voice grows more concerned. "Sun is going down. I don't think I'd want to be there in the dark if the sheriff was up and about. People only go talk to Black Nick during the day. No one goes there at night."

"I'm due back at Quantico in the morning. I don't really have a choice. Black Nick isn't in any of the reports."

"Fine. Just don't get lost," she tells me.

An hour later, I've parked my car at the edge of the road and started hiking up the hillside. A thin path leads over a ridge and into a copse of trees. Before my cell phone signal vanishes,

I decide I should call headquarters and tell them where to find my body.

"Black Nick?" Ailes's voice cuts in and out.

"That's what they call him," I reply, surrounded by forest. The faint blue light of the sky is barely visible through the trees.

The woods have a quietness about them, but I get the feeling I'm being watched by dozens of small eyes.

"Isn't 'Old Nick' a name for the devil?" he asks.

The signal goes dead.

I realize he's right. I tell myself it's just a coincidence.

8

THE TRAIL TO Black Nick's cabin is more of a dried-up gully than a path. Shards of white stone poke out of the earth like whale teeth, telling me I'm on the right track—at least, the one Kris told me to follow. Every few hundred feet there's a fork in the trail, marked by rocks, intended to lead the bad spirits astray.

My dad and I once took a trip to the Winchester House in Northern California, a sprawling mansion that had stairways leading to the ceiling and doorways opening to brick walls—all of it to confuse the spirits that the widow of the Winchester rifle magnate imagined were after her. This trail reminds me of that.

The sun is setting and the frogs have started chirping from deep inside their soggy homes. On the fringes of the trail, creatures scurry in the bushes. Out of the corner of my eye I catch long shadows of twisted branches as I go farther up the hill. They reach out to me across the trail as the sun sets.

Crows, an awful lot of crows, perch in the trees. Watching me with their beady black eyes, they turn their sharp beaks toward me as I pass.

Kris had mentioned a rock shaped like a skull without a jaw. The setting sun makes its shadowy eye sockets and gaping nose stand out.

I make my last right turn here and come to flat ground, where tall grass gives way to a ring of white stones. A shack stands

56 ANDREW MAYNE

at the end of the clearing. Covered in plastic bottles, aluminum cans and knots of foil, it looks like a house built by a giant magpie—the same creator who made the twisted twig-man on the Deputy's porch.

A blue rocking chair sits on the porch next to a wind chime made from spoons and forks. It sounds like the bells of a Lilliputian cathedral in the breeze.

The only churchgoers are the silk black crows still watching me. What do they make of the sound? Is it meant to scare them or invite them closer?

As arresting as the shack is, my eyes are drawn to the mound of bones as tall as the roof piled off to the side of it. I spot antlers, cow skulls and the femurs, ribs and spines of a hundred other stark white creatures. Nothing human that I can see.

I hope.

I can't imagine generations of Hawkton children *not* having stories to tell about this place. Even without the threat of a cannibal sheriff looming somewhere out in the woods, it's eerie. I resist the impulse to touch my gun under my jacket and take a deep breath.

The shack's one window, made from different-colored pieces of glass joined by thick solder, is blocked from the inside by what looks like a burlap sack. There's no sign of life except for the smell of burning.

There's a small fire of charcoals in front of a tall oak tree that was old when this was still Indian country.

White stones keep the smoldering briquettes from setting the dry weeds around them ablaze.

There's only the ringing sound of the spoons and forks in the wind and the occasional caw of a crow in the distance. Telling the others I'm all alone, I assume.

"You da witch?" a deep voice asks from behind.

I suppress a gasp and spin around to find the source. In the

fading sun and dim glow of the fire, I almost miss him. Tall,
real tall. Thin like a scarecrow, Black Nick is dressed in stitched
slacks, a sweater as random as his house, and a black blazer with
patches on the sleeve. Well-worn, but not dirty, he reminds me of
a survivor from a postapocalyptic movie. Old—hard to tell how
old—he's got deep blue eyes. White-blond hair sits on his head
like a bad toupee. His feet are bare.

"I wouldn't call myself that," I reply, more calmly than I feel.

Black Nick steps out of the trees and takes a seat on a rock by
the fire across from me. "Dancing up in trees in the middle of da
storm, pitch black night, if that ain't a witch, I dunno what is." He
stirs the coals with a stick.

"You saw me in the tree?"

"I didn' say I did. I just said whats you were doin' last night. Yo
business is yo business."

His accent isn't West Virginian, but it's not quite Southern,
either. It's a mishmash of pronunciations I can't quite place—
maybe with a hint of Minnesotan Swede.

He gives me a close look in the firelight. "You ain't no witch.
Just a fool."

"I'm an FBI agent."

"Same thing. I see why people think you a witch. You got a
mysterious way about you. Coming up here in the night. Things
out here. Dark things." He's reproachful, but not menacing.

"I came to talk to you about that. Has anyone asked you about
what happened at the church?"

"Lotsa people. Coming here to ask Black Nick for some help.
Wantin' totems to ward off the wickedness. Ignore me forever.
Call me names behinds my back. But when the evil come, then
they all want Black Nick."

"Has anybody like me come to talk to you?"

He stabs the stick into the fire, sending up a shower of sparks.
"Fools aplenty."

"I mean a law enforcement officer, a cop. Has anyone asked you for a statement?"

He draws a circle in the ashes with his poker. "What would I state? You seen what happened. Not much else to tell."

"What did happen?" I hope that, even up here, he may have heard something we didn't.

"Didn't you see nothing with all your tree climbing? Something evil happened."

"Yes, but because of whom?"

He scratches the rough skin of his chin. "The *whom* is da Sheriff Jessup. I suppose you know that already."

There's a way he emphasizes 'whom.' "Is there someone else involved?" I ask.

He stirs the flames again. "Supposing you knock this stick from my hand into the fire? My hand done let go of the stick. But it's yo hand that done the knocking."

"Is there someone else involved?"

"Supposing."

"Can I ask you if you know something about this?" I reach for my phone to show him the photo of Bear McKnight's chest.

He raises a hand. "Don't show me that. Might as well call him over to supper. I know who you're talking about."

"Is that who's behind this?"

"That troublemaker has been to these parts before. The Indian-folk had their own name for him. And the folk before them, and before them. He's playing his tricks, as expected."

Tricks. It's a weird word for evil. Oddly, that's how many cultures see the devil: as a trickster.

"What else has he done?"

His blue eyes stare into mine. "You read your Bible? Plenty. Ask old Abraham."

"So you think he's the cause of what happened?"

"I didn't say that. I say he's involved. But if you let the door open for him to step inside, your fault for leavins the door open."

"The door?"

"He don't just show up unannounced. Someone brought him here," he replies matter-of-fact.

This drunk Yoda act is getting on my nerves. "The sheriff? Did he open the door?"

"Why'd he do a fool thing like that?" Nick's blue eyes flash at me like this is the dumbest question in the world.

"Maybe he's crazy?"

"If'n he's crazy, he don't need the troublemaker's help. Crazy people do awful things all the time. The troublemaker just sit back and laugh."

"So someone else made the sheriff do these things?"

"I reckon."

"Anyone around here?"

"No one here knows about how to use a man's fears to open the door. Nothing."

"Except you . . ."

"Excepting me."

"You and the sheriff get along?" I take a cautious step away from Black Nick, wishing I'd brought backup.

"We get along fine. When those prisoners bust out the lock-up, Black Nick help get them. When kids get lost up here because they want to spy on Black Nick, I make sure the sheriff find 'em. When the fools decided to camp out on Lighting Peak and got a taste of the 'tricity, Black Nick carried them down the mountain. Me and Jessup get along fine. I've no need to open the door on him. Wouldn't open it no how, even if I did. You never get it closed."

"What about Reverend Curtis?"

Nick shakes his head. "He's a Christian man just like me. No quarrels. I ain't got none. If you're trying to ask me polite if I had anything to do with what happened to those poor folks, the answer is 'no.'"

He reaches into a trouser pocket and pulls out a handful of moss. He drops it into the fire, then tosses a copper penny from his jacket into the middle of the flames. White smoke shrouds the penny and begins to drift upward. Black Nick fans it with his hand. "No one round here knows the magic."

Growing up in a family of magicians, I've met plenty of people who believe in the 'real' kind and have their own rituals. I stop myself from distracting him by asking what he just did. "Can you name someone who might know that kind of magic?"

"Lotsa folks. I been a bunch a different places before I came here. Hill folks, like me. Keep to theirselves. Following the old trails. The ones the Indian-folk found when they came here. Trails left back in the days when the angels were all getting along." He points toward a cluster of trees. "Trails like that."

I glance at the thick gnarl of bushes and trees protruding from the edge of the clearing. "It doesn't look like much of a trail to me."

"Cause you can't see. Like I said, lotsa folks can. None around here no more, save me." He stands up and beckons me closer.

I hesitate.

"Come on. Black Nick ain't going to bite ya. We need to say a prayer."

"For who?"

"For poor Sheriff Jessup. So his wandering soul will find its way home and he won't disturb nobody more."

I relent and take his hand. He's more bone than muscle. I'm sure I could take him in a fight, especially since I've been spending extra time at the gym these last few months. Maybe too much time.

Black Nick clasps my other hand. I feel like the root of an oak tree has grown around them. He lowers his head. "Lord, forgive there Sheriff Jessup for what he's done. Find him safe passage and protect all them folk." His grip tightens. I try to pull away gently, but he won't let go. "See to it this one finds her way. Make sure she don't get lost in her own long shadow." He releases me. "All right. I should take you back to your blue car down at the end of the trail. I don't want you gettin' lost up here and running into you-know-who."

I'm not sure if he means the devil or the sheriff. Neither one would make for an enjoyable encounter. Although with the sheriff I'd be able to do something within my mortal jurisdiction.

A HALF-HOUR LATER, we reach my car. Black Nick managed to guide me without the use of a flashlight. He said it just invites troubles—it is better to not be seen.

"Things agonna work themselves out. But you gonna keep putting your nose where it don't have no business." He takes out a shard of black glass from his pocket. "I get these up on Lightning Peak. When the 'tricity hits the ground, it leaves these behind." He hands it to me.

It's heavy. He's ground the rough rock into an edge like a blade. A hand knife made from a bolt of lightning.

I'm uneasy about the gift. "That's okay. You don't have to."

His eyes widen. "I do have to. You go running into trouble, some of that trouble is going to come running toward you." He throws his hands up in the air and won't take it back.

He waits for me to get inside my car before turning back to the trail that leads up to his shack. Unafraid of the dark, he vanishes in the night with the determination of someone who knows his own destiny.

9

"LET'S TALK ABOUT demons," says Ailes as I walk into the conference room at Quantico.

"Wonderful," I reply, taking my seat. The chair, like the building, is decades old. Off from the main FBI campus, we're in our own corner.

Gerald, my lanky, mop-headed coworker who looks like a teenager who got lost on take-your-kid-to-work day, is sitting at his laptop pecking away at a furious speed. Behind them is a full-screen video wall. In the center is the Hawkton church.

"Oh, so now we're interested?" I remark.

"I'm always interested. No, it seems Mitchum wants some more information about demons."

"What gives?"

"This," replies Ailes. He nods to Gerald. The church erupts into a fireball on the monitor. The roof rips apart and then the entire building explodes. When the smoke settles, the structure is spread across the ground in a thousand splinters, just as I saw from the helicopter.

"Where'd we get this footage?" I ask, surprised. I didn't know anyone was filming at the time.

"We made this. Gerald took all the laser-mapped 3-D data and put it into one of our number crunchers."

"Impressive." I feel a bit silly for thinking it was real. I glance at Gerald and nod. He gives me a meek smile.

"You haven't seen the half of it." Ailes picks up a laser pointer and aims its red dot on a small white plank in the bottom left corner of the screen. "See that?"

Gerald moves his cursor over the board and the image zooms in. The individual grains in the wood become visible. He runs his finger across the track pad and the board flies into the air, reversing the trajectory of the explosion. Seconds later, I'm looking at part of a wall inside of the church, which has magically reassembled. There's a cork bulletin board a few feet away from the plank. The camera spins around, showing us the entire interior of the church. Not all the details are there—some areas are pixelated chunks—but overall it's convincing.

"We have to fudge a few things," says Ailes. "But it's useful."

"I'll say. It's like a time machine. So what's with the new interest in demons? Mitchum take another look at the smudge I found on McKnight?"

"Not quite. Roll forward," Ailes tells Gerald. The camera flies back to a bird's-eye view of the hellmouth. He points his laser at a patch of ground in the field across the street. "Zoom."

The camera pulls close to another plank. This one is darker, like flooring. On its edges are several deep gouges.

"Look familiar?" asks Ailes.

"No. Not really."

"Roll back, Gerald." As before, the board shoots through the air to fall back into place inside the church. Several other planks nestle down on either side. The gouges continue on to the other boards, and next to each other, the jagged carvings form a name: *Azazel*.

The same name in English that I saw written in Hebrew on McKnight's chest.

"Who wrote this?"

"We think that perhaps one of the victims carved it with a house key." Ailes points to the blood stains on the floor in front of it. "Maybe Mrs. Alsop. Now we have two people saying the same thing. Both of them alive long enough to tell us something."

"Yet none of them said, 'Jessup'?" I ask.

"Nope. Kind of odd. Even Mitchum realizes that now."

There's a small victory for me she'll never acknowledge. At least not in a positive way. "Where's the forensics on Alsop? Any bite marks?"

"Gerald, we got the live feed from the forensics lab?"

Gerald turns the screen to a live view of one of our new autopsy rooms in DC headquarters. Two robot arms move over the body of what looks like Reverend Curtis. A separate window shows the super high-resolution images the cameras on the arm are capturing. At this magnification, the wrinkles on Curtis's skin resemble vast canyons. Hairs shoot out like black tree trunks. Each pore is a pit that fades into the earth.

"We're building a 3-D model of each victim," explains Ailes. "We're also capturing infrared so we can see the kind of blood vessel rupturing. The abrasions might tell us another story. It's time-consuming."

"You're scanning the body?"

Gerald points to the skin detail. "We're making a 3-D map."

Ailes nods. "So far, cause of death appears to be our missing sheriff."

"But nobody thought to implicate him in their last dying breath? Instead, they name a demon?"

Ailes shrugs. He's still trying to figure things out too. "That sums it up. You wanted weird, you got weird."

"What I wanted was a nice tidy case I didn't have to be involved in. What we got was inconvenient reality. What about this 'Azazel'? Any other meaning besides a demon?"

"He's a popular character in fantasy literature and gaming," replies Gerald. He pauses for a moment. "Also one of the members of the Brotherhood of Mutants."

———

"GREAT, JUST PUT an APB out for Magneto. Case closed."

Gerald gives me a smile, appreciating the reference.

"How'd your interviews go in Hawkton?" asks Ailes.

"The town is more eccentric than you can imagine. I even got a souvenir." I set Black Nick's blade on the table.

Ailes picks it up and looks at the unfinished handle. "Nice fulgurite."

Of course he'd know what it was called. I'd had to Wikipedia it. "That's from Black Nick."

"Ah," replies Ailes. He gives it a tap. "Iron? That's rare." He hands it back to me. "Careful with that edge. I read the local reports on him. You think he figures into this?"

"I don't know. He seems pretty harmless. He wasn't wearing shoes when I met him. I also don't think he climbed up any trees. I doubt he'd be able to get the bodies up there without a pulley, unless his crows helped him."

"Pardon?"

"Never mind. With enough patience, he'd be worth talking to again if we have more questions. I suggest someone with a gentle touch. He's real backwoods."

"What was his assessment?"

"He says the devil was involved, but not the instigator. He took pity on Jessup. He thinks the sheriff wasn't under his own control."

"Interesting . . ." Ailes's eyes drift up to the side as he starts to think about something.

"How interesting?"

He slides his open laptop over. "Our sheriff took quite a few bites of McKnight," he says, pulling up an autopsy photo on the screen of McKnight's mangled neck. "In one of those bites, he managed to chew into the side of his own mouth. We found his DNA."

"I can tell you that hurts." I touch my cheek, more than one bad memory resurfacing.

Ailes zooms into the wound. "We pulled separated tissue out and ran it through a dozen different screens. Cheek cells, unlike hair or skin cells, can tell you a little bit more because they're in the mouth. In this case, we found something unusual. Just a trace, but enough to make a spike." Ailes points to a graph. "Psilocin."

It takes a moment for me to remember my pharmacology classes. Psilocin is a psychedelic. "Psilocin? This was in Jessup's sample? You mean he was on mushrooms?"

"That's the closest match. But it's something different. The conventional toxin screen wouldn't have noticed it. Hold on." Ailes taps away at his keyboard faster than I can think. "Here . . ." A chemical structure floats on the screen.

It's just a bunch of ping-pong balls to me. "Care to dumb it down? I'm just a former showgirl who learned a few card tricks."

He rolls his eyes and points. "Hardly. That's the phenyl ring. Almost all of the psychoactive drugs we have involve some variation of this. Jessup had something in his body that's a close match to psilocin, something similar to what you'd find when a magic mushroom breaks down."

"So the sheriff did get high off mushrooms?" We've reached my limit of crazy for the town.

"No. I said close. That's the funny thing about chemistry. Rearrange an atom or two and decongestant becomes meth. Substituted phenethylamines are a whole family of molecules that can interfere with your neurotransmitters in a variety of ways. It's why synthetics aren't always precise. A right-handed version of a molecule might be a nausea-alleviating wonder drug, but the left-handed version could have the same effect and cause birth defects, like Thalidomide."

"So the sheriff was on some kind of synthetic drug?"

Ailes shakes his head. "Not necessarily. It could be a natural substance that hasn't appeared in our databases yet. We're still finding new and different ways to mess with our brains. Archeologists have even found what appears to be psychoactive moss in ten-thousand-year-old graves. Its main ingredient is a substituted phenethylamine we hadn't seen before." He traces his finger around the molecule. "There could be a billion permutations. Each one affecting the brain in a slightly different way. One might slow down processes in the calcium channels, while increasing the response between auditory neurons." He looks at me like the result should be obvious. "Words would sound distorted to you, slow and drawn out."

"Is that a real thing?" I ask.

He shakes his head. "It's an example I just made up. My point is that there are a billion ways to mess up our perceptions."

"I think you may have missed your calling. Could the sheriff have ingested this accidentally?"

"You were there, what do you think?"

"If there hadn't been an unexplained explosion and bodies in the trees, just violence, I'd say *maybe*. But everything together doesn't quite match the behavior of one man on the worst trip ever."

"No, it does not," agrees Ailes. "This suggests something larger."

"How much larger?"

Gerald snorts.

I glare at him. "What's that supposed to mean?"

"He knows where you're going next."

"Where's that?"

A map pops up on the screen, replacing the graph. The center is a town called Tixato. I've never heard of it.

"Why would I be going there?" I ask, trying to figure out their private joke.

Ailes starts talking in his professorial voice. "In any crime scene you find a thousand pieces of evidence that are interesting, but lead you down false alleys. A blond hair from a dead prostitute gets tracked in because the cleaning lady lives in a bad apartment building. A Syrian passport found in a plane crash is actually from an overnight express envelope and not a terrorist onboard. Odd things that seem like one-in-a-million occurrences. In reality, every event has a million different one-in-a-million occurrences. The important ones are those that connect to other one-in-a-million events without an obvious reason.

"That molecule we found in Jessup's tissue? It's not a synthetic. There are only a dozen places in the world where the bio databases say animals that could produce it might live. Tixato is one of them."

"So why Tixato? Because it's closest?"

"Because of those mud samples you brought us. From the footprint you found in the tree. Our other one-in-a-million fact. Guess where it comes from?"

I see where this is headed, or more literally, me. "Tixato too?"

"Exactly. Tixato. Tixato, Mexico."

10

I'VE BEEN MEANING to ask my grandfather about what happened after the Buick followed me home for a while, but now just doesn't seem like the time. My flight leaves shortly for Mexico, and Grandfather has his own agenda he seems to be dancing around.

We were able to meet at the airport as he was flying in and I was flying out.

He takes a puff of his cigar, exhales and makes it vanish in a cloud of blue smoke. Behind us, an airport police officer is walking through the crowded lounge trying to figure out where the smoke is coming from. She gives the Belgian college students piled around their backpacks and trays of Chinese fast-food and cheese-dripping pizza slices a suspicious look. They smile innocently back.

"My stepfather was an asshole," Grandfather says. "A pious man. I don't think he ever read a book in his life, besides the Bible. And even then, I think he only read it selectively. We lived on a tiny farm in the middle of Oklahoma. The world seemed so big, yet our lives so small."

"That's why you ran away to the circus," I reply. He's told versions of this story a thousand times in my presence.

"The circus makes for a more romantic story to how I became a magician. The truth is a little more complicated. I guess my point is, I wasn't running to something, just away from that tiny, narrow, little life. I know what it means to run away." He looks right at me.

"I never ran away," I retort sharply. Although, truth be told, I've been avoiding my family since I was twenty. I don't call myself Jessica Blackstar anymore. Born into that legacy and everything that came with it, I realized that world wasn't for me. Ironically, the last time I spoke to my grandfather at any great length, was years ago in Mexico, when I almost died. And now, my plane leaves in an hour to take me back.

Grandfather's cigar rematerializes at his fingertips and he takes another draw. Hand to chin, it's his reflective pose. He's got dozens of them. Combined with his strong features, which evoke those of an aging 1940s matinee idol, he has *presence*. These are traits he taught himself. He wiped away the Okie farm dirt to create a polished, erudite man who can, in a simple sentence, convince you that he alone possesses the greatest secrets of the universe—and all that it takes to witness them is the price of admission.

I try to imagine my grandfather as a young teenager, sitting in a dark movie theater alone watching movies, trying to pronounce his words like Richard Burton and Cary Grant.

"I know you too well, Jessica. You've always had that defiant look about you. Tell me, are you happy in the FBI?"

My happiness has never been a topic of discussion. "I enjoy my work."

"Even when it almost gets you killed?"

"I don't remember our business being all that different."

"The illusion of mortal danger isn't the same as the reality."

"Suffocating at the bottom of a lake seems like more than an illusion to me."

He shakes his head and looks away. "Things were under control . . ."

"No, they weren't."

"I've never wanted anything more for you than your happiness," he says, with too much conviction. It sounds like a line from a play.

"But that's the problem," I explain. "You can't see what makes other people happy. You only understand your own. You think someone without ambition is wasting their life. You have Dad convinced he'll never amount to anything because he can't live up to your legacy."

Grandfather rattles the ice cubes around in his glass of scotch as he stares up at the massive modern art mobile dangling overhead in the cavernous atrium. "Do they accept you?"

"Who?"

"Your *peers*."

He says the word "peers" dismissively, drawing it out. Uncle Darius liked to point out that Grandfather could add more syllables to a word than there were letters. "We get along great."

He raises a bushy eyebrow. Grandfather's judicious use of words is matched by his scrutiny of how other people choose them. "'Great' . . . Do they accept you? Do you get invited to watch Sunday football? Drinks at the bar after work?"

"I get asked."

"Mostly by men looking for something? Husbands wanting to step out on their wives?"

I shake my head and roll my eyes. "You're a bastard," I try to say the words calmly, but fail.

He inhales his cigar and swiftly sleeves it as the police officer walks past our table. She looks over her shoulder, smelling the smoke, and Grandfather gives her a smile before turning back to me. "I know what I am. Do you know what you are?"

"A cop."

"Like that fool?" He points to the airport officer. "Hopelessly wandering around here, trying to figure out how to confront me?

While I enjoy my smoke, she'll keep circling me, ignoring that man over there on his way to the Philippines to engage in illegal acts with minors. Or our Middle Eastern friend three tables over sitting next to his veiled wife who has bruise marks on her wrists. Are you that kind of cop? Ignoring the things you feel helpless about?"

"I've told old fools to put away their cigars and I've put away murderers and wife beaters."

"You're a garbage woman with a badge," he replies, swiping his hand in the air.

"I see it differently."

"Is there any less trash in the world?"

"Statistically? Yes. Crime rates are down. Are you arguing against the profession of law enforcement?"

"No. Just you being in it."

"Because I'm a woman?"

"Hardly. I'd stack you up against just about any man I know. No. Because you're," his voice halts for a moment. The carved scowl softens. " . . . because you're my granddaughter."

"Every woman is someone's granddaughter."

"None of them are a Blackstar."

"Well, actually, I'm a Blackwood."

"I left that name back in Oklahoma on the farm. You should too. You're not like them. You're not like any of them." He waves his cigar around, gesturing at the world. "You're special."

"The FBI is where I belong. I've never felt better about what I was doing than now."

"But do your peers really accept you? Do they consider you one of them?"

No, I think to myself. *I'm still the outsider.* Knoll and Ailes respect me. I get along with the others, but I'm not a part of their social circles. They're polite, to be sure, but nobody tries to set me up with their friends. The female agents keep their distance. I could be resentful, but I know it's not them. It's me.

"What would you have me do?"

"You're famous again from that whole Warlock business. You're interesting. At least for a moment."

The way in which he says "famous again," as if it's everyone's ambition to see their name on a magazine. "Then what?"

"Write a book. You could probably get a television show while you still have your looks. Run for office. It's a great place for photogenic people who grow old. Anything. Just something bigger. It's an opportunity."

"Then what?"

"Don't be childish. The Attorney General has less experience and intelligence than you. You could pass the bar, run for Senator, and have his job before you're forty."

"You make it sound easy."

Grandfather smiles. "For you, it should be. These people, they know nothing about themselves, much less how people like us think."

I've never heard my grandfather speak of success like this before. "I thought you were going to try to convince me to do Broadway."

"I know you well enough to see where your heart is. I recognize my own stubbornness when I see it."

"Then why can't you accept me doing this?"

"Because . . ." He pauses for the right words. "Because it's too small."

"Small?"

"Small for someone with your talents."

This is his special way of giving a compliment. He tells you you're so good, you must be failing at something larger. "I'm good at it."

"I'd bet you're one of the best. You are my flesh and blood. That's why you need to do something that challenges you. Something where the payoff amounts to more than putting some sad person in jail for doing something to another sad person." He points to the retreating airport police officer. "Let her take out the trash."

"Wow." I shake my head once more. "I knew you had an ego. I just had no idea." I was a fool for thinking we could have a simple talk without drama.

"It's not egotistical to want something better for you than I had. Magic must seem silly to you now. It does to me. But to that boy back in Oklahoma, it was everything. Our adolescent dreams shape the adults we become. I should have dreamed bigger. I think I really could have made something of myself." His voice trails off as he looks away.

"Could have?"

He stubs out his cigar in his empty drink and gets to the point. "Even the man that defies death has to acknowledge that it's just a trick." He sighs. "I'm sure you guessed. I have to go into the hospital. The doctors say it's treatable. I'm optimistic. But it just puts things in perspective . . ."

"And that's why you wanted to talk to me?" I notice he conveniently waited until my flight was about to be called to deliver this news. I have a million questions now, but I know him well enough to know he's said all that he'll say on the matter.

"Among other reasons. I like to see your face. Even when it's scowling like it is right now. In my advanced age, I've begun to realize my single greatest accomplishment."

"What's that?"

A smile forms. "You. Somehow this family of misfits brought us you." There is a goddamn tear in his eye. Is this what old age does to you? I don't know how to respond. His large hand reaches out and pats mine.

"Jesus Christ, are you getting soft?" I try to make it sound like a joke.

"Don't count on it. I just don't want any of us to die with regrets. It's bad enough to live with them. I've got plenty."

I give him a hug as my alarm goes off. "You're a complicated bastard," I tell him before walking to the gate.

"Jessica," he calls out. "Should we be worried about this hell-mouth thing on the news? You're not involved, are you?"

I pause for a moment. "No," I lie.

"Good. Risking your life once was enough."

"Twice," I correct.

"Yes. I guess our Mexican debacle counts too. Did you know I almost died there once? And your uncle spent some time in prison there. Nice place usually, except for us Blackstars. We always seem to have bad luck there."

I've only told him I was heading out of town on business, not where.

"Let me know if you need anything."

HE RETREATS DOWN the walkway. Suddenly his gait becomes clumsy. He bumps into the man he singled out as a wife abuser. He drops a lit cigar into the man's pocket before moving on. A minute later, the police officer walks by again and corners the man as his pocket spews smoke.

Grandfather looks back and gives me a wink.

11

"DO YOU KNOW why they call it the Caves of the Dead?" asks Dr. Moya as he sloshes through knee-deep water. His body is just a short silhouette in the blue glow of his flashlight. Giant daggers of shadow slide across the walls as we pass stalactites stretching from the ceiling to the surface of the water. Moisture glistens their ragged edges making it feel like we're in a reptile's mouth.

"I thought it was just 'cave' and not 'caves'?" I protest as the cold water pours over my borrowed boots, soaking my socks.

"There are many Caves of the Dead here." He points his light toward a dark passage. "Some of them are connected. Maybe all of them. But, back to my question." Dr. Moya speaks perfect English. Educated in Mexico and the US, he's got that Socratic way of asking you questions instead of telling you things.

With Ailes, it's earnest. With Grandfather, it can be condescending. I think Moya is just being himself.

Apparently, my FBI badge didn't impress him. I'd asked him about the source of the psilocin variant we found. His answer was to take me into the cave to help collect his sample kits. With his research assistant filling in at a nearby school for the underprivileged, he drafted me as an able-bodied helper. If I wanted his assistance, I would have to climb down the thirty-foot ladder.

I admire his pragmatism.

"Is it the Caves of the Dead because of all the dead things they find down here?"

I can see Moya's cherubic smile in the shadows. "All caves have dead things. Every cave could be called the Cave of the Dead. Skeletons were piled as tall as you at the mouth of this one when we first found it. Jaguars, cattle, coyote, a hundred other animals that fell down the hole and died."

"Didn't they find human remains in one near here?"

"*Si*. Where the church stands. The priests there took those bones and buried them nearby and renamed their cave "The Healing Cave." A little girl said she saw the Virgin Mary bathing her feet there once, and people have been coming there ever since. The church does quite well by the traffic, you could imagine.

"But no. The Caves of the Dead are much older than that. The people who lived here before, the Yucatecan, used to come down into the caves when they needed advice. Not the kind you got from throwing chicken bones on the ground or eating peyote with the elders. The Caves of the Dead was a place for matters of war. A shaman would be chosen to make the journey. He wouldn't always make it back."

"They'd get lost down here?"

"They'd lose their minds. The *Iluicatl michin*, as the ritual was called, was supposed to open a door. On the other side you could see the realm where the dead lived. If the Old Coyote was digging many graves above, then you knew they were about to be filled. Sometimes the Old Coyote didn't want the shaman to return and kept his mind down here. The man who came back had the same body, but was filled with the spirit of the trickster and did wicked things."

"The trickster?" Black Nick had used that phrase.

"A native term for the devil. In primitive cultures good and evil weren't as black and white. Even the Greek and Roman gods were capricious."

"What was this ceremony?"

Moya turns out his light. The cavern is completely dark, darker than black. "What do you see?"

It's cold and damp. For the briefest moment I'm afraid this man could try to cut me or do something that'll require a violent response on my part. "Nothing."

"What do you hear?"

"Water dripping."

"What else?"

There's a faint splash. "Just water."

"Would you describe this cave as a living place or a dead place?"

"It feels somewhere between."

"That's what they thought." Moya flicks on his light, revealing a smile. "But to get to the other side, they needed the *Iluicatl michin*."

"And what was that?"

"It's what you came here for. It's the source of the chemical you asked me about."

"The paper you published didn't say where it came from specifically, just that you had isolated it from biological samples."

"That was a precautionary measure."

"For what?"

"Toads," he replies.

"Toads? I didn't know they kept up-to-date on the latest scientific literature."

Moya's boisterous laugh fills the cavern and continues to echo. Evidently he's been spending a lot of time by himself. He wipes away a tear. "I am sorry. I imagined a little toad reading *Nature*. When people found out you could get high by licking the skin of certain toads, young people and mental incompetents started doing this. I didn't say where I found this because I didn't want the same thing to happen. There are drug tourists who seek out these things. I couldn't care less about the fools that want to do a stupid thing, but I'm worried about the creature. This substance is very powerful. It's unlike other hallucinogens. It literally takes the mind to a dark place.

"There are stories of shamans coming back from the *Iluicatl michin* and killing entire villages. The dark spirit was powerful in them."

"You mean the drug?"

"Perhaps. But most drugs simply lower our resistances. We say things when we're drunk that we secretly hold in our hearts. A drug doesn't make you creative as much as it stops you from *not* being creative. It lets out what's inside you. But when it comes to this, where does that evil come from? Some might say it's a doorway. But although I'm a rational man, I can't understand why a man who never had a violent thought in his life would act out in such a way."

"Are you suggesting possession?"

"Which frightens you more? That each of us harbors in our soul the potential for evil, to do such wicked things as murder others? Or that real evil, the kind you came here to find, comes from outside and that we're safe as long as we remember we're fallible and don't invite it in?"

"I didn't expect this metaphysical discussion from a scientist."

Moya aims his beam in the water. "Look. Just wait." After a moment a small school of fish swim by. Tiny, each no bigger than my fingernail, they pass in and out of the light in a flash. "What is the water to them? The cave? If they have minds, do they have any concept of what's above their heads? What's an ocean to them? The universe? What are our legs to them? Do you imagine that for even a glimmer of a moment, they think we're something like them? No. We're part of their world. Transient. In a fraction of a second their brains will have moved on to some other stimulus.

"We're like that. We don't have the attention to focus on problems for a long time. We ponder things, we make equations until something new comes along. The deep questions, the big mysteries, you're not going to find the answers in the words of any one man. Not even the questions. You have to take the long view. What questions have we been asking collectively? What have we observed in tiny fractions, but can't describe as a whole? I think of these as slow questions. You know the parable of the blind men trying to describe an elephant as they touch it? Each one feels something different: the trunk, the tail, a leg? None of them see the whole. Science is good for specific questions. It's not so good at seeing elephants.

"Still, I don't believe in the supernatural, Agent Blackwood. I believe in science. I believe the universe can yield answers to our questions and our experiments. I'm just not sure if we really know how to ask the right questions yet. The slow ones."

I get a little of what he's trying to tell me. You can learn a simple sleight-of-hand and fool someone, but never fully understand why holding your hand a certain way as opposed to another evokes an almost mystical experience—a suspension of disbelief. It's not just that you tricked their optic system. Something happened that struck a primal chord in our relationship to the universe.

"Fortunately for me, I have simple questions. I just need to know the source of the chemical."

He veers down another passage. "Yes. Yes. *Iluicatl michin*. It means 'fish ceremony.' Our tiny little friends just swam past you. They're the source. The toxin is a defense mechanism they developed to keep hungry predators from eating them. When a coyote or a lizard travels down from the surface and swallows them, they release it. The animal then gets disoriented and lost. It dies down here, its body decomposing and feeding the bacteria that feed the fish. The fish have their revenge, as the corpse provides for their children."

"The circle of life," I reply, the song from *The Lion King* playing in my head. "Do you have any samples I can take with me?"

"Like psilocin, it breaks down in hours. You'll have to take some living fish with you. I'll help you get some tonight."

"Tonight? Why not now?"

"They like to sit in the pools of water where the moonlight reaches them."

Were-fish. Of course.

"It's so they can know when the bats come home. The fish eat their droppings."

"Delightful." I shake my head and follow him to the next chamber. "Moonlight, dark caves, bat *guano*, psychoactive fish. Quite a job you have."

"Gracias."

12

"THIS CAME FROM a bad place. You don't want to go there," says Patience Viñalon as she scrutinizes my mud samples from the tree in Hawkton. Moya had said she was the local expert on soil. He wasn't kidding. Where I just see mud, an expert like Patience can spot the color, clay content and environmental makeup on sight. She puts her books into her bag and hugs two waiting girls before they run to the playground outside. Tall, with long black hair, she's just over twenty. Her intelligent eyes suggest she doesn't have any trouble keeping up with Dr. Moya. She'd started doing field research into the geology of the area before she was a teenager. Moya picked her over scores of graduate students because of the quality of her undergraduate research.

A little boy with dark hair in his eyes wanders across the classroom, stares up at me, and whispers something under his breath to Patience as if he's too scared to say it out loud. My Spanish is barely passable enough to understand the whisper.

"He'd like to give you a hug," Patience translates.

I lean down and let the boy wrap his arms around my shoulders. He flashes me a gap-toothed smile, then runs after his friends.

There's a soft pang in my stomach. I remember that need for affection. My house wasn't a hugging household. If I initiated one, it would be politely reciprocated, but never more than that.

I was jealous of the cat because Grandfather and Dad would absentmindedly pet him if he happened to sit near them on the couch. Of course, when the poor beast sat in Grandfather's chair and got hair on it, he'd find himself tossed across the room by the scruff of his neck with the threat that next time it would be *"into the fireplace!"*

I watch through the window as the boy climbs onto a swing set. I'd pity him if I wasn't a little envious of the attention he seems to get from Patience and the other staff here. I feel guilty for my envy. I had it better than most kids, I'm sure.

"Some of them have parents. Some don't. We try to do the best we can for them," Patience explains as I watch the children through the window. "When I'm not helping Dr. Moya, I come here and teach science."

"We have foster programs in Mexico, but they're still quite new," says a woman standing by the door. Her English is perfect. Short, dressed in a blouse and slacks that I recognize as being more expensive than they first seem, she looks like a plain woman—the exception being a Parmigiani watch on her wrist. Her hair is pulled back to reveal a face with simple makeup. She has a soft face, making her age difficult to tell.

Patience makes the introductions. "Sister Marta, this is Jessica."

"Hello, Sister," I reply.

Marta politely smiles. "What do you think of our school?"

"It's quite nice," I respond with sincerity. "The children seem very happy here."

"Lots of hugs. We make sure these children are very loved." Marta gazes out at the playground filled with new swing sets and toys. Her smile seems genuine.

"They look it."

"What brings you to Tixato?" She eyes my bags sitting on the desk.

"I'm on vacation and a friend asked for a favor."

"A favor?"

"He's a geologist and wanted some samples." I feel guilty lying to a nun, but it's important to keep a low profile. You don't know who knows who.

"Oh." Her expression changes to one of suspicion. "Are you a scientist too?"

"No, no. I'm a bookkeeper. Between jobs, actually."

Patience doesn't know as much as Dr. Moya, but she knows I'm not telling Marta the truth. Although she keeps silent, her eyes narrow as I lie.

"I'm sure something will come up." She nods to the window. "Tixato may not be much, but it's a special place." Marta gives Patience a pat on her shoulder, then leaves the classroom.

"Sister Marta is wonderful," Patience says enthusiastically. "She's the reason this place exists. She found the money and made it possible for these children to have something special."

"They're fortunate to have you."

"They're like my little sisters and brothers. Are you close to your family?" She'd have to charge by the hour for me to tell her the full story on that. "My mother left when I was young." I've used this truth before to end the conversation.

Patience's face turns sad. "Were you raised by your grandmother?" Her expression shows how deeply she cares.

"Um, no. Mostly my dad and my grandfather. My grandmother died before I was born." It's an odd subject for me to address. Dad never spoke too much about his mother. He was in his teens when she died. Grandfather would mention her name in passing, but they were divorced years before she passed away.

I think I learned from their example when it came to dealing with the absence of my own mother.

"Cousins?"

"I never had much contact with my mother's side of the family."

"None at all?"

"It's . . ." I decide not to explain to her my mother came from a difficult background. She was young when she had me. Younger than Patience. I've never been really bitter about her departure. After all, I barely remember anything about her from when I was a child.

I pick the mud samples off the desk along with the printout from the lab. "You were saying this came from a bad place. What do you mean? Dangerous?"

"Yes." She gives me a solemn nod.

"Could I at least see it?"

She thinks it over for a moment. "Okay. You'll understand when we get there. But we must take my car. If they see someone from not around here, that would be bad."

Twenty minutes later we are on the other side of the small range of hills dividing Tixato. I see what Patience meant by a "bad place." Hundreds of shanty houses pile on top of each other up a red dirt hill, above which it looks like part of the mountain has been scooped away. Assembled from rotten plywood, pieces of plastic and metal siding, the houses embody the poorest side of Mexico. I remind myself that even the United States still has pockets like this.

One paved road runs through the area. Half-naked children hide behind doorways while scowling teenagers linger on carcasses of rusted cars, shooting suspicious glances.

"What's that?" I ask. "X-20" is spray-painted on a number of walls. I know it's one of the fastest-growing gangs in Mexico and now the American Southwest, but I want to hear Patience describe them.

"It's a gang. Many of the young people who live here are in it. It's not as violent here as it is elsewhere, thankfully. It was started by some former members of our special forces. Most of them are dead now."

"Who runs it now?"

Patience shrugs. "I don't know. They used to just be involved in street trafficking. Now they're supposed to be in narcotics across the border. I don't pay attention to those things.

"They don't like outsiders here. Tixato is mostly a safe place, but if you went wandering around here alone, it would be no good."

"Is this why you say this is a bad place?"

"No. There, see the side of that hill? That's why." She points to where the vegetation and rock give way to the reddish earth that slopes down into the shantytown. "There used to be another village here. Then they had mudslides and the whole hill came down on them. This village was built on top of the wreckage."

"That's horrible," I reply, trying to imagine the houses buried under the ones I'm staring at. My chest tightens at the thought.

"You don't understand." Patience's voice descends to a whisper as she points to the ground. "They're still down there. Over a hundred people, children. The old orphanage. They just built over them. They never dug them up. At the top of the hill there's a small marker. That's it, and even that marker has been covered by graffiti.

"It was bad. They killed one of the rescue workers because it took so long to get here. Officials barely checked for survivors in the buried homes. Government ministers won't even come here for fear they'll be killed. It's like this place doesn't exist."

The dirt is the same color as my mud. "This is where the dirt sample came from?"

"Yes. You can tell by the mixture of clays and volcanic ash. Soil composition is like a fingerprint."

We reach the end of the road and Patience turns the car around. On the second pass I see more than the weariness of poverty in the eyes of the people watching us: anger and resentment burns. These are people who feel betrayed not only by society, but also by God.

I don't know how the mud got from here to the tree in Hawkton, but I have no difficulty understanding how they could be connected in some way. Both places of devastation, Hawkton and Tixato are linked by anger.

Patience drops me off at my car by the orphanage. Sister Marta waves to us as she pushes the boy who hugged me on the swing. I wave back and head to my hotel to call Ailes. Hopefully I get a cell phone signal. I've been out of range almost since I got here.

13

Back in the hotel, I click on my television and don't like what I see. The Spanish version of CNN is showing the aftermath of the church explosion juxtaposed with images of the sheriff. You don't need to know Spanish to understand the words *"caníbal"* and *"zombi."*

It's futile to point out that technically, the sheriff isn't a cannibal. He just used his teeth in the attack. Of course, the fact that if he *was* in the explosion he would be dead by now doesn't deter the zombie theories. Not that anybody takes them seriously. Scratch that, nobody serious takes them seriously. Unfortunately, there are a lot of people out there that do.

The television cuts back and forth to clips of helicopters buzzing over the hills of West Virginia, Virginia, Ohio, Maryland and Pennsylvania. Tracking teams with dogs are scouring the ground. Even heat-sensing drones and satellites have been called into the search.

"This is getting out of hand," I tell Ailes on my check-in call.

"Wait until the details of the satanic symbols gets out. We're going to move on from half-joking zombie panic to something worse."

We saw this happen before, with the case of the Warlock. A case too sensational to be true is irresistible to the media. "And I thought things here were crazy," I say, dreading the escalation of things.

"Anything come of Dr. Moya?"

"He says the toxin is from a cave fish. They're nocturnal and only come out in the moonlight. We're getting a sample tonight."

"Of course," he replies dryly. "What about the mud?"

"One of his students showed me the area it came from. It's a shantytown barrio. They collected samples after the last mudslide buried half the village. They're hoping to find some kind of shrub or tree with deep roots to plant there to keep it from happening again."

"Anything to suggest how that mud got tracked all the way to West Virginia?"

"Tixato has a strong gang presence. Especially in that barrio. It's X-20 territory. We know they're involved in cross-border narcotics smuggling. If I was going to hire a killer, that'd be where I'd look."

"The Hawkton incident seems a little more sophisticated than a gang-style slaying."

"True. But X-20 has a number of former Mexican Special Forces guys. Our sixth man may have grown up in Tixato, gone off to serve, then come back. I'm sure X-20 pays better. Some of those Mexican troops were involved in Indian scuffles. There are rumors of death squads doing heinous stuff. Nothing that'd be out of place in Hawkton."

"True, but how is our lead suspect, the sheriff, connected to them?"

"Directly? I don't know. But Moya told me the chemical we found could cause very violent auditory and visual hallucinations. Somehow there's a connection. That might explain Jessup's strange behavior."

"The X-20 lead is interesting. It gives us another angle besides looking at locals. Maybe the sheriff did something to piss them off?"

"Like ticketing an X-20 lieutenant?"

There's a pause. "Sorry, dealing with another crisis. Maybe."

"Here's the thing I've been trying to wrap my head around. This . . . *whatever* isn't a gang-style killing intended to warn off others. It was about the people who died, not the ones they left behind. They were the target."

"Interesting perspective. Behavioral analysis has drawn a similar conclusion. If it's not just the sheriff, we might be dealing with a more complicated person than we realize. Several people with resources change the picture quite a lot. Has anybody ever explained how X-20 has been able to get hundreds of millions of dollars of narcotics across the border?"

"No," I reply. "They're sophisticated. I guess that's the military training playing its part. They know how Border Patrol and the DEA work."

"They appear to be a complex operation."

"Yeah. And how widespread, if we're finding literal footprints in West Virginia? Speaking of which, any word from my friend Black Nick?" I ask.

Ailes hesitates. "I was going to wait until you got back to tell you."

"What?"

"We sent some field agents to do an interview. When they got there they found his shack burned to the ground."

"What? And him?" He was "out there," but he had grown on me. He was helpful in his strange way and seemed to be concerned for me.

"No sign of him. It looks like he may have set the fire."

"Christ. Crazy bastard. Keep an eye out for him. I'm pretty sure he's harmless. Pretty sure . . ."

"You've said that. I hope that's the case. I'll make some calls to Customs so we can get your fish across the border. How is the chemical extracted?"

"It isn't. Moya said the shaman would eat the fish whole and they'd produce the toxin in the stomach. Apparently, because they've evolved to the harsh chemistries of the cave, they can swim for a while in your gut and keep producing the hallucinogen."

"Delightful. Well that raises the question of how one got into the sheriff's stomach."

"Hawkton's not known for its sushi."

"Wouldn't be the strangest thing you could find to eat in West Virginia. And if the fish have to be transported live, that does play into the X-20 connection. They'd certainly have no trouble getting them across the border. Psychoactive fish . . ." I can practically hear him shaking his head.

"Remember, these gangs compete in horrific ways to torture each other. Have we had anyone follow up on what the deputy's daughter told me, about strange stuff going on?" I ask.

"Actually, yes. It's hard to make sense of things. Digging a little deeper, we're getting stories ranging from odd lights in the sky to Jesus visitations. Some people talked about the feeling they were being watched. Apparently the Alsops had called in to Jessup several times about trespassers, then their dog was killed. McKnight too. We're looking into the more unusual sightings."

"Didn't he say he found hoof prints near his house?"

"He told Deputy Baldwin he saw glowing eyes outside."

"Christ."

"It all stopped on the night of the explosion. People say they haven't felt the 'presence' since then. The one upside, if you can consider it that, is they're not talking to the press about it."

"I think they have enough attention with their cannibal zombie sheriff on the loose."

"Did you talk to anyone down there about the case?"

"Not in specifics. I told Moya what you told me to say. I've kept my purpose here close to the vest."

"Hold on . . . Interesting . . ."

"What's interesting?"

"We just got a tip passed on to us from our Mexico City office. I'm watching the wires for Mexico while you are down there."

"What is it?"

"A name of a possible suspect. Nèstor Albó. He has ties to Tixato and has been arrested for dealing in the US. He calls himself a 'shaman' and sells mainly to college kids in the North East."

Now I shake my head. "I hear more of that now. Drug dealers calling themselves 'shamans' so everyone feels more enlightened about the experience of getting high. What do you think?"

"It's an interesting lead. He's been to the US and Tixato. No known ties to X-20, though."

"Hard to imagine anyone involved in drugs who has links down there *not* being connected to them," I reply.

Ailes, cautious about jumping to conclusions, points out, "He could be in a rival gang, or we just don't know the connection."

"Curious. Any idea of where he is now?"

"We're looking into him. We believe the US. The Mexican police are known for not wanting to go out of their way to tell you where their sources come from."

"I'll let you know what I hear." I glance out the window. "Got to run. It's dark out. I think the bats have left the cave. Time to go get our fish."

"Blackwood, be careful."

"Hopefully your tip works out and the sixth man is a long ways away from here, off in the woods with the sheriff."

14

WHEN I PULL up to Moya's location, his Ford Explorer is parked near the mouth of the cave. The tailgate is open and the coolers he uses to carry samples are still sitting there. His headlights are on, cutting through the darkness into the brush. His toolbox of scalpels, pipettes and other instruments is wide open, but there's no sign of him.

I take a closer look at his toolbox. I spot a drop of blood on the plastic. It could be nothing, but . . .

Just beyond the front of the SUV is the cave entrance. A hole in the ground, in the moonlight it looks like a black puddle with the top of the aluminum ladder poking through.

"Dr. Moya?" I shout below.

There's no reply except for my echo. I go back to his SUV and rummage around for one of the powerful flashlights he uses in the caverns. A branch snaps behind me. I wheel around and see the outline of someone standing in the dark.

"Are you a friend of Dr. Moya's?" the stranger asks in slightly accented English.

"Yes. Who are you?" I keep close to the SUV. I have a gun under my jacket, but his hands appear empty so I don't reach for it just yet.

"I'm Officer Esteban. I'm with the Ministerial Federal Police. I came to check up on the doctor. I'm a friend of the family."

He steps into the headlights. He's young, in his mid-twenties. Dressed in slacks and a tailored shirt, he looks like he'd be more at home at a Mercedes dealership than in the police force. He carefully pulls out a badge and shows it to me. I notice the gun under the hem of his shirt. "I'm a cop, like you." He gives me a broad smile of perfectly veneered teeth.

I nod back at him. "I was supposed to meet Dr. Moya. There's blood here. I think he's in trouble."

Esteban walks over and takes a look at the splatter. "Is there a first-aid kit here?"

I see a white box with a red cross and remove it from a plastic crate. Esteban pulls out a flashlight, walks over to the hole, and aims the beam into the dark. "I can barely see the bottom. We should go and check on him."

I join him with the first-aid kit. Then something dawns on me as I turn my back on him, about to climb down the ladder: How did Esteban know I was a cop?

How did he even know to speak to me in English? With my dark hair, I often get mistaken as Latina.

I don't trust him.

He's a little too concerned with me, and not so much Dr. Moya.

Something is wrong.

"Ladies first," he says smoothly as he points to the ladder.

I glance back and give him a bashful grin. "You go. I'm a little unsteady with heights."

"I'll hold the top of the ladder for you."

I could just be hysterical. Maybe Moya told him about me? If Esteban wanted me dead, he could have shot me from the trees. Unless . . .

My mind goes into overdrive. If he needs to make it look like an accident . . . An FBI agent found dead with a gunshot wound would certainly bring more attention than Esteban wants. An accident is different. If I fall down the ladder and get killed, that wouldn't raise an alarm. Especially because there's no reason anyone down here should want to kill me, at least that I know about.

Killing cops who are chasing down clues only brings more cops. The surest way to look suspicious is to do something dumb like that. It doesn't make any sense right now.

I was abducted once before. Ever since then I've been a little paranoid. Maybe that's why I've been dwelling on the Buick recently. I swore I'd never let it happen to me again. Much of my free time since the incident has been spent at the Academy, working on my martial arts skills.

I take a breath. I need to test Esteban before giving in to my paranoia full-force. "Hold on. Let me call a friend before we go down there. Better that someone knows where we are if we get lost too."

"Sure thing. Good idea," he agrees, as relaxed as can be.

He doesn't make any effort to stop me from pulling out my phone. Now I wonder if I *am* overreacting. I decide to follow through with my ploy anyway, and walk over to the bumper of Moya's SUV to sit with the first-aid kit on my lap. I call Ailes's direct number. While I wait for the connection I absentmindedly sort through the open toolbox, keeping an eye on Esteban.

The phone keeps ringing, but there's no answer. I try the FBI direct line next. The call doesn't connect.

"Trouble?"

"I can't get through." Great.

"The signal here sucks," Esteban says. "If Moya is hurt, we really shouldn't keep him waiting."

"You're right." I come back to the cave mouth and hand him the first-aid kit. "You go down while I try to get through."

He takes too long to respond. "I really wouldn't know my way down there."

I play up my helplessness. "Neither would I."

"There's no point in both of us getting lost." He reaches for his phone. "I might get a better signal. Why don't you go down while I call?" There's an urgency to his voice that he didn't have before.

This is a setup.

I reach for my gun. Esteban is faster getting his out. He points it at my head. I freeze.

"Sorry, sister. Too slow." He drops the helpful act.

"Is Moya even alive?" I ask.

"Probably. Now go down the fucking ladder." He's lost his smoothness. There's more than anger in his tone, maybe even desperation.

I don't move. One twitch and I could be dead.

Esteban grabs me by the neck with his left hand and pushes his muzzle to my temple with his right. "I said move, bitch!"

I have to think my way through this. What does he want? "You squeeze any harder, you're going to leave a bruise. Tell me that won't look suspicious?"

He relaxes his grip and moves the barrel a centimeter away from my temple, then uses his left hand to grab my ponytail. "Don't do what I say, and by the time they find you, it won't matter." He yanks my scalp toward the hole. "Down."

I flash back to that moment outside the Texas church when I let my guard down. After I was rescued, I'd vowed never to make the same mistake. That determined vigilance has affected me in a lot of different ways.

Now, when I feel the hint of something odd, I find myself subconsciously preparing for an attack.

I think it's my past playing into it too. Magicians practice a coin vanish or a card sleight to the point where we aren't even conscious of doing it. The first step is to practice until you can fool an audience. The final step is to fool yourself. You work to get so good, you don't even know you did it.

I know theatrical pickpockets who have to make embarrassing phone calls to the booker after they get home and find an extra watch they slipped off a stranger's wrist at an opportune moment.

Instinct.

There's something cold and metallic in my sleeve. While I was trying to reach Ailes on the phone, I stole a scalpel. As I kneel, Esteban reaches for my gun. He sees the flicker of reflected moonlight as the blade appears at my fingertips.

15

I MISS HIS JUGULAR and hit Esteban's collarbone. The blade still goes in and he screams. He pulls away from me and out of reach. I hear something metallic splash in the water below.

My gun.

It slipped from my waistband.

Fuck. It must have fallen into the cave during our struggle.

I could run for the trees, but I won't get far in the dark. He's done with the game. He'll shoot me before he lets me escape. There's only one place to go.

I jump into the hole and hit the ladder hard. It buckles on me, nearly throwing me off. But I hold my grip and keep climbing down, pulling my body into the dark.

Gravel stings me as Esteban runs to the edge of the hole and points his gun into the shadows. Silhouetted by the moonlight, I can tell he's trying to decide what to do. His original plan must have been to push me off the ladder when I climbed in at the top, but now I'm out of reach. I slide down the last few rungs and slip out of the light.

He aims the flashlight he took from the SUV around to spot me. Because he has to use one hand to brace himself over the edge to keep himself from falling, there's no way for him to simultaneously catch me in the light and aim.

A dark drop of blood falls from above through the beam of his flashlight and splashes into the water. It's not the torrent I'd like, but I know I've hurt him just the same.

"Coming down?" I taunt. I want to make him hesitate. I need him to think I have the upper hand. My eyes slowly adjust to the dark. Sticking to the shadows, I go to my knees and start feeling around in the water for my gun.

The pool is only a foot deep, but the bottom is a murky gunk of sharp rocks, rotting vegetation, and the small bones of animals that fell down here and died. Slimy things slither past my fingers. Sharp objects poke into my hands.

The torch beam disappears for a moment, then comes back. I duck to the side just as he fires his gun. That's his plan: wait for me to step into the moonlight as I look for my gun, then shoot me.

I shrink against the wall, out of his reach, and my leg touches something soft. It's a body. Dr. Moya is slumped against a rock. I put a hand to his throat and feel a pulse. He makes a small moan and says something in Spanish. I'm glad he's still alive, but I have no idea how I'm going to be able to help him.

Esteban's shadow is visible in the circle of light cast on the water by the moon. His roaming flashlight beam falls on the ladder and inspects the area around its feet. He can't wait much longer, because I could go deeper into the caves. I might get lost and die, but there's a small chance I'd find another way out, or be able to outlast his patience.

He's not going to let that happen.

What he can't comprehend is that there's no way I'm leaving Moya alone right now. That's my biggest weakness. But whatever kind of sociopath Esteban is, he doesn't see that.

The ladder shakes as he takes his chances that I haven't found my gun yet. I haven't. I keep digging into the horrible ooze to no avail. It's most likely right in the moonlit middle of the water, where I can't search.

Esteban is the only one that's armed right now. And I think he's past the point of making my death look like an accident.

He takes another step, then pauses, pivots and points his torch into the dark recesses of the cave. I pull a rock free from the bottom and throw it across the pool.

Esteban fires at the moving target, but then he realizes the trick and aims at the direction it came from.

I'm still out of range for now. Unfortunately, there's nowhere behind me to go. If I want to move, I have to run through the light. Which would be suicide.

Still on the ladder, he has the higher ground.

Normally that would be an advantage . . .

He descends to the next rung.

I think.

What makes him vulnerable?

Gravity.

I run for the ladder.

I leap into the air and kick it with both feet.

The bottom of it buckles, gets knocked free from the ground, and slides out from underneath him. I hit the water on my side and roll free as the ladder comes toppling down. Esteban falls the full thirty feet and slams into the rocks. There's a sickening crack followed by a splash. His screams are muffled by the water as his head goes under for a moment.

Broken, sprawled out, he flails. I stagger to my feet, ignoring my bruised hip, and pry the gun from his fingers. He lets out a howl as he tries to lift himself on his broken arm. I pistol-whip him unconscious so I can find my gun before he does. It's a savage thing to do, but this is a matter of survival.

"Remind me to stay on your good side," says a weak, but alert, Dr. Moya.

I cross over to him and grimly smile in the moonlight before probing his arms and legs for broken bones. "Who is he?"

"A policeman, I believe. He looked familiar."

"Seriously?" I was hoping the badge was a fake. Now I've done it. This is even worse than I thought. I may have just killed another cop.

16

Eꜱᴛᴇʙᴀɴ ɪꜱ ᴀ dirty cop. They're like cockroaches: where there's one, there's more. I've met some hardworking Mexican police who risk their lives every day to bring justice, but all it takes is a few corrupt ones and you no longer know whom to trust—the whole system falls apart. I've got nowhere to run.

Esteban had kicked Moya down the ladder just before I got there. Fortunately for the professor, he landed on his arm and got only a mild concussion. Esteban himself is in slightly worse shape. He shattered a leg, his arm, and at least one rib.

I right the ladder to fetch some materials from Moya's SUV so I can make a splint for his sprained arm before helping him up out of the hole. I wrestle with leaving Esteban at the bottom of the cave. It would be the safest course of action, but it's not a moral or an ethical one.

My phone still isn't working, so I can't call for backup. If I leave him, he'll probably be alone for hours before any help can be sent back to him. His wounds are severe enough that he could die.

I couldn't live with that.

My only choice is to use the winch on Moya's SUV to pull Esteban up. I sling the cable under his arms, padding it with a blanket. Moya controls the motor as I guide Esteban's body up the ladder. He screams bloody murder before passing out, which makes the most difficult part a little easier.

With Moya covering him with his own gun, I put Esteban's arm and legs in a splint using duct tape and broken branches. To be safe, I handcuff his free wrist to a handle in the back of Moya's SUV.

"If he moves, hit him," I tell Moya, who is now sitting in the passenger seat, as I turn the ignition.

"Gladly." Moya is holding up better than I expected.

"Where's the nearest hospital?"

"There's one in Tixato, but there might be a problem . . ."

"Right. It's next to the police station?" I recall. "That's a little inconvenient."

"*Si*. Most of them are good men, though."

"But we don't know which ones he knows. We also don't know who he's working for. Hell, I don't even know why he wanted to kill me."

"He was after you?" Moya gives an exaggerated sigh. "There's a small mercy for me."

"How far is the next hospital?" I ask.

"About thirty miles."

"Damn. They could be waiting."

"How do you know?"

"It's what a good cop would do. Or a bad one. If Esteban was supposed to do this for someone else, they'll be expecting a report telling them that it's taken care of. When it doesn't come, they'll know something went wrong." I check my phone again for a signal. I still can't get through. "Does your phone work?"

"It got broken in the fall."

"How about Esteban's?"

Moya reaches into the backseat and rifles through the barely conscious Esteban's pockets. The old man is tough. He barely grunts as he makes the effort. "I found two."

"Of course. One's a burner."

He checks them both. "Neither seem to be working right now."

"What is it with the cell phone signal around here?"

"Sometimes it goes down. I've heard the gangs will take out towers when they want to keep the police away."

I slam the steering wheel. "Christ!" I can't call Ailes for help, and I can't go to the police.

We reach the end of the dirt road and get on the highway. I head north, more out of instinct than any logical reason. Almost midnight, the road is deserted. There aren't any streetlights, so Moya's headlights provide the only illumination other than that from the clouded moon. Another car could be ten feet behind me and I'd never know.

As we drive I try to think of a plan. I need to get both of them medical assistance. If I find a working phone I can call for help then leave them to be found. The trouble lies in trying to track down a landline this late and in this day and age.

"What was that?" Moya breaks my concentration.

"What?" I stare into the darkness beyond the road.

"Something went past the window. Like a big bat."

"Maybe it was a big bat? You said they live around here."

"Not that big. Maybe I'm delirious," he replies and shakes his head.

"You holding up okay?" I ask. I'd never even asked my grandfather that at the airport. Do people have to be physically hurt in front of me for me to notice their pain?

"I've done worse. I'm getting too old to be stumbling around in caves."

"You're not going to make it out of here," Esteban says weakly from the back. "There's no place to go." His hoarse voice is full of pain.

"Who are you working for?"

"It doesn't matter. We're all dead now."

"I can get you help."

He laughs faintly. "You can't even make a call."

"Tell me what this is about. We can make a deal." I angle the rearview mirror so I can see him and keep my attention on the road.

"There aren't any deals. None of us will see dawn."

"They're going to kill you because you screwed up?"

"Essentially," he replies.

I try to push him into giving up more information. "So how's it feel to know you're about to die?"

He raises his head and looks out the window. "For what it's worth, sister, my heart was never in killing you, I hope you know that. I didn't have much of a choice."

"Who? Who put you up to this, Esteban?"

He doesn't respond.

"If you think you're going to die, why not tell me?"

"If I keep my mouth shut, I'll get a merciful death. They'll leave my family alone."

"What did Moya see outside?"

"A bat," replies Esteban.

"Bullshit." He's hiding something. I'm on the verge of pulling over and aggressively interrogating him.

"Bat . . ." He lets outs a laugh. "They're watching us. Right now, men are on their way to kill you. You won't even make it to the next town."

There's a small glow in the distance. "Is that the town?"

"No," says Moya. "It's a bodega. A market with a little kitchen. A woman and her father run it. They live in the back."

I pull into the parking lot. It's a small cinder-block cube of a building. The front is tiled? plastered? with a rainbow of signs for sodas and candy. The only opening I can see is the glass door, its exterior covered with metal bars. The inside is dark.

"Can you walk?" I ask Moya.

"Yes, I'm good. I think my arm is only bruised. I will get the key for the store."

Moya returns with the confused woman and her father. They see Esteban in the back of the SUV, and Moya gives them an explanation that's too rapid-fire for me to know if he's telling the whole truth.

I write down Ailes's number on my business card. "Go with them. Don't go to a hospital. Go to a friend's house and try to call this number from there."

"What about him?" He points a thumb at Esteban.

"He's staying with me." I look to the dark sky. "Hurry before their bat-thing sees you." It may be nothing. It might be a drone.

After helping me to drag Esteban into the store, Moya talks the reluctant woman and her father into taking him to a safe place. I park the SUV behind the back of the store so it's not visible from the road.

Esteban could be all talk about roadblocks and other people coming after me, but I don't want to take the chance. If I come across a roadblock, they will gun me down before I can slam on the brakes. It's also too dark and there are too many dangerous curves in the roads. I don't know my way around here.

My safest bet seems to be hunkering down in a secure place. The bodega looks like a World War II pillbox if you ignore the flashy posters and colors. I decide we're better off waiting for help in here than out in the open.

I bolt the main glass door from the inside and drag a refrigerated case in front of the opening, then I push the freezer from the kitchen across the store's back entrance. To see out, I use a screwdriver I find in a toolbox under the counter to scratch holes in the poster that obscures the glass above the refrigerator case. Finally, I yank the racks from the shelves and wait.

Esteban slumps in the corner, silently watching me.

Just as I feared, forty minutes later I hear a truck pull into the gravel parking lot in front of the store. Through one of my poster holes, I spy five men in army fatigues climb out. A second pickup truck, with a heavy machine gun mounted to the bed, parks directly across from the front door.

A voice calls over a loudspeaker in accented English. "Agent Blackwood? Are you okay?"

"Looks like you've been rescued," says Esteban.

I give him a sharp look. If this is the cavalry, why do I feel like I'm an Indian?

17

THE FBI TRAINED me to handle hostage situations—but not the kind where *I'm* the one holding the hostage.

I push my face closer to the glass and shout, "This man says he's going to hurt me. He says he wants to speak with the American authorities."

"What are you doing?" Esteban hisses through pained groans. Crumpled like a rag doll, he's too weak to even raise his voice.

"Calling their bluff." The longer we can pretend Esteban is holding me hostage, the longer I stay alive.

"These men are here to help you."

"And you're a Ministerial Federal Police officer who was just trying to kill me. You do the math."

Beads of sweat pour down his face. "You're being a fool."

I need to buy some time. I can't trust anyone until I hear a familiar voice. Esteban fights through the pain to slide his body closer to me while my attention is on the armed men. "There's something you need to know . . ."

I give him a sideways glance and kick him in the shoulder. Then I pull a wad of paper towels from a roll and shove them in his mouth. "Don't even think about yelling," I say as I drag him behind the counter. Not taking any chances, I open a package of zip ties from the toolbox and bind his wrist to a drawer.

A man calls out my name again. He sounds sincere. Almost.

I cautiously resume my position by the door. "This policeman wants to speak to my superiors," I shout back. "He wants you to get them on the phone."

"Agent Blackwood, we're trying to reach them right now," he replies, still standing behind the headlights.

When this is over, I'll either look like the biggest fool or see their bluff called. So I use the time to prepare.

Back in hostage-rescue training, they taught us how to handle a variety of scenarios. If I was dealing with a hostage situation and had to enter a building, I'd send agents through the front and the back at the same time. The heavy refrigerator and freezer I pushed into place as barricades will slow these men down, but won't stop them. The key is to make the terrain difficult so they get pinned down.

Outside they're hesitating because they don't know what's waiting inside of here. You can practice a raid using a known floor plan all you want, but if you don't notice the coffee table in the middle of the room you're liable to trip and get yourself killed.

My survival depends on making this open space hostile and unfamiliar to them.

For a planned military maneuver you have barbed wire, barricades and a variety of other resources. This is a situation where I have to improvise. In training they showed us a variety of films and instructional videos depicting the different ways to act in a critical situation. They shared case studies about soldiers pinned down behind enemy lines who used everything from dead animals to car tires to make barricades.

My favorite example came when our instructor brought out a DVD case titled *A Narrative Example of Unconventional Domestic Defense Techniques Utilized by a Non-Combatant*. We were expecting another dry video, but it was *Home Alone* followed by *Die Hard*. Our teachers wanted us to understand that although these

Hollywood examples may not be the most practical, thinking outside of the box is an essential survival skill.

In the back kitchen of the bodega I knock down two shelves from the wall and stack them on top of the freezer in front of the back door. If the men make it through, they'll have to climb over that. This could give me the opportunity to take a shot.

There's a propane tank under the stove. I unhook it and place it behind the butcher's block.

I pull racks of merchandise behind the freezer and pour motor oil over them. Hopefully this will make navigating the obstacles even more difficult.

I'm changing the store into a briar patch.

For added protection, I kick over a squat freezer filled with popsicles and face the opening toward the back of the counter so it acts as a barrier. There's a bathroom I could retreat to, but that would leave me pinned down with no way out.

"Agent Blackwood," calls out the man hidden behind the lights. "Our phones don't seem to be working. Please tell Mr. Esteban there's little we can do. If he lets you go, we can bring this conflict to an end."

Esteban's eyes plead with me to agree.

I wonder if the military men actually believe that Esteban is holding me hostage. Given his fear of them, it's not an outrageous theory. If they do, it means that things are very compartmentalized within whatever organization they're working for. Distrust is my ally, for the moment.

It's all game theory. I'm alive right now because Esteban wanted to make my death look like an accident to avoid suspicion. In not taking a clear shot when he could have, he put himself in a position of vulnerability. These men might accept my claim because they think it's possible Esteban is using me for leverage after he screwed up killing me.

Even if they don't believe me, they could be playing along in the hope that I might come out willingly so they can still stage their "accident."

But for how long will they play?

The longer I stall this out, the better my chances are of getting help. At this point, my best strategy is to ignore them. Let them decide if Esteban is being difficult, or if it's me who is complicating things.

"Agent Blackwood?" Back at the front door, I steal a quick glance through the hole. As the man steps to the side and the light catches his shoulder, I can see he's wearing a sergeant's uniform. "Can we speak?"

I say nothing. Every minute of delay helps.

"We're having trouble with our phones," he repeats.

Of course. They could just use their radios, but there's no point in me telling them this. Doing so would tip my hand.

I take Esteban's phone from my pocket. There's still no signal, but it gives me an idea. I shout to the man outside, "Esteban wants you to bring a charger for his phone so he can make a call. He says he'll let me go then." I try to sound as vulnerable and desperate as possible, but to be honest I'm not sure how much of that is an act.

The charger is a simple request, yet it's bound to buy some time as they discuss it. If they agree, they'll have to find a charger. Assuming they don't have one in their trucks, the nearest one for miles is on a rack by my head. But I'm not telling them that.

"Hold on, Agent Blackwood. We'll get you out safely." His voice is so genuine. He's continuing the ruse with conviction—or I'm making a horrible mistake.

Twenty minutes go by. The real cavalry has yet to show up. I retreat from the front door and keep my back to the wall and my eyes on both entrances. In a real hostage crisis, the goal of the police is to rescue the innocent. But if these men are crooked like I think, they're not going to care who they hit when they burst through the doors. My only protection comes from making the idea of entering the bodega a very dangerous prospect for them. None want to risk a bullet if they think they can talk me out of here.

"Agent Blackwood, we'd like to speak to Esteban, please."

This is a stalling game. I ignore him.

"Agent Blackwood, please. We'll give him the charger if he speaks to us."

I make up an excuse to explain his silence. "He's afraid to come near the door."

"Tell him it's okay. We can bring his wife here to talk to him."

His wife?

Shit.

They just called my bluff. They've made it clear they have a hostage of their own.

Esteban stares at me with rage. He knows they'll kill her if I keep up this charade.

18

E STEBAN'S WIFE IS going to be murdered if I don't do something. He's a piece of dirt that can get shot in the crossfire for all
I care, but his wife is another matter. For all I know, she's a civilian with no part in this. My job is to protect her.

The only way to keep her out of this mess is to admit my bluff.
As long as they think Esteban is running things, she's in danger.

Esteban's eyes lose their anger and fill with pleading. There is
someone who cares inside of there. "She's got no part of this!" I
shout outside.

"Are those your words or his?" asks the sergeant. Once more
at my lookout, I can see the outline of his body as he stands in
front of the headlights. "You are holding a federal agent hostage,
Blackwood. This won't end well if you don't surrender."

"Let me speak with someone from my agency."

"Is Esteban even alive?"

I need to buy time. "Yes."

"What's his favorite football team?"

I run over to him, pull the wad of paper towels from his
mouth, and place my pistol against his temple. "The only way
you stand a chance of surviving is by telling me the truth. You
understand that?"

"Yes. Yes. Thank you, for my wife," he whispers through
twinges of pain.

"I'm not a monster," I tell him.

"Nor am I. Mallorca. They're my favorite."

Back at the front door, "Mallorca!" I shout.

The man steps away from the headlights and fades into the darkness. Right now he's assessing his options.

Now this isn't a hostage situation anymore, and I've made it clear that I won't walk into a trap that could make my death look accidental, they just want me dead.

Probably the easiest way to do that would be to start a fire.

Fortunately, however, the walls of this building are concrete and the roof is metal. Getting it to burn isn't going to work so well for them.

I take inventory again. On the rack where I found the motor oil is a stack of air filters. I pull them from their casings and start layering them.

Outside, there's the crunch of boots on gravel as men walk around the building. They're planning their attack. I have the advantage inside here, and they want to minimize that.

Using a box knife from the toolkit, I carve up an empty two-liter soda bottle and place the air filters inside. It's not the best gas mask, but it should protect my lungs if they use smoke grenades. I also spot a pair of children's swim goggles and I put them on my head, ready in a moment's notice to keep the tear gas out.

None of these measures is ideal, but each will give me a slight edge when they storm the building. I'll be more alert than they expect. I'll be able to shoot one or two of them as they come inside. Covering both doors will be a challenge, but hopefully my little obstacle course will slow them down.

"Who are these men?" I ask Esteban.

He knows there's no longer any point to hiding that information. If I survive this, I'll find out anyway. "Army," he says. "A special unit that combats narcotics in this area. They're all corrupt."

"Shocker. Friends of yours?"

"No," he shakes his head. "They had a choice."

"So did you."

"Things are complicated here. You heard them mention my wife. What would you do? What if you knew some of your superiors worked with them? Who would you go to?"

Suddenly, I don't have an answer. His world is different from mine.

"Imagine that on your first day at your job you see your boss picking up a bribe for his boss?" Talking is hard for him, but he wants to make his point. "You know that if you say anything to anyone, it's more than likely going to end up getting you hurt, or worse."

So Esteban considers himself as a victim. Reluctantly, I see his point of view to a degree. I need to play on this. "Can you help me?"

Sweat trickles down his brow and he winces. "There's nothing I can do."

"We can give you protection if you tell me who is behind this."

"Can you protect my wife? My family? Her family? You can't even protect yourself right now."

Yeah, that. "I don't even know why they want me killed. I'm not DEA. I don't know anything about X-20."

"I don't know why either. I was simply told to kill you."

"You accept orders without explanation? By who?"

Esteban ignores the question.

"How long before they storm this building?"

"They're waiting."

I glance through the hole. "On what? Me?"

"Permission. Permission to kill you."

I keep holding out, waiting for the real cops to arrive, but I might be even more alone than I thought. "Are they watching the roads? Waiting to see if someone comes to help me?"

"They could . . ."

"What does that mean?"

"They don't need to. These men outside, the ones who are waiting on permission to kill you, they're the ones who would be sent to rescue you. Even if Dr. Moya called your bosses, they'd contact your Mexico City office. They'd then contact these men. They're the ones who are supposed to save you." Esteban gives me a weak smile and shakes his head in frustration. "Welcome to Tixato."

Christ.

"Right now," Esteban continues, "they're deciding that if they can't make it look like an accident, they need to make it look like I did it."

"But that would still look suspicious."

"An accidental death is a convenience. Not a necessity. If the suspicion ends with me."

"Why me?"

"Why me?" He closes his eyes. "Why any of us? Sometimes there are no reasons."

In the mirror over the counter, I see the headlights move. They're putting their trucks into a different position. Something is going to happen. "Time to move you." I grab Esteban by the shoulders.

He screams with pain as I shove him into the bathroom. I don't want him to get hit in the crossfire, because if we survive this, there might be a way to get him to talk. And part of me, even after what he did to Moya and tried to do to me, is sympathetic in some way. Maybe he wanted to be a good cop, but the system wouldn't let him.

I push his legs past the doorjamb as a cinder block hits the front doors. The glass shatters, but the bars are too thick to let anyone through and the refrigerator is still blocking the opening.

I pull the goggles down and place the filter over my face. In a hostage situation, the next step would be tear gas.

Only this isn't a hostage situation.

An explosion rocks the front of the store.

This is war.

19

THE FIRST GRENADE blast is so powerful it knocks the door off its hinges, and my refrigerator back a foot. Shards of cinder block sting my cheeks. I feel like I'm inside an oven. My whole body just got punched. I don't hear the second explosion because my ears are ringing. The back door smashes into my kitchen barricade.

These are the critical few seconds that can make all the difference. If I freeze up, they'll be on me in seconds.

Stunned from the blasts, I just want to lay still and recuperate.

That way leads to death.

I force myself to crawl toward the middle of the store.

The smoke is dense, but I can see light coming through the back. However, there's not enough room for a man to climb in. I tense up for the next barrage. Seconds go by that feel like hours.

Something small flies through a gap in the glass and lands inside the front of the store. I flatten myself against the ground behind the counter. The concussion of the flash grenade slams into me, hard.

The first round was to push back the barricades. This one was to catch me off guard. Fortunately, the counter absorbed the blast. If I'd been in the open store I'd be on the ground, unconscious with bleeding eardrums at best.

The refrigerator and freezer are simultaneously pushed

backwards as armored men rush into the store. I jump up and blindly fire two rounds into the swirling smoke toward the front, and two more at the back door.

The barriers stop moving. I've bought myself a few more minutes. I think.

For what?

Right now they're assessing the situation. They were hoping the blasts had knocked me out, and my gunshots proved otherwise. I also don't think they were planning on my fortifications. They won't last, but they got me this far.

If these men really are my only hope of rescue, I'm screwed. I've only got Esteban's gun and my own, plus two extra clips. With four spent rounds already, I'll run out of bullets before they do.

Quitting is death.

I climb out from behind the counters to reposition the freezers at the door.

As I push the refrigerator, through the broken glass and wire of the entrance, I spy the sergeant standing out in the open next to his relocated truck. My defenses took them all by surprise, but he's clearly confident that he has me pinned down and that he'll get me sooner than later.

I angle the muzzle of my gun between the freezer and the open door frame and fire off two rounds. One hits him in the chest and the other takes out his knee. He crumples to the ground, screaming, "*Puta!*"

I guess he was wearing body armor. But that hit to the leg tells me that for him, soccer is only going to be a spectator sport from now on. His men rush to his side and pull him into a truck.

There's a lot of yelling, followed by a burst of vengeful bullets. It's futile on their part. I'm already clear of the door.

Tires squeal in the distance as they drive him off to the hospital. Shooting him was cold-blooded, but I have to be to survive.

With him taken out of the equation, these men aren't going to be making the most rational decisions. They'll either wait for instructions from their superiors or try to get me now.

Other than my own deep breaths and the ringing in my ears, it's silent for a moment. Then I hear vehicles being moved around again. Another truck pulls up.

I wait.

They wait.

I crawl over to the bathroom and open the door to check on Esteban. He's still where I left him. "How many are there?"

He waits a while before gasping, "Eight, maybe ten. They could get reinforcements."

"Fuck."

I drop to the floor as gunfire erupts, so loud that it makes the grenade blasts seem like a pleasant memory. They're shooting that truck-mounted .60 caliber machine gun at the front of the bodega. Bullets rip through the concrete walls like it's soft plaster. Dust and debris flies into the air. I lay as flat as I can. The heavy bass of the gunshots sounds like hell ripping apart. The gun sweeps back and forth for a full minute until coming to a stop.

Beams of light stream through the hundreds of holes in the storefront. Eddies of dust swirl around like gray ghosts. Through the bullet holes and cracks, I can see the men's silhouettes race around the building toward the back.

"Make room." I push myself into the tiny bathroom, leaving the door ajar. Esteban cowers by the broken toilet. I get to my knees and keep an eye on the front and back door through the gap.

"How do you like Tixato so far?" he says dryly.

I put a hand over his mouth. The light is now mostly coming through the back, and it grows brighter. Something slams into the back entrance and the whole store shakes as a truck crashes into the opening.

Three men slide across the hood and land in the middle of the kitchen area, their legs trapped in the shelves. Standing up is difficult because of the motor oil.

From where I'm hiding, I have a clear view of one of them as he tries to raise a leg over the racks. He's got several cylinders strapped to his chest . . .

Some of the other men fire their weapons into the front of the store. I duck behind the bathroom door and wait. They fire again. Bullets hit the wall behind my head like blows from a hammer.

Through the crack in the door, I shoot at the man wearing the flash grenades over his body armor. There's a blinding burst of light, followed by another. The door to the bathroom buckles and slams into me.

Flash grenades aren't meant to be lethal. They're also not meant to be exploded on your chest. The man's plastic armor catches alight and a fire begins to rage in the kitchen.

Something else explodes, maybe a gas pipe.

I yank Esteban up onto his good leg and press his face near mine, against the small air vent. It's the only way we'll keep from suffocating. He groans again. I cover his mouth with my free hand to silence him.

The men in the burning kitchen scream. Metal crashes as they pull themselves from the blaze. Others holler as they try to help.

This wasn't their plan.

I wait. Minutes go by. Through the vent I hear a truck drive away, presumably taking more men to the hospital. The other vehicles remain. I pull away the bug screen for a better look. My view is limited to a narrow area on the side of the building, but I can see the shadow of a man on the .60 caliber gun. That probably means at least two more men are waiting in back.

They pull back a dozen feet or so, but don't leave.

We're still trapped.

My only hope now is to play dead and pray they give up.

Unfortunately, I'm sure they're not leaving until they see my corpse.

Hours pass. Esteban struggles to stay upright. I keep him pressed against the wall near the vent so he doesn't suffocate in the smoke. I take long, slow breaths and hope nobody sees the air vent.

Sometime later in the night, with dawn still a few hours away and when my legs are stiff from standing so long, I hear gunshots go off near the back of the store.

The smoke has cleared, so I look through the gap in the warped bathroom door. I can't see any movement in the front or the rear.

I wait.

There's the sound of scuffling feet.

More shouts.

Screams.

Silence.

I remain frozen. None of the shots seem directed at me.

Esteban has passed out. I check his pulse to make sure he's alive. He's still there, but he needs a hospital or he risks a fatal infection.

The sun finally crawls over the horizon sending golden rays through the Swiss-cheese front of the store. It's been quiet for over an hour. I finally venture from my hiding place.

Through the broken front door, I see a man slumped over the machine gun mounted to the back of the truck.

I assume it's a man.

It's hard to tell.

He's missing his head.

I push what remains of my barricades out of the way and cautiously walk over the threshold. Two more men lie behind the truck, guns still in their hands. Their necks also end in stumps and puddles of congealing blood.

Dead.

They're all dead.

Esteban somehow finds the energy to drag himself out of the store. I point my gun at him. "Take a seat."

He falls to the gravel and leans up against the front wall. "I'm not going anywhere."

I pull out my cell phone and get a signal at last. I've never been happier to see two faint little bars.

"Jessica? Are you all right?" asks Ailes frantically. "Did the rescue team find you?"

Blood is splattered on the trucks and ground all around me.

I try to inhale deeply, but can only manage shallow gasps. The full enormity of what happened is finally hitting me. "Yeah, they found me. The question is, who found them?"

20

Assistant Director Breyer has summoned me into a conference room at DC headquarters, in front of a dozen other people, to explain things *again*. That's what I've been doing for the last three days. I've gone over the events ad nauseam.

It took a miracle to get me out of Mexico. We bypassed Mexican authorities entirely. Ailes sent a DEA unit, escorted by two FBI agents from the Mexico City office, to meet me at the bodega. They arrived just as another police unit was pulling up. We didn't stop to talk.

Our liaison with the Mexico City office took custody of Esteban just outside of Tixato while I was rushed to the airport in an unmarked car and flown back to the US on a DEA jet.

If I'd know the storm that was waiting for me here, I would have stayed in Mexico.

Back in my days as a patrol officer, one of my instructors told me something that has stuck with me. Always tell the truth. When in doubt, you can say you don't recall. If you're afraid you might incriminate yourself, shut up. If you didn't do something wrong, be honest. Even if it makes you look bad. If you want to nail someone to the wall and the evidence is lacking, you use the investigation process to trap them in a lie.

Right now, they want someone to blame for this mess. And the first person to get caught in a lie is going to take the fall.

Everyone is pissed. The Mexican government is embarrassed and wants to pin the debacle on me. The FBI is angry that I let myself get into this situation in the first place.

Convoluting things is the fact that nobody knows what the hell happened, including me. I was involved in an altercation with a Mexican federal agent and got into a shoot-out with their army, who then ended up decapitated. You know, just a normal day.

I try to comfort myself with the fact that, as much as they want me to be at fault, the Mexican government has little evidence that I did anything wrong. The soldier I shot in the knee hasn't been seen since his men presumably drove him to the hospital. And Dr. Moya backs up my account of Esteban's hostile actions. Last I heard, Esteban is in a secure location somewhere in Mexico City and isn't cooperating.

The official theory, at least according to the Mexican media, is that an unnamed FBI agent got caught in a gang turf war. It doesn't fit with the facts, but it's a narrative that supports what everyone wants to believe.

To Americans who have grown accustomed to the narco violence that happens south of the border, it's just one more bizarre, grisly story.

Breyer pushes his copy of my statement away from him across the conference table, as if that will make the matter disappear. "What the hell happened, Blackwood?"

We haven't spoken since I delivered my final report on the Warlock case. He's too senior to be involved in day-to-day investigations. I'm not sure if his presence here is good or bad for me.

I go over my account one more time. "I went to Tixato to source two samples we found at the Hawkton crime scene. I was there only a few hours. When I went to meet Dr. Moya, as previously arranged, to pick up the evidence I'd been asked to return to Quantico, Moya wasn't there. I was approached by a man presenting himself as an agent of the Mexican Federal Police. After behaving suspiciously, he drew his weapon on me. We had an altercation."

"An altercation?"

"I stabbed him with a scalpel, then knocked him off a ladder."

"Is it possible there was a misunderstanding?" Breyer asks.

"Pardon me?"

"Did you misread his intentions?"

"The gun to my head? That was pretty clear."

Breyer sorts through the other papers in front of him and pulls a sheet to the top. "According to Esteban, he had spoken with you earlier in the day and the two of you, his words, 'made a date,' to meet later. He said that he was amorous with you, as you had led him to believe it would be welcome."

Jesus. Christ. "You've got to be goddamn kidding me."

Breyer shrugs. He confers with one of the Justice Department attorneys by his side. "His words. Made under oath to a Mexican Grand Jury."

"His oath? Huh. I never met him before he showed up at Dr. Moya's site. His intentions were anything but 'amorous.'"

"The Mexican government says they have three witnesses who have also sworn to seeing you meeting with him earlier in the day."

"Of course they do."

"What's that supposed to mean?"

"Have they found the soldier I wounded? Or the other men?"

"They say they weren't on duty that night."

"What about Dr. Moya?"

"He can only speak about what happened after you found him. His last memory was leaning into his truck. He says Esteban may have knocked him down the ladder. Esteban says Moya slipped and became disoriented."

It's not even a full alibi, yet here I am, defending myself.

"Did they explain my reasons for hauling Esteban out of the hole in the ground and trying to get him medical attention?"

"Esteban claims you kidnapped him and held him hostage in an attempt to cover up what had taken place. The army unit was trying to rescue him. Would you like to change anything in your story?" Breyer looks over his glasses at me.

"No." I'm not taking the bait. They're trying to get me to lose my shit and say something I've been holding back.

God knows I've used the same tactic on dozens of suspects.

It's always different when you're the one whom the fingers are pointed at. I keep my mouth shut and measure my words carefully.

I keep my clenched fists below the table. Slow breaths.

"The Mexican government is indicating they would like to have you extradited to make statements. Are you sure you don't have anything to add or to change in your statement?"

Nothing printable. More deep breaths. Keep calm. "I've given as full of an account as I can. I will answer to anyone I'm legally obliged to. I did my job." I feel my blood rising, but I'm doing my best to keep my anger to myself. This is the FBI, they're supposed to have my back.

Breyer folds his hands behind his head. He gives a glance to the other people in the room, most of whom are his aides and assistants. "Quite a mess, Jessica."

Ailes takes a seat at my side. I never noticed him enter the room. "Excuse me, Assistant Director, but what do you think happened?"

Breyer's eyes narrow on Ailes. He wasn't expecting to be put on the spot himself. "I wasn't there."

Ailes nods. "And the only surviving participant who we have reason to trust is sitting right here. She could have invoked her right to an attorney, but she hasn't. I think that says a lot about her confidence in the facts supporting her version of events."

"Hiring an attorney isn't a sign of guilt," replies Breyer.

"Not bringing one is either a sign of hubristic stupidity or a certainty of the process working itself out. So what do we think? Is Jessica stupid or telling the truth because she trusts us and the Bureau?"

"That's what we're trying to determine."

Ailes reaches down into his briefcase and retrieves a newspaper. The front page is in Spanish, and the lead image is a photo of the market. Bullet-ridden, charred, and surrounded by covered bodies on the ground—it looks like a war zone. "What does this image tell you?"

I have to turn away. The experience is still too vivid.

Breyer gets an uncomfortable expression on his face. "They wanted her dead."

"They wanted to kill one of your agents. Unfortunately for them, she proved rather tenacious. I think if Agent Blackwood had exercised anything less than optimal judgment during this trip, we'd be discussing the return of her remains. I sent her down there. She did everything exactly as requested."

Breyer takes the newspaper from Ailes and shakes his head. "I believe you, Jessica. Although I'm not sure you handled it in the most ideal way. You could have gone straight to our Mexico City office."

"They had an army unit," I reply. "There could have been roadblocks. I also have reason to believe they're using drones for countersurveillance." The simplest explanation is the best right now. No need to embarrass him with all the holes in his suggested course of action.

He drops the paper and waves his hands in the air. "I read that in your report. That still doesn't answer the outstanding questions. Why did they want you dead?"

"I don't know." I'd been wracking my brain trying to think of a reason. "Dr. Moya didn't tell me anything that I wasn't able to relay, or that we didn't already suspect. They may have thought I was an undercover narcotics officer. But even then, the response doesn't make sense."

"If I may interject a little game theory," Ailes suggests. I like that he's shifted the attention from my actions back onto those of the people who wanted to kill me.

"Please," replies Breyer.

Ailes adopts a professorial tone. "Either they were acting rationally or irrationally. If they were irrational and just wanted her killed, they would have simply shot her in an ambush. Esteban had ample opportunity. There would be no advantage to making it appear to be a murder. Another agent would have followed up, bringing more scrutiny. Therefore, we have to believe they were trying to act rationally. Either off a valid assumption or an incorrect one.

"The assumption being that Agent Blackwood obtained information they didn't want relayed back to us, even though she says she didn't observe anything that wasn't already communicated."

"So they made an incorrect assumption?" Breyer asks.

"Not necessarily. She may have seen or heard something that she didn't deem important at the time. A small detail. Perhaps when she took the detour through the barrio."

"Or somebody just didn't like me," I reply dryly.

"There is that possibility. Although X-20 isn't known for making irrational choices. The order to kill you was a high-level decision."

"Which would explain the influence we're seeing from down there," admits Breyer. "Informally, our contacts within the government are calling bullshit on Esteban's story."

"You could have mentioned that a few minutes ago," I snap. After all I've done and sacrificed, he still made me sit through this interrogation.

"I just had to hear you say things to my face." He pauses for

a moment and casts a glance to the other people sitting around
the conference table, then back to me. "We needed to be certain.
We'll put a pin in why they wanted you dead for the moment.
The next question is, who the hell cut off their heads?"

"What about the rival gang theory?" Ailes asks.

"Their forensics says there was one assailant. We're not aware
of any gang making that kind of intrusion into X-20 territory, let
alone one capable of taking on a military unit. It may have been
internal, X-20 bosses punishing them for not killing you."

I sigh. Ailes shoots me a look. He should be impressed that this
is my only external sign of frustration.

"In the meantime, I'm taking you off the Hawkton case for
your own safety," Breyer declares.

I'm about to protest, but Ailes lays his hand flat on the table,
signaling me to keep my mouth shut. I clam up. I owe him that,
at the very least, and wait until after the meeting to say my piece.

"THEY CAN'T PULL me from this," I exclaim in our own conference room in Quantico an hour later. Gerald is elsewhere, so I
don't mind letting him hear the emotion in my voice.

"Blackwood, you were never on the case officially." Ailes ignores my mild tantrum.

"Yes, but . . ." I don't know where to go with this argument.

"What about the decapitations? Somewhat convenient," he
says, as if implying I know more than I've let on.

"Very. I'm not sure I'd trust their forensic report."

"Was it him?" he asks, catching my eyes and holding them.

Now we're getting to it. I didn't even want to think about this.

By "him," he means Damian Knight, my ex-boyfriend-slash-
guardian-slash-stalker who can be best described as serial personality disorder. I'm pretty sure Damian has killed to protect
me in the past, although I've never been able to prove it. I haven't
heard from him in months, not since he sent me flowers when

I was in the hospital. He's vanished out of my life for years at a time. Each time he resurfaces he has a new look and a personality to match. But each time, he lets me know he hasn't forgotten me.

"I don't know. I've told you everything and you *know* I always report it when he contacts me."

"You didn't mention anything in this report."

"Because I don't know anything and he didn't contact me! And now I'm being kicked off this."

Gerald knocks on the conference room door before sticking his head in. "Sorry to interrupt, but you guys see the thing on the news about the reverend?"

"Reverend Curtis?" I ask.

"No. This other guy. He just offed himself on live television."

"What?" I look to Ailes. He shrugs.

"You need to check it out."

"I don't think I could stomach that right now." I've got too much murder and death to deal with.

"I'm sorry, but I think he said he was possessed by a demon. The one we haven't named publicly. Your demon . . ."

21

"A sin is like a scratch on your soul," proclaims Reverend Groom. In his mid-forties, his head of dark hair is coiffed like that of a television anchorman. Dressed in a casual collared shirt and slacks, he doesn't look like a man of the cloth. He could be a well-groomed school principal, or your next-door neighbor dressed up for a block party.

There's something desperate in his voice as he leans on the lectern and tries to make eye contact with the viewers on the other side of the screen. I've seen that pleading look in the interrogation room from someone who wants to explain how he or she ended up in that horrible situation. Desperate to be believed. Guilty.

"If you ignore that sin, the wound gets wider. We do things to ignore the pain. We medicate ourselves. We deny it's even there. Maybe others don't know about it. Maybe they can see the effect. But you know. The wound grows.

"If we don't treat the wound, we die with the wound. We die imperfect. God looks down on our broken souls and says there's no place in heaven for us. Had we found the courage, we could have healed the wound, but we chose not to.

"But that's not the worst part. A wounded soul is an invitation. An opportunity for infection. That sin calls out to evil, and sometimes the evil answers. When we let the evil in, it makes us commit more sin. Sometimes evil takes over. It's too late then. There's nothing left to do."

He closes his eyes for a moment, then says, "I have sinned. My wounds are beyond repair. My soul is broken. In my weakness, I have let evil come into me. Even now it's making me do things I'm powerless to stop.

"I have become that evil. For I am Azazel. I walk the dark path. I live in the shadows."

Reverend Groom opens his eyes and looks out into the studio while reaching under the lectern. He pulls out a revolver and places the barrel in his mouth. A shocked tech runs onto the set to try to get the gun away, but Groom pulls the trigger before the man can wrestle it from him. Red sprays from the back of his head, hitting the stained-glass window behind him. Drops of blood and brain fall on the floral decorations lining the set.

Groom's body slackens. He collapses onto the lectern, a smoke trail rising from the hole in his head in high-definition video.

Somewhere in the control room a technician finally has the sense to throw the live feed to a standby image of the station logo.

We sit in silence for a moment in the bullpen. Gerald finally speaks up as the recording stops. "I just looked him up. He lived near Hawkton about twenty years ago."

"Did he know the people in the church?" asks Ailes.

"It's a safe bet. It's a small town," Gerald replies.

"Tragic."

"Why 'Azazel'?" I ask. "We haven't released it yet."

Gerald shrugs. "Details like that can leak."

"Where was this recorded?"

"A studio near Atlanta."

I turn to Ailes. "I'd like to go there."

He hesitates, then shakes his head. "It's a suicide, Blackwood. There's no apparent connection to the murders."

"There's a connection to the victims. Maybe."

"I don't know. Breyer wants you off the case."

"He said *Hawkton*. This isn't Hawkton and if it is a suicide, then it's not part of the case . . ."

Ailes rolls his eyes. "Another damn lawyer is all we need around here. If I say 'yes,' what do you expect to find?"

"A connection to the murders." I can feel it more than I can describe it.

"What kind of connection?"

"I don't think it was a suicide," I reply, without any idea how I can back it up. Sometimes the pattern recognizes you before you recognize it.

"Pardon me?"

"I think someone made him do it." Something about the video just reads wrong to me. I try to figure out what.

"Azazel?" Gerald raises an eyebrow.

I have to talk it through aloud, just to hear myself think. "Of course not. It's just . . . there's something about him that seems off. And I don't just mean because he's obviously flipping out. He almost seems coached. Roll it back. Pay attention to his eyes."

We watch the recording again. As Groom speaks, his eyes start darting from the camera off to the side in an unprofessional way. Like he's distracted I pause the video mid-glance. "See that? It's like he's looking for someone."

"Someone to stop him?" asks Ailes. I've got his attention now.

"No. I'm trying to think of an example. You know those hidden camera shows? Ever notice how people react when they find themselves in the middle of a really weird situation? It's that look."

"I'm not sure I understand. Did he think he was in the middle of a joke?"

"I don't know. Maybe he wanted someone to intervene? Or what if he didn't think the gun was loaded?"

"This sounds a little dinner-theatre-murder-mystery to me,"

Ailes replies. "Someone there knew he was going to use the gun as a prop and put a real bullet in it?"

"I don't know. But already we have a hypothetical situation in which Groom's death wasn't a suicide, or at the very least influenced by someone else."

"Maybe . . ."

"If it was a suicide, he was obviously distraught. In any event, he probably knew our church victims. The Azazel connection ties this to them. That alone should tell us there's something they shared. Something that killed them and made a man kill himself in the middle of a live broadcast."

"Do you mean the sin he was talking about?"

"Yes. Don't you want to know what he did that was so horrible he felt he had to risk God's wrath by blowing his brains out in public? Something you kill yourself over might be something someone else would murder for. So what was their sin?"

"Their sin?" asks Ailes.

"The Hawkton victims. They're all being punished. That's the connection I was trying to put my finger on before. The church murders were retribution. I think Groom's suicide may have been instigated by someone else."

"Where do you see the sheriff in all of this?"

"He's part of what happened. We know there was a sixth man at the Hawkton scene, but I don't think he's the sheriff's accomplice. I think he was the one putting things into motion.

"What we need to know now is whether there was someone whispering something in Groom's ear. Was he being pushed? And if we can link this to Tixato, that would also tell us there's something more here."

"What?"

"I don't know. Groom's death came out of nowhere. We already talked about how revenge killings continue." I think this over for a moment. "Is someone else next?"

THE FAVOR

THE WOMAN WHO opened the front door smelled like a perfume counter. That overwhelming scent is my strongest memory of Julia Vender. Dressed in a bright silver evening gown and draped in more costume diamonds than there were crown jewels in all the kingdoms, she exuded a calculated, over-the-top opulence. From the bright smile with which she greeted us and the way she kissed him after calling out, "Petey! *Dahhhling!*" I thought she had to be a friend of Grandfather's.

Grandfather grumbled a response through his gritted teeth. I would learn later on that Vender was, in a sense, his arch nemesis. A celebrity psychic to the stars, she and he had faced off more than once on a television interview couch: Grandfather as the crusty skeptic, and Julia as the effervescent charmer swatting aside his comments about her being a charlatan.

"Dahhhling, my clients have more money than they know what to do with," she'd say with a smile to the audience at home.

After the showdown, Grandfather would drive back from the studio hoping the appearance might get him another Atlantic City booking and put butts in seats. She'd count the money flooding into her 1-900 line.

Grandfather had watched her con her way into the lives of anyone important in Hollywood. Having spent years using magic to entertain, he was frustrated to see her manipulate its methods to scam people out of their money. But it wasn't really the lavish gifts given to her by brain-dead celebrities that bothered him. It was knowing that, every time she appeared on a talk show, thousands of vulnerable, desperate people would call her pay line or buy her books with money they couldn't really spare. The live readings, or "demonstrations," she held in major cities, where people who really couldn't afford it would pay five hundred dollars for the chance to ask her a question in a crowded room and maybe hear that yes, a departed relative still loved them, were the worst.

A con-artist extraordinaire, Julia Vender was also the most connected woman in Hollywood. From the struggling actress just off the bus from Nebraska to the studio chief who could make or break someone in a pen stroke, she knew everyone. Grief, pain and desire are universal.

Julia turned away from Grandfather and gazed down at me, broadly smiling. "Aren't you the most adorable creature!"

Too afraid to leave me alone at the house after the Buick incident, Grandfather and Dad had brought me along tonight. I'd followed them inside to endure Julia's embrace, and then sat quietly in a chair that looked to me as old as the pyramids, pretending to read a book while I listened.

"I was delighted when you called!" she effused. "I wish I saw more of you socially, Peter. I always think our banter makes for so much fun!"

"Yes, our encounters are lively," replied Grandfather stiffly, trying to avoid a confrontation.

"So what is it that Peter Blackstar the Magnificent needs from Julia the Merely Interesting?" She grabbed his hand and slowly turned it palm up. "Come for a reading?"

Grandfather jerked his hand away. "Not quite."

"What are you afraid of?"

"Contagious charlatanism," he muttered. Dad gave him a nervous glance.

Julia's loud laugh nearly shook the chandeliers. "Oh my, Petey. You have such a wit. Why waste your time with the magic baubles? I think you missed your true calling."

"Perhaps." I could tell coming to her had been very difficult for him, and she knew it. She was reveling in the moment that was, for him, a humiliation.

"Seriously then, what can I do for you? Or is this to be the first of many friendly visits?"

Grandfather ignored her last comment, folded his hands under his arms, and stared at the floor. "I know we have our . . . professional differences . . ."

"What was it you said on *Merv Griffin*? Oh, yes, you accused me of being a fraud and a cheat, I recall. You said I fleece the innocent. You must know that my lawyers are always after me to take you to court. But I say, 'No, leave poor Peter alone.' What would be in it, anyway?" Her eyes narrowed as her tone changed. "A ramshackle house? Some moth-eaten magic things. No, Peter, I don't let those things get to me. I'm better than that."

"Better than that?" asked Grandfather, his voice rising.

Dad shot him another look from across the room, and Grandfather tried to regain his composure.

"We have very different ways of looking at things," he finally said, in his most diplomatic manner. "I can be blunt . . . I don't think you're an evil person."

"That's a relief! Especially coming from a man whose posters depict him with devilish imps sitting on his shoulders."

Grandfather shook his head, barely controlling his anger. I could tell he was on the verge of giving up, but then he glanced toward me in the corner. His face softened. "I won't pretend I don't like what you do. But . . . I know there's a good side to you."

"Likewise," she replied halfheartedly. "But you're not here to mend fences. You're certainly not asking for a loan. Are you? Oh, how I'd love that."

Grandfather bit his tongue. "They're threatening Jessica."

Julia's face slackened. She turned to me, then back to Grand-father. "Who?"

"Brutani's outfit. It's complicated."

"With him, I would imagine it is. Whyever would he hurt that precious little girl?"

"Because of me." Dad spoke up for the first time. "He invested in a show that fell apart. He wants his money back and we don't have it right now."

"Oh, dear." Julia seemed sincere for the first time since she'd greeted us at the door. She smiled sadly at me. "Do you need money?"

"No!" Grandfather replied sharply. "We'll settle that ourselves. We just need some time, a way to talk to his people before things get out of hand. When Brutani's kid came out here he didn't say it was mob money he was loaning us, or we never would have touched it. Now we're in this pickle. I was hoping you might know somebody. Someone we could talk to."

"Someone who Brutani answers to?"

"Yes. Maybe help us set up a meeting."

"He's East Coast. I don't really know anyone out there. I don't run with those types anyway."

"You don't have anything?" Grandfather pleaded.

Over the edge of my book I watched Julia's face soften. She could tell how hard it was for him to ask this. She also keenly understood the value of a favor. "Maybe . . ." she replied, with her finger in the air. "I have a friend who might know something. Sometimes we exchange information about clients."

Much later, I realized she'd been obliquely referring to the psychic mafia, a tight-knit group of mediums who exchange inside information on their clients in order to better fleece them. There's a book: a directory of the wealthiest clients and their dark secrets, the triggers to pull. As people hop around from psychic to psychic, they are consistently astonished at how much each one already knew about them.

The truth of the matter is that the moment the appointment is booked, the psychic will be on the phone with a colleague gleaning as much information as they can. This isn't something they do for garden-variety readings with bored housewives. This is what they do when they had real whales, clients who had too much money and spare time.

"I *might* be able to help you," Julia continued, after thinking it over for a moment. "But I'll want a favor."

"What?"

"An endorsement."

"Out of the question." Grandfather stood up and motioned to me and Dad. "Time to go."

She tried to reason with him. "Just words, Peter."

He shook his head. "Words are everything. Can't you understand that? If you don't speak truthfully, where is your integrity?"

"Integrity? I'm not the one in deep shit with the mob."

Grandfather made a show of taking my hand as we headed toward the door with Dad in tow. I looked back at her and waved, then followed him out the door.

"Dad," my father said as we walked to the car.

"Not now," Grandfather growled.

"Dad!" he insisted.

"Get in the car!"

I buckled myself into the backseat as we headed down the long driveway. When we reached the gate, it refused to open.

"For Christ's sake!" Grandfather got out of the car to try to pull it.

In the headlights I saw a flash of gleaming diamonds as Julia ran up to him. They quickly exchanged words, then she pushed something into his hand before retreating back into her house. The gate opened and Grandfather climbed back into the car.

"What was that about?" asked Dad.

"The old broad took pity on us. She said to talk to Father Devalo. She gave me his number. He's a former priest and a spiritualist. Brutani's uncle goes to him. The uncle is the real weight in the family. Julia said that if we can get Devalo on our side, then maybe we can get Basso, the uncle, to leave be."

"A spiritualist?" Dad asked.

"Basso goes to him to hear from his dead mother. If we can get Devalo to invite me to the séance, maybe we can ask Basso's mother to forgive the debt."

"Are you goddamn kidding me?" snapped Dad. "This is the plan? More mobsters?"

Grandfather shot him a deathly stare. "This is the mess we made."

"What if she says 'no'? Christ, what am I saying, she's dead." He turned back to me. "I'm sorry, kiddo. I'm sorry your pop is such a screwup."

22

WHAT WAS GROOM'S sin? Why did he have to kill himself in such a public way? I'm hoping the church, which is actually a run-down television studio on the outskirts of Atlanta, can give us some clue. Agent Knoll was able to hop on a flight out of Reagan with me, with the promise we'd get him back to DC that night. Ailes pulled him off the sheriff manhunt to help me out—and, I suspect, keep me out of trouble.

While the local detective assisting us talks to the station manager about turning on the floor lights, Agent Knoll stands behind the podium inspecting the scene of the death. Sitting in the front row of chairs set out for the live audience, I watch him search for some physical clue: A piece of tangible evidence that ties what happened here to what happened in Hawkton.

Knoll looks like he'd be more suited to leading a platoon of soldiers than detailed investigative work. Appearances are misleading. I've seen how his mind works. He's not known for sudden flashes of insight; instead, he builds the whole case together in his head and then surprises you with the most minute, but key, observation that everyone else had missed.

I'm afraid there won't be a breakthrough piece of evidence like our muddy footprint on the tree. The autopsy report already came back negative for the chemical we found in the sheriff's tissue. Whatever happened to Groom was psychological in origin. Or, if you believe the religious rumormongers, super-natural.

Reverend Groom's suicide has made national news. Not quite supplanting the "Zombie-Sheriff-on-the-Run" story, but definitely enhancing it. Once it got out, his Hawkton connection was too powerful to ignore. The claim of possession made it so sensational that it was impossible not to sensationalize it even more.

The lights in the studio finally come on as Knoll leans down, flashlight in hand, to have a look under the podium. How Groom got the gun is still a mystery. Not licensed in his name, it's an artifact that came out of nowhere. Forensics found only his fingerprints. The bullet casing and everything else was clean. He only touched the gun when he removed it and placed it in his mouth. It's as if the gun didn't exist before that horrible moment.

Knoll stands up and crosses his arms. I can tell he suspects something else is at play here. "What do you think?" I ask.

Knoll wrinkles his brow and stares at the floor. "I think it was planted. He could have just brought his own gun. The placement here? It's like someone else put it there."

I agree. The problem is that the studio has an audience of a hundred people during their broadcasts. Probably a thousand people go through here every week. Bussed in or lined up at the door, there's no record of who has been here. They have footage of all the people in each audience, but there's no way to stop someone from walking in with the crowd and leaving before the show starts.

Detective Stafford, an affable cop from the local police department who met us here, takes the seat near me. "You folks need to see anything else?"

"What kind of man was Groom?"

"A bit churchy, of course. Not as much as some of the other folks here. It's a bit of a racket," he continues, apparently not afraid of being overheard. "They get old folks in here and work them for donations. They do okay with the call-in contributions, but the real money is when they bring in their 'special guests' and pray over them."

"Sounds sleazy," I reply. In both my former life and my current one, my history with these kinds of people goes way beyond my first encounter with Julia Vender.

"It is. Nothing we can do about it from a legal point of view. Groom got involved years ago. He helped build up the church. He was doing healings and claiming God was speaking through him. Sometimes he'd tell people stuff about them he couldn't have known. That was a big draw."

"A faith healer," grumbles Knoll, who's been listening.

"When it's fashionable. He started doing more of that lately. Ratings, I guess."

"Nobody noticed anything odd about him recently?" I ask.

"People here say he kept to himself. He'd show up for his tapings, do a meeting or two, then just go home. He's a private man."

"Any chance his so-called 'sin' might be something criminal?"

Stafford shakes his head. "He doesn't have a record other than a couple DUIs. Which is bad enough, but he never hit anyone or did damage. He doesn't have a reputation, like some of them do, for engaging in the kind of behavior they admonish."

I look over my shoulder. The three of us are alone for the moment. "What's the word around here? Why do the employees think he did it?"

Stafford scratches behind his right ear and makes an earnest face. "Hawkton. He knew those folks. It was just too much for him. Some think he had a devil in him. Others think he was afraid *of* the devil and just went nuts."

"Did any of the people here say anything about him witnessing strange things, like we've been hearing out of Hawkton? Maybe like he was being followed?"

"No. None that I spoke to."

If Groom was a private man, he probably would have kept that to himself anyway. With the multiple DUIs, he's apparently got an alcohol problem. From wrestling with some inner turmoil?

"What about his regular followers? Did anyone have a grudge against him?" asks Knoll.

"There were complaints from the families of some of the viewers they fleeced. Angry children who found out their parents had given up their inheritance to the church. But nothing I'd think would lead to anything like this." Stafford pauses for a moment. "You think there's something more to this suicide?"

"While it appears open and shut," I reply, "we're having a hard time closing the book on Hawkton. Our sheriff is still on the loose and we think others may be involved."

Stafford looks at me. "Do you know what caused the explosion?"

"We're still working on that. It looks like a gas explosion." I don't tell him the latest setback, which is that we can't conclusively prove it was propane. The lab results have yielded some crazy findings.

"Could you see if Groom made any 911 calls from his cell phone in the past few weeks? Just look for outbound. He may not have left a name."

"Sure. I can get that in a few minutes." Stafford gets up and walks over to a corner of the studio to make the call.

I join Knoll onstage and look out into the empty studio. The chairs are cheap fold-up aluminum ones, the type that makes your ass hurt after ten minutes. I can't help but notice that all the chairs onstage have plush padded pillows. "What are you thinking?"

"A bat," he replies.

"A bat? The thing I saw in Tixato? What was stalking the people in Hawkton? Maybe he was being surveilled?"

"Maybe. We're getting more of that kind of thing." Knoll is methodical. He doesn't always see eye-to-eye with me on my leaps, but during the Warlock case we developed a mutual respect. Coming to Atlanta was a favor on his part as well as Ailes's. Knoll has his own cases, but he's always ready to roll his sleeves up.

Stafford lowers his phone. "Well, that's odd."

"Anonymous reports of being followed? Noises around the house?" I suggest.

"Yes. Yes, indeed. There's a photo too."

"A photo?" My ears perk up.

"Someone calling from Groom's number reported something was following him as he drove home. A deputy answered the call but couldn't find anything. Just to be safe, he went to a convenience store on the route and pulled the security footage from that night. It ended there. They're sending me the photo now."

"A photo? Of what?" Knoll asks.

"What they saw on the footage from the night Groom says he was followed," responds Stafford, who is just as confused as we are. "They say it looks like a demon."

23

As soon as Detective Stafford receives the file, we sit around the studio trying to decipher the image. Opening the file on his phone, he'd revealed a single frame from a time-lapse video showing the street in front of the convenience store. In the darkness, the only light on the street came from an overhead source mounted somewhere high.

Grainy, hard to see for sure, but it's there and it's got a defined shape. A big shadow with wings. To my eyes it looks like a bat. A large one—as wide as a car.

"Things weren't this weird before you came along," Knoll whispers to me.

"Or as interesting," I shoot back.

Stafford zooms in on the image then opens a browser. "You have other sightings of this?"

"Possibly," I reply. "We haven't made it public yet for obvious reasons." I'm not even going to go into my Mexican misadventure.

"Yeah, I don't think we need to tell people there's a flying demon on the loose that chases people before they die." Stafford holds his phone screen up to me. "Have a look."

It's a picture of a drone. Similar in shape to the shadow, but not quite the same. Close, though. The image and its caption confirm my earlier suspicions.

"We used ones similar to this for recon when I served in Afghanistan," he explains. "That was a long time ago. Who knows what they look like now."

"Let's forward this to one of our military experts," suggests Knoll. "Some of the newer ones look more and more like real creatures."

"Good thing demons aren't real creatures . . ." Stafford offers.

"Maybe we could tell people it's an angel?" jokes Knoll.

"Remember, only two creatures have wings in the Bible: birds and demons," I point out.

"Well, if they're fallen angels, how do they get the wings? You'd think those would keep them from falling."

I take one last long look around the studio before going to the car to call Ailes. I'm sure there's something more here that I'm not noticing. Maybe not a physical clue, but I can't forget the way Groom kept looking around the studio. His last moments play over and over through my head. All I can see is the three cameras, the glass-walled control booth, and a mirror on the back wall. If someone had been standing there, threatening Groom, someone else would have seen him.

"Are you two sitting down?" asks Ailes over speakerphone.

Knoll glances at me from the driver's seat and shrugs. He doesn't like what we've heard so far. The forensics lab was finally able to make progress on the source of the explosion, but the answer just leads to more questions.

"The explosion has all the hallmarks of a gas explosion," Ailes explains. "A distributed agent that was able to push out on all sides with enough force to rip the church apart, as opposed to a pipe bomb or a high-yield, which pushes with more force on one part than another. So we know that is what we are looking for.

"If you don't find a ruptured propane tank, as in this case, you look for incomplete combustion, things that didn't burn all the way, and do spectral analysis to see if you can identify any suspect chemicals. That comes back incomplete. So the lab starts cutting into the wood fragments, hoping that they are porous enough to have trapped the propane from the compression wave of the explosion. There isn't any propane gas to be found.

"The next step, which would have been the first step if it hadn't initially looked like a gas explosion, is to examine the residue. This is where it gets strange.

"In a house fire you have several kinds of propellants, the things that keep the fire burning. There's the wood. There's the furniture, carpet and wall coverings. In some cases there's another foreign propellant . . .

"We think this was an aerosol explosion. A fuel air bomb, of sorts."

"What was the fuel? Why didn't we see it right away?" asks Knoll as he tries to follow along.

"Because it was an aerosol. That is what baffled the lab. At a hot enough temperature, our fat burns. If it gets even hotter, it can explode if it turns into a gaseous state."

At Quantico they'd given us a pretty good understanding of the kinds of explosives we might encounter on the job. Growing up in the family I did, I'd tried more than a few in the backyard, nearly singing the rose bushes. This was something new to me.

"Fat? Like human tissue?" Knoll is as confused as me.

"Yep," says Ailes. I can tell he's beside himself about this one too. "Vaporized into the air, aerosolized and ignited. The questions are severalfold. First, other than Jessup, we're not missing anyone. Second, it'd take a *lot* of human fat to do this. One person isn't just going to burn up and cause this. You'd need to isolate the fat, use a small explosion to disperse it, then ignite it. If the igniter is somehow removed from the scene of the crime or it self-destructs, all you're left with is an explosion of fatty tissue. And this leads us to the perceptual problem. We may think of it as a 'fat bomb,' but people have another way to describe what happened."

I see where this is going. "The simplest explanation is that the explosion was caused by a person spontaneously exploding. Spontaneous human combustion. We've got a zombie sheriff, demons and now this? What's next, ghosts?"

"It's an inaccurate conclusion, but it's the one we're afraid the press will run with when it gets out. Someone prone to believing such things are possible will probably assume the supernatural hypothesis. We have to get ahead of this and explain the fuel-air bomb mechanism before discussing the propellant. A reasonable mind will understand."

I wish I shared his optimism. Some people still think the Warlock murders were divine acts. "We're sitting outside the building where someone, by all accounts in possession of a somewhat reasonable mind, blew his brains out on live television because he thought it was real. Who else is going to react this way?"

"That's what we need to know. The connection to Hawkton is more important than ever. Do you have anything yet I can pass on?"

Knoll and I exchange glances. "You're not going to like this if you're worried about an optics problem. Remember the reports of odd sightings from Hawkton? And the thing I said Dr. Moya saw following us?"

"The bat?" Ailes recalls.

"We got a photo."

"Of a drone?"

"Of a shadow of something that could be a drone . . ."

"Or a demon," adds Knoll. "I'm just playing devil's advo— poor choice of words. I'm just saying that's how some people are going to see it."

"Well, that is interesting. Can you send us the image? In the meantime, I have more mixed news," Ailes continues. "They want Knoll back in West Virginia. There's been a lead in the manhunt for the sheriff. They found a blood sample from him."

"Where?" I ask.

"On a fulgurite near Black Nick's cabin that had been carved into a blade like the one he gave you. Evidently, before the cabin burned down there may have been an altercation between the two."

"Between Black Nick and the sheriff?"

"It looks that way."

"Still no trace of Black Nick?" Please, let there be no more victims in this nightmare.

"No. I take it as a good sign that he was able to avoid getting killed by the sheriff. Find out what you can about Groom, Blackwood. The bat is an interesting lead, but I think this whole case is going to get shut down when they find the sheriff. They don't have a lot of patience upstairs for this kind of stuff."

I grab the phone off the dashboard. "What do you mean? What about the sixth man or Tixato?"

"Bureaucracy favors simple explanations. Bring me something back from down there. Otherwise it's going to be ruled a coincidence and you'll be put on something else."

"That's bullshit!"

"Yes. But they're always going to choose the simplest line between two points."

"And ignore everything else?"

"Some of them think that's what they're paid to do."

24

WHEN I WAS little, Dad worked as a technical consultant on movie sets when magic was involved. Most of the jobs came about through Grandfather's connections. Seeing my father as more of a technician than an artist, he had no qualms about lending his son and the family name to teach some Hollywood actor to palm a card or saw a woman in half convincingly enough. Because of this, I got to spend some time roaming studio back lots.

While the Wild West towns and New York backdrops were fascinating in their way, it was the small-town-USA neighborhoods that held my interest. I'd sneak away to play on the suburban sidewalks in front of the perfectly manicured houses. Even though they were little more than empty shells, they were a strange source of comfort to me.

Our own house deep in the Hollywood hills was in a perpetual state of disrepair. It was filled with its own mysteries, which I liked to explore, but it never felt like how I thought a home *should* feel. Those back-lot houses, a glorified ideal of the perfect family life, did.

Reverend Groom's house resembles one of those empty shells. Located in a nice suburb, set back on a small rise behind a picket fence, it looks picture-perfect. There's the feel of a facade beyond the flower gardens and landscaping. It's meant to be looked at, not looked out from. It's a mask.

Mrs. Groom greets me with a polite smile as she lets me into the home. She's clearly distraught about her husband, but appears to be holding it together. Attractive, and too well dressed for the dish gloves she's wearing, her reserve hides her shock.

"Thank you for letting me speak with you." Going into this kind of job, they don't tell you how much of your time will be spent talking to people who have lost someone, or the people who caused that loss. It gets easier, but you can never be callous about it.

"Of course. Alec never spoke about his time in Hawkton. I met him after he moved to Atlanta." She offers this right off the top, then shakes her head. "I didn't know how deeply he felt." There's suddenly a distant look in her eyes.

"If you don't mind my asking, are you aware of what he said before he died?" I follow her into the kitchen.

"I haven't watched the video. But I know he was talking about sin. I know some people think he was under some kind of influence." She's obviously still trying to understand. Now she's alone in this house, her quiet moments must be filled with thousands of questions.

"How do you feel about that?"

"Do I believe my husband was possessed?" she snaps, not too shocked to be insulted.

"My apologies." I take a breath and speak more carefully. "I meant to ask if you thought there was some motivation behind that."

"Ms. Blackwood, I'm a religious woman, but I'm not as . . . naive as some of the people Alec worked with. Neither was Alec, for that matter."

"Didn't your husband sometimes speak as if God was talking through him and do faith healing?"

She waves away the question with a dish-gloved hand. "He had a flair for drama. Some people like rock bands in their church. Others want the old-time preacher."

And some people want to live in million-dollar houses, not caring where the money came from.

"May I have a look in his office?"

She hesitates for a moment and then peels off the gloves. "Sure, I'll be upstairs if you need me."

She leads me to his study, opens the door and departs. Bookcases line two walls. One section is filled with religious texts while the remainder holds military thrillers and popular fiction.

One wall is covered with photographs of Groom and his wife with smiling children from around the world—proof of his outreach ministry. I've heard of more than one preacher who raises funds to help the impoverished in far-flung places, only to spend the majority of the money on underage prostitutes and expensive hotel accommodations. Just a few hundred dollars donated to a local orphanage gets you your photo-op that proves to your donors what great work you're doing.

I'm sure most aren't like that. I suspect that Groom's intentions were to a degree sincere, although the photos and the other items in his office look like props for someone playing a part.

In the top drawer of his desk I find a stack of letters, fawning testimonials from people thanking him for his prayers and telling him what a wonderful person he is. The top drawer is an interesting location. While the photos are for visitors, he kept these affirmations within his own arm's reach.

In the next drawer down I find a copy of a men's magazine filled with women in swimsuits. It wouldn't be a dark secret in any other man's office, but in a minister's study, it's understandably out of sight.

Below the magazine I see something familiar, and more career damning than the girlie magazine. This is the reading material he *really* doesn't want people to know about.

It's a book of magician's techniques for reading minds. We call these acts mentalism, a mixture of sleight-of-hand and psychological principles that makes it look like you have ESP, or must be getting information from a supernatural source.

Groom was making sure he kept up on the latest methods. He'd bookmarked a section on getting people to fill out forms with personal information, under the guise of a contest, in order to use it later. I suddenly feel less sympathetic toward him.

I set the book back and look elsewhere.

His trashcan is empty, except for a discarded package that once held AA batteries. No crumpled suicide note. No threatening letter made from cut-up newspaper print.

I walk up the stairs to find Mrs. Groom. Along the hallway a slightly open door leads to a boy's bedroom, and I take a peek. A Spider-Man poster adorns the wall. An antique computer sits on a desk next to a television and a Nintendo game console. On a table by the bed, a Walkman sits on top of a stack of comics.

"This was Cedric's room," says Mrs. Groom from behind me.

The posters, the computer—It's all almost a decade old.

I don't get it. Then it hits me.

This is a shrine to a dead child.

I notice the sheets are ruffled slightly. "Did your husband come in here?"

"This is where he prayed. I haven't cleaned it since he . . . he passed."

I pity her. Despite the fact her good fortune was based on defrauding the innocent, she's been dealt so much tragedy. First her son, and now her husband. There's never going to be a normal day for her.

"I'm so sorry," I tell her, knowing she's heard this a thousand times.

"It's His will," she says, as if trying to convince herself this is all part of a greater plan. "I'll be in the other room if you need anything else. I hope you can see that Alec was a good man now." Her words trail off as she tries to hide her tears.

"I'm sure he had a good heart."

Cedric had to have been ten or so when he passed away. After Mrs. Groom vanishes down the hallway, I take a step into the room, morbid curiosity getting the better of me. It feels like I've just traveled back in time—like the clock froze on the day he died.

It reminds me of my old bedroom, down to the Walkman. Mine was a hand-me-down from my father, complete with his cassette collection of music soundtracks.

Wait a second . . .

I'm older than Cedric would be now.

The Walkman seems out of place here. It was already on its way out when I was a teenager, replaced by compact discs and soon after that, MP3 players.

I'm about to dismiss it—after all, I had kept mine long after it was out of fashion—when I remember the empty battery package in the trash downstairs . . .

Making sure Mrs. Groom isn't around, I violate the sacrosanct atmosphere by taking the Walkman from the nightstand. I place the headphones over my ears and press play.

25

Low and guttural yells are followed by swearing. Male and female voices repeatedly cry "hold him." Things are knocked over. There are footsteps and the sounds of exertion. Someone reacts in pain, and the screams start again, high-pitched this time and then lower. Unintelligible shouting.

Abruptly, the screaming comes to a stop. Then, chilling and deep, "I am the one who walks in the dark path. I am the one who lives in the shadows. I am Azazel. I am the devourer."

I have to pause the playback for a moment. This doesn't sound like a Hollywood movie. This sounds real.

Barely audible whispering. A man begins to recite the Lord's Prayer. The screaming and thrashing starts again.

"I said *hold him!*" a man shouts.

The hysterical screams are muffled, there is scuffling, and then they come to an end. There's a long silence in the room. The last voice to speak says, "Oh God." Then the tape ends.

Lost in what I just heard, I sit on the bed staring into space, trying to make sense of it. Mrs. Groom finally knocks on the door to get my attention. "Everything okay?" She gives me an odd look, but says nothing about me sitting on her dead son's bed.

"I'd like to take this." I hold up the Walkman. "I'll make sure you get it back."

"Okay . . ." She seems more confused by the expression on my face than the presence of the tape player.

Ailes looks up from the cassette player resting on the conference room table. "Did his wife know where the tape came from?"

"No. She said she'd never heard it before. One of the voices I think is Groom's."

"Yes, I recognized that too."

"I counted at least five other people, maybe more."

He knows where I'm going with this. "You want to match them to our victims?" he asks.

"Yes. I'd also like to go to Hawkton."

"You don't need to go there to do that."

"Maybe not. But the other voice, the screamer, I think it's a child, a boy. I'd like to know who that was."

"Groom's son?"

"No connection that I've found. The tape is at least twenty years old. Groom's son died of leukemia ten years ago, when he was ten. I don't think there's a connection there. This is separate." My eyes widen. "I think this even may be what binds everyone together."

"And the boy on the tape is the subject of this . . . exorcism?"

There it is. I wanted him to say it first. Exorcism.

It's a loaded word, conjuring up images of horror movies and scary novels. For believers, it's proof that supernatural evil is real. For nonbelievers it's a stark reminder that in some ways we still live in the Middle Ages, a time in which someone with psychological problems can be ill-treated and abused instead of getting the care they need.

"Whoever this boy is, he may be the key. If this tape was made in Hawkton, then he has a connection to everything. He could be at the center of it all."

"How?"

"It's the first time we hear 'Azazel' in connection with them."

"Is the boy on the tape our sixth man? Do you think this disturbed child turned into a killer?" he asks.

"I don't know. Maybe this goes deeper. But everything ties in here, I think. If the other voices are those of our church victims."

Ailes taps the table. "You know what this would look like if we were religiously inclined . . ."

I've thought this through over and over. "Yes. A demon returning to kill the people that exorcised him."

He contemplates this for a moment, staring at the ceiling. "Why do you and I see that as absurd, when others would accept it?"

"We're rational."

"Are we? What does rational mean to you?"

"Never closing the door on questions."

"We all shut the door at some time. We just choose to pursue some things and not others." His talk of doors reminds me of Dr. Moya.

"I know. There's something else that bothers me. It's the way the tape ended."

He nods. "I've got some signal processing people I know in Silicon Valley I can have take a look. There's a lot of information in there. We'll also have audio forensics see what they can pull from it. From an audiotape we can tell approximately how far away someone is from the microphone. We can probably identify what was used to record the audio. Which can give us some idea of where everyone was in relation to the recorder. Echo will give us an idea about the size of the room and even furniture. Not in great detail, but it will tell us if there's a mattress in there, a hard floor. The more audio to work with, the better. A lot of it is trial and error. The program will anticipate models and then reconfigure until it creates a virtual match, but we should be able to get a 3-D reconstruction of the room and an idea of how many people are in there."

I pretend to know what all that means. "I'm worried about how it all finished. Something frightened them even more than what had been going on."

"Me too. And Blackwood?"

"Yes?"

"Between us skeptics, it's okay to be a little disturbed by the tape. It creeps me out too."

Ailes seems as resilient as a rock, yet it's a relief to have him tell me he's vulnerable too.

The screams haunt me. "I know it's just a child pretending. But I'm not sure what bothers me more: the idea of why, or the fact that those people took it seriously."

"Find this boy for us. Maybe he can explain what's going on."

26

CLASS PHOTOS GOING back over forty years stare back at me from behind Principal Kitson's desk. He was a fifth-grade teacher at Hawkton Elementary School around the time the tape was recorded. Now, in his late fifties, he seems more at ease in an office than a classroom.

I play a sound file on my phone for him. It's just a selection culled from the full-length audio, but it's still disturbing. Kitson looks up at me. "Is this a joke?"

"No joke. I just need to know if the boy sounds familiar."

"I don't think it's even his real voice," he replies, well familiar with childish pranks.

"I know. It's a long shot. The kid may have been a class clown, or he may have been the shy type who never said anything."

Kitson looks to the side for a moment, then shakes his head. "We've had lots of those. But I can't think of anyone specific who sounded like that."

"What about the Alsops or Jessup? Any of them have any kids around that might have done that?"

"No. None that I recall. I was just a math teacher back then. I didn't see all the students."

"How many teachers are still around that might know? Maybe the principal?"

"She's in a nursing home. Alzheimers. But I can give you some names."

He makes me a list and I spend the next several hours making calls and knocking on doors. There are a few vaguely suggested names, of boys that may have been troublemakers back then, but nobody says anyone stands out.

Those names turn out to be dead ends, but Mitchum's investigators circulate samples of the audio and manage to positively identify Adam Alsop, Curtis, and McKnight, confirming what I already suspected. Of the other voices in the room, none of them can be definitively identified as belonging to Natalie Alsop.

The remaining unnamed voices are troubling. Everyone on the tape we *can* identify is now dead. Are there others marked for death?

More direct questions about the exorcism are met with blank stares and shrugs, even from people who knew the victims. This town has seen so much. The last thing they want to talk about is how far back these troubles began.

Driving down the street or walking past stores in the small downtown, I get strange looks everywhere I go. The sheriff still hasn't been found. The mysterious events at Black Nick's cabin have only added to the overall sense of unease.

Nobody knows whom to trust. Even though I'm supposed to be one of the good guys, they're still in shock over the implications surrounding Sheriff Jessup. He was their good guy.

The local radio stations are going nuts. Information about the blast having a still-secret, mysterious explosive has fuelled the hysteria of a zombie on the loose. Footage of Reverend Groom's suicide plays endlessly on national news, anchor invectives about its graphic content only hyping interest in the clip. YouTube videos of Groom speaking in tongues and faith healing have begun popping up.

The sheriff comes across as the Boogeyman, but oily televangelist

Groom, who conned people in television broadcasts, is also a complicated victim. Many see his suicide as divine intervention.

Theologians fill the airwaves discussing every aspect of the case. The notion of avenging angels has been brought up. Fortunately, our video frame of the demonic shadow chasing Groom hasn't gone public. I can only imagine how that might go over.

When I check in with Mitchum's task force at their office, I notice more crucifixes around necks than is normal for the FBI. Several Bibles are scattered around, open to passages describing possession.

The armed search teams still looking for Sheriff Jessup are reporting strange stories about "lights in the woods" and the feeling of a "presence." I chalk that up to paranoia, although they won't change their minds.

What presently frustrates me the most is not being able to identify the boy on the tape. Our victims are all dead ends. The Alsops didn't have any children. Curtis and McKnight had none the right age. After the teacher interviews went nowhere, Kitson had given me a list of students from that time who still live around Hawkton. My cold calls are repeatedly met with "no comment." I don't get the impression anyone is hiding anything from me on purpose, but I think the past is just so distant, and the present so stressful, that they are reluctant to think back.

Ailes calls me when I get back to the motel after spending the day in the City Hall records wing going through the births. "Any luck?"

"No," I reply as I take off my flats and lean back on my motel bed.

"Mitchum is raising a fuss," he sighs.

"Over what?"

"You."

"I didn't do anything." I feel my back spasm. "I stopped by the task force for maybe forty minutes to drop off some interviews."

"That was enough, apparently."

"Christ. I'm not even technically on her case. I did that as a courtesy to the team doing backgrounds. Groom's suicide isn't even an FBI investigation. It's not even a local one."

"I know. But once we ID'd Curtis and the others on the tape, it became part of Mitchum's investigation. She wants to call the shots on this too."

"You're kidding me, right?"

"It's bullshit. I know. She's frustrated because they haven't found the sheriff. The manhunt isn't hers, but people want closure on this thing."

"Closure? Or a whitewash?" I snap.

Ailes ignores my comment. "And there's the other problem with the tape . . ."

"What?"

Ailes pauses. "It got leaked," he replies.

"Christ."

"Some blog has the full audio. It's on SoundCloud now, and YouTube."

"Terrific." This could make things that much more difficult.

"Mitchum is saying you leaked it."

"*What?*" I shoot off the bed. Jesus. Christ.

"I know you didn't." He doesn't say anything about my other superiors. "She was cornered by a journalist. She made a comment about 'publicity seeking' people attached to the case."

"I didn't do that." My fingers clench the phone so hard I'm afraid I'll break the screen.

"I know. But the director is in a tough spot. Your Mexican adventure and now Mitchum raising a fuss. We can't have you two fighting."

"I'm not fighting! I'm just doing my job," I protest.

"I know. I know."

"All I'm doing is chasing down the leads she's ignoring. I'm just filling the gaps."

"No one is pulling you in yet, although that may change in the next day or so. It depends on how much of a fuss Mitchum raises."

"Do I just drop it?" I ask, knowing there's no way in hell I would now.

"No. Keep going, stay clear of Mitchum."

"What can I do?"

"Find the boy. Get someone still alive who is on that tape."

"I'm trying. Mitchum has to realize she'd never even know about him if I hadn't stuck my nose in things."

"I know she knows. But here's the difference between you two: You just want to find out what happened and get the guilty party. She sees this as a competition. In her mind, any success you have comes at her expense. Time isn't important to her. If she has to elbow someone to win, that's okay by her."

"That's horrible."

"That's politics. It's why you're a great field agent and would make a horrible manager."

"I take that as a compliment."

"It is."

We hang up and I lay back down on the bed, trying not to think about what gross acts have taken place on the comforter. I'm at a dead end with the boy on the tape. My next step is to start knocking on random doors and barging into houses. I'm sure Mitchum will love that.

She's incomprehensible to me. I can't even bring myself to hate her. I just don't get it.

My phone rings again. I answer without looking at the display, expecting Ailes. "Now what?" I blurt.

"Something naughty, I hope," replies a voice that's definitely not my boss's.

27

Damian. Of all the people to hear from now. He's got a radar for locating me when I'm in a bind. "Hold on." I send a text to the working group assigned to track him down.

call trace this dk number

"You're such a good girl, Jessica," he replies in his calming voice. "In the future, I'd be happy to go through the FBI switchboard if that'll save you the trouble of having to tell them every time I contact you."

"Where are you?" I ask flatly. This is one more complication, one I can do without.

"Safe."

The events that took place less than a week ago in Tixato are fresh on my mind. "Been to Mexico recently?"

"Why would you say that?"

"Just a hunch." I don't have too many vigilantes that like to follow me, leaving bodies in their wake.

"What would it say about your employers if I am able to reach you more quickly than they can in a time of crisis?"

"Were you there?"

"Certainly . . . in spirit. Let's change the subject."

"Let's not. Why did you follow me down there?"

"Hypothetically, I'd only go there if I thought you were in some kind of trouble."

"And how would you know that?"

"Hypothetically?"

"Whatever?"

"Ever wonder how your phone knows how to ring when someone calls you?"

"No. Not particularly."

"Now you will. You see, your phone broadcasts an identifier. It tells the nearest tower you're in its zone. The tower then alerts the network and that's how they know where to send the call.

"If you are resourceful and you care for someone, you might find a way to make sure that you know the moment their phone vanishes off the network. Of course, when you turn a phone off or its battery runs down, it has the same effect as a disappearance.

"Even if said person is visiting a foreign country, in particular a region with a very nasty criminal element, you might still assume a phone going off the network is just their charge running out. But if you realize that every phone in the area has gone down with no explanation, and that the bad people might be the ones doing this, you might have cause for concern."

This is as close as I'm going to get to an admission.

"Thank you." The words come out of nowhere.

"Pardon me?" Damian is taken aback.

"I said thank you." I don't believe I'm saying this.

"I thought you were going to tell me you had it covered. That you didn't need any help," he replies.

"I don't know. I was scared. I was really scared." I haven't confessed this to anyone, not even Ailes. I'm not sure why I'm choosing Damian. He's dangerous. He's psychotic. He's probably a murderer. Twice now, maybe three times, he's killed for me.

"I don't know what to say. Do you think . . ." he starts.

"No, Damian. I will shoot you on sight," I reply forcefully.

"I love your foreplay."

"I'm serious."

"Are you ever not serious?"

"I said 'thank you.' I'm going to hang up now."

"Don't you want to know why I'm calling?"

This is the game he plays. He knows something but wants to tease me. He wants me to ask him. He wants me to let him know I need him. "Why, Damian?"

"Besides the sound of your voice? Speaking of voices, I heard that little audiotape you found. Heck of a performance. That kid had potential."

"A faker after your own heart?"

"Indeed. A tragic waste of talent. I'm sure you can relate. Have you found out his name yet?" he asks.

"No. I don't suppose you have?"

"I can't do everything for you, Jessica. But I do know someone who can help you."

"Who?"

"He's a collector by the name of Max Ripken. He lives in Virginia."

"What does he collect?"

"Ones and zeroes."

I don't have the time for this dance. "Yeah, um, helpful."

"You have no idea. He has so many of them, you'll need something to start with. A name would help."

He's already drawn me in. Why do I encourage this?

I know why . . . I just can't admit it to myself.

"If I had a name I wouldn't need him."

"Are you so sure? You've already looked at the name of every child who lived in Hawkton that you could find. Any luck? If you have the name, Max can help you make a connection."

"I don't have the goddamn name!"

"That's because you're thinking like an adult."

I hate his games. "Damian, give me the name."

"I don't have it. What you need to do is take a nice long hot bath and relax. The name will come to you. Or, at least the path to the name."

"Damian . . ."

"It's important you do it this way. It's important for you to keep thinking differently than everyone around you. That's how you caught the Warlock. If you're chasing ghosts, then you have to think like one."

"Ghosts aren't real."

"Exactly. But if I force-feed you what's going on, you won't see the whole picture."

"And you do?"

"A little bit. I know something about ghosts, and about how lost boys bide their time. Have I ever led you astray?"

"You're the definition of astray."

"I'll leave you with this parting thought. It's actually something that has been concerning me."

"What?"

"Between the 'event' in Mexico and the unfortunate experience you had a few months ago, you seem to be getting in harm's way quite a lot."

"And?"

His tone changes from teasing to serious. "Is it me?"

"What do you mean?"

"Are you taking these risks because somewhere, deep down, you think you have a protector?"

"No. Don't flatter yourself. I'm more afraid of you than anyone else."

"Jessica, I'd give my life to save you. You know that. Unfortunately, I may not always be there. You need to know this. I'm just a man."

NAME OF THE DEVIL

"A disturbed, psychotic man."

"Who loves you more than he can ever express."

"Turn yourself in if you love me so much."

"For what? I'm just a person of interest right now. That's rather boring. I can't even get conjugal visits. Unless . . ."

"I'd sooner shoot you."

"There was a time when you felt differently about me."

"I was young and didn't know the real you." There was a time when things weren't so complex, or at least I thought they weren't.

"Perhaps you did. Looks like it's time to go." The line goes dead.

Damian and his damn hints! He has a particular way of seeing things. I don't trust him, but I can't ignore him. He's been right before.

I lock the door and search under the bed and in the closet. He has a thing about violating my personal space.

Satisfied that I'm all alone, I start the bathtub and undress. The power of suggestion was too much. Damian knows scalding water and steam are my happy place. I place my gun and phone on the toilet seat within arm's reach and step in.

I relax against the cold tub as the water trickles over my toes and try to think of what I'm missing. Damian said to approach this from a child's point of view. I'm not sure what that means.

I've looked at every record I can find in the town. There is no way to track down children who were visiting relatives, or staying somewhere nearby.

What am I not seeing? I let the water pull me down into the suds and stare up into space.

The warmth begins to lull me asleep.

Something catches my eye and my spine chills.

The bastard.

He was here.

He was in my goddamn room!

I don't know if I should feel afraid or secure that he's nearby.

There are numbers written on the mirror, probably with soap. The steam has made them visible.

793.809

291.216

282.451

My phone rings.

"Agent Blackwood?"

"Did you get the trace?"

"Yes."

"Was it from here?"

"No. Miami, actually."

"I'm sure he's nowhere near there."

Self-consciously I get out of the tub and wrap a towel around my body. There's a shiver at the back of my neck.

I write the numbers down and wonder how far away Damian really is.

28

A T FIRST GLANCE, the numbers don't mean anything. They're not a location. They can't be phone numbers. I stare, trying to decipher them. A code? I give up and just Google them all at once.

Nothing.

Next I try the first one by itself, and get somewhere. The top result is a card catalog designation from a library.

So is the second, and the third.

Library card catalog numbers . . .

$$793.809 = \text{Magic.}$$
$$291.216 = \text{Religion.}$$
$$282.451 = \text{The Occult.}$$

NOTHING ELSE. No names. Just three Dewey decimal system categories that are already at the forefront of my mind. Damian's clue seems pointless.

But seeing things from a lost boy's point of view . . .

What are those numbers to a child? They identify book categories, just like they do for me, but they also represent something else . . .

The basement of our house held my grandfather's huge library. It was poorly lit and home to too many spiders, and I was

afraid of going down there. Unfortunately, my favorite books—
the ones Grandfather and Dad had little use for—were shelved
all the way at the back of the basement. When I wanted to read
Grimm's Fairy Tales or *The Wizard of Oz*, I had to venture to the
library's darkest recesses. There was only one lightbulb there,
and it was always burning out.

A scary home for fairy tales.

These numbers are not just a system. To a child, they're locations in a library.

This is the connection to the lost boy.

I barely bother drying off. I quickly put on a pair of jeans and
a sweater as I call the local deputy still on duty and tell him to
find someone with keys to the Hawkton Public Library *right now*.

Forty minutes later, an older woman with her hair in a
net and a bathrobe around her plump shoulders meets me at the
door of the small building.

"I'm so sorry," I tell her, showing my badge.

"No, no. Whatever I can do to help." She understands that this
must be important, and that it has something to do with the explosion.

The library is one of the older buildings in town. Made from
red brick and concrete, its shelves and furniture resemble a set
from a Frank Capra movie.

I hand her the numbers and she leads the way. We grab all
the books from the relevant shelves and set them on a table in
the center of the reading room. In total, there are thirty books,
worn but clean. They don't look like they've been opened in ages.
I take the first one, *Hoffman's Book of Magic*, and flip through the
pages, hoping for some kind of clue.

"Anything I can do?" the librarian asks.

"Look for writing in the margins." My previous search for the
child came up in a dead end, but what if he had been actually

hiding here the whole time? "Better yet, do you have records of who checked these books out?"

She shakes her head. "We never went to an electronic system. It's been hard enough keeping the doors open."

"Damn." That would have made things so much easier.

She takes the second book off the stack and flips to the back. "All you need to do is look here." She removes a card and hands it to me. "Each book has its own card. When you check it out, you sign your name and leave the card at the desk. The card goes back into the book when you return it."

The card has a dozen names in handwriting styles of varying legibility. Next to each name is a date, some going back to the 1970s. Every person who ever checked the book out is listed here.

"Can I have copies of all these cards? Wait, I can just take photos with my phone."

"If it will help you, take them." She starts to pull cards from the books. "I'll sort them all later."

"Thank you. Do you have records of library-card holders? If I found a name, could I match it to someone?"

"They only go back twelve years. After that, all those records are gone."

"Shoot. I'm sorry. Thank you." I collect all the blue cards from her and lay them out on the table, quickly dividing them into three piles according to topic. There are hundreds of names. The one I'm looking for should be in all three stacks, next to a date of at least twenty years ago. It's really a job for a computer.

In magic, there are formulas and techniques for sorting. We call it "culling." None of them ever held my attention for very long. Uncle Darius, on the other hand, could strip out the aces and high-value cards as he shuffled a facedown deck. He had some time to practice in prison.

"Are you looking for someone in particular?" she asks after watching me try to sort them for several minutes.

"I'm trying to find a name in all three of these piles. Somewhere in the 1980s, I think."

She picks up the first stack and runs through it, glancing at each card before setting it on the table. She picks up the second and flips through it the same way, selecting three cards. She returns to the first pile and culls four. Finally, she goes to the last stack and pulls two cards.

"Impressive," I tell her. "My uncle has a photographic memory." I don't mention how he used it.

"Is he a librarian too?" she asks.

I shake my head. "Only when he's in jail."

"I see." She leaves it at that and points to a name on a card. "M. Rodriguez. He's in all of them."

"Does he sound familiar?"

She taps her temple. "I'm not so good with faces. Numbers are my thing."

That name never came up in any of my school-related interviews. "Would he have had to be a resident to have a library card here?"

"No. We're quite liberal about that. All he would have needed was a resident relative who could sign for him. To accommodate children visiting over the summer and that type of thing."

Of course. Nobody at the school knew him because he probably never went there. "Thank you. May I hold on to a few of these cards as samples of his handwriting?"

"Sure. Sure. I'll hold the books for you too."

She helps me search through all the school yearbooks, just to be certain. M. Rodriguez is nowhere to be found. All we have is his childish signature and a list of books he liked to read.

I email Ailes the name so he can put in a search request for state and county records. Unfortunately, for older records that could take weeks. We'll be able to prioritize the search, but it'll still have to be done by hand.

I'm at a dead end until they can run it.

Or am I?

I remember the name Damian gave me, of the collector of ones and zeros: Max Ripken.

A quick web search finds someone with his name identified as a curator of the "Archive."

It's late, so I send him a brief email.

After a couple of minutes, my phone rings.

"Hello?"

"Jessica? Freddy told me to expect your call. I'm at your disposal whenever you're ready." Freddy? Must be one of Damian's weird jokes. His voice is friendly and youthful. He kind of reminds me of Gerald. "Can I give you a name over the phone?"

He hesitates. "I'd prefer we handle this in person . . . you'll understand why when we meet. Freddy told me I could trust you."

I look at the tables of books around me. I feel so close. To leave Hawkton now? "It's a little inconvenient."

"I know, but I'm just not sure about talking to someone from the FBI over the phone about what I do."

"I see . . ." This raises all kinds of red flags.

"You'll understand."

I better.

29

"A LOT OF this is in a legal gray area," Max says after I give him a reassuring smile at the door.

"Unless I find a meth lab, I think we're fine." I peer over his shoulder with some hesitation.

"Freddy said you're okay. So I'm glad to help." He has a pleasant smile and the round, boyish features I often notice on men who find themselves working with computers all day. His hair, the color of sand, is slightly receding, suggesting that he's probably a little older than he looks. Between the ten-speed in the corner and the rock climber forearms, I can tell he manages to keep active.

He leads me inside and down a long row of metal shelves filled with electronic parts in plastic bags. Hard drives and floppy disks of all kinds are stacked everywhere. It's a history exhibit of data storage evolution.

He lives in a recently built mansion in rural Virginia. The "Archive," as he calls it, is his collection of disk drives, with which he's filled the house and an add-on building.

From my brief Google search, I'd gathered he was some kind of software millionaire, but I wasn't able to find out anything more specific, or anything about him personally.

We pass deeper into his home, past bookshelf after bookshelf of hard drives in static-resistant bags, as he explains how his current "occupation" came to be. "After we sold the company, I was looking for something to do. A friend of mine wanted me to invest in a company that bought old computers and broke them down for scrap. There's gold, palladium and a lot of other re-usable metals in there. That's how I found out about the black market for old hard drives. Criminals buy them to steal banking information, which got me thinking: What else are we throwing away besides credit card numbers?"

He's probably told this story a hundred times, but seems to enjoying retelling it to me. "We make a big deal about television shows and movies that are lost forever. But what about data?" He walks over to a hard disk the size of a large toaster. "This has hospital data from a Northern California payment processor in the early 1980s. One of the first to computerize. It doesn't actu-ally have patient charts, those weren't digitized yet, but it holds billing information. This lists prescriptions, what tests were done. Everything you'd pay for. You know that you can make a vector of the spread of HIV from that information? Think about it. While we were trying to solve that mystery through other means, we could have discovered right here what was going on. There's a pattern in the data.

"It would have been illegal to have done that in the early 1980s. So I guess it's even sadder that the HIV epidemic exploded under our noses. We'll pass secret laws if we think terrorists might be a threat to an infinitesimal percent of the population, but we can't do anything remotely like that to stop something that harms far more people."

We walk down another corridor and come to a room con-taining something the size of a large washing machine. A single track light illuminates it like it's an art exhibit. Max's face bright-ens. "I found this in Guam. It's from a naval tracking station that monitored the moon landings—secretly. It's also got all sorts of spy satellite intelligence in there too. Satellite orbits, images of

Soviet bases." He looks at me anxiously. "Don't worry. I told the Department of the Navy about it."

"What'd they say?"

"They still haven't got back to me. That's the thing with this information. We'd rather pretend it doesn't exist. I'm afraid we're going to lose it all before we know what we have. It's disposable."

I'm not too surprised. A colleague and I had recently found a crashed MiG jet in the Bayou that our military never bothered to track down.

"My biggest project now is buying up old phone books and digitizing them. For a hundred years we've been tracking the migration of people from rural areas to the city without even realizing it."

I get the sense he could go on for hours. I find it, and his enthusiasm, fascinating, but I'm trying to track a killer. Mitchum could have me completely removed from this case at any moment. "I don't think the person I'm looking for had a phone number," I reply, steering him back on topic.

"We'll see what we can find. I have all kinds of random records. Not a complete life record on any one person, but everybody and I mean *everybody* is in my system somewhere. Even you." He gives me a half grin.

"I'm afraid to ask." I feel self-conscious.

His expression changes and he flushes. "I didn't look you up. That would have been rude. Some of this data is very personal. I'm just saying that we leave footprints everywhere."

We step into an office that's empty except for a computer sitting at a desk next to two padded chairs. "Where is all the data stored?" I ask.

Max suppresses a smile. "That's a secret. Freddy said I could trust you, but I still would like to keep that to myself."

"Of course." He's still cagy about the fact that I'm in the FBI. This data could be a legal minefield.

He points me to a chair and sits down at the desk. "What do we know?"

"A boy around 1985. His name is M. Rodriguez. He was in Hawkton, West Virginia, around that time. I'd guess an age between ten and thirteen."

Max nods. "Okay, anything else? Any other people?"

"Yes." I give him the names of the victims.

"Oh." Mentioning Hawkton was all it took to link this to what's all over the news. "This boy is connected?"

"I can't say how." It's a polite way to ostensibly deny knowing anything while implicitly confirming to him that he's correct.

"I understand." Max types for a moment, then leans back. "That's it?"

"Basically. It's not quite a search in the traditional sense. The Archive isn't just a database. It's a piece of artificial intelligence software. There's way too much noise for the signal. It has to make educated guesses and then keep approaching the data in different ways."

"I was expecting a printout or zip file or something."

"Well, that's the problem. Most people either rely too much on human intelligence or too much on big data. That's the difference between the CIA and the NSA. The best answers come from somewhere in the middle. Ask smart questions, then use your smarts to examine the data." Max looks at the screen. "I could give you a list of the seven thousand M. Rodriguezes near West Virginia around that time, but that won't do much to help you find the one you're looking for. Sometimes the information is in the gaps.

"Say, for example, I wanted to track you down from all the other Jessica Blackwoods using phone records. Maybe there are twenty? I'd find your latest address and note when you got that address. Next, I'd look for when a Jessica Blackwood disappeared from a phone directory in some other city. It's highly unlikely that two people with your name moved at the same time. I can then go backwards all the way until I find your first phone number."

"What if I have an unlisted number or no landline?"

"There are lots of other ways. Subscribe to a magazine? Ever ask yourself how junk mail finds its way to you? Same thing. They sell that information to advertisers. And that's just the legit data. I'm more interested in the gray data. The things people don't realize are important." He glances at his computer. "Hold on . . . I think we have something. What do you know about the couple named Alsop?"

"A little. Why?"

Max studies his screen. "That's your connection. M. Rodriguez shows up in a database of kids who were in the West Virginia free- and reduced-lunch program."

"He never enrolled in the school at Hawkton."

"No, because he lived there during the summer. But they start that paperwork early."

"How do you connect him to the Alsops?"

"They have about a half-dozen free- and reduced-lunch students in the system."

"But they never had children!"

"Not of their own. But from 1980 to 1985, it looks like they were foster parents."

This was a new revelation. "Foster parents? You have those records?"

"No. Just the lunch records. But that's the deduction the software makes. It's making a guess.

"All those databases aren't tied together. Especially ones from back then. A child-services database might wipe out all the information after the kids reach a certain age and never get imported into a new one."

"Yeah, it's just that nobody mentioned this in the background check or the interviews."

"1985 was a long time ago."

"True. Before my time."

He checks his screen. "Marty Rodriguez left Sparrow Oak Elementary in North Carolina at the end of the 1985 school year and then vanishes from the rolls altogether."

"Wait, so how do you tie him to the Alsops?"

"ACME Fun Toys has a card with his name and their address. It was scanned and added to a database."

"ACME Fun Toys?"

Max clicks through some information. "He responded to an ad in the back of a comic book, listing their home address."

"Any idea what for?"

"Hold on. It's an old database, but they might have kept it. Yep . . . it was for one of those books on how to throw your voice."

"Ventriloquism?"

"Yeah."

This is interesting. The allegedly possessed boy on the audiotape had been reading up on the occult, magic tricks, and also how to throw his voice.

A little faker, indeed.

But where is he now?

30

"I THINK WE may have our sixth man," I explain to Ailes. I trust him enough to share the broad details on how Max helped me identify Marty Rodriguez. I can hear him type the name into his own database on the other end of the line.

It took an uncharacteristically long time for Ailes to get back to me after I called and left a message. I know something is up, but I don't want to pry. It might be personal.

"Interesting . . ." he replies. "We've been working on the 3-D reconstruction of the audio environment. We've got all the main players in there, but there's still another voice we're trying to track down."

"That could be crucial. If we don't find Rodriguez before our missing man finds him, there's no telling what's going to happen."

"Yes . . ."

I hear his uncertainty. "What is it?"

"I'm looking up the name. I don't show any arrest records in West Virginia for a Marty Rodriguez in that age range. It'll take me a moment to get the other data."

"Maybe he stayed out of trouble. And foster kids move around a lot. What about a driver's license?"

"Nothing that matches what we're looking for. Foster family records will be harder to get, but doable if we can look through actual paper files."

"It's him. It's got to be him on the tape." I'm certain. My gut tells me that all the pieces fit.

"I'm sure too."

"Then what's with the hesitation? You seem unsure about something."

"It's the acoustic model, Jessica. We've been able to enhance certain parts and extrapolate reconstructions to test against what we're listening to. The moment where the voices stop . . ."

"Yes?"

"We picked up a sound in there . . . We've checked it against various potential sources. One match stands out more than any others . . ."

"What are you saying?"

"This isn't easy." There's anguish in his voice. "It's in no way certain. We have software that shows bullet trajectories and other kinds of physical trauma. You can also use it to create sound models. But it's not a precise technique."

"Tell me."

"That sound may be the boy being crushed. The data model matches the noise made when a ribcage collapses."

"Jesus." I have to stop to take a breath. "You mean they killed him?" The thought hits my heart like a hammer. I'd never even considered that possibility.

"We don't know that he's dead. It's just a computer model. But now that we have a name . . ."

I suspect Ailes is searching through death certificates as we speak. If his acoustic model is correct, Marty Rodriguez didn't grow up to become a criminal mastermind as I suspected.

He died a little boy.

A foster kid, shunted from home to home and desperate for attention, he came up with a gimmick. It was a game for him. A prank that went too far when some terrified people tried to rid him of the "demons."

I've heard other stories about children dying during exorcisms. Adults, while trying to hold back their small and flailing limbs, lean on them with too much pressure and kill them.

It's murder.

"Oh . . ." His voice trails off. "On October 20, 1985, a Marty Rodriguez died of suffocation. Oh dear . . ."

"What is it?" My stomach churns.

"Cause of death is listed as accidental. The report says he fell off his bunk bed in the middle of the night and it landed on top of him."

"They killed him, Jeffrey. They killed him!" I can barely breathe. "That little boy . . . they murdered him!"

"We don't know yet." Ailes tries to soothe me. "This may have happened afterward. It could be a coincidence. The report doesn't say anything about broken ribs."

He's rationalizing. "You've heard the tape. Tell me that's not the sound of him dying? This kind of thing has happened before."

There's a long pause. He has kids. I can tell he's just as affected by this as I am. Part of me feels guilty for wanting to think Marty was somehow responsible for all the evil that came afterward. I tried to make him into the next Warlock.

He was just a victim. The only truly innocent victim in this whole sad story.

"The death certificate was signed by the sheriff."

"Jessup? Of course. Anyone else named on there?" He had to have had an accomplice in his deception.

"Just the coroner. He died several years ago."

"It's a goddamn conspiracy! They killed the kid and they covered it up."

"We don't have any proof. All we have is an audiotape and some shaky computer modeling. We can't definitively tie the two events together."

"So we leave it?!" I yell. Sometimes Ailes's dispassionate, logical approach makes me want to strangle him.

"I'm not saying that. We're just in a hard place here. If we go out with allegations that all the victims, as well as our missing sheriff, were culpable in the murder of Marty Rodriguez before we can substantiate them, there will be hell to pay. We need to have this locked down."

"This could be the link we need, though. It might help us find someone else willing to come forward who knows something." I'm trying to cling to some single fact we can hold up. "Wait, what about the body? Could we get an autopsy?"

"No. It says the body was cremated."

"For fuck's sake. Of course. The sheriff knew what he was doing. Damn it. Somebody has to know something! I'm not going to let this go. They can pull me off this. I'll goddamn spend my vacation time out here."

"We won't drop this." He means *he and I* won't drop this. "But that still leaves the larger question unanswered . . ." He trails off at the end of his sentence, bringing my attention back to the center of all this.

Of course. In my frustration, I'd forgotten there still has to be someone behind all this. Part of me wants to believe there is an avenging angel serving out retribution for Marty's death. I don't know that any of our victims deserved what happened to them, but I do know that they needed to be punished.

"Who is behind this?" asks Ailes.

"I don't know. I just don't know." There's so much to process here. I couldn't even tell you my phone number right now, let alone the person I think we should be pointing the finger at.

"There's something we shouldn't lose sight of either," he continues.

"What's that?"

"This tape, what happened, it may have nothing to do with any of this. It could just be one more coincidence that ties them all together. We can't let our emotions dictate our perceptions."

"They murdered that kid. It has to be related." Ailes may be correct logically, but ignoring this feels wrong.

"Yes. I believe so. But who killed them? Is it our sheriff, acting out of some weird delayed guilt? Is the sixth man just hired help?"

"Is that what Mitchum is going with?" I'd bet anything she's pushing for a self-contained case in which all the parties are accounted for.

"I think so. Easiest path."

"Damn it. So the sixth man becomes a minor player. A footnote and then they bury this thing. We can't let her do that."

"We need more, Jessica."

"I'll find something. I can't . . ." I have to put down the phone. I don't want him hearing me get emotional.

I regain my composure. "I can't let them just throw that child away."

31

How the hell do you prove a murder took place twenty years ago when all the witnesses are either dead or missing, and the victim has been erased off the surface of the earth?

The one person we know was involved in the cover-up, if not the actual murder, was the coroner who signed the death certificate, Dr. Kinder. But, as Ailes discovered, he died several years ago.

The county medical examiner's office was only able to provide me with the slimmest of files for Marty Rodriguez. Inside is the death certificate, stating Marty Rodriguez died of asphyxiation, and the standard black-and-white photocopy of an outline of a human body.

The attached photo of Marty is a slightly faded Polaroid. It looks like it was taken in some government office. Probably Child Services. He's got a light brown complexion, dark hair, and the uncertain look of a child who has no idea what life holds for him. Hopefully a future better than what came before.

I take a picture of the photo with my phone. I want to remember this face whenever I have my doubts about carrying on.

Dr. Kinder's notes are sparse. They don't identify a first responder by name, only that the sheriff's office was called. This is peculiar on the surface, but according to the map, the nearest emergency room was ten miles away at the time.

The first responder, presumably Jessup, stated the boy was found unresponsive under the mattresses and collapsed bunk bed. The Alsops had been in the other room watching television when the accident allegedly took place. No other witnesses are cited.

The medical examiner reported that the cause of death was consistent with asphyxiation. Trapped under his blankets, unable to get enough air into his lungs with the heavy mattresses on top of him, Marty couldn't breathe.

There is no mention of any other injuries. This is a red flag to me. What hyperactive ten-year-old boy doesn't have a skinned knee or a bruise somewhere? The omission makes me suspicious, as does the absence of x-rays or photographs accompanying the report. Marty's body was delivered, the medical examiner signed off and then Marty was sent to the crematorium.

Why would Dr. Kinder sign off on this, unless he was somehow involved?

Could he be the other man in the room we haven't identified?

Without any hospital records to confirm he was on call at the time, the only person who might be able to give me some insight is his widow.

She greets me at the door of her small house, which is set back behind a well-kept garden in a town fifteen minutes away from Hawkton. As orderly and composed as her yard, she's exactly what you'd expect a retired rural doctor's wife to be.

She offers me coffee as we have a seat in her living room. Photographs of children and grandchildren adorn the walls, their smiles less forced than the ones in Groom's office. And I'm about to imply the man they love, who is no longer around to defend himself, was an accomplice to murder. I'm not sure how to begin.

"I assume you've been following the events." I know it's a stupid question.

She gives me a curt nod. "I'm not sure what to think. The people in Hawkton are nice folks. A bit rural, but sweet."

"You're not from here?"

"No. I was raised in Northern California. I met George when he was going to Virginia State. We married when he got the job out here."

"I need to ask you something about his job. I'm trying to track down some information about a case that happened a long time ago."

She shakes her head. "I probably wouldn't know anything about his work. He kept it to himself. Have you called the office?"

"Yes. But they don't keep call schedules going back that far. I just want to know if you can tell me whether your husband was working a specific night." Finding out if he could have been in the room when the death occurred is the first step in understanding his involvement. "This would be Sunday, October 20, back in 1985."

I'm surprised when, without hesitation, she replies, "Oh. George was working that night."

"You remember?"

"I know that because he had weekend shifts during that time. Our night out was Monday."

I make a note on my pad. At least he probably wasn't there when it happened, which makes me feel slightly less hostile toward him. Though that still leaves the question of why he'd help conceal a murder. "What was his relationship with Sheriff Jessup?"

Mrs. Kinder sets her coffee cup down a little forcefully. "Not good."

"What do you mean?"

"I'll be honest. My husband had his flaws. Jessup liked to . . . exploit them."

"Oh? How so?"

"George battled with alcohol. He was a really sweet man, but his job was very stressful. The sheriff pulled him over more than a few times. At first Jessup was doing him a favor, but then he started expecting something in return."

"Like what?" This is an angle to Jessup I hadn't heard about.

She shrugs. "Having a county medical examiner in your pocket makes certain things easier. Abuse could be ignored. Injuries could be exaggerated. This tore my husband up." The words just flow, as if she's made this speech in her head a thousand times. She's been waiting to tell someone. "It's why he drank himself to death. It was having to lie in court that got him the most. He didn't have much choice."

"That must have been difficult for the two of you." I've seen this pattern before, of one small thing cascading into a nightmare.

"He tried to never let it affect us or the kids. He was good that way. But you could see he was suffering."

"What do you remember about that Sunday night?"

She shakes her head. "Nothing in particular."

I could swear she was on the verge of revealing something. The admission about Jessup confirms everything I'd suspected, that the sheriff had to have something on Kinder to get him to go along with faking a death certificate.

Mrs. Kinder picks up her cup, takes a sip and places it back on the saucer. "What you meant to ask me was what happened on that Monday."

"Monday?" I sit up. She knows something after all.

"Yes. That's when Jessup asked my husband to go in and do a medical examination, even though it was his day off. I wasn't too happy about that."

"What happened?"

"He came home a wreck. I'd never seen him like that before. Sullen, but never . . . furious, I guess is the word." She points to a threadbare easy chair in the corner. "He sat there and drank until the sun came up."

"Did he tell you why?"

"Not specifically. But I knew what it involved. The Alsops' foster child who died. That's it. George took what happened with him to his death."

"You never asked?" I try to restrain my anger at her apathy.

"I couldn't. I wasn't sure if I would have been able to forgive him."

"I understand." I have to see it from her point of view. She has her family on one side, and the sheriff on the other. "Did he by any chance keep a diary?"

"No," she replies.

"I was afraid of that. All the records are gone. There's nothing left," I admit out of frustration.

"What about the body?" she asks.

"Cremated. They didn't leave anything behind."

Mrs. Kinder looks straight at me and shakes her head. "No. It wasn't."

"What?" There's yet to be one shred of physical evidence in this entire case that ties the explosion to Rodriguez's death.

"George was very drunk, and he kept saying something that didn't make sense at the time. Later on, I understood."

"What?"

"He substituted the child's body for that of an indigent who was to be buried at the county lot. He lied to the sheriff. He couldn't bring himself to destroy all trace of the boy . . . Marty's still out there."

I almost spill my coffee when I put my cup down on the edge of the saucer.

32

MY OLD FRIEND, Special Agent Danielle Barnes, greets me in the parking lot next to the graveyard well after midnight. "We have to stop meeting like this," she says, giving me a hug. We first met on our way to another crime scene in a cemetery. This time, she drove all night to come help me on a whim. Sweet-natured, with a spunky personality that matches her red hair, I like her a lot. Outside Ailes's group and Knoll, she's one of the few I truly get along with.

She understands my quirks, and how to deal with all the bureaucracy around her without losing her cool. I've seen her treat senior agents like one of her out-of-line teenagers, and watched as they sheepishly apologized.

It's not she's *motherly*, per se. She's more like a coach everyone respects and loves.

Ailes put in the request to exhume the body, but we got immediate pushback from the county. They're already stretched thin with the current lines of investigation into Hawkton. Trying to start another one was met with unsympathetic ears. They were going to make us jump through all the hoops. Dr. Kinder had done us a favor by making sure that Marty's body wasn't destroyed. The problem was that burying him in someone else's grave made exhumation a legal nightmare.

All I have is hearsay from Kinder's wife. The evidence is flimsy and only tangentially related to the current investigation, so no amount of string-pulling will work. That's why I asked Danielle to help me.

The thing about FBI departments is that they like new toys, and also justifying the expenditure on said toys. As the head of computational field analysis, Danielle gets the newest and shiniest ones. She's also a great forensic expert. After I gave her the rundown, she agreed to help me because this will be an interesting field test for some new equipment she has. But she met me in the middle of the night because she's a saint.

"Are you sure this won't get you into any trouble?" I ask. I don't want any blowback to hit her.

"If this boy is buried here, and what you think happened happened, then they can kiss my butt for all I care."

I lead her over to the grave where Kinder's widow said Marty was buried. Honer Jackson was the transient found dead of heart failure under a railroad trestle the day before Marty was killed. His unfortunate demise gave Kinder a place to hide Marty's body out of sight, unbeknownst to the sheriff.

Danielle stops at the marker and looks warily into the shadows of the trees surrounding the graveyard. "How long you been out here, hon?"

"Not that long," I lie. I'd actually spent the last few hours waiting near Marty's grave. I can't imagine anyone has ever visited. The thought of a forgotten child lying there, alone, for thirty years nearly brought me to tears. I'm getting soft.

I raise my flashlight over my shoulder as Danielle starts unpacking equipment. "I'd be scared to death to be out here alone."

We haven't really talked since what happened in Mexico. To be honest, I haven't spent much time dwelling on it. It's something I'd rather not think about. "This place is fine," I reply. "It's the living that give me the most problems."

She sets four round black discs the size of DVDs at the corners of the grave, then sticks a metal rod about a foot long into the soil. "The transponders will give us the image. The spike tells us the soil density." She takes a seat on one of the cases and puts her laptop on her knees.

Lights blink on the transponders, but I don't feel the low pulsing I expected after seeing the transducers she used in the Michigan cemetery on the Warlock case. "Is this a different system?"

"Sonar is so passé." She gives me a grin. "Microwaves. This takes a bit longer. The antennas have to calibrate. They reinforce each other and create a kind of virtual waveform. The tricky part is establishing a baseline. Fortunately we have one here with the coffin. If it knows there's a flat plane down there, it can interpolate the return signals that much faster."

"Obviously . . ."

She smiles. "You have your tricks, I have mine. It's kind of like trying to make sense of a blurry photograph. Calculating all those photons is next to impossible. But if I tell you the image is supposed to be a face, a computer can figure a lot of it out." She presses a button, then changes the topic rather suddenly. "So, how's your love life?"

"Nonexistent."

"I don't mean to pry."

My face flushes. "Oh, no. I mean there isn't one at the moment."

Danielle is easy to open up to. It's obvious that she cares. As she sits there waiting for her machine to tell her what's down there, life goes on.

I envy her ability to multitask. Or is it multi-emotion?

"What about the pediatrician?" she persists.

"It didn't really go anywhere."

"I'm sorry. He seemed like a nice guy. You didn't steal his watch at the dinner table?"

"No . . ." Regrettably, I had told her how that led more than once to a disaster. "I just . . . didn't really follow up on things."

"Oh. Well, you've got options. Your looks aren't going any-where," she replies, as she fiddles with her controls.

"Thanks. I was hoping to find someone who loves me for my mind."

"Oh, that's adorable. That's not the way it works, darlin'. Men have to fall in love with you despite all that. Here we go."

I move to watch her laptop screen as the image develops. It's just a big fuzzy block. "What's that?"

"Everything. Hold on. Let me subtract the dirt using the den-sity formulas."

The blocks begin to disappear, cube by cube, from the top to the bottom as if we were down there digging away the soil. A rectangular-shaped object is what's left behind. I assume it's the coffin. To be honest, the image isn't as clear as ones I'd seen on the older system.

"Not impressed?" Danielle has a sly smile on her face. She presses a button and the rectangle instantly resolves into a coffin. The detail is sharp. The handles, and even the wood inlays, are visible.

"Wow." I look at the ground beneath our feet, trying to un-derstand how we got all that information. "This is real magic."

"It helps that we know what we're looking for. Now, let's erase the coffin."

It vanishes, revealing the outline of a small body inside. Too small to be Honer Jackson.

It's Marty.

Mrs. Kinder wasn't lying to me.

His clothing a pixelated jumble, he looks like a mummy wrapped in plastic.

"All we'll really get a good look at is the bones and the major organs. Until we get one of those positron imagers . . ."

"What?"

"Wishful thinking. We'd need a truck just to carry the anti-matter containment system."

"Good lord. What can you show me now?"

She taps her keyboard and the chest area and his clothing fades away. Bones begin to emerge. His lungs are two large black voids.

"Can you zoom into the chest area?"

"Sure."

The image reloads and expands to show the rib cage. Two of the ribs are at an odd angle. One of them appears to dissolve into the black lung area.

"Is that what I think it is?"

"Yes. This boy has a ruptured lung. The rib snapped and poked right into it. Probably filled with fluid right there. Poor thing."

"Oh, lord." My nails claw into my palm. All this primal anger and nowhere to direct it.

"Did they report any of this?" Danielle asks. Her voice is flat, all the cheer gone.

I'd only been able to give her the broad strokes beforehand. "The death certificate says he suffocated under a mattress."

"A mattress wouldn't do this." She shakes her head. "The medical examiner would have seen the broken ribs." She points to them on the screen. "Even without an x-ray, it'd be obvious he died from a blunt force trauma. There would be blood in the lungs as well. There's no way he could miss this." Shaking her head again. "No way."

"The coroner covered it up."

"Bastards. I'll make a copy of this data for you."

"Thank you." I lean against a large memorial and send Ailes a text to let him know what we've found.

There's a message from him in my inbox, saying that they've definitely isolated another male voice on the audiotape that doesn't belong to any of the Hawkton explosion victims. He thinks enough of it has been captured for us to start looking for an identity.

The break offers a little relief. But it doesn't make up for finding out what happened to Marty.

This last man could be the only other person who knows exactly what happened and, just as important, what's going on right now.

I help Danielle load the equipment back into her truck. "Have time for coffee?"

"I got to head home and see to it my boys get off to school," she replies.

"When do you sleep?"

"Sundays." She smiles.

33

AFTER MY LATE-NIGHT sojourn with Danielle, exhaustion takes over and I fall asleep in the motel room. An hour before dawn, I'm startled awake by a suffocating dream in which I'm buried alive. I can't tell if it's trauma of my own I'm trying to work through, or the thought of Marty buried in the lonely grave.

I get up, walk to the window and slide the curtain back. I crack it open a bit and gaze across the parking lot that's bathed in the yellow light of the street lamps. Cars crunch grit on the highway, early risers going about their daily routines.

I imagine that not all of them ferry convenience store clerks driving to work, or night-shift employees heading home. Maybe some of the passing cars contain a normal family headed somewhere on an eagerly awaited family vacation.

I want to hope the occupants of those cars will all go on to have happy, if mundane, lives that are unaffected by tragedy. It's a naive notion. We all have to face some kind of adversity. However, a few of us, like Marty, get far more than our fair share.

It'd be nice to know that somewhere out there are islands of sanity. I think of Danielle on her way home to make sure her boys get off to school before she heads in to work. There's so much about her I admire. She's a good agent and, as far as I can tell, a great mom. There's work, and then there's her home life.

I don't doubt which is more important. The day she thought her family would suffer, I'm sure she'd take a leave of absence—or even give up her career—to make sure what was really important to her survived.

She knows the center of things. I don't even know the shape of my life. There's work, and then everything else. Lately, the "everything else" part has been pushed so far out of my mind that I'm not even sure how to have a non-work moment.

Seeing a movie, grabbing dinner with old friends, trying to kindle a relationship: It all feels so wasteful and pointless.

I sit down on my bed and open my laptop, which I fell asleep next to, and read through the latest reports. According to our forensic audio experts, our unknown man on the tape was in his mid-forties and approximately five-and-a-half feet tall—I have no idea how they deduce that. The words he says that we can make out with certainty are "restrain" and "must confine."

The significant thing is that English isn't his first language. His accent indicates either a Polish or Austrian background. The linguists say his pronunciations suggest he may not even have been a US resident. His English is more akin to British than to American.

This information has also been passed on to Mitchum and local law enforcement, but nobody has a clue who this man could be. None of the residents who recognized the other voices on the tape have the vaguest idea.

The team that went through town records couldn't find anyone living there in the last eighty years who matched that description ever. Expanding the search to records in neighboring towns has so far proven fruitless.

Apparently, neither the Alsops, McKnight nor Curtis had any friends or relatives that we could find who matched. There's a possibility this man may have been someone Sheriff Jessup interacted with, so investigators are now combing through arrest and court records trying to find some clue as to who he could be.

Other than if he's a stranger, the second-worst scenario would be if he's just a friend of a friend. This makes the potential circle huge. Ailes explained the permutations on this based on the research of a British scientist named Robin Dunbar. The average person has about 150 stable friends they keep in contact with. When you include old classmates and relatives, the number increases to around 250. An average couple may have 400 unique acquaintances in all. These are people you might have over for dinner or otherwise spend time with socially.

If the unknown man was a friend of a friend, perhaps of a former classmate of Alsop's in college, he'd be one of 160,000 possible people—that's assuming the connection wasn't completely random. And assuming that between all five victims at least three separate social groups exist, our unknown man is one of 500,000 possible people.

Even if we knew everyone that the Alsops, Curtis, McKnight and Jessup knew, we'd still have to conduct a half million interviews to find our man. It's an impossible job. It's too much data. It'd take a miracle . . . or at least someone who can work magic with numbers . . .

I email my new friend, Max.

My phone rings a minute later. "What do you have on this man?"

Max is well inside my circle of trust after leading me to Marty. I give him the description from the audiotape and the inferences our experts made.

"Hmm . . ." He mulls this over. "That's thin. What else can you tell me? It's a Bayesian thing. What are your gut instincts?" Like Ailes, he reminds me of my college professors.

I wonder if this is how *I* sound to other people when I explain things. I'd never thought about that before.

I think for a moment. "If he's a stranger, he'd be someone they feel comfortable bringing into the situation. Maybe a psychologist, or a doctor. He probably wasn't from there, but he might have been visiting and was asked to stop by."

"Hmm. Visiting?"

"I know, that makes it harder."

"Not necessarily. It could be easier. If he was from a nearby state and just drove there, that would be hard to trace now. However, if he flew there, or into some place close by, that's a little easier. Footprints . . ."

"Airline records?"

"Well . . . ever hear of a system called SABRE?"

"The online ticket system?"

"Yeah. It started as a project between IBM and American Airlines in the 1960s. It stands for Semi-Automated Business Research Environment. Sexy, huh? Anyhow, in the 1970s they opened it up to travel agents, who could dial into the system and book flights. The system was so huge it took up a football field. Of course, you could fit that data into your pocket now. The problem is, they'd purge the system every few years for space, so technically it no longer exists."

"Technically . . . You don't have a secret cavern somewhere hiding this, do you?"

"No. Actually, I've been thinking about buying a salt mine. But that's not where I'm going. So, here's all this data they have. Now imagine an agency, *not* the NSA, which has to do a lot of interesting computing. They've got a bunch of computer scientists working off the books on big data projects, at university research centers and think tanks with funny names and no visible means of support. You've got all this funding for hardware. That part is easy; you just call up IBM or Tandem and put in an order for whatever you need. Now you have acres of computers at your disposal. But what about the data? You need data to run experiments on and test out spy software. You can't just fill the disks with *lorem ipsum* or a million "John Does." Real data is a mixture of random information that contains patterns you don't think about at first glance. It's not just smoothly random. Do people in Michigan have longer last names than people in Arizona? For a period, yes, they did. Eastern European immigration. You get my point.

"So, real data is better than fake data. Anyhow, this not-the-NSA agency funds a group to make a copy of the entire SABRE database every couple years. Only they don't purge the data. They just keep adding to the system. Hard disks keep getting smaller, and their budgets keep getting bigger. They've got the room. It's government money. Then one day, at the dawn of the tech boom, the people that run that project all go off to start some Internet company, abandoning a system full of data that is in a quasi-legal area because not-the-NSA never classified it."

"So you're telling me you've got airline records going back that far?"

There's a pause on the line. "Further," Max replies, "I could tell you what seat Marilyn Monroe sat in when she flew into Washington National to hook up with JFK."

"Who?"

"What?"

"Who sat next to her?"

"Oh. I never actually looked. I can get back to you on that."

"That's okay. But that's amazing. You should write a book." I can only imagine what someone less ethical would do with this information.

"I'm not sure I'd live to publish it. I like data, not secrets. Anyhow, I'm going to take a look and see what I can find. I should be able to give you some names."

"I don't need all of them . . ."

"Don't worry. I'll help you find him. I'd guess a few hundred at most. I can pare them down a bit. But I'll have to think around a few things." He stops. "It'll cost you though . . ."

"What?"

Max hesitates again. "Freddy said you have to teach me a magic trick and let me buy you dinner."

There's something endearing in his struggle to ask me out. He's like a nervous kid in class. "Max, it's a deal. And I'll buy dinner."

He's not my type, but there's an earnestness about him. God knows I could use more of that right now.

34

WHILE MAX WORKS his data wizardry to find the unknown man, I concentrate on what happened to Reverend Groom and whether or not it involved the man who put the bodies in the trees in Hawkton. Something tells me the sixth man isn't our unknown voice on the audiotape. But I do think he had something to do with Groom's suicide.

The trouble is that there are few clues with Groom. We don't have any mud or other physical evidence like corpses and broken branches. By itself, Groom's suicide would be an open-and-shut case. It's plain as day he shot himself. We're only concerned about why because of who his friends were.

All I have to go on is his behavior right before he killed himself. On camera he acts like he is following a script he doesn't understand.

On a lark, I give my grandfather a call. I haven't spoken to him since we met at the airport. I never even followed up on his hospital visit either.

Ugh, I suck at people.

"Jessica, is everything okay?" he asks after I say hello.

It's not a sign of strong family relations when that's the first thing the other person says. "I'm fine. Um, how are you?"

"Good. Good. The medical thing is under control."

"Oh . . . um, good." I don't know if I'm supposed to press

further. What's the right thing to do? I just ignore the situation. "So, I have a professional question I wanted you to think about."

"Hold on. Let me write this down."

"What?"

"The time and date you asked me to help you." It's a gentle tease, but I can tell the old man is pleased.

I laugh with relief. I got him on a good day. "I could just call Dad, or Uncle Darius."

"Amateurs," he scoffs.

"They learned from the worst. I'm working on a case and I need your thoughts. There's something familiar about what's going on."

"Of course. Of course."

"Have you seen the video of the reverend who killed himself?"

"Good riddance." Grandfather's opinion on faith healers is as strong as my own. I have to resist telling him why he may be justified in his response.

"Yeah, um, but have you actually watched the part before he kills himself?"

"I haven't seen any of it. I only read about it."

"Could you do me a favor and take a look? I could send the video to you."

"Why don't I just pull it up on my iPad?"

Grandfather has an iPad? "Yeah, I guess so. You know how to find it?"

"Found it. Give me a minute." I hear the audio playing over the phone. It cuts off before Groom pulls the trigger. "Interesting. I see what you're saying. There's something off about him, isn't there?"

"Yes. I'm trying to figure out what."

"Let me think for a moment. Hmm. You may have been too young to remember this. In fact, you may not have even been born yet. For a while we had a bit in the show called 'The Antics.'

It was a hypnosis pickpocket act. Your uncle actually came up with the idea.

"I'd invite a man up onstage and tell the audience I was going to control him with my mind. Volunteers would put earplugs in his ears and make sure he couldn't hear a thing. He was behind a table with a bunch of props and I'd then stand at the foot of the stage and show a series of signs, only to the audience, explaining what the man was going to do under my control.

"One sign might say 'He's going to choose to put on a green hat.' The man would then pick up a green hat from all the others and place it on his head. The next sign would say something like, 'I'm now going to make him pour out the glass of beer or stand on one leg.' He'd do everything as I commanded it, without me asking him directly.

"The table holding the props had a big cloth over it. People would assume there was someone hiding underneath telling him what to do, so the next sign would say he's going to yank it away. You get the idea."

"Sounds clever."

"It was hideously boring. But it was deceptive. Nobody knew why he did the crazy things that I predicted he would do. But there's a reason that they never saw."

"What was the method?"

"We just had little signs on the back of all the objects telling him what to do. 'Step one: put on the green hat. Step two: pour the beer onto the ground.' There was more to it, but you get the idea. It was stage cuing.

"The problem was that it was dull, and the participants kept looking to me to make sure it was okay to go on to the next step. That's what your reverend looks like. He's waiting for his next instruction."

Exactly. I couldn't put a finger on it, but Grandfather nailed it.

"Was there anyone cuing him?" he asks.

"I think we'd know. There was an audience there. Someone would have seen something."

"Not all cues are visual. He did a bit of cold reading on people, didn't he?"

"Yes. He'd tell them the names of their children and stuff."

"That's a lot to remember. Remember when Randi exposed that televangelist on *Carson*?"

"The one using the earpiece with his wife?"

"Yes. That's the one. Do you think this man had one of those in his ear when he killed himself?"

Did anyone bother to look? "I can ask the coroner. If he did, someone could have been talking to him via radio. But still, how do you get someone to kill himself on live television?"

"When we did 'The Antics,' we tried a lot of different gimmicks. Some people did anything we asked, including undressing and waving around prop guns. But if someone doesn't do what you ask, what's your next step?"

"You threaten them."

"Exactly. Would you put a gun to your head if you were afraid someone you loved was about to be killed?"

"I'd have to believe the threat was real." Would I do this for Grandfather? Ailes? Gerald, even? I think the answer is yes. What about Damian?

"Was the reverend close to someone?"

"His wife."

"Where was she at the time?"

I think back to notes taken by the officer on the scene. "She said she was in a different part of the building."

"Why wasn't she in the audience, or in the studio?"

Good question. "Or was she?"

"If he's using a radio to do his mind-reading bit, there needs to be someone somewhere feeding him answers."

I think about the layout of the studio. At the back there was a large mirror.

I'd ignored it when I saw it. But it could have been a one-way window. "Grandfather, you're brilliant."

"I know."

I GIVE DETECTIVE Stafford in Georgia a call, and ask him to pull up the file on Groom and pay a visit to the studio again.

Two hours later he calls me back. "All right, Blackwood, care to tell me how you guys figured this out?"

"Actually, it was my grandfather. What do we know?"

"When Groom was examined, they removed a hearing aid from his ear and returned it to his wife. I checked and there is no record of him having a hearing problem. So I asked around the station. They were kind of cagey on the matter until I made some threats. They were afraid to admit what they knew about the mind-reading act. The station manager showed me the closet where Groom's wife would hide during the broadcast. The mirrored window looks right out onto the audience and the stage."

"After Groom went onstage, someone could have been on the radio telling Groom he was in there with her and was going to kill her if he didn't say what he told him?"

"Possibly . . ."

"She would have never known what was going on." Up there onstage, all he had was the voice in his ear. I think about what would tip him over the edge. "Groom was a tormented man for a long time. It could have been the voice of Azazel telling him this . . ."

"Maybe. If Azazel uses a cell phone with a Mexican long-distance plan," replies Stafford.

"Pardon me?"

"After I found the earpiece you told me to look for, I sent one of our techs to the studio. We found a small antenna in the ceiling, almost impossible to see. Connected to it was a box with a transmitter and a cell phone."

"A cell phone?"

"Yeah. And a thick battery. The last call to the phone was from Mexico. The whole thing was done remotely."

"Wait, did you say *Mexico*?" Groom was being communicated to from miles away. Someone used his little earpiece against him.

"Yes."

"Was it from Tixato, Mexico?"

"Hold on. Let me check the area code. Yes. We traced the tower to there. How did you know?"

My pulse is pounding. "Long story. Send me everything you got."

Tixato!

What the hell is it with that town? Why is someone from there killing these people? And why do they want to kill me?

35

AT AROUND FOUR-THIRTY yesterday morning, local time, Esteban was taken from the secure wing of the La Palma Mexican Federal Penitentiary, a prison used mainly for police employees and judges caught taking bribes, and led to the secure block's holding cell, which adjoins a hallway to the main prison.

Someone—a trustee, a guard, maybe the warden, who knows—left the door to the main block unlocked. At 4:44 a.m., Esteban was found stabbed over a hundred times. His head was nearly severed from his spinal column. The trail of blood traced back to the cell of a seventeen-year-old inmate who'd been in La Palma for all of seven days. He had just four months left on his sentence. He was a member of X-20.

Under intensive questioning, all he would, or could, say, was that he'd received orders to murder Esteban on a folded piece of toilet paper placed under his pillow. The instructions simply said to kill the man at the other end of the doorway at the allotted time.

Esteban was the last living witness who could reveal a connection between our case and X-20. During his incarceration he'd been kept away from the other prisoners because he was a cop and a potential witness against the cartel, but all it took was one prearranged "screwup" to get him sent to the wrong holding area and shanked by a seventeen-year-old.

Someone involved with X-20 is behind it. This much we know. Everyone I've encountered who was associated with the gang is no longer living. Although the last group, my "rescuers," were likely killed thanks to Damian's hands.

Damian . . .

I dial the last number he called me from.

"Assistant Director Breyer's office. How may I direct your call?" replies Breyer's front-office assistant.

Brilliant. Damian is forwarding any calls to that number right back to my boss. A man-in-the-middle hack. "Sorry, wrong number."

I could call Max and ask him for "Freddy's" current contact information. Before I have the chance, my phone rings.

"Hello?"

"I wish you'd call more often," Damian says in his chipper voice.

"Hold on." Per procedure, I send a text to log the call.

"Aren't we ever going to have any moments just between us?"

"I hope not." At least, that's what I tell myself.

"That's no way to ask for a favor."

"I'm sorry."

"First a thank you, and now an apology?"

"The army unit in Mexico . . ."

"I never met them."

I don't press him on that detail. Is it because I don't want to corner him in a lie?

"If someone you know did, by any chance did they take anything off of them?"

"Besides their heads?"

"Ugh." I suppress a shiver. "There is nothing funny about this conversation."

"There's nothing funny about what they wanted to do to you, Jessica. We live in a wicked, wicked world where evil men walk among the innocent."

"The difference between the good and the bad is the law."

"No, Jessica," Damian replies sharply. "The difference is that the good look out for the innocent and protect them from the wicked."

"Is that what you do?"

"If I were to break a law, it would only be of the kind that are designed to inconvenience. Law, like God, is only real when people believe in it. When you know the truth—that it's really just the good and bad we do to each other that really matters— you see things differently."

"Sounds perfectly amoral."

"No. Amoral implies I have no morals. I do. But they're not yours, or anyone else's. Legalities are like speeding on a desert highway when you know you're alone at night."

"Enough. Tell me about the Mexican militiamen. Their phones. None were found on the scene. Did you take them?"

"Their phones? Why would you be interested in those?" There's a touch of mischief in his tone.

"I want to know who they talked to. Did you take them?" I ask him curtly.

"I deny everything. Although you may have just won an eBay auction you didn't realize you were bidding on."

"Come again?"

"Buyer pays shipping," he replies.

"What?"

"All right. You're a tough customer. Just leave me a good star rating and I'll FedEx them for you."

A text alert from eBay pops up on my screen. I click the link in the message to read the lot description:

FIVE USED CELL phones. Perfect for narco trafficking and receiving orders for assassination attempts. Complete call log included. Previous owners physically incapable of using them. May be bloodstained. Actually, definitely bloodstained.

Auction ended 1 minute ago.
Seller: EternalUndyingLOVE
Bidder: MagicGirlDangerLover

"DAMN YOU, DAMIAN!"

He's already ended the call.

My phone rings again. "Agent Blackwood?" I recognize the voice of an FBI agent from our call center.

"Yes. Where'd the call come from this time?"

"The Vatican."

FEDEX DELIVERS THE package to my motel the next morning. Inside are five cell phones wrapped in plastic. Conveniently enclosed with each one is a printout of all the data on its SIM cards.

Damian not only went through the trouble of printing the information out for me, he also circled all the calls to the United States. He has drawn stars next to one number in particular.

The rest are to Mexican border states. This number's area code is in Virginia.

Like the phone found in the TV studio, these are all throwdowns designed to be untraceable to an owner. They would only have been used to call other burner phones, which would also be tossed aside after a few days.

It's a well-known fact that the prepay segment of the telecom industry, which makes and provides services for "dumb" phones just capable of calls and texts, is heavily supported by drug trafficking. I'm sure lots of regular people use these phones too. They just don't buy a new one every week.

The number he circled isn't traceable to any person in our database. Through an FBI records request made via a DEA task force, I am, however, able to get a cell tower log that tells me where the phone was located when the last call to it was made.

Not in Hawkton, surprisingly. A town in Virginia called Red-ford, about thirty miles from Quantico.

At least six calls were made from the militia phone and this number while it was in that area. The militia that tried to kill me must have been pretty high up in the X-20 org chart, and it doesn't surprise me that someone at that level would be running a contact stateside. I pull up an online map that breaks down cell towers by zip codes and addresses.

A Federal watch database shows me a list of convicted felons registered at addresses within the area of the calls. There are several dozen—too many to sort through. Trying to trace an untraceable call to an untraceable person is as hard as it sounds. Tapping phones only works when your suspect can't just walk into a 7-Eleven, drop fifty dollars and walk out ten minutes later with a new phone.

On a whim, I type the block of zip code addresses tied to that tower into an internal database of news reports.

Redford is a small town. Too boring to get much attention. The biggest item is the suicide of a former Air Force specialist two days after the Hawkton explosion. I click on the link to see if anything stands out.

Interesting. The victim had a technical background working on avionics and explosives.

Rene Deland has no obvious ties to organized crime. Dead of a drug overdose that coincided with a despondent text message sent to family members, there isn't anything overtly suspicious about his passing.

Except . . .

His job description is a little peculiar. According to the local paper's obituary, his family said he worked as a private security consultant overseas. People who handle private security and have serious drug problems often work for clients who are on the other side of the law. It's a red flag.

Deland suddenly interests me. If I was a lieutenant for a narco-trafficking organization who was placing calls to the US, they'd probably be to someone like him.

"I need to go to Redford, Virginia, to check on something," I tell Ailes over the phone.

"What have you got?" he asks.

"A wild hunch. Real out there . . ."

"How far out there?"

"One of our decapitated soldiers may lead to our sixth man . . ."

36

Retired Army Sergeant Charles Conner, who lives next door, pulls open the wooden gate to lead me inside Deland's compound. Dressed in a polo shirt and shorts and unfazed by the cold wind, Conner still has a military bearing about him.

"Deland sure liked his privacy," I remark as I notice the entire property is encircled by the wooden fence. A long driveway ends at a garage set apart from the house. Deland's pickup truck is parked in the well-kept grass between the two buildings.

The grass still looks fresh underneath. This doesn't appear to be the usual place for the truck, but the first responders could have moved it—or Deland, for unknown reasons. I file that observation away.

"Quiet guy," replies Conner. "Gave me a set of keys for when he was out of town. His sister is coming next week to take care of the place."

"Did you talk much?"

"A beer every now and then. He'd come over to the house for a barbecue when we had them."

"Ever see anyone else here?"

"A few times. Usually his only company were the strippers he'd date." He shakes his head a little.

"Strippers?" There's a correlation between men in high-testosterone lines of work and women in adult industries. I'm not sure what to make of it.

"Good looking, but lots of mileage." He pauses for a moment, looking at me sideways as he wonders if he's said something politically incorrect.

You don't last long in my field calling foul every time some guy talks like he's in a locker room. I give him a pass. "Did he ever talk about his work?"

"Said he did avionics consulting. A lot of people around here do consulting work they can't talk about. Nobody presses them."

"The coroner's report said he died of a drug overdose. Did you know he was a user?"

"Sometimes he'd have bloodshot eyes. Some of the girls looked like they were. He didn't come across as hardcore. I was surprised to see the needle in his arm when I found him. But not shocked."

"Why is that?"

"Once you open that door, anything can happen."

Again with the doors.

I notice Conner answers my questions like they're checkboxes on a tax form. They're all "yes" or "no," without any elucidation.

"I'll leave the keys with you," he offers. "Just put them in my mailbox when you're done."

I LET MYSELF into Deland's home. The police had done a quick check, I'd learned, but nothing thorough. Without any reason to suspect foul play, this wasn't treated like a crime scene. His death seemed pretty straightforward, with no reason to think it was anything other than an overdose.

After I got off the phone with Ailes, I'd called the investigator in Redford who'd handled Deland's case. I was curious if they'd found more than one cell phone among his belongings. If the phone the Mexican soldier used could be matched to a phone in Deland's possession, we'd have a clear connection. Unfortunately, the only phone they catalogued among his possessions was the one found in the bedroom, which he'd used to send his final text message before he died. But they weren't really looking for a second phone.

His house is small compared with the size of the yard. Uncluttered, it's almost too compulsively neat. Of course, I'm the one that uses the floor of my closet as a laundry basket.

There's a living room dominated by a flat-screen television and a brown leather couch. The kitchen looks like it was used for breakfast and little else.

A plastic sheet still covers the bed where Deland's body was discovered by Conner. The bedroom is just as sparse as the rest of the house. I'll attribute the tidiness to Deland's fastidiousness, but my gut tells me someone went through here and cleaned out a few things. There's not even a laptop to be found.

That's peculiar to me. I'm not sure what kind of avionics expert doesn't need a computer.

Conner didn't seem like the kind of guy who would steal from the dead. There's also the paramedics and cops on the scene to consider. It's a horrible thing to accuse your peers of, but it happens far more often than we want to admit.

The top drawer of his dresser holds a row of watches that each cost more than my car. I assume the investigators decided there wasn't anything suspicious about the lack of a computer because anyone wanting to rob Deland would have taken the watches. If he'd been killed violently, then that would be a different matter. But opening a criminal investigation every time you notice an apparent suicide victim is missing something is impractical. It's common for people spiraling down to give things away. If they're in a financial crisis, they hawk them.

As far as I'm concerned, I'm now reasonably sure this could be a crime scene. I take a pair of gloves out of my field forensic backpack and slip them on before going any further.

Out of curiosity, I reach behind the nightstand and feel two wall plugs attached to cords. One of them is an iPhone plug, the other a micro-USB.

Deland's phone, at least the one recovered by the police, was an iPhone. The other plug is for a different device. Could that device have been another phone—a throwaway that was removed from the scene along with the laptop?

Killing someone via a drug overdose is an easy affair if the potential victim is already a drug user. If Deland knew his presumed murderer, all the killer had to do was spike a drink with a soluble amphetamine that would then make Deland less resistant to an injectable amphetamine of a much higher dosage.

A quick toxicology report, the kind the county does when no foul play was suspected, wouldn't show the different amphetamines. Investigators would find what they were looking to find: drugs in the system. Case closed.

If I can find more evidence, which can reopen the case, then I can lobby for a more precise test. Most counties keep blood and tissue samples on file for at least a year after death. Ideally, we'd look at the body before Deland's sister claims it.

The extra phone cord is informative, but not conclusive. I need something else.

The rest of his house doesn't reveal anything to me. I check the closets for special hiding spaces, but there's only a locked safe in a fairly obvious location. It takes me three minutes to open it. Inside I find a stack of bills, mostly hundreds. Maybe twenty thousand dollars from my quick count. There's nothing else. But then again, no good criminal would use that to store his dirty laundry.

This is get-out-of-town-fast cash. Now there's a thought.

I take out the bills and have a closer look. They're brand new and smell fresh. We need to check with his bank and see if he made a recent withdrawal. If he didn't, then this may be a payoff. If he did, then he might have been nervous about something.

I sit back and gaze around. The house feels like a realtor's show house; I can't find anything to provide some kind of record of who Deland was, or what happened to him.

The money and the missing laptop and phone are suspicious. But if he's just a standard crook, doing things like making custom police scanners for marijuana dealers, his death is not really an FBI matter, or anything even the locals would care about all that much.

Back in the kitchen I take a final pass and notice some photographs on the side of the fridge. They're of Deland on the beach and at bars with attractive women. My catty side notices that they do all look like strippers. Too tan, too much boob on display and heavy makeup hiding hard living.

Underneath, almost hidden, is an older photograph of Deland in his Air Force uniform. He's posing with a wrench in his hand. Behind him is an aircraft. Long, dark fuselage, no cockpit. It's a drone.

I haven't got a copy of his service jacket yet. I didn't realize Deland had been a drone technician in the Air Force.

Interesting . . .

I RETURN TO the living room to take a look at the backyard. As I walk across the carpet to the window, something catches my eye. The low sun is casting shadows across the shag, turning it into a tiny forest. It highlights four deep impressions next to the wall. Something heavy must have been there until quite recently.

I glance around. None of the other furniture seems to match the dimensions of the carpet dents. This was taken from the house—and not that long ago.

Kneeling on the floor, I stick a pen in the gap between the carpet and the wall and slide it from left to right. Something clicks against the plastic. I pull the object free and it lands on the carpet.

It's a dull blue rock, worn smooth. I squeeze it. Hard like quartz, this isn't a drug like meth or crack.

It's the kind of stone you put in an aquarium.

Deland had a fish tank.

Someone took the fish tank out of here.

That's what the investigators didn't see. A missing fish tank.

This could have been where Dr. Moya's psychoactive fish were kept.

Through the curtains I see the sun dip behind Deland's free-standing garage. I wonder what's in there?

Well lit, Deland's garage is actually more like a machine shop. It has the same sense of order as his house. I can see the clear spaces on the floor where two tool chests must have sat, but they've been removed too. The center area of the shop is devoid of clutter. He'd been working on something here.

The truck parked on the grass suggests that whoever took what was in here must have had to back up to the large door to get it out. They either forgot about, or didn't bother, moving Deland's truck back.

What *was* he working on? It's impossible for me to tell because of the missing tools. Whatever it was, it required the full space of the two-car garage. Maybe forensics can find something if they go over it with tweezers. A sample of mud took me to Tixato, and a phone call from Tixato brought me here. So who knows what's waiting to be found.

I do need to be wary of trying too hard to make Deland fit. The aquarium stone is interesting, but it's not enough to link to anything here. The last thing I want is to get an FBI team out on a wild-goose chase. One blue rock is all I have; the missing laptop, phone and wild theory about a fish tank aren't enough.

I close the door to the garage back up. My best bet is to get the local police more interested in what Deland was up to. If they find something, then maybe I can persuade Ailes to stick his neck out and channel some more resources into uncovering the connection.

As I'm about to lock the garage, I spot a crumpled drop cloth hidden behind the door and stop. My dad used to lay one out on the driveway when he wanted to paint a magic prop. I would often help him, fascinated by how the overspray formed an outline of whatever he was making. Boxes, circles, rabbits. It was like a giant after-the-fact blueprint—a kind of negative of whatever he was building.

A blueprint . . .

Deland's project may be gone, but not all its traces.

I take the drop cloth outside and unfold it across the driveway.

As it unfurls, it reveals dozens of random paint marks outlining Deland's different projects. One stands out more than the others: a large triangle.

It's shaped like bat wings.

It's much larger than the shadow in the convenience store video frame from Reverend Groom's 911 call. But it's obviously from the same family.

Besides housing exotic cave fish that may have sent the sheriff into a prolonged psychosis, Deland was using his military training to work on a drone. A large, demonic-looking drone.

37

FURIOUSLY TAKE PHOTOS of the drop cloth, afraid the paint will somehow fade away like a print in a darkroom, and almost trip on a lawn sprinkler while running back to my car to shoot an email off to Ailes with the images. The mere suggestion that Deland might have been working on something that could be used by a drug cartel, particularly one with terror links, should be enough to justify a thorough search of the premises along with an extensive investigation into his activities.

There's a voicemail on my phone from a West Virginia number.

"Miss Blackwood, I'm callin' you so you can set the folks straight on what occurred." This is a voice I remember vividly, Black Nick. By the roaring of the cars in the background, he called from a pay phone by a highway. "Ole' Jessup came by my cabin, I reckon you know that cause uh the fire and all. He had the idea old Black Nick had somethin' to do wit his troubles. He's all out of sorts.

"I prayed for him. I tried to get him to do the Lord's Prayer too. He'd have none of it. Kept talking 'bout how the trouble-maker had his soul no matter what. Said he was an avenging angel, doing right by God's hands.

"He chased me all the ways up to Lightnin' Peak. That's where you gonna find him if you bother looking. Not that there much to look at no more. He got what was due.

"Now I suppose folks wanna talk to me. I ain't having none of that. I done what I done and no man can say I didn' try saving his soul. It wasn't having no saving.

"I'm going backwoods, back with the other folk who live in the deep parts. I said my piece. I hope you still got the bolt I gave you. There's more dark out there. The troublemaker ain't done with you."

I've had many strange phone calls in my life, but I'm pretty certain this will never be topped. Nick's warning unsettles me.

It takes me a moment to process everything before I call Knoll and tell him he should have the team handling the manhunt go to Lightning Peak.

An hour later I'm back at Deland's, persuading the local cops to seal his property as a crime scene, when Knoll calls me back. "They sent the chopper. The pilot spotted something." His voice is matter-of-fact. He'd probably narrate a boxing match like an autopsy.

"Jessup?"

"We don't know yet. Definitely a body, charred though. There was a storm last night and multiple flashes on the mountain."

"Jesus." The image is . . . biblical.

"How'd you know where to find him?"

"I'll send you the voicemail message. Our sheriff had an 'altercation' with our crazy Swede witch doctor."

"An altercation that involves lightning? Christ. I'll let you know when we get a preliminary report. He called you?"

"Yup."

"The crazy ones sure love you."

"Story of my life. Takes one to know one, I guess." I say it with a half smile. "I think I got a lead on our sixth man." I tell him what I've found at Deland's house.

"So the circle is complete?" replies a hopeful Knoll.

"Hardly. We don't have a motive nor any idea who the Tixato connection is."

"They'll come up with one."

"What's that supposed to mean?"

"If this briquette is the sheriff and Deland is the man who put the bodies in the trees and created the explosion, then I think they're going to say the case is closed."

"But it isn't. We don't have proof Deland did it or know who killed him. We don't know who is behind all this. This keeps getting bigger, not smaller. I mean, who wanted me dead in Tixato?"

"You know they're going to pin this on Deland if they can make a connection. You check his shoes for mud from Hawkton or Tixato?"

I'd gone back and checked after getting off the phone with Ailes. "His shoe collection was small, intentionally sparse. I used a roll of tape to grab some carpet samples from the truck and closet. I left enough for a proper forensic exam."

"Gut feeling?"

"He was in both places at one time or another."

"They're going to pin this on him."

"Who? Agent Mitchum?"

"Her, everyone. It's easier to close the books when everyone is dead."

My blood is beginning to rise. "What about X-20? How do they figure in on this?"

"What will Mitchum go for? She'll admit he worked for them, maybe. When you came snooping around someone made the connection. Even if we find out Deland was killed, it'll be just another gang-on-gang crime. Drug-related murders don't count like real ones, as far as the public is concerned."

"That's bullshit. I can't believe you're saying this."

"It's not my case. Mitchum and the Bureau want closure on this. The longer it's open, the more expensive it gets and other things don't get done. Despite their obstruction, you brought them all the pieces they need to make a circular case."

"There's no motive for Deland!" I protest.

"He's a bad guy. They do bad things. I'm just preparing you for what I see coming. This whole case is totally out there. It's too much to wrap our heads around. They're going to go with Occam's razor and apply the simplest explanation."

"Occam's razor doesn't say anything about excluding facts! They can't really be going this way?" I know Knoll is trying to just be straight with me, but I can't help taking it out on him.

"I'm afraid so. That's my gut. Ailes will tell you the same."

My elation over finding Deland is crushed by the prospect that all Mitchum wants is a person to pin this on. I may hate her after all.

To her, the question of who put the transmitter in Groom's studio, who wanted me dead in Tixato, of what really happened the night Marty Rodriguez died, are details she's going to ignore because the facts are too weird.

MAX CALLS ME on my drive back to Quantico. "I've got a list for you," he says eagerly.

"How long?" I try not to let my sour mood show.

"Sixty names."

"That's not bad." Thank God someone is taking this seriously. God bless Max.

"I've also pulled up a list of events and conferences going on in that area at the same time."

"How'd you do that?" I ask, impressed.

"Internet."

"In 1985?"

"The Internet, not the web. The Internet is the thing that connects it all. That was around a long time before."

"Yeah, of course. Was it a Listserv?" I dig up a term from a college class on computing.

He lets out a small laugh. "Yeah. Old message boards for swingers."

"Pardon me?" I take my eyes off the road for a second to stare at my phone on the dashboard.

"People back then, before Tinder, Grindr and Craigslist, would put announcements on online message boards about where to hook up. Got an insurance convention at the Hilton in Raleigh? Somewhere, someone is going to post something to a board suggesting a rendezvous. I found a bulletin board system that still had listings in that area. Maybe there's something helpful."

"Thank you, Max."

"You sound down. Everything okay? You don't have to do the dinner thing. I was just . . ."

"Max, that's still on. I need some sense of normalcy." Just the thought of passing an hour talking to someone who doesn't spend their time staring at dead bodies, or carry around a pair of handcuffs professionally comes as a relief.

"Normal? Me? Your world must be something strange."

"You have no idea."

38

THERE'S A STORY one of my favorite high school teachers loved to tell about selective blindness. I don't know if it's true or not, but it makes an interesting point. When Spanish ships first appeared off the shores of the Americas, some of the Indians couldn't see them. The ships were anchored right there in the bay, but the tall-masted vessels were so utterly foreign that they simply couldn't acknowledge them.

In a modern culture, where every commercial break is filled with visual computer animations of alien attacks and mythical creatures that assume you already understand a dozen bizarre concepts, the notion of pretending something isn't there because it defies explanation seems almost laughable.

Yet, every day, science reveals things that were right in front of us: bacteria actually cause ulcers, animals can indeed sense earthquakes, your house cat may be infecting you with a virus that makes you hoard things, including more cats.

The events in Hawkton are like this in some way. Because we couldn't see what was there, because we had to fit it into what we understood. At first it was an accident. A little bit of investigation revealed it was a murder with someone else possibly involved. Maybe there was a tinge of conspiracy, but nothing that went beyond small-town politics.

This is the explanation that conveniently fits the facts. It's the explanation investigators cling to because they prefer it over others being put forth by people who see the fantastical in every dark corner, who believe Satan walks among us. But their prejudice has forced them to choose an explanation that's also at odds with reality.

The middle ground isn't clearly marked. There's no map for me. I know there's something more here than what my colleagues want to acknowledge. I also know the supernatural explanation just isn't rational. To accept that would be to give up on the very notion of intelligent query. I can't fault someone who chooses to believe the dinosaurs lived alongside the Egyptians. But I can't tell them with a straight face that they're thinking like an adult. It's a childish worldview to choose what to believe and what not to in the face of the evidence. Playing peekaboo with the facts doesn't make them disappear.

However, being too quick to rule out a hypothesis is just as misguided. Although dinosaurs died out millions of years before the first primate walked upright, the early Egyptians were putting capstones on their pyramids while wooly mammoths were alive and well on a tiny island near Siberia untouched by man.

In trying to tell people there's something more here, they think I'm pointing at dinosaurs. I'm simply saying mammoths might be involved.

I've also drunk half a bottle of wine while flipping between the science channel and the news. Back in my apartment lying on the couch in my pajamas, I'm trying hard not to be a cop for a moment.

The investigation isn't going the way it should. Ailes just called to tell me it's unfolding the way he feared. To his credit, Knoll saw this coming. Mitchum is giving a press conference announcing the case has for all intents and purposes been effectively solved.

Solved. *Right*.

Mitchum is standing at a podium outside the Hawkton sheriff's department. There's a crowd of news trucks and crews that's
easily bigger than the single-story brick building. She thanks the
laundry list of agencies involved in the case. Flanked behind her,
symbolically representing the unified face of law enforcement,
are the remaining Hawkton deputies.

"We have concluded that the body we found is indeed that of
Sheriff Jessup. This brings the manhunt to a close," she says. She
smiles with pride, but she looks tired. Real tired.

"Are there any other people involved?" asks a reporter from
CNN.

"We have a person of interest who we think may have been an
accomplice." She means Deland.

"Is this person in custody?" presses the reporter.

If you count a mortuary table, sure.

She hesitates, not wanting to say he's dead. That would make
the case a little bit thinner. "This person is not at large."

I'll say.

"What about the connection to Reverend Groom?" another
reporter interrupts.

"We believe this person is connected. That's all I can say."

Yeah, that fits, except that the phone call to Groom came from
outside the country when Deland was in Virginia.

"What about allegations of involvement with Mexican drug
cartels?" asks an NBC correspondent.

"We have no evidence the sheriff or any of the victims were
involved in anything like that." Mitchum gives the journalist a
sharp look, frustrated with the line of questioning. She keeps
trying to form a bubble around the case and the reporters keeping poking holes.

"Was the shootout in Mexico, between Jessica Blackwood and
alleged cartel-aligned military, related?"

"There's no evidence for that. She got caught in the crossfire with a rival gang. Wrong place, wrong time. We're just glad she's safe."

Oh, that's what happened. Thanks for clarifying.

Her words are too clipped to be sincere. I'd swear she flinched when my name was mentioned.

"What about the satanic connection and the mention of demons?"

Mitchum rolls her eyes. "Likely planted by the perpetrator to instill fear."

In dead people? I want to shoot my television. Not her, just the TV. I think.

"Is the sheriff a suspect or a victim?"

"We have reason to believe that he may have unwillingly been under the influence of a substance that caused erratic behavior."

And that substance came from where? My bruises from the cave are still a nice shade of purple, but hey, you're welcome.

"Of course, there are more details to come. But we confidently feel that, with an end to the manhunt and the hard work of my colleagues in locating the other person of interest, we can bring this matter to a close."

Thanks for the name check, sister.

Mitchum prays for the back and forth to end. She just wants to go home with a pat on her back and no loose ends.

"What was Jessica Blackwood's involvement?" asks another reporter.

Oh. As much as I hate my name being mentioned, it's worth it to see Mitchum cringe a little.

She definitely flinches that time. "There are hundreds of people who've worked hard on this case. Singling them all out would take too much time."

She sounds colder than she means to, I think. Oddly, I almost feel bad for her. Almost.

"Will there be an investigation into the audiotape that was leaked?"

"I can't comment directly on evidence that may or may not be relevant to the case."

Relevant. As in, throw it in a drawer and forget about it.

The press conference ends and the news camera cuts away as she retreats back into the sheriff's office. I go back to my pile of printouts containing the information Max sent. I should probably be looking at them with a clearer head, but that's not going to happen for a few hours.

Flipping through the list of events in the Hawkton area, I try to find something that might bring an outsider into the world of the Alsops and their troubled foster kid. There are no psychology or medical conferences, but the Star Trek convention held at the War Memorial auditorium twenty miles away certainly opens up the possibility of intergalactic operatives.

The bulletin board system (BBS) announcements are somewhat cryptic. People want to hook up with others, but also don't want to expose themselves too much. I have to look up a few acronyms to understand what's going on. Even modern online dating is a mystery to me. I go back over the first list and find events that stand out and compare them against the BBS records. This catches my attention after my third drunken pass of the BBS logs:

Purple Collar looking for similar attending the Interfaith Rituale Romanum Series at Gregory College

APPARENTLY, "PURPLE COLLAR" appears to be a code name for a gay priest. The Rituale Romanum sounds boring, but the window is open. I do a Google search anyway.

Holy crap.

Of course.

Here I am, getting wasted while I bemoan my colleague's ignorance, and I can't even acknowledge the mammoth.

The *Rituale Romanum* is the religious text that Catholic priests use for exorcism rites. It's for dealing with the possessed.

Confronted with a possible case of juvenile possession, Reverend Curtis could have gone to the interfaith conference in search of guidance.

The unidentified man on the audiotape is a Catholic priest.

I go through Max's reduced list of twenty names from the SABRE records. Three of them departed from the airport in Rome.

One name looks familiar, but I'm not sure why.

I don't know too many priests. Was he on a list of witnesses we already went through?

I do a system search of the files on my laptop. No . . .

The middle and last names throw me off at first. At a loss, I type the full name into Google.

There we go. The first result is a priest identified by the European spelling of his first name and a truncated surname.

But that's not his name anymore.

Holy shit . . .

I knock my wineglass over and ignore the pooling red liquid as I pull my laptop onto my knees.

My hands almost don't want to type as I pull up a YouTube clip of him speaking.

I'm getting that buzzing feeling in my head.

Same voice.

He's the man on the audiotape.

Fuck.

Holy fuck.

It's got to be the wine.

It can't be.

I'm drunk.

I'm dreaming.

This is insane.

Jesus. H. Christ.

Reverend Curtis didn't just find himself an expert on the *Rituale Romanum* at the conference; he talked the man into coming to the Alsops' house and delivering the rite himself.

And not just any man. The expert at the time.

A man who would keep going up the Vatican ladder.

Thirty years later, that man is now the pope.

The pope.

No. This is insane.

I take a deep breath and try to clear my head.

I find another YouTube clip of him speaking. I recheck Max's records.

I sober up fast.

My head isn't spinning so much. I have focus now.

This all points to the same thing.

The current pope was there that night in Hawkton when they tried to exorcize Marty Rodriguez.

The pope helped kill Marty Rodriguez.

Maybe not kill, but Marty is dead and he was there.

And now someone is killing everyone who was responsible.

There's only one survivor left.

The pope.

The goddamn pope.

Christ.

I need another drink before I tell Ailes.

39

ASSISTANT DIRECTOR BREYER sits behind his desk and has me go through the entire sequence of events that led to my conclusion. After I'd drunk two cups of coffee and showered, I wrote what I thought was a reasonably cogent email to him and Ailes.

Breyer replied by asking me to meet him in his office on a Saturday. I still haven't heard from Ailes and that has me really concerned. Usually he has my back on these kinds of things. I guess this is part of the growing-up process.

Breyer is wearing a polo shirt, which makes the meeting seem a little more casual. But that's a deception. I'm here alone with the most ridiculous allegation of my career.

"The pope?" asks Breyer. There's no humor in his voice. No trace of sarcasm.

"Yes."

"There are only two audible words on the entire tape from this man and you think he's the pope?" He asks me this as if he's a father questioning me, his teenage daughter, about the dent in the family car.

Do men see these power relationships in the same way? Do other women? I put that question on the side burner.

"Yes . . ."

He sits back and folds his arms. "Could you run through how you arrived at this conclusion again?"

I make sure to detail this point by point. I don't even have to look at my notes. I had to prove this to myself first, and I'm the most skeptical person I know. "Travel records show he was in the area at the time the audio recording was made."

"What records?"

"I have access to the SABRE database from that period."

"You have access?" He sounds suspicious, and rightfully so.

"An informant has access."

He raises an eyebrow. "Is this person an official informant?"

"No."

"How do you know this database is even real?" replies Breyer.

"I don't, but I trust the man who provided me with the information. He was the one that helped find the Alsops' foster child, Marty Rodriguez."

"And how did you come to find this person?"

Oh boy. I didn't want to go there. At least Breyer knows about Damian. I don't have to explain that again. Once was embarrassing enough. "The individual known as Damian Knight contacted me."

Breyer looks straight at me. "You've been in contact with Mr. Knight?"

"Yes. He still contacts me. I've logged every call. You can check with the unit tasked with tracking him down."

Ailes has taught me to do things so by the book that it's too heavy for them to throw it at me.

Breyer pauses for a moment to process all the information. "So, Blackwood, let me understand this. A man we believe may be a felon, with a demonstrated pattern of psychotic behavior, puts you in touch with another man, whom you refuse to name and has dubious access to restricted information, and that man says the pope may be guilty of manslaughter?"

"No. I drew my own conclusions."

"Put yourself on my side of the desk. How does this sound?"

"Ridiculous. Utterly absurd. But we have the audiotape."

"Yes. I had the lab run a comparison first thing this morning."

"And?"

"It shows a sixty-three percent match to the pope's vocal pattern."

"Isn't that enough?"

"No. If you compare the voice sample to our linguistics database, it matches over twelve thousand recorded voices. It could just as well be a false positive."

"We can check, right? He's older now."

"We can make inquiries into the pope's whereabouts in 1985, but that's going to raise some questions. The Vatican has no reason to tell us. Especially if our reasons for inquiring are because we think the pope is guilty of manslaughter."

"Wait? We're not going to do anything?" My voice rises a little too much.

"I can make an inquiry through diplomatic channels. That will take time and sensitivity. The more urgency we put on the question, the more suspicious they'll be."

"We may not have time . . ."

"Why do you say that?"

"Everyone else on the tape is dead."

"Nobody else on that tape gets driven around in a bulletproof popemobile. I think his eminence is safe."

He's not getting it. I was up all night doing my homework. "Pope John Paul II got shot by a rumored KGB operative, stabbed by an angry priest, and then almost blown up in the Philippines by Al-Qaeda. It's the most dangerous head-of-state position there is. Safe is not a word I'd use."

"I get that. But assuming for the moment he is on the tape, what can we do? You still haven't given me a suspect."

"X-20. There's a connection. Every step of the way, they're involved."

"Who? Why them?" He holds the fiasco in Tixato against me. I know he's not a stupid man, but that wasn't my fault!

"I don't know. Someone close to the boy."

"The boy was an orphan. We pulled his records. No known father, his mother died shortly after he was born. There was no family or close friends. If there had been, he probably wouldn't have ended up in the foster-care system."

"What about the tape? That's evidence of a crime."

He waves his hands in the air. "It could be coincidental. Or, who's to say this didn't start with the sheriff?"

"What do you mean?"

"He was there at the exorcism. He heard the demon's name there and it stayed with him until he went insane."

"He was drugged. We have the evidence."

"Whether it was his idea or Deland's, they're both dead."

"Maybe he's a victim? What if the sheriff wasn't in control of himself? Toxicology research says that hallucinogen could provoke extremely violent reactions. It wasn't his fault."

"At this point, we're not going to prosecute him posthumously."

"You know there's more here!" I insist, and immediately regret pushing my point so forcefully. Breyer has cut me some slack so far.

He shoves a finger at me. "Don't tell me what I know and don't know! You come in here with evidence but you can't tell me where, or who it came from. You imply a connection to one of the most powerful people in the world. Then you tell me he's going to be assassinated? Let alone what happened in Mexico.

"You've done good work. Although I think Ailes gives you too much leeway. You have solid intuitions some of the time. But at a certain point you have to realize when you're overreaching. We all want that career-making case. You had yours with the Warlock. It's time to consider the fact that the rest of your time here is going to be filled with the same monotonous work we all have to deal with."

"You think I'm making this up?" I try to keep my voice level. The words come out haltingly as I contain my anger.

"I didn't say that. I think you see a very, very tenuous connection and you're letting the enormity of it get away from you."

I take a moment to try to calm down. "So now what?"

"I'm not going to ignore this. I'll forward the information on to our European liaisons."

"It'll get buried."

"What else can I tell them? You don't know who is behind this. What are they supposed to do? The FBI can't just call over there and say they think maybe somebody wants to harm the pope. They get those calls every day. We're the FBI. We need evidence. In absence of that, we need a suspect. You have neither."

"I've said it already, X-20. One of the most powerful cartels in the world. They're behind this."

"That's just a name. Who is behind them? Why would they care about the pope?"

"I don't know." I know I should have had more before I sat down here. But I couldn't just sit on this!

"Exactly. You've done a dutiful job. I'll make sure you get the credit you deserve for the Hawkton case."

I shake my head. Why can't people understand? "I don't want credit. I just want justice."

"For who? The boy is dead. The pope is unreachable. You just want to be proven right."

"That's not fair. There might be more victims . . ."

He doesn't waste time putting me in my place. "The case is closed as far as you're concerned. Furthermore, if I catch you leaking any of this to the press, your career here is over."

On that threat, he ends our meeting by gesturing to the door.

———

I MANAGE TO make it to the bathroom before letting my face show my rage. It takes ten minutes of sitting in a stall with my eyes closed before I can go back into the hallway. I need to talk to someone who understands.

I call Ailes's office number. Gerald answers instead.

"Where's Ailes?" I ask.

"He's at the hospital." His voice is somber.

"What? Is he okay?" I feel like I just got a blow to the stomach. The last leg under my chair just got kicked away.

"It's his wife. She's been going through some medical problems. I think there was a complication."

His wife? I'm ashamed to admit that I had no idea Ailes was dealing with this.

He never complains when I pester him at all hours of the day and night. Little did I know he was dealing with other drama. I'd noticed he'd been a bit off, but I didn't stop to think what could be going on in his world. I was too distracted . . . or is it self-centered?

"Will she be okay?"

"I don't know. We sent some flowers."

"Oh."

"I put your name on the card."

"Thanks." The gesture makes me feel even more guilty. I realize I still don't even know why my grandfather had to go into the hospital.

I'm terrible at people.

I push them away, or ignore their problems. Someone only exists for me when they're in my sphere. That's the definition of selfishness. Then I find myself in a situation like this. No Ailes. What do I do?

But now?

I have to focus on the case.

Breyer was specific with me.

But maybe a little *too* specific.

"Can you meet me in our office?" I ask Gerald.

"I can be there in a couple hours."

40

E VEN WITHOUT A suspect, I have to warn someone that the pope may be facing a serious threat. But if I call someone in any official capacity, Breyer will have my head. If lives are at stake, the moral thing might be to run to the media and tell them what I know, but I can't bring myself to do that. I'll be out of the FBI before the newsprint ink dries, and then I won't have access to any of the resources I need to find out who's behind this.

Blowing the whistle is useless if it doesn't save the lives you intended to.

My hands are tied. Breyer wasn't trying to be an officious jerk. He just doesn't sense the urgency of what I see. It's a string of tenuous connections. I feel as if I'm standing in the middle of a lake on a rock just below the surface, and I got here by hopping across rocks only I can see.

The pattern is obvious to me. Why isn't it to Breyer?

I think back to Ailes's conversation with me about finding two one-in-a-million events that are connected.

I believe the pope is in danger because I feel the Hawkton murders are an act of revenge. The audiotape gives me a motive. Deland is the accomplice I needed to make it possible. He's got demolitions experience and is obviously comfortable with build-ing things. He'd be the perfect bomb maker, even of unusual ones given enough resources. Getting the bodies into the trees wouldn't be a problem. He might have had some help from another X-20 operative. Maybe the one that killed him.

So I know someone is angry and why, but not who.

It would be easy if Deland was at the center of everything. But he seems like a puppet.

I keep trying to connect him to Hawkton before the recent events and there's nothing. He appears to have lived in a separate universe from the victims.

He was brought into all of this by a connection to X-20. It has to be someone in that gang driving the agenda.

I have to ask myself, though: What if the tape is a false lead? What if this isn't about Marty's death?

But I just can't see how that could be the case. Marty named the demon. Groom kept the tape all these years out of guilt. The medical examiner hid the body from Jessup for the same reason.

If they held onto a reminder from the event, I wonder if McKnight or the Alsops did as well? I'm sure Jessup would be too smart to hold on to anything that tied him to the murder. But maybe they did?

It probably wouldn't be something as obvious as a piece of physical evidence, like a body. In Groom's case, the tape was a way to punish himself. What I should be looking for are scars of the psyche, not buried weapons.

I take the Metro to clear my head before I drive back to Quantico to meet Gerald. Am I acting unreasonably?

I know my life and my mind aren't in the right place right now. I'm still getting over what happened months ago with the Warlock. Tixato is too recent for me to even process. This might be what shock is about. Every time I think about that night, the memory plays out in snapshots taken by a third party. I've disassociated. I've tried to keep rolling along. Truth is, I don't know which way is up.

As a street cop, you can find as much crime as you want. But at the end of the day you have to go home and take a break. The older you get, the more you realize how important it is to learn when not to be a cop. The teenage girl walking briskly out of the drugstore with a guilty look on her face probably just stole something. If you're on duty, you have a responsibility to intervene. If you're not, do you still stop her under suspicion of shoplifting just so you can arrest her for stealing a pack of condoms so she doesn't get pregnant? It's a judgment call. You have to shut down that part from time to time. Danielle can do it. I'm still trying.

Everything becomes more complicated when you see how the world really works. As a detective, you know that nothing is ever simple. You read about a home invasion in the news, only to read the case report and find out it's one drug dealer ripping off another. You get called in to investigate a kidnapping and realize the crying parents have a suspicious amount of hydroponics equipment. Do you investigate that as well?

This case is like that. The easy thing is to just walk away. Breyer doesn't see any urgency. He also thinks the pope is safe. He gave me permission to move on. He ordered me to. I just can't. He doesn't see the shape of things.

Intuition, in the blind sense, is a dirty word to me. If I can't explain things objectively, then I tend to think things aren't rooted in reality. Intuition can be another word for bias.

What's my bias?

My suspect, X-20, isn't some underfunded, fringe terrorist group. They've made their money, a lot of it, by openly defying the US and Mexican governments. They have entire regions in their pocket and were capable of sending a death squad, composed of an active army unit, to kill me. I think they're a formidable challenge, even for the pope.

My Metro train comes to a stop. I pull my coat tight around my body to shield against the wind and emerge a few blocks from my destination. I use the walk to prepare what I'm going to say. This is awkward. I have no idea how it's done, other than what I've seen in movies.

Breyer was clear with me. But I don't think he realizes that I'm an escape artist. I'm always looking for ways out of impossible situations.

"I CAN SEE you're new to this," says the priest on the other side of the latticed screen.

The voice is friendly. "Avuncular" comes to mind. He reminds me of my Uncle Darius, to whom I could tell anything without judgment.

The booth is dark, but not in a frightening way. It feels like a secure closet you can hide inside. I can smell the oiled wood and an air freshener.

"Technically I'm not here to confess my sins, Father."

"Are you Catholic?"

"Not even close," I reply.

"There are easier ways to talk to a priest if you have questions." I'm sure he gets more than a few curious tourists straying into here.

"I need a certain amount of legal immunity."

"Oh boy, this will be interesting. Now I'm worried. Is this a matter for the authorities?" His manner becomes more serious. He's probably heard variations on this a few times.

"In a way." I take my badge from my pocket and press it against the screen.

"If it's about the sacramental wine, I can explain," he jokes.

He's smooth. I take note of how he turned this situation into a lighthearted moment. He'd be great in an interrogation room.

"I wish. Legally, what I say is between us?"

"Well, technically, I'd need to be your confessor."

"My confessor?" I ask. I know a little bit from my law classes, but I want to hear his understanding of the legal definition.

"The person you go to to confess your sins. It's during the act of confession that the legal boundary is the clearest. You can't just tell a priest anything and expect the court to respect that as being between you and God. Otherwise, I suspect, mobsters would be in a rush to get ordained."

"Oh. I get it. I have to make a genuine confession?"

"Yes. That's a start, I guess."

I can tell he seems a little confused by my questions. I can't blame him. I'm not so sure either.

I need a sin to confess . . . Maybe I'll just go with something recent. "I had impure thoughts about a man I saw in the coffee shop this morning. Good enough?"

"Er, yes. I'll absolve you when you come up with something better. What's this really about?"

"Do you recognize me?"

"Your identity isn't supposed to be known to me."

"How does that work in small towns? Never mind. My name is Jessica Blackwood. Sound familiar?"

"Yes, from the news. The FBI agent. What can I do for you?"

"You know I'm a credible person. Well, reasonably. I wouldn't be here if I had any other option. So I'm just going to come right out and say it. I believe a Mexican cartel, called X-20, is plotting to kill the pope."

There's a long pause on the other side of the screen. "Well, that is quite . . . something. Why are you telling me this?"

"Because the evidence is thin and I've been told by my superiors that we need to go through proper channels. Unfortunately, I don't think they understand the seriousness or urgency of the matter. Time is very critical. Hours could make a difference."

"Interesting." He's taking me seriously, thank God. "Is this connected with his eminence's upcoming visit to Miami?"

"Possibly. I don't have any specific information yet. It's just important that the people who handle his security know this."

"Why are you telling *me* this?"

"Because we both know this particular church is a phone call away from the Vatican. This is the top church in the country?"

"Not all would agree. But I get your point. I'll see what I can do."

"I'm serious, Father."

"I believe you. Trust me, I believe you are. Tell me again what I need to know."

41

KNOLL HURRIES TOWARD me as I exit the parking garage elevator at Quantico. Something is wrong. "Follow me," he says, without looking in my direction.

For a moment I panic and think word already got back about my trip to the confessional. It can't be. Nothing works that fast around here.

We take a turn across the Quantico campus toward the recently finished tactical operations building. You would think it was a New England college if it wasn't for all the trainees in FBI sweat suits running around while carrying guns.

The Tactical Operations Facility was previously located in the main building in downtown DC headquarters. It handles live operations around the world.

As we cross the sidewalk, I notice Knoll's eyes darting upward from time to time. I count at least eight men in sniper positions on surrounding rooftops. They're watching the sky.

Damn.

This isn't any drill I'm familiar with.

This is something serious.

An agent in tactical gear holds the door open for us and secures it after we enter. Once we're inside the lobby Knoll turns to me. "We've spotted a small drone flying over the campus. Sharpshooters are preparing to take it down."

"A drone?"

"A small one. It looks like it's designed for surveillance. It could still be weaponized."

"Who the hell sends drones over the FBI?"

"Exactly," replies Knoll. "Could be a prank, but we're taking this very seriously. But we have a bigger problem."

Bigger than someone penetrating FBI security? I get queasy just thinking about that. "Now what?"

He shakes his head. "Remember when I made the joke about you attracting the crazy types? Follow me."

We take the elevator to the third floor, clear the security checkpoint and enter the operations theater.

Agents are gathered around a large wall screen displaying a map tracking some kind of trace from parts around the globe. The leader of the group turns to me. With buzzed gray hair and a squat, powerful build, he looks like a SWAT team veteran. "She's here," he barks into a headset. "Put the audio on the intercom."

"All right then. Let's get right to the point," a voice booms over the loudspeaker. I freeze before I even hear him say my name. "Here's a puzzle for Ms. Blackwood and company. Pretend I've placed a half ton of plastic explosives inside an SUV, which is sitting inside a parking garage somewhere in the DC metro area. I'll give you the address in a moment, but you need to know a few things first."

What the hell did I just walk into? I want to start asking questions, but have to keep my mouth shut. Knoll already knows what I'm thinking and writes something on a pad and shows it to me: "Call came in twenty minutes ago."

"This is a game," the speaker continues. "There are rules. Play by the rules and nobody gets hurt. Break the rules and I promise you, people will get killed. The name of this game is 'Stop me from killing Jessica Blackwood.'"

I exchange glances with Knoll. Other people in the command center watch me from the corners of their eyes.

I feel the blood drain from my face as the nightmare continues. I want to sit down, but can't show weakness. Not here. Not in front of my peers.

"Rule number one: Nobody, and I mean nobody, should approach the vehicle and make me suspect that the bomb squad is about to try to deactivate the bomb. If I see someone act a little suspicious, *boom*. That said, this is a parking garage. People come and go. People doing things that look normal won't set off the bomb.

"Rule number two: If I see you evacuate the occupants of the building, *boom*.

"Rule number three: If I see emergency vehicles, police or even hear a whisper of something on the radio, *boom*. You have to assume I'm watching everything.

"Rule number four: I'll let you in on a secret, I've been using a cell sniffer outside Bureau headquarters to listen in on mobile phone identifiers. If my sniffer near the bomb detects an unusual number of cell phones belonging to FBI agents, *boom*.

"Rule number five: This is the most important one of all. If I see Ms. Blackwood anywhere near the location, *boom*. I want you to assume that the goal of the bomb is to kill her. Although, after the bomb explodes, someone claiming to represent a ridiculous militant group will call and take the blame, saying there's no connection. But make no mistake, this purpose of the bomb is to kill Ms. Blackwood.

"So, to play this game right, when the bomb goes off I want to hear on the news you saved the people but she died helping the bomb squad. I need to hear she's dead.

"You have less than four hours. Any questions?"

His voice as calm as steel, a gray-haired agent speaks up. "This is Agent Winstone. To whom am I talking?"

"Call me Boy Scout. But that's not important right now. By my count there are one hundred and twenty-two people in that building. If you accept the rules, I'll give you the address and an unsecured IP for the security cameras in the garage and elevators."

"If we don't accept?" asks Winstone.

"The bomb *is* going to go off. The question is, who has to die with it. Remember, if I see this on the news, hear a radio dispatch or even suspect this has been leaked, *boom*."

"This game sounds stupid. Can we negotiate? Can you tell us why?" prods Winstone.

Negotiating a hostage situation is tricky. Winstone is trained how to find someone's weaknesses. Calling the game "stupid" is his way to see what kind of response he can elicit from Boy Scout. A more erratic, scattered mind would take this as a challenge and try to defend himself.

"I'm hanging up," says Boy Scout, clearly in control.

"We need the address."

"Do you understand the rules?"

"Yes."

"2392 Kentucky Avenue."

"Is there a chance we can negotiate some terms?" He's still matter-of-fact and as cool as ice. In most hostage situations only the negotiator has had prior experience. Winstone has been involved in dozens.

I don't have his nerve right now. It's too personal. I feel dizzy.

"He's off the line," calls out a tech. "The call came in through an Internet phone service. We'll try to find the origin, but it's not likely."

A map of the location fills the main screen.

I don't need the map.

I know exactly where it is.

2392 Kentucky Avenue is the address of the apartment building where I live.

Winstone turns to me. "Any idea what this is about?"

I'm still in shock.

The voice was modulated but familiar, very familiar.

Boy Scout is Damian.

42

SECURITY CAMERA FOOTAGE of my parking garage is now visible on the command-center screen. A Toyota pulls into a space near an SUV and a pregnant woman gets out. We watch her as she struggles with the groceries in her trunk and then waddles to the elevator with her bags. I can't tear my eyes from the screen.

My heart is beating its way through my chest. A pin drop would probably give me a stroke right now.

The elevator door closes and she's gone. I breathe a sigh of relief.

Nothing happens. That's what we were hoping for.

Five minutes later we get a call in the ops center. Winstone has it patched through the loudspeaker. "This is Agent Bancroft," says the woman we just watched.

"What's the status?" Winstone asks.

"We're hot for EMF. The truck is broadcasting. I repeat, the truck is broadcasting. Backup has picked me up from the lobby. I'm heading to the lab with the sample I got when I brushed up against the truck. The field sniffer says there's a high probability of explosives inside the SUV."

"Did you get a look inside?"

"Negative. The windows were tinted."

Dr. Chisholm, the head of behavioral analysis, is ushered into the room by one of Winstone's assistants. Winstone briefs him on the latest details. Chisholm nods his head slowly, occasionally glancing at me.

Damian was a career liability before. Now . . . I can't even begin to process what I'm thinking. I thought I knew him, the real him.

Finally, Chisholm walks over. "This is rather . . . unexpected behavior."

"No kidding." I'm trying to understand why in the world Damian would do this and can't come up with an explanation. I heard what he said, but it just doesn't feel right. Maybe that's the wrong word. Nothing about him is "right."

"Mad bombers don't usually call you and run through what they'll do in different scenarios and then advise you how to protect the target." He pauses for a moment and looks directly at me with his analytical gray eyes. He lowers his voice just so I can hear him. "Is this real?"

"If Bancroft thinks there's a bomb in the car, then there's a bomb there."

"Why?" asks Chisholm.

"I don't know. Damian is insane, but this doesn't make any sense." There is something about the wording he used. Damian loves his wordplay. He chooses what he says carefully.

"Do you think he'll blow the bomb if he sees you go near it?"

"I don't know. I don't think this is an exercise in reverse psychology, if that's what you mean. The threat is real. I think the conditions are exactly as he stated them."

Winstone steps over to us. "Any suggestions as to how your boyfriend expects us to pull this off?" I ignore the taunt. I can tell Winstone is on edge. It's a situation you can't prepare for.

This is a fucked-up place to be, and I'm right at the center. I can say Damian's obsession isn't my fault, but I haven't done everything under my power to stop him. And to be honest, if I had, I'd have died back in Mexico or in the caldera of a volcano.

Jesus. When this is over, I need to think seriously about going back to doing magic tricks for a living.

"We have to get the people out without anyone seeing. There are no open cameras in the building itself, just the garage." I point to an aerial image of the complex in the corner of the screen. "However, assume the streets are being watched. We need to get everyone together and make sure they don't call for help."

Winstone nods. "I can get a couple dozen people inside the building in the next half hour. We'll drive them in and have them walk in as residents and visitors. We'll use radio silence."

"No cell phones either," I remind him. "He was specific about that."

"We can go door to door and have the building cleared in twenty minutes. But then what? How do we get them out?"

"There's a bus stop at the end of the street. What's the schedule? Can we park a city bus in front of there and just move everyone out?" asks Knoll.

Winstone shakes his head. "He'll be watching for that. It needs to be something more clever. We need a trick." He turns to me. "That's your department, isn't it?"

"Solving them." I gesture to the screen. "Not this." Magic? Hmm, maybe I need to think this through like it's a trick? Is that what Damian wants me to do?

"This is an unconventional situation. We need an unconventional solution."

Now I remember where I know Winstone from. He was one of the special operations people who rescued me from a similar situation in a Michigan warehouse. Only this time, I'm not the one in danger.

He shrugs dismissively then turns to his head of tactical operations. "We need to move people to the safest part of the building then prepare for an evacuation."

"The roof? Helo them out?"

"It'll have to be fast."

I can't believe they're going to do this. "They'll die! The moment a helicopter is spotted the whole building is going to get dropped!"

Winstone jerks back around to face me. His eyes narrow. "You have a better idea?"

It's a fair challenge. "Hold on." I have to let my mind work on this in the background. "Any word on the drone spotted over the campus?"

Knoll lowers his phone. "Snipers took it out a few minutes ago. The thing was a smoking mess when they pulled it from the trees. We got some still shots of the thing. Big lens on it."

"What about the cell sniffer?" Winstone glances up from a display.

"It could look like anything," replies Knoll. "It could just be a plastic rock sending out bursts every twenty minutes."

I hadn't factored in our campus being under surveillance. "If the bomb was meant for me, then we shouldn't touch it if we find it. It could be set for when I leave the campus."

"What if you don't leave?" asks Winstone.

"I'm sure the bomb will still go off at some point. He was clear enough on that."

Winstone gives me a suspicious look and grunts. "For fuck sake, who is this guy?" He's asking if I can be trusted.

Chisholm speaks up. "He's clever. I've been thinking it over. I don't think he wants to kill Agent Blackwood, but I wouldn't assume anything he said is an outright lie."

He suspects what I do, that there's something more at play here. The one thing I know for certain is that all the people in my apartment building are in danger unless we figure out a way to get them away from the bomb as quickly as possible.

Assuming all the entrances and exits are being watched, which isn't too difficult with readily available fifty-dollar wireless webcams the size of lipstick cases, we have limited options.

A tactical specialist unfolds a large printout of sewer tunnels on the table. He points to a pipe conduit. "We could try to enter through here."

"Is there access from the building?" Winstone leans over to study the plans.

"No. We'd have to blow a tunnel using a shape charge."

"They'll know something is up," I reply. "We can't go digging our own subway tunnels through there. The moment they see us trying that, they'll blow the whole building."

"You keep saying, 'they.' Do you believe he's working with someone?" asks Chisholm.

"I don't know any more than you do." If I try to defend Damian right now in opposition to the facts at hand, they'll lose all respect for me. "And that's not relevant right now. We can't do anything that would suggest we're doing some kind of tactical operation."

The tactical commander looks up. "We can take over the feed of the cameras and send it to a loop."

I shake my head. "Any glitch and they'll know. We have to assume they'll be looking for that."

"Are you sure?" asks Winstone. "It worked before."

He's referring to my rescue from the Warlock's warehouse. "To be honest, I'm not sure it did. We don't have any room for error.

"We have to assume they're as smart, or smarter, than us. If we can think of a trick, they'll probably already have figured out how to watch for it."

Knoll points to the garage. "What about loading people up into cars, packing them in, and taking them out that way?"

"All the cameras in the garage are on the same open network," I reply. "There's one in front of the elevator. They'll see that happening."

"We're running out of time," says Winstone. He gives me a

sharp glare, "Unless you have any ideas, we're going to have to try running people out the front as quickly as possible."

All eyes are on me. The pressure crushes down. The people in the building are my neighbors. I don't know them well, but I see their faces every day. One mistake and they're gone. All of them. "You can't . . ."

"Then how?" He needs a plan, not just a list of reasons why they all suck. There's an edge to his voice he didn't have before.

How?

How do I make one hundred and twenty-two people just vanish from a building when it's being watched from every direction?

Maybe I'm looking at the problem the wrong way.

I do it when I'm not being watched.

"I got it . . ."

"What?" asks Winstone.

"It's time for really out-of-the-box thinking."

Sometimes your only choice is to destroy the box.

"Meaning what?"

"We blow it up ourselves."

CRISIS

So MUCH OF the way I think about things is influenced by what I learned watching my father, my uncle and my grandfather sit around the large table in our kitchen and dissect a problem to come up with a solution. Usually they were fun problems, like the creation of a new illusion. Occasionally, there were not-so-fun ones, usually financial ones. The worst nights were those they spent drinking large cups of coffee while trying to figure out what to do about Brutani.

My father is mechanically inclined. He tends to see things as physical problems, to be solved with physical solutions. How could you use a mirror to hide someone onstage?

My uncle is more psychological. His mind would leap to how you could hide someone in plain sight, maybe through a visual distraction.

Grandfather likes to see the problem as a matter of theater. How you hide the woman is irrelevant unless you have a good reason to make her disappear. Simply vanishing a woman has no dramatic value. Vanishing a woman an instant before she is about to be pierced by a rack of swords creates dramatic tension, and a climactic solution with meaning.

After Grandfather and Dad met with Julia Vender, they spent several nights trying to figure out how to use the information about Father Devalo. Arranging a meeting with Devalo, who lived in a sprawling estate near Lake Tahoe, was a challenge unto itself.

Before I could walk, Dad and Grandfather taught me how to hide inside the razor-thin magic tables and secret compartments magicians use. They'd had no idea they were also teaching their little girl to be a ninja capable of spying on them from any room, even if it wasn't bordered by a secret corridor. I'd wedge myself behind cabinets, under tables, or just disappear quietly into a dark corner.

This was how I followed their conversations with visitors and people on the phone as they tried to deal with the crisis.

Before becoming, and then "unbecoming," a priest, Devalo had lived in Sicily. He left the Church and started his own, almost cult-like, following in America when his passion for women got the better of him. His mother had been a half-gypsy tarot reader back in Sicily, and Devalo adapted and expanded this skill considerably for his own ends.

Criminals are probably more superstitious and religious than anyone else. You only have to look at the tattooed crucifixes and Virgin Marys on gang members to understand this. Devalo soon found himself doing psychic readings and even acting as a confessor of sorts for a number of high-ranking mobsters. All of them, without fail, wanted to speak with their departed mothers. From there he built himself a reputation as a spiritual adviser to some of the roughest criminals in the country. Always discreet, he was rewarded lavishly.

About a week after our meeting with Julia Vender, the phone rang late one night and I was ushered into the car for the drive to Devalo's estate. Dad and Grandfather were still too scared to leave me out of their sight. The introduction came from an old actor friend of Grandfather's.

I slept in the backseat most of the way to Lake Tahoe but woke up as we pulled onto the gravel drive that led to the three-story stone mansion. I remember it looking like a castle, but not an

NAME OF THE DEVIL   263

inviting one like Cinderella's Castle at Disneyland. More like a Roman fortress. I stayed in the car with Dad as Grandfather met with Devalo for what seemed like several hours.

Finally, as the sun came over the horizon, Grandfather climbed into the car. He was tired as hell from being up all night, but was all set to head back to Los Angeles.

"That is the strangest man I've ever met," was all he would say as we drove off.

Sometime later, Dad prodded him for more information. "What do you mean?"

"I had to spend an hour convincing him I wasn't Satanic. I showed him a half-dozen card tricks and had to explain how I did each one. The man has no idea how conjuring works," replied Grandfather.

"But he's a fraud, right?"

"A peculiar kind. Not like Vender. He did a cold reading on me. I think he genuinely believed it was divinely inspired."

"You sure it wasn't an act?" asked Dad.

Grandfather was too exhausted to call out the question as stupid. "If so, he's the greatest actor in the world. I think the mob guys go to him because he doesn't go in for the blackout spook-show stuff. Apparently he talks in the voices of the dead. All these guineas want to hear the same thing from their dead mothers, so it's not hard to keep them happy. I think Devalo genuinely believes he's channeling their relatives."

"Is he going to help?"

"He's going to let me come to a séance with Basso in a week. He says I can ask for intervention there."

"You mean, ask Devalo to pretend to be Basso's mother and ask for intervention?"

"I don't know."

My father glanced at me in the backseat, where I was pretending to sleep. "That's not good enough, Dad."

"I know." Grandfather sounded almost defeated.

"If all you had to do was ask their dead mother to forgive a debt at a séance, there wouldn't be too much point to loan-sharking. I get the feeling they're not in the habit of saying 'yes,'" my father continued, agitated.

"You don't think I don't goddamn know that?" Grandfather shot back tersely. "Where were you with all this wisdom when you were telling me to take Brutani's money? Huh?" Under his breath, he muttered, "Just one more goddamn disappointment."

"Don't say that in front of my daughter," my dad snapped, trying to keep his voice low.

"Your daughter? Heh. Whose roof is she living under? Where's her mother? You're a child. A goddamn child. I have three children."

"You're an asshole." My father turned back and gave me a guilty look when he realized my eyes were open and I was awake. "Sorry, hon, we got carried away."

I just stared back at him, not sure what I was supposed to say.

"She knows that. Christ, the girl sees everything. Don't you know that by now?" chided my grandfather. "Always watching, never speaking. She sees *everything*," he emphasized. "I wish you had a fraction of her common sense."

These moments were my least favorite ones. I could handle it when their criticism was directed at me, but not when it was pointed at each other. Especially not when Grandfather would rip into my father.

I love my dad. He is, at heart, a sweet man. But I think I sometimes look down on him because of the way my grandfather talked to him. You can't help but notice someone's flaws when somebody else is constantly shouting them to the world on a megaphone.

Dad would rarely defend himself. He would just take it all in, quietly accepting that he was a failure. Uncle Darius is different.

He would have no qualms about calling Grandfather a righteous bastard to his face. Grandfather would retort that he was a cheat and a thief, but Darius would just throw up his hands and say he had no trouble admitting what he was. At least he knew.

But what was I? Who am I?

I am all of them. The good and the bad, I think. Right now, I need the good.

43

WINSTONE SWEATS AS he watches the monitor. My fists are coiled so tightly, I'm afraid I'll draw blood. The tension is carved into Knoll's face. But Chisholm is rock steady. He's watching me. I can tell he's trying to figure out, as always, what the connection is between me and Damian. It's not so much from suspicion—I've told him just about everything and I think he believes me—as much as from clinical fascination.

ESPECIALLY RIGHT NOW, there's no solace in knowing that Damian's mind is just as much a mystery to one of the world's leading psychologists as it is to me.

Tapping into the building's surveillance cameras give us multiple views of the street around the apartment complex. Occasionally a car comes and goes. Nothing indicates that inside are one hundred and twenty-two people worried that they're about to be blown to hell.

A blue Honda Civic pulls into the parking garage and appears on the open network cameras. Our bomber is seeing the same thing we are. The car takes the ramp to the lowest level and pulls into the space directly behind the SUV.

Everyone in the room leans in and squints at the screen as it draws closer.

The driver of the Civic misjudges the gap as he backs up,

overestimating the distance beyond his rear bumper, and heads straight toward the SUV.

Someone in the control room gasps. It might have been me.

It's a slow-motion crash in real time.

The Civic is one foot away from the back of the SUV when the camera feed goes dark. Switching to an external view on the monitor, we see an explosion rip apart the front of the apartment complex, blasting through windows and sending shards of glass and smoke into the street. It's so loud our microphones make a garbled chirping sound. Cars waiting for the light to change vanish in billowing clouds of dust.

The building is obscured as the smoke conceals the entire block.

No one in the operations theater speaks.

We stand in stunned silence and wait.

Seconds feel like lifetimes. I think of the little boy who always holds his sister's hand as he takes the elevator. I think of the retired couple who send me a Christmas card every year. I think of all my neighbors. How many of them do I really know? Have I ever invited any of them over, even once? They live there. I just take up space. And they are in peril because of me.

"All clear," calls a voice over the open radio channel.

"Our driver?" Winstone immediately inquires.

"Some broken glass in the back of his legs. He's fine."

"The occupants?"

"We've got them into the lobby across the street. We're now moving them to the next building."

A cheer erupts in the control room. Knoll nods at me. A flicker of a smile crosses Chisholm's face.

The smoke begins to dissipate, revealing the street and parked cars covered with debris. It could be a scene from the aftermath of any other terrorist bombing, except the cars are empty. The first five floors of windows are blown out, but the building structure is intact.

"What about emergency crews?" asks a technician.

"Hold them back," says Winstone. "We need to send in the bomb robot." He turns to me. "Is your guy going to blow it?"

Before I can answer, we're interrupted by the agent monitoring phone calls. "Boy Scout is on the line."

"Put him through the loudspeaker," Winstone growls. "Is this what you wanted, Boy Scout?"

"It's exactly the kind of thing I hoped you'd do. I don't need to ask who thought up the clever solution. But there's no telling what the actual bombers will do when they realize what you've done."

Winstone looks confused.

"Actual bombers?" he asks Damian.

"Yes. The ones who put the device there. I've already gone through the effort of outing them, now that everyone is safe."

"Pardon me?"

An agent holds her phone to her shoulder. "We're getting reports that the media has already received calls from a group claiming responsibility."

"Who?"

"X-20. It's trending up on Twitter. Hold on . . ." The agent puts the phone back to her ear and listens for a moment. "Now we're getting reports that the Filipino Marxist Muslims are taking credit."

"What the hell is going on here?" Winstone demands.

"I took the liberty of calling out the real culprits," says Damian. "I also sent time-encrypted emails to the editors of the major newspapers claiming responsibility for this bombing on behalf of X-20 in advance of the certified letters this afternoon."

Winstone looks to Chisholm and Knoll for an answer. "I don't understand."

"I don't imagine you would," replies Damian. "Was the fake explosion Jessica's idea? Low-yield charges to blow out the windows? Smoke bombs. Very clever. It looked quite convincing. Hopefully, the real culprits are second-guessing detonating the bomb now they've realized that the car didn't hit the truck and it was all a ruse to get everyone out under the cover of the smoke."

"What are you getting at?" Winstone asks.

"I've messengered the assistant-director the passport I lifted from a Colombian bomb maker I spotted leaving Jessica's building yesterday. His brother-in-law is a known affiliate of X-20. The details aren't important right now. Well played, Jessica. We'll be in touch." The line goes dead.

Winstone turns to me, confused and angry. "What the hell was that about?"

I'm only beginning to understand what just happened. I try to piece everything together. "Damian figured out X-20 was going to try to kill me by planting a bomb in the parking garage of my building. He knew the only way to save everyone was to explain how to fool X-20. The only way he could get us to believe him and follow his instructions, was by acting as if he planted the bomb."

"He could have just called it in," Winstone barks.

I shake my head. "To DC metro police? If they'd even taken him seriously, X-20 would have blown the building the moment a uniformed officer showed up. If he tried calling us as someone passing on information, it would have taken hours to reach the right people. This was the only way he could get our attention."

"Why?" asks Winstone.

"X-20 wants me dead. After Mexico, they can't target me directly now. I'm sure the alleged Filipino Marxist Muslims pointed out in their message are meant to imply that the officials from the Filipino embassy who live in my building or the US envoy who lives there is their target. It's a cover.

"The last thing X-20 wants is for themselves to be connected to this. By telling the media X-20 was responsible before they could pass the blame, Damian put this right on them. They wanted to kill me and have no one trace it to them."

"By taking out a whole apartment complex?"

Knoll speaks up. "Anything too targeted would look suspicious. Instead of just taking out Jessica, take out a hundred people in the first major act of terror here since 9/11." He's still letting it all sink in. "This is . . . insane."

Winstone glances up at the building on the monitor. "Are they still going to blow the bomb?"

"I don't think so. They've already been outed. There's no point to detonating the bomb to get rid of any evidence. We know they did it. We know why they did it. And I'm not in the building." And never going back if I can help it.

"To kill one FBI agent."

"Yes. I just don't know why they want me dead." I stare at the street filled with our staged devastation, glad it isn't real.

"I would think finding that out would be of paramount importance right now," replies Chisholm in his gallows voice. "And yes, I know who you think their next target is supposed to be. The only thing about your hypothesis that lacks credibility is the name of whomever is behind the threat. Who wants you dead, Jessica? And why?"

Who would kill a hundred innocent people to get me out of the way so they can kill one man?

44

"Tell us more about Damian Knight," says Agent Arron, who has the defeated look of a man who knows he'll never get to the bottom of the stack of files on his desk. He wants me to tell him something that'll neatly tie Damian into the building explosion, the missing pieces of the Warlock investigation and possibly the disappearance of Amelia Earhart.

I wish I had those answers too.

I touch a pen to the pile of briefs I've already filed. "Is there something specific you want to ask me?" I've sat in this working group a half-dozen times. Every month or so, Arron and Kinsey, the other agent on the case, look at their calendar and get together to discuss what little progress they've made. They keep bringing me in, hoping I'll reveal the vital clue they can't find from their desks.

I'd call them lazy, but this could be me in a few years. They've got a decade or so in the Bureau up on me. And with that, more cases than they can manage. This is just one more headache. And I'll bet anything that after Damian's stunt with the building, they got called into their supervisor's office and yelled at for not making any more progress.

DAMIAN'S NOT ACCUSED of any specific crime—yet—but he holds the distinction of being the most interesting of all of the FBI's persons of interest.

"Give us something," pleads Kinsey, trying to play the less-exasperated cop to Arron's completely exasperated cop. They both have the sallow complexions of guys who sit around drinking too much coffee and giving themselves stress ulcers.

"Look, guys, he enjoys outsmarting me as much as you."

"But you manage to summon him like a genie whenever you need him," Arron points out.

"Not quite." I hold up my phone. "You have all the numbers he's called me from. If you dial them, he won't pick up. But if I do, he'll call back."

When you're dealing with a clever person, phone traces are useless in the age of Skype calls and burner phones. "Could you call him right now?" asks Arron.

"For what?"

"So we can ask him some questions directly."

"Like where he is," jokes Kinsey.

"I'll do whatever the Bureau asks me to. But if this is just for your own amusement, keep in mind I'm pretty sure I only get to pull that card so many times."

"What if we set up a network trace in advance? Monitor IP traffic, TOR networks, the full NSA treatment?"

"If you can get authorization, I'll cooperate. Of course."

"Despite your personal history with him?"

I don't know if I should be offended or not. If one of them had a female stalker, or a jealous ex-girlfriend, would they be acting like their loyalty as an agent had been compromised? They can pretend the situation would be the same, but we all know it wouldn't be treated that way.

I tell myself I cooperate because I'm a good cop. The real reason? They'll never catch him.

"I would specifically *because* of my personal history."

"You know, Jessica, I've seen these kinds of obsessions before." Arron folds his hands on the table.

Oh my God. He's pulling the paternal routine on me. He should know my history with father figures. I tense my jaw to stop myself from blurting out that I'm not his daughter on prom night.

Kinsey weighs in. "This guy is more into you than you can imagine."

I can imagine plenty.

The two of them are clearly playing out some routine they concocted before I got here. This is why Damian won't be caught anytime soon.

"The Wikipedia stuff is just weird," says Arron, following their script.

"Wikipedia?" I reply. What are they talking about?

"You don't know?" he counters, a little dramatically. He's happy he caught me by surprise.

"He's constantly updating your web page. He's your number one fan," adds Kinsey.

"We just want to make sure he's no Mark David Chapman."

Their use of a John Lennon reference reveals just how unaware they are of the generational gap. At least Selena was alive while I was.

"What about Wikipedia?" I ask again.

Arron pulls up the page on his laptop. "You have an admirer that's constantly editing your page and deleting disparaging comments. We can assume it's not you."

"And you think it's Damian?" This doesn't sound like him at all. He has much better things to do with his time.

"He goes through quite an effort to hide his IP address. Sounds like your boy."

Sounds like half the hackers I know.

Arron turns the computer so I can read the entry. It's pretty benign. There's nothing there that Damian would care about, as far as I can tell.

Then I see that there are at least a half-dozen photos of me, ranging from my teenage publicity shots for magic shows to snaps of me at crime scenes. Someone has been very obsessive.

I knew this was out there. It's hard to be confronted with it.

One of the photos seems odd to me. I click on the larger version. It takes me a moment to see what is out of place.

I pull out my phone and dial without even telling Arron and Kinsey why.

Knoll answers. "What's up?"

"Are you in the building?"

"Yep. Need me?"

"Conference room 2-232. Now."

"What's going on?"

"I think the Warlock is trying to send me a message."

Arron and Kinsey give me a stunned look.

"Shit. I'll be there in five."

45

Knoll leans over my shoulder to see the screen more clearly. We're looking at my Wikipedia page, specifically at an image of me holding a fan of cards, faces out. In it I'm sixteen or seventeen, wearing a silvery sequined gown and too much stage makeup. It's from some European magic magazine that had a circulation of about two.

"What am I supposed to be noticing?" he asks.

I look up from my notepad where I've been making a graph and point to the fanned spread of cards. "See them?"

"Yeah?"

"I always fanned the cards in new deck order. Ace through king, king through ace, spades, diamonds, clubs, hearts. In fact, for photo shoots, I'd glue all the cards together. That was something Grandfather taught me. But someone Photoshopped these cards in a different order. See the queens next to each other? Or here, there are two four of clubs."

Knoll nods, telling me he believes I believe I see something, but he has no idea what the hell I'm talking about.

"There are fifty-two cards in a deck, not including jokers. You can assign each card to a letter of the alphabet twice. That means you can spell anything with one deck if you never use a letter more than twice. There are more complicated schemes using letter frequencies, but this is pretty simple. They just used the same four twice."

Arron speaks up. "The Warlock, or rather Heywood, doesn't have access to a computer. He's currently awaiting trial for kidnapping and electronic fraud while we build the other case around him. He's not allowed anywhere near a computer."

Knoll ignores him and takes a seat beside me. "Why do you think it's him?"

I want to say "a hunch," but that won't fly in this room. "Give me one second." I pull up the file info on the Wikipedia image. It shows when it was uploaded. There's probably even fingerprint data within the Photoshopped file itself. Every photo-editing software program used in a correctional facility embeds a special watermark. I save the image and send a copy to Gerald with a quick note.

"Can you call the Beaumont penitentiary? Ask for whoever has the prisoner logs," I tell Knoll.

Arron and Kinsey are both slack-mouthed. They can see Knoll, a senior agent, is treating this seriously.

Knoll puts his phone on speaker. "This is FBI Agent Knoll. I'm here with Agent Blackwood. We have some questions about inmate Heywood. I can get his number . . ."

"No need," replies a woman's efficient voice. "I have it here."

"Has there been any change to Heywood's computer privileges?" asks Arron.

The woman types for a moment. "No. There's nothing here. Still not allowed around anything electronic. We even dial his calls for him. And those are under a subpoena order."

Arron looks at me and shakes his head. "Maybe he asked someone else to do it." He's trying to throw me a bone.

"Can you pull up his movement log? Where was he on . . . hold on," I call out the date from the image upload data on Wikipedia.

"One second." More typing. "I have him in the print library. There aren't any computers in there."

"Oh, thank you." It was just a hunch. I want to take this up later, but beating an apparently dead horse in front of Arron and Kinsey would be bad right now.

"No problem. Anything else?"

"That's all," Arron replies, barely hiding his satisfaction at proving me wrong.

"Okay . . ." She pauses. "Hold on. Wait a second. This is odd. Huh. I'm looking at the log on that date. Heywood was moved to another location before returning to his cell. He was in the room assigned to vocational training. It seems like there was a half hour before they realized their mistake."

The Warlock had access to a computer for a half hour.

The man who hacked the FBI's computer network.

Shit.

This is bad.

Real bad.

"Actually, it looks like that's happened a couple of times." She seems confused, but unaware of what this means.

Knoll gives me a look. I know what he's thinking: The Warlock may be paying off someone in the prison to get him in front of a computer. It could be a low-level clerk, or handled through some other exploit he figured out.

"Can you access IP logs?" I ask. "I want to know if there was any outgoing traffic to Wikipedia."

"Yes, one second. We have key-logging software. I show a session during that time period. A couple megabytes of upload."

"It's him," Knoll grumbles. He raps his knuckles hard against the table.

Gerald has already emailed me back, confirming that the watermark on the image matches the serial number assigned to the copies of Photoshop in the Texas federal corrections facility.

I'm trying to solve the code on the cards.

I have the first three letters.

Y O U

46

THE CONFERENCE ROOM is now full of agents who are working on different aspects of the Hawkton case. Word travels fast.

Knoll is on the phone with Assistant Director Breyer, asking him to put some pressure on the Texas prison authorities to find out why one of the worst hackers the FBI has ever encountered has been getting computer time.

What bothers me the most is that the Warlock clearly didn't care that we found out. He wanted to remind us how smart he is. Why would he ruin a good thing?

There's only one answer, and it rattles me.

Because he has a better thing going.

Right now there's a dedicated machine in the FBI computer center trying to solve his last puzzle. We're at least a year or more from breaking it. Some think it's a red herring; others think he really has some final plan that transcends everything else he's done.

I don't know what to think.

"What do you got, Blackwood?" Knoll is understandably antsy. We all are.

I wish Ailes could be here. He'd make sense of it. Or at the very least, be a source of reassurance.

I double- and triple-check my decoding. He used a simple cipher designed to capture my attention. A third grader would know how to figure it out if they realized it was there.

I hand my work to Knoll to check. He stares at it for a minute before speaking. "You believe him?"

"That's a question for Dr. Chisholm. My gut says he's not lying about this."

Actually, my guts are twisted in a knot right now.

We're getting sharp looks from the others in the room because we haven't shared the transcription.

I hold up my notepad. "The code says, 'You will know it when it is me.'"

"What's that supposed to mean?" snaps Arron.

"Hawkton isn't him," I reply.

"And you believe him?" he asks skeptically.

"I believe he's a homicidal megalomaniac. Emphasis on the megalomania. He wants the world to know how smart he is. If Hawkton was him, then he'd either keep his mouth shut or take credit."

"So why doesn't he come out and say it?" asks Kinsey.

"Because he still denies being the Warlock," Knoll answers. "Heywood insists he's an innocent man, wrongly framed. He's only hinted that he's connected to the Warlock."

"So he tells you," Arron points to me. "You certainly attract the weirdos. They love you."

"This one wants to murder me," I remind him.

"There's a lot of that lately," he says, almost as an accusation.

I keep my inner voice buried deep. *Screw you.* I didn't ask for any of this.

"Why didn't he kill you in the warehouse?" Kinsey prods. There's a skeptical tone to his voice.

"He implied it was under surveillance. But, yes. I believe he could have killed me, but chose not to. That was also when he thought he was way ahead of us and we didn't stand a chance of catching him."

"But you did," says Kinsey.

"We did," I correct him. "We did. But he still held me responsible and tried to have an associate kill me. I have no doubt he'd try again if he had the chance. He hates me." I saw it in his eyes when I last spoke to him. It's why I sleep with a loaded gun under my pillow. It's why I spend Friday nights in jujitsu classes. It's why I survived my trip to Tixato.

His anger is what keeps me going. I'm afraid if I stop, it'll all be over.

"If he hates you so much, then why did he want you to find that message?"

"For starters, I didn't, you did. I never would think to look at my Wikipedia page. Second, the message isn't necessarily for me. There's a whole cult of people now out there, obsessed with deciphering his messages and reading into his murders. I'm sure they're all over his case like ghouls looking for any clue or new detail."

"Can I offer a theory?" interjects Dr. Chisholm from the corner of the room. I never even saw him enter. "He did it on your page because you're the only one he respects. Yes, he hates you and wants to kill you, but you're also the one who outsmarted him. Putting this message in an image of you, on your page, is a way to subvert you. An extension of a magic ritual using a personal object. He's using you to get his message out. He's trying to tap into your power."

"My power?"

"Heywood is all about mystical iconography."

"Do you believe him?" Knoll asks bluntly.

Chisholm ponders the question. "Yes. In this instance. He gains nothing from telling us this. It only reinforces his sense of ego. The Warlock never wanted to make his methods appear material, of this world. Nothing he did was personal," he nods to me, "until Agent Blackwood interfered with his plans. Hawkton is extremely personal."

"So we don't need to worry about the Warlock anymore?" Kinsey seems confused.

Chisholm raises an eyebrow. "Quite the opposite. This stunt tells us he's still got influence outside the walls of his cell. He wasted a good gimmick just to tell us not to be fooled. I'd be relieved if he tried to take credit. Now I'm even more convinced he has something else planned. But not now. Not for a while." Then Chisholm turns to me. "Given recent events, I think you need to be even more careful. If he can change a web page while in maximum security, he can just as easily ask one of his acolytes to try to reach you again."

They're coming at me from all sides. What started as a joke of a meeting about the Benny Hill efforts to catch Damian has turned into a stark reminder that even if I ever get to the bottom of Hawkton, there's an evil man biding his time, waiting to kill me.

47

I SET THE HAT and blond wig on the table next to Gerald's computer. I have a growing collection of disguises, a sign of how complicated my life has become. He gives them an amused glance and shakes his head. "They find the sniffer?"

"Three so far." Because of the X-20 threat and the new developments with the Warlock, I've been ordered to wear a disguise any time I'm out in the open at Quantico. I've been living in the office and sleeping in the dorm. There's no telling if the drone we found was the only one. Now, nobody doubts their connection to the attempted bombing.

"You'd think the FBI would keep better track of stuff like that around here," replies Gerald. "We're supposed to be the counter-surveillance experts."

"We also live in a country where law enforcement is generally trusted and government agents aren't active targets of criminals. X-20 is from a different part of the world. Snooping on agents coming and going isn't new for them."

"The location is," Gerald points out. "I mean, here of all places? Does upstairs finally acknowledge their connection to Hawkton?"

This is still a frustrating point for me. "Tenuously. We need more evidence. I'm hoping there is something in the exorcism tape we've missed. Maybe another person."

"Besides the pope?" Gerald arches an eyebrow.

"You don't buy it either?"

"I believe that you have credible reason to believe that it's him. I just think the chain of connections is quite . . ."

"Tenuous . . ." I add. There's a lot of that with this case.

"Yes. The 'T' word. Christ. Who knows. I mean, they did try to kill you twice and also one hundred other people. It's just . . ." He shakes his head.

I don't want to say it out loud, but if Ailes were here, he'd back me. He'd find some way to prove my theory through computational or logical jujitsu. Gerald is a good guy. He's bright and every bit the thinker that Ailes is, but he's just not able to make that extra leap.

"What do we have with the reconstruction from the audiotape?"

"Here's what we've got so far. We matched the voices to multiple people in the room." He presses some keys and 3-D people appear in a virtual room on his screen. "We can tell approximate location and position." Gerald points to the characters. "Here are the Alsops, Jessup, Curtis, McKnight and our other person we'll call 'Peter.'" Little captions with their names float above their heads.

"As in Peter the Apostle? I guess that's better than nothing."

"Like I said, I'm prepared to believe you. I've added a child on the bed for Marty." He clicks the mouse and a bed with a small child appears in the room. "As you can see, the people are gathered around him. There's likely some heavy blankets being used to hold him down. People tend to thrash and claw in the middle of an exorcism and you don't want to take your chances."

"Is there room for anyone else in the room?"

"Possibly. But watch this . . ." Another click and footsteps appear on the ground like tracks in fresh snow. They all end at people who already exist in the scene. "We matched any footfalls on the tape to the locations of the people. Someone else could theoretically be in the room if they were still and didn't say anything during the recording." He hits some more keys and circles radiate from the mouths of the people and various other points in the room. "These are all the audio sources. We can track just about every single one to somebody or an object in the room."

It's almost like time travel. "How are you able to get this much information? What's real?"

"Ears."

"Ears?" He's picking up Ailes's Socratic style. I need to check if I'm starting to do that too. It can be annoying if not done right. At least Gerald is sincere.

"Your ear is more than a funnel for sound. It shapes sound and changes it as it goes through the cartilage. It's how we can tell whether something is above or below us, and not just to what side. We actually hear in three dimensions. Even with one ear.

"Our brains know what a voice is supposed to sound like. It's pretty good at guessing if that sound bounced off your earlobe first, or the top of the ear." He waves toward his computer. "We estimate dimensions and make a virtual room, and tell the computer how human voices behave. We plug in what kind of flooring, etcetera, and then it makes some guesses. Let's take a look? Right now it's going to show us the sources for all the voices for the whole tape."

Circles bounce from the virtual people. Occasionally one appears to hover several feet over the bed. "What's going on there?"

Gerald looks sheepish. "I was afraid you were going to ask about that. This is more art than science. I have almost all the voices tracked to the virtual people. But I think we got a glitch." He clicks his mouse and Marty's body floats up to the bubble.

"I'm pretty sure he wasn't levitating," I reply.

"I know. I know. The computer is assuming he moved. But they have him under blankets and are pressing down on him.

The bed would creak if he stood up. My guess is an echo bounced off a bookshelf or the headboard, confusing the algorithm. There are so many assumptions going into this."

"Because levitation would be ridiculous."

"Right? I mean, it's not like a ten-year-old kid could pull that off."

"I could . . ." I give him a sly grin.

"Uh, there's that. Say, didn't you find the kid because he bought a book on ventriloquism?"

"Yeah, but that doesn't actually throw your voice. It's just a way to synchronize it or change the volume to make it sound farther away."

"Oh. That would have been convenient. Anyhow, I didn't pull the levitation out of the simulation because something about the voice seems to be throwing everyone off too. Whenever it appears, they all get a little more agitated. It seems to coincide when the pitch changes. If you listen to the tape, it really is creepy."

"Could someone else be speaking, other than Marty?"

"They'd have to be in the room, and it's real close to Marty, so I don't see how that could be possible."

"Could they be under the bed? Hiding from them?"

"No. We'd be able to tell from the audio sample. I don't know how they couldn't see another person unless the lights were out, which I don't think they were. Although, we do hear them describe a flickering."

"This was peculiar."

"Old houses?" Gerald responds.

"Yeah."

"I've been reading up on poltergeists and possession. This kid seemed to know all the tricks."

"He'd been doing his homework at the local library. To be honest, I really feel for him. Kicked around from home to home, this was his only way to get attention."

"He sounds like a psychopath on the audio. I don't think I've heard someone say 'fuck' more times in one minute."

Gerald had never been backstage with Grandfather when something went wrong. "True. And he's getting away with it. The adults are convinced he's not in control of himself."

"I guess I had it easy. Is that the point of acting like this?"

"I don't know. A kid like that has so little control over his life. He doesn't even know if he'll be able to sleep in the same bed the next night. Maybe doing this allows him to feel like he's got some power. Making the adults look like idiots gives him that." I had an uncertain life, but at least I had regular fixtures in Grandfather and Dad.

"You sure he's not bipolar?" asks Gerald.

"That'd be a question for Chisholm. To me, this is a kid putting on a show. You sure that other voice is an echo?"

"Or a levitation. Without the actual room layout, it's hard to know for sure. Remember, all of this is a virtual reconstruction from a crappy, thirty-year-old audiotape. We make a lot of assumptions—like the room is square, a certain size, there's not drapes."

"Would photos of the room help?" Gerald sometimes thinks a little more theoretical than practical.

"Yeah. You have some?"

"Give me your car keys."

"What?" He stares at me, confused.

"I can't use my car because they'll be following me if they have the chance. Also, I'll need a spare phone."

Gerald tries to convey a stern look. I can see concern in his eyes. "You can't be serious. You shouldn't even be leaving Quantico."

"Gerald, not too long ago over a hundred people almost bought it because of what X-20 thinks I know. Maybe it's time I just figured that part out for certain. Forget the pope, they'll kill anyone in their way."

He reluctantly pulls the keys from his pocket and tosses them on the table along with his phone. "Just bring it back with a full tank of gas."

"Thanks," I reply, heading to the door.

"Hey, don't forget your disguise. And, uh, be careful." He waves the hat and wig.

"Oh, those. If you hear from Ailes, try not to worry him too much."

48

MY HOPE THAT Hawkton would feel any less creepy now that the sheriff's reign of terror has come to an end is sadly dispelled by the fact that any rural town in the dead of night is raw fuel for nightmares.

Set in the middle of twenty acres, the Alsop farmhouse is away from central Hawkton. That would explain why having a foster child went unnoticed. The back end of the property sits on the county line. An open gate sits across the entrance from the road. Their gravel driveway winds between hills, gradually slanting up. A rope with frayed ends dangles from a tree, a chew toy gnawed by a giant. I assume a tire swing was once attached.

In the moonlight, the property is quietly foreboding. Small things with glowing eyes jump into the tall grass as my headlights catch them off guard.

In better days, in better light, I imagine this wouldn't have been such a bad place to grow up. To a foster kid shuttled around from home to home, the Alsops' property would be filled with wide-open spaces for adventures.

But life on a farm eventually grows dull. If the Alsops were anything like the other denizens of Hawkton I've met, I can't imagine the slow pace of life here being something a kid with a hyperactive imagination would be able to stand for very long.

A basic magic trick or two, learned from a book, would have shown Marty how easily these churchy folks could be conned.

When I was in college, my freshman roommate was a sweet girl studying biology, who I'd thought was sheltered, a bit naive, but not stupid. However, when she found out about my background in stage magic, she reacted as if I'd confessed I was Hitler's niece. She even told me she'd pray for me. Try as I did to explain to her that invisible thread and palmed cards weren't the same as drawing pentagrams in the basement and letting a goat have its carnal way with me, she didn't—or couldn't—see the difference. In her eyes, pretending to have supernatural powers was the same as being in league with Satan himself.

She and I passed the remainder of the semester as polite friends. She spoke no more of my magic, and I politely ignored the sounds that came from under her blankets when her equally devout study partner "accidentally" fell asleep in her bed.

I pull Gerald's car to a stop a hundred feet from the Alsops' ranch-style house. There are no lights on. The security light above the porch doesn't even activate as I come within range of the motion detector. The power must have been shut off.

Still wary of eyes in the sky, I put on the wig and hat. To anybody watching, I'm not sure how hard it would be to figure out what was going on. Either I'm me, or some cheap woman wearing slept-in clothes who stole an FBI agent's car and drove three hundred miles.

The front door opens with a quick jiggle of my bump key and pick. In a town like Hawkton, locked doors are more of a formality than a necessity. The real theft deterrent is kept loaded in the corner.

The floorboards creak as I enter. My flashlight reveals glimpses of a house arrested in time. It's the 1980s, complete with pine paneling, thick carpets and garishly upholstered furniture with hideaway drawers to conceal remote controls and hold drinks.

It's the kind of place that keeps Thomas Kinkade in business, I think, then I realize I'm making too smug of an assessment. My own taste in art doesn't extend beyond my Pinterest page.

The television is an old-style tube set in the middle of an entertainment center. Photographs framed under glass reflect my light back at me. Smiling kids that look like Mrs. Alsop open presents and mug for the camera. These were probably her nephews and nieces.

Beyond the family room lies the master bedroom. I peer inside and see their bed, all made up and waiting for them to come home. Did they make the bed together? Or did Mrs. Alsop push the pillows back into place every morning as her husband went about his daily business?

The house is silent, even more so than you'd expect in the still of the night. The trees and the hills baffle the noise of the wind. The croaking of frogs is muffled by the tall grass. I can understand why the Alsops looked forward to the sound of some other voices here besides their own. It's a lonely place, miles from anywhere.

They must have thought this could be a great home for an unfortunate child. Under different circumstances I think they would have been right. Their devout beliefs aside, I think I would have been comfortable here. This place has the stability I always desired.

I loved the mysteries of my family's house, but not the rise and fall of our family fortunes. The drama between my father and my grandfather instilled a fear in me that even when I became an adult the conflicts wouldn't end. I was afraid I'd be trapped in their dysfunction forever—always in their shadow.

I walk toward the hallway leading away from the bedroom. There are six doors. One leads to a closet. Another leads to the laundry room and garage. The third goes to a bathroom.

I open the first door on the other side of the hallway. There's a small bed frame in the middle of the room. The walls and shelves are bare. A child's dresser stands to the left of the entrance, its empty drawers slightly ajar. It's too sparsely decorated to even be a guest room. This feels like the room where the audiotape was made. The tape recorder probably sat on the dresser, a foot from my head. Above the dresser is an empty frame, probably belonging to a mirror that had been the target of a childish tantrum.

There's no headboard on the bed frame or bookshelf. I go to the far wall to get a closer look and run my fingertips across the surface. I can't find a trace of nail holes. The paint doesn't reveal the telltale signs of something that's been covered over.

This was where Marty was killed. But the absence of a bunk bed suggests this isn't the room where they said he died.

Everyone involved in the events that night had their own reminder. Groom had his audiotape. Dr. Kinder had Marty's corpse. The Alsops had absence.

I venture down the hall to see the other rooms. The next door leads to a water-heater closet. The last door leads to the room where they'd said Marty was found dead after toppling over in the bed and getting tangled in the mattress and blankets.

Sparsely furnished like the other room, the bunk beds are still in there. Pushed against the far wall, the mattresses are covered in plastic. I step inside and try to imagine how they could have conceived of Marty getting trapped. The room is much longer one way than the other. If the bed was where it stood now, I'm not sure how he could have been trapped. Placed against the wall by the door, it might have been possible.

I look around for evidence of moved furniture. At the opposite end I spot scuff marks suggesting how the bunk beds had previously been positioned.

My flashlight catches something. Blood rushes to my head

as I experience the sensation of a missing puzzle piece landing squarely in the center of my field of vision.

Of course.

How could I have been so stupid.

It's right in front of me.

49

I'M LOOKING AT a metal vent about eighteen inches across and twelve tall. Painted the same beige color as the wall, it's easy to miss at first glance. Underneath the vent are faint abrasions from when the bunk bed's railing had been pushed directly below.

I slide the bunk bed back across the floor so it's directly below the vent and climb up.

The four screws that originally held the metal grille in place are missing. I set my flashlight on the mattress and pry it free using my fingernails, then pick the light back up and aim it inside. A long duct goes over the water-heater closet and to the other bedroom, where there's a matching vent opening.

The mysterious voice didn't come from a levitating Marty or even an echo off a bookshelf or headboard. It came from here.

I push my head into the crawl space. Layers of doodled drawings line its sides along with randomly placed stickers. There's a Yoda, a Princess Leia and a herd of colorful ponies. Candy wrappers, picked clean by insects, litter the narrow floor.

Like my own corridors, this was a secret place. This was where a child could peer unseen into another room to watch the adults acting like scared buffoons. I pull myself forward along the duct and see the outline of the bed frame emerge below the vent.

Remembering the geography of Gerald's reconstruction, I see

that the slats of the vent slope downward, aiming sound toward where the bed was that night. Anyone of adult height would just see the grille and not the grinning face behind it.

Relying on a little too much experience in tight spaces, I carefully back myself out of the duct and call my digital historian, disregarding the hour. This is too big to wait.

Probably a night owl himself, he picks up right away.

"Max!" I shout into the phone.

"Hello? Jessica? Is everything okay?"

"Marty Rodriguez . . . is there anything in his foster records about having a sibling?"

"What? Oh, hold on. They didn't always keep those items on there. Let me check. Give me a second. Um, here it is. No."

Evidently, he was up. Or he sleeps next to his computer.

"Damn." I think for a moment. "Can you see if the Alsops had any other kids staying with them?"

"One second. I can check the reduced lunch schedules. Wait. I have to do a cross search. What's with the number you're calling me from?"

"Long story. I'll explain over dinner."

"Oh, cool. Um, here we go. Interesting."

"What?" I ask impatiently.

"There are records of Marty being signed up in the government lunch program multiple times with another child, including in Hawkton. Neither actually enrolled in the school. Got the name here, which is interesting. It's another Rodriguez. If they were cousins, they might not have put that in the record. Or even if they were half-siblings. Sometimes they leave things out, maybe because of incest or other extenuating situations. Other times they're just sloppy. No shock there."

"This other Rodriguez, what's his name?"

"Her name. She's a girl. Hold on. Martha Rodriguez. Her name is Martha. I'm not sure how we missed that. It's a safe bet they're probably brother and sister if they moved them around together."

"Can you get me a photograph?"

"One second. After we talked last time, I got some school year-book publishers' databases. I'll take a look. I can match them to the lunch database and the school, so that should rule out the false positives . . . hold on . . . I think this is her. I'm sending it to the number you're calling me from."

I stare at Gerald's phone, willing the image to come quickly. There's something at the back of my mind, a mental tickle. I don't want to encourage it. It could still be a coincidence . . .

The phone chirps. I click on the icon and open up the new message containing the image. Her face is similar to Marty's. There's a serious look to her. She stares straight ahead. Like Marty's Polaroid, this photo captures a child who is unsure what new disappointment the adult world is going to bring her.

I know this face somehow.

"I'm not sure how we missed her," says Max, frustrated.

"I told you to look for boys because of the library books. I just assumed the 'M' was a boy. It could have been her. Hey Max, do those schoolbooks list anything like nicknames?"

"Yeah, hold on. Let me pull up the image of the page. Not all the text is entered. Here we go. Martha 'Marta' Rodriguez."

"Holy shit." I lean back and almost fall off the bunk bed.

I've been so blind.

She was right there.

"Are you okay?" Max is concerned.

"Yeah! I got to go. Thank you!"

I jump to the ground and buckle to my knees.

Marty's death had a secret witness.

Marta Rodriguez.

His sister.

Sister Marta.

I know her.

I've met her face-to-face.

I shook her hand.

The saintly woman of Tixato, helping the orphans, is Marta. In her expensive blouse and nice watch, I wrote her off as just a woman from a wealthy family trying to do some earthly good.

She is wealthy, but she didn't inherit her money. She earns it the old-fashioned way: she's a criminal.

Sister Marta is close to, or very likely the center of, X-20.

X-20 . . .

It was right here that Martha "Marta" Rodriguez watched from her hidden passage her brother get murdered.

That day was October 20.

10-20.

X-20.

I look around the barren room. One of the most vicious criminal cartels we've encountered was born here on that night.

Who knows what dark thoughts Marta had before then, or what traumatic experiences she'd already endured, but after what happened here, her only connection to society was severed. She watched her caregivers, the law and even the church kill the one person that understood what she was going through.

No wonder she's bitter. I'd be raging like hell if that happened to me.

Marta was probably even the real mastermind behind Marty's "possession," the misguided prankster who read magic books and studied how to manipulate people. She knew someday she'd have her revenge.

And she will let nothing, not even me, stand in her way.

50

I RACE DOWN THE Alsops' gravel path so I can refill Gerald's tank and make it back to Quantico before the rush hour traffic starts piling up on Virginia's highways. The glossy metal of a black car reflects back from the road directly in front of the open gate. I slam on the brakes and come to a halt. Stones ping the underside of Gerald's car.

As the dust settles, my headlights catch the man as he gazes back at me, unfazed. Older, dressed in a well-cut suit, he takes a drag off his cigarette but otherwise remains perfectly still as he blocks my exit.

I put my hand to my gun and scan the surrounding field to see if there's an ambush waiting to happen. I've been caught off guard like this before. However, something about his casual demeanor tells me this isn't the church in Texas all over again.

I exit the car with my hand on the butt of my pistol, leaving my headlights on in his face. He gives me a polite nod as I walk toward him. "Good evening, Agent Blackwood." He speaks with a trace of a European accent.

He obviously sees past my thin disguise. I glance around to see if there's anyone else nearby. The shadow of a driver is visible through the passenger window. "You have me at a disadvantage," I reply.

"Perhaps. Did you see anything interesting in there? Any old ghosts with stories to tell?"

"Who are you?" I still have my hand on my gun at my side, ready to draw.

"That's not important." He takes an arrogant puff of his cigarette. "Let's just say we have a mutual friend in Rome."

"I don't know anybody there."

The man makes the smallest of smiles. "Well, let's just say he thinks of you as a friend and is grateful for bringing a certain person to his attention."

I decide to stop dancing around the issue. "So the Vatican knows there might be a plot against the pope?"

"Yes. By my presence, you can assume they treat this credibly. The question now is a matter of opportunity and method. Our mutual enemy is rather unconventional. Recent events in your own neighborhood have our friend concerned that others may be hurt."

"I wouldn't put anything past these people."

"Nor I. That's where you can be of assistance." He delicately reaches into his pocket with his free hand and removes a DVD case. "Between you and me and the moon, there's a bit of a spiritual debate among our friend's inner circle. I'm hoping you can discreetly offer a professional opinion."

"Religion isn't my strong suit."

The tip of his cigarette glows bright orange in the dark as he inhales. He lets out a stream of smoke that drifts across the headlights like a dark blue phantom.

"Precisely. But that's all they're capable of seeing. I'd like to interject a more secular viewpoint into the discussion."

"Over what?"

He holds up the disc. "Watch the video. When you're finished, call the number inside. We might be able to arrange some kind of trade."

"Trade for what?"

"Answers."

I point back toward the house. "Did your friend tell you what happened in there? Did he tell you the part he played?"

"I'm aware that things are often more complicated than they appear on the surface. Our friend is a good man. Sometimes good men find themselves in difficult situations."

"A difficult situation? A dead child is more than a difficult situation." I glare at him.

He casually waves his cigarette in the air. "Dwelling on the sins of the past won't help us stop the evils of the present. Our mutual enemies have shown us that many more children may die before they're done.

"I'd like to take something back to our friend tonight. I'll give you a piece of information if you'll give me one in return."

"What is that?"

"I understand that the church explosion wasn't caused by any conventional method. I'm told it appears as if someone had spontaneously combusted. Given the amount of damage, I find this hard to accept. Yet, there hasn't been a counter-explanation put forth."

They're confused by how it happened. I can't reveal too much about what we know. I have to parse my words carefully. "You can engineer an unconventional explosive from anything that burns, even cocoa powder. We have no reason to believe there was anything about this explosion that can't be explained rationally."

He nods, as if he's already come to this conclusion. "And the sheriff's behavior? Was it psychological or pharmacological?"

I'm not telling him about the psychoactive fish. That's too important of a lead. But I can allude to the explanation. "My guess is both. A predisposition toward one made him especially vulnerable to the other. If your friend is having delusions, I'd be concerned."

The man nods toward the disc I'm holding. "Let's just say we are concerned."

"What's on here?"

"The contents of the disc are as important to us as the method. If there is an explanation, then the content is irrelevant. If there isn't . . . well, that would be of great concern."

"What do you have for me?"

"A name," he replies with a certain amount of gravity.

"What kind of name?"

"If you're dancing around in the moonlight by yourself, it's obvious to me that your superiors don't take the casual connections you've made between Hawkton and Tixato very seriously. Am I correct?"

"Perhaps . . ." That may change when I reveal Marta's existence. Or at least it should.

He nods. "Jackson Lamont is a man you'd like to speak with."

"Who is he?"

"He knows our mutual enemy. Currently, he's in a federal prison in Virginia. With some encouragement, he might provide you with the information you need.

"But please, your attention to the video would be greatly appreciated. Mr. Lamont will only be able to confirm what you already know. I doubt he'd be able to help you find our mutual enemy now."

"Why is that?"

The man checks his watch. "An hour ago Interpol declared her a suspect in an unrelated crime, one she didn't actually commit."

"Why did they do that?"

"It was a favor . . ."

"To your friend in Rome?" I ask.

"No." He looks right at me. "This was a favor to you. I'd like her to leave you alone. As long as she thinks only you know the relationship between her and these events, you are a liability.

Your superiors don't even have the evidence to name her a person of interest. Fortunately for you, someone owed me a favor."

I get the feeling that exchanging favors with this man could lead down a perilous path.

He gets into the town car and it drives away, leaving me alone in the dark.

I have no idea how long he'd been waiting for me to show up. Having already been inside once, his friend in Rome understood the significance of this place. I suspect he figured it was only a matter of time before the connection between Hawkton and the pope became evident to someone else.

51

"Is that Hebrew?" asks Gerald, furrowing his brow as I play him the DVD of the pope, who is visibly shaken and speaking almost incomprehensibly. To me, it's obvious he can't understand why he's saying what he is.

"No. According to the text file, it's a version of Aramaic."

"Like Bible-times talk?"

"Earlier."

"Does it say what he's saying?" Gerald takes a seat next to me at the conference table.

I push the printout I made toward him. I've been trying to follow along in the video to discover when exactly the pope goes off track. Unlike Reverend Groom, he doesn't gaze off to one side. He just looks disturbed and angry with himself.

"Whoa," remarks Gerald as he reads the transcript. "This is some level thirty D&D bullshit here. The kind of thing you hear a demonic kid say in a found-footage horror movie."

"Only it's the pope saying it."

"Do you think he's being fed lines like Groom?" he asks.

Our current theory is that Groom was told over his earpiece that his wife was going to be killed if he didn't do exactly as he was told. We may never know what was really said, but at least it's plausible.

"I don't know. The pope isn't in the habit of doing television mentalism and magic tricks. So I doubt he's wearing an earpiece that can be jammed."

"What about a hearing aid?"

"That's what I'm thinking. I'm putting together a list of questions. Here's the other part." I open up a directory and show Gerald other similar clips of the pope giving speeches and interrupting himself, apparently against his will, to utter the strange phrases.

"This is really messed up. Why hasn't this gotten out? I think it would be all over." Gerald asks.

"Good question. These were all low-level appearances. Minimal coverage. If I had to guess, the man who gave us this disc probably carries some weight. He might be with Papal security. Did you contact the car service?"

I'd managed to write down the license plate before he drove off.

"Yeah. The car was rented by a company named Tranquilo Partners. There was no passenger name."

"What is Tranquilo?"

"Some kind of investment firm located in Europe. I looked it up and that's where things get a little conspiracy."

"Let me have it," I declare.

Gerald sighs. "You asked for it. Ever heard of the Dictato Serviam? All the Tranquilo board members belong to it."

"Let me guess. Is it some kind of Opus Dei thing?"

He shakes his head. "Not quite. More of a lobbying group for the Church. If you could call it that. The Vatican is every bit as dysfunctional as any other bureaucracy, with the added benefit of being two thousand years old. The Dictato is a group that influences Church position."

"How exactly do they do that?"

"They select priests and cardinals with a record of supporting views with which they agree and want to advance, and donate heavily to their parishes. More money means more influence. The priest who benefits is able to do more works and attract more attention."

"That sounds kind of corrupt."

"It's all a matter of perspective, I guess. But remember, this is the organization that defined modern corruption. The aim of the Dictato is to reward the parts of the Church that they think are serving the true intent. The unintended, or intended, consequence of their influence is that you get priests modifying their application of the Word to suit the Dictato."

"And what is the Dictato's position?" I ask.

"That's where it gets tricky. It changes over time. Not necessarily toward a more progressive view, or a conservative one. The clearest explanation I can see is in how they affect the political viewpoints of clergy. They're not so much interested in the Church itself as much as the Church's power within the rest of the world.

"For instance, an African bishop changes his negative assessment of a dictator with a human rights violation record to a slightly more positive one. That shift is enough for that regime to open up foreign-oil exploration. Care to guess the name of the consulting firm that gets the payday?"

"Tranquilo. So that's who this guy is . . ."

"Maybe. Maybe not. There's another interesting connection. Did you notice his accent?"

I think back to the conversation. "It could have been Italian or German."

"What about Swiss?"

"Maybe."

"There are anecdotal stories about senior members of the Swiss Guard serving as a kind of Secret Service for the pope."

"Don't the Swiss Guards have their own plainclothes units?"

"Yes. I suppose the description for this might be more of a SEAL team for the pope."

"To do what?"

"Priests and agents of the Church inevitably find themselves in various situations. Sometimes aggressive back-channel diplomacy is needed."

"What's the connection between them and the Dictato?"

"If I had to guess, funding. Running those kinds of operations is expensive. The Dictato foots the bill and gets the ear of the pope."

"Things are starting to make sense. I think." My visitor in Hawkton went through a lot of effort to find me.

"So what's going on with the pope?"

"The first speech happened before Hawkton. So that rules out the idea he saw it on the news and went nuts and started speaking in tongues. There had to have been some other trigger."

Gerald nods. "Okay. But what was it? What made him speak that way?"

"I don't know. It could be psychological. But there's too much similarity with Groom's outburst."

"I'd think the pope would be harder to get to than a local televangelist."

"Me too. I'd like to know more about Marta Rodriguez. She's still the center of this. Any word on Lamont?" We'd tracked the tip about the informant down to where he was incarcerated.

"I called the warden. You can speak to him later this afternoon. Do you want to do it in person or over the phone?"

I think about it for a moment. I always get more in person. I want to hear from someone who knows the real Marta firsthand. "It's a hassle, but I'll go over there."

"I'll tell them."

"Thanks, Gerald. You're more than helpful." Despite my doubts, he's really stepped up in Ailes's absence. I'm not sure if I have.

"Until the old man gets back, someone has to keep you from falling on your face."

He has no idea how true this is. "Any word from Breyer about the Marta Rodriguez connection?"

"His office says they're looking into it. The information has been passed on to Mitchum."

I roll my eyes. "That'll do a lot of good." Breyer is following procedure, of course. I'm just not sure he gets how much of a stick in the mud Mitchum is.

"I know. I tipped off Winstone, who is heading the investigation into the bombing at your complex. He seemed more eager to have someone to dive into."

"Well, that's encouraging." Winstone may have been kind of a jerk to me, but at least he's looking more deeply into this.

"Knoll is going to do some digging too."

I smile. "Look at you. Ailes is gone a couple of days and you're already subverting our superiors."

"I like to think of it as rerouting the network around the weakest points." Gerald returns a boyish grin then buries his head into his laptop.

I replay the pope video a few more times trying to figure out what's going on. His delivery sort of reminds me of watching someone trying to lip-sync words as they listen to them.

I don't even notice Gerald leaning over my screen until he clears his throat.

"What's up?" I take the buds out of my ears.

"Ever hear of speech shadowing?" he asks excitedly.

"I don't even have a clue what that means." But I have a feeling it's important.

"There was a Soviet researcher named Chistovich who discovered that if you played people's voices back to them with a slight delay, it basically shuts down their ability to talk. It kind of overloads the brain."

That would explain the pope's expression on the freeze-frame in front of me. "Interesting. Did he discover anything else?"

"She. Chistovich was a woman. It turns out twenty-five percent of women could ignore it and keep talking."

"Watch it," I reply.

"Don't blame science. Well . . . that's not the end of it. Over here, there was that whole MK-Ultra government mind-control project. Who knows what else they came up with? This opened up a whole new area for speech and cognitive research—and manipulation." He points to his computer. "It turns out you can use this method to do things like speech shaping, influencing what people say."

"Yeah, but the pope didn't have an earpiece as far as we know."

"True," Gerald admits. "But you wouldn't need one to do this. We can project sound like a laser. All you need is a flat device, like a dinner plate, aimed at the person. They'd be the only one who heard it."

"So you render them mute first? Then maybe feed them lines?"

"Yeah. Something like that. I'll ask around. But I think this could be the basis of a plausible explanation."

"Hell yeah. See if you can find me a way to demo this." I think about the sound projection idea. "Could you just project the sound off their face?"

"Yeah. That's one application. Are you saying you might not even need the speech shaping?"

"The pope's lips seem to match. Hold on a second." Something hits me. "This could just be a high-tech version of the ventriloquism trick Marta and Marty played. Maybe a mixture of both techniques."

"Oh, man. I can see how that could work. I see a trip to Radio Shack in my future." Gerald enthusiastically types away on his computer as he tries to reverse engineer what we think is Marta's trick.

I call the number on the disc. The man from Rome didn't exactly tell me what his hours of business are, so I don't bother doing the math to figure out what time it is over there. He seems like the type who'll pick up the phone if he wants to.

52

"Hello, Agent Blackwood." His voice is just as deep and confident as I remember. "Have you seen the contents of the video?"

"Yes . . . Mr. . . . . What should I call you?"

"You may call me Mr. Oberst. And what is your professional opinion?"

"My professional opinion? Your pope is acting nuts." There's no other way to put it. He's one *Drudge Report* headline away from a global scandal.

"Yes. There's cause for concern. Do you have a possible explanation?"

"Other than a psychological breakdown?"

"I can assure you that this man doesn't know a word of the language he spoke, let alone how to string a sentence together."

Without Gerald's technological discovery, I'd find this hard to believe myself. "What does he say happened?"

Oberst hesitates. "It's a complicated question."

"How so?" I don't have any patience for this kind of verbal dancing. Lives are at stake. "You ask the man what happened and he tells you. It's really not that hard, I do it a hundred times a day."

"Yes, I imagine you do." He pauses. "These things must be broached more delicately. There is a chance for people to misinterpret the response. Words may be taken out of context."

God, more insider politics.

"You approached me."

"Yes. Yes, of course. Our friend says he heard the words inside his head in his own voice. He wasn't aware that he was repeating them out loud. In fact, he wasn't quite sure what was taking place. It was . . . It was as if someone else had control over his speech."

And thus the fear over the identity of the "someone."

"But he does remember the experience?"

"Yes. Vividly."

"I don't suppose someone hijacked a teleprompter?"

"No. On these occasions, one wasn't even present. We considered all of the obvious possibilities."

Obvious is a subjective term. "Is he on any medication?"

"Nothing that would cause this. After the first episode we began monitoring everything that went into and out of his body."

I need to rule out the obvious conclusions first. "Does he have a hearing aid?"

"Yes. But we checked it for interference and in the second speech he went without."

"Are these the only times it's happened? And they were all in public?"

"Yes, and mostly. The second time was with a group of about a hundred people in Majorca. The third time was in a museum in Vienna where he was speaking at the opening of an art exchange with the Vatican gallery.

"After the first incident, we've been certain to thoroughly search everyone who comes near him. We've also used scanners to listen for illicit transmissions."

"Anything?"

"Just cellular signals."

"And this has never happened in the privacy of his own quarters or in parts of the Vatican with no public access?"

"No. Never."

This suggests a method that can't work when security is too tight. "Hmm . . ."

"Why is that interesting to you?"

"I don't know yet. But it simplifies things to a degree. Can you send me any photographs or video you may have of these locations? Any shots or information about the crowd would be helpful."

"Do you think there's a connection to what happened with Reverend Groom?"

"I don't know. We think he may have been coerced to pull the trigger. He may not have thought he was possessed. We may never know."

"Interesting. Hold on a moment." Oberst muffles the phone. There's the faint sound of someone talking. "Would you have any suggestion for how to stop this?"

"If I had to guess? Earplugs."

"Earplugs?" he asks, confused.

"We think Groom was being extorted to do what he did by someone hacking a radio receiver in his ear. In the pope's case, we think either the sound could have been projected off his face in sync with his speech. Or it's possible he was somehow hearing his own voice, modulated and time-delayed, played back at him."

"I'm not sure I understand."

"Try it yourself, it's very uncomfortable. You can use a sound mixer to delay your voice a half second or so. If you try to listen to this as you talk, it confuses the speech center of our brain. If you alter the sound and then play the words to the person in this way, they try to form them with their mouths. You can shape someone's speech in this manner.

"Watching this video, I'd guess that's what might be happening. It's some kind of psy ops trick. A mechanical device involving speakers. But you said you searched everyone?"

"In the second and third speeches. Hold on . . ." He speaks to the other person. "So you're confident that there is a scientific explanation?"

"Yes. Very. We think there are a couple explanations. The actual method may be different, but I'm sure we only have to ask the right questions."

Oberst speaks to the other person for several minutes. I scan Gerald's emails about sound projection and voice shaping. The more I read, the more this theory fits the bill. It also has the sting of being the same trick that got Marty killed. Marta has decided to use it to discredit the pope and make him fear for his sanity.

"Agent Blackwood, we'd like you to come to Rome."

Rome? Is he kidding? "I don't think that's possible. Technically, I'm not assigned to this case right now."

"It would be a great service to us all if you could come here and share your explanation in person. It could also be very advantageous to you personally."

I'm not sure he understands how my life works. "Like I said, I don't think that's practical."

"I can have a jet ready for you in a few hours. The flight is quite pleasant. I made it this morning."

"I'm speaking to your Mr. Lamont this afternoon."

"After that then? Surely your superiors would let you take the time off for this?"

"It's not about that." I don't like their poorly veiled attempt at wielding power. It might impress some, but it only annoys me. As far as I'm concerned, once we get done with the X-20 matter, I plan on pursuing Marty's murder. And that means finding out how involved Oberst's boss is.

"You can't be convinced?" He asks with the hint that it's merely a challenge.

"I'm sorry."

"Hold on." Oberst whispers to the other person in the room.

"All right. We appreciate your assistance. I'll send you the information about the venues in which his holiness has spoken."

I can't end this call without pointing out the elephant in the room. "I'd also like to know what happened the night Marty Rodriguez died."

"That's not relevant," replies Oberst, a little more curtly than usual. "Thank you and good-bye."

Gerald gives me a look when I hang up. "What's up?"

"Ever have one of those conversations where there's clearly another person in the room calling the shots?" It's just become obvious to me whom Oberst was speaking to.

"Yes. Annoying. Who was it?"

"I think it was the pope." I set my phone on the table and stare into space, wondering what the hell I got myself into.

THE PACKAGE

ABOUT TWO WEEKS after our drive to Tahoe, I was awoken one night by the rumbling sound of a truck engine in the back driveway of Dad's workshop. I crawled out of bed and crept through the house to the kitchen window to see what the noise was about.

Dad and Uncle Darius were pulling a large wooden crate out of the back of a pickup truck. Uncle Darius had been gone for several days so I rushed out onto the driveway to greet him.

"Uncle Darius!" I shouted.

He looked up from the crate they were struggling to lift and smiled. Dad scowled at me. "Go back to bed!"

Hurt, as he rarely raised his voice at me, I ran back inside and defiantly climbed onto the counter in the darkened kitchen. I listened to them argue for several minutes. I couldn't quite make out the words.

"Spying?" barked Grandfather from behind me.

I turned around to face him. "What's in the crate?" My curiosity was stronger than my fear of being caught.

"It's not important."

Obviously it was, but I knew better than to challenge him on matters like that. I climbed down from the counter and padded toward the hallway.

"Jessica," called my grandfather. He was half lit by the light of the driveway through the window.

"Yes?"

"Do you know the difference between sheep and wolves?" he asked.

"Wolves eat sheep?"

"Yes. What else?"

"Sheep are gentle?"

"Gentleness isn't always a virtue." He leaned on the counter, staring out the window into the dark. "The difference between a wolf and a sheep is that a sheep will stand by and watch a wolf devour its own lambs. If you threaten a wolf's pup, it'll rip your throat out. Wolves are foul, vicious creatures. But it's better to be a wolf pup than a dead lamb. Now good night."

I returned to my bed with some horrible images churning in my head, but they were nothing compared with what I saw early that morning when I got up before everyone else to go to Dad's workshop. I can never remember a time when my curiosity didn't get the better of me.

Bigger than a toy chest, the crate was in the middle of the floor. Made of wood planks, there were foreign words stamped on its side and I stood there trying to imagine what was inside.

I could see from the scraped wood where Dad and Darius had opened it last night then sealed it back up with four small nails. I grabbed a hammer off the workbench and clumsily pried the lid off the top of the box using all my weight as leverage.

I had to know.

The box was stuffed with straw. I pulled fistfuls aside to see what Uncle Darius had gone away to get. At first I thought it was a ceramic vase because of all the padding.

When I pulled away more straw, I revealed fine black hair. Below it was the thin brown skin of a scalp.

A body.

I didn't scream. We had shelves of fake body parts in our house from the show. I could look at this dispassionately as if it was a severed head I'd placed into the magic guillotine bucket.

On another level I registered the dried-out leather smell invading my nostrils. This wasn't latex and rubber. This was rotted flesh and blood.

That was the first time, but sadly not the last, I experienced a dead body. I say experience, because the scent penetrates you.

This was a dead thing.

A dead person.

Uncle Darius stole a body.

I replaced the lid and shoved it back on the crate and hammered the nails in the exact spots, using small strokes so I wouldn't wake anyone.

I crawled back into bed, still trying to understand everything. I knew this had something to do with me and the man that had me followed after school.

The corpse was old and withered. I couldn't imagine that it was anyone Uncle Darius would have killed. This was an old thing dug up from some cemetery—a cemetery in a faraway place.

Grandfather and Dad had been talking about things late into the night over the oak table. They always waited until I was in bed before they had their discussions, and even if I didn't creep out to my usual spots the sound of their arguing voices carried all the way into my room.

A few weeks after the Buick followed me, we started receiving calls at all hours. I picked up the first time and heard a man panting. After I described this to Dad, I was forbidden from answering the phone. Grandfather had them all unhooked except for the one in his study. The calls kept coming. One time I heard him yelling at the man on the phone. A little while later the phone rang again and Grandfather started screaming, only to stop abruptly when he realized it was someone he knew.

I imagined it was Uncle Darius calling from some exotic location. I may have heard the word Sicily. It's hard to remember.

The body was real, I was sure of that.

I also vividly remembered the previous night, when my grandfather told me I was being raised by wolves.

53

Jackson Lamont smirks as he's led into the room on the other side of the thick glass divider. "At least you're more fun to look at than my lawyer," he says as he picks up the receiver.

During the half hour it took for them to dig him out of lockup, I'd been reading the file on him. With short-cropped hair and Air Force insignia tattoos emerging from the sleeve of the orange jumpsuit on his left arm, he now looks like a weathered version of the clean-cut young man in his government file folder. Currently serving time for intent to distribute, his life has been one spiral after another.

Kicked out of the Air Force for possession of controlled substances, Lamont knocked around various jobs ranging from telephone solicitation to hauling portable toilets. Probably seeking something more out of life than verbal abuse and trucking other people's waste, he was let go from the telephone job under suspicion of stealing credit card numbers.

I get to the point. "Martha, or Marta, Rodriguez. You know her?"

Lamont gives me a long stare. His eyes dart to the door where the guard went through. "What about her?"

"Do you know her?"

His eyes narrow on me. "There may have been a person by that name in my Air Force unit."

Marta was discharged eight months after Lamont. She was let go with a general discharge, the kind they give to somebody they suspect is up to no good, but don't quite have the goods on. "It says here she was interviewed by the Air Force Security Forces when you were apprehended with controlled narcotics."

"Narcotics. There's a funny word. Do you know how much they found on me?"

"I'm sure I can find it here somewhere . . ."

He waves his hand in the air. "I'll save you the trouble. Less than what they send a pilot up with when he's in combat."

"I don't think the pilots generally intend to distribute while they're in aerial combat."

He shrugs. "Why are you here?"

"Marta Rodriguez. What can you tell me about her?"

"Nothing." He smiles smugly.

"What if I speak with your prosecuting attorney?"

"Don't waste your time. If he agrees to knock the time in half, I'll still be seventy before I get out of jail. That's assuming, of course, she doesn't have me killed first."

"She can do that in here?" I already know the answer, but I want him to tell me what he thinks she's capable of.

"What do you think? Let me just go on the official record as saying she's a wonderful human being."

"You were arrested with two kilos of cocaine in the trunk of your car. It doesn't say where you got it from."

"It was planted." He rolls his eyes.

"Of course. How's that defense working for you? What if I told you we found a fingerprint on one of the bags that belonged to Marta?"

"Bullshit." His eyes lock on me. I know I have his attention.

It's a calculated lie. I gamble that he still thinks the X-20 operation is a complete mystery to us. "An informant, one of the drone pilots, made sure she touched the bags before it went over the border."

NAME OF THE DEVIL

"An informant?" he asks skeptically.

"Former Air Force. Marta contacted him like you. I'm sure you know who I'm talking about." I want to vaguely insinuate Deland, but I'm not sure if Lamont knows he's already dead.

"If I talk, she kills me. I was clumsy and got caught. That didn't fly so well."

Marta has been cleaning house. She knows it's only a matter of time before we work our way to someone who knows her. "She's going to try to kill you whether you talk or not. If you do talk, there's another level of protection. You don't get mixed in with the regular population."

"They can still get to you."

"It's much, much harder in the federal system. If you have a lot to say, we can put you in witness protection. The only people who get killed there are the ones that stray. Keep your nose clean and you'll be fine."

He shakes his head. "I don't know. They found a lot of shit in my car."

"Yes. Yes they did. They also want Marta for something much more serious." In the back of my mind I'm putting together an arrangement for Winstone. The DEA can get a solid sentence for Lamont; not the lifetime they want, but five years or so, and we can get enough information to connect Marta to the bombing attempt and X-20.

"More serious than being a trafficker?"

"Let me put it this way, if you'd known where Bin Laden was hiding, they'd have flown you out of here on Air Force One. We let people operate poppy fields in Afghanistan just so we can get intel on Al Qaeda. Marta is a terrorist now. We're not above making deals with drug lords to go after them."

"What will this information get me?"

"Probably a much shorter stay here. You'll still be able to re-member why you wanted out."

Lamont mulls this over. I can tell he was already fearing the prospect of Marta reaching him inside of here. "I need to talk to my lawyer."

"Is this an attorney provided to you by the state? Or is it someone recommended to you?"

"Why?"

"If this is someone Marta's people suggested, you're screwed. They don't hire attorneys they can't buy body and soul."

"So you're telling me not to talk to an attorney? I'm not sure that's legal."

"I'm saying you probably need new counsel. Ask to speak to the DA directly. Ask him point-blank if you should get a different attorney."

"Why the hell would he give me a straight answer?"

"If he says 'yes' and agrees to a potential delay, then he's shooting straight. That's assuming he thinks you'll be more likely to make a deal with a different attorney."

"Meanwhile, you want me to tell you everything?"

"I don't care about how you got stopped or what happened. I need to know about Marta. See the explosion on the news in DC?"

"Yeah?"

"That was her. There were over a hundred people in that building. Thankfully, none of them were hurt and the building is still standing. You're still alive because you're not worth her attention, for the moment. So help me out. Who is she, really?"

54

LAMONT KNOWS HE'S in a hell of a bind. He needs to make some kind of deal. I can tell this was already weighing on him. Whether he promised his silence or not, if he screwed up the transfer of the cocaine Marta already has all the justification to have him killed while really trying to protect her own identity.

Running a criminal enterprise is filled with human resource challenges. If you had everyone killed who had potential evidence on you and was at risk of turning State's witness, nobody would work for you. Lamont wasn't a worry for Marta as long as prosecutors and cops weren't waving her photo and asking about her. Now she knows her invisibility is coming to an end. Loose ends have to be tidied up.

Lamont leans back, crosses his arms and stares at the ceiling. "Marta? Which one? I knew three of them. There was the Marta that went into the Air Force. She was an eighteen-year-old girl coming off the streets. Managed to get her GED and enlisted because some judge thought it'd help a smart kid find some discipline."

"Did it?"

"Discipline was never her problem. Authority was. Here's the thing about the military; it's like a razor. It cuts right through you. On one side you get people who want to be part of something. They need that gung-ho attitude and want to be told what to do. They're the do-gooders. On the other side, you get the fuck-ups, like me. We sign up because we think it's going to straighten out all that shit that's wrong in our lives. Only it doesn't. We coast along and avoid getting in trouble for a while, but then we figure out how to beat the system or at least push it a little. What's only a small infraction on the outside is a big one inside. Get caught with a joint in your pocket outside a club? In some cities the cops will just trash it and tell you to go home. In the Air Force, you're looking at time in the brig, and that's if they don't kick you out.

"Marta figured this out early on. Lucky for her, she wasn't much to look at. Any half-decent chick in the military is getting chased by a dozen cocks every minute of the day. Know what the STD rate is for a woman in the service compared to the average? My point is, Marta showed up with a grudge. She didn't like being told what to do, which is a bad attitude to have in the military. She took some shit from a couple COs and that's when the second Marta emerged. Bad Luck Marta. Shit had a habit of happening to people who crossed her. One CO who wrote her up for breaking curfew had his brakes go out. He ended up driving through a red light and getting T-boned. Another one who noticed parts were going missing and probably showing up on eBay got electrocuted by a bad light switch before he could start a formal investigation. Weird shit.

"She was always somewhere else. You could never pin it on her. She was good at getting other people to do stuff for her. Look at my dumb ass. I got to hand it to her. Anyhow, Bad Luck Marta realized the Air Force was too small for her. By that time she was smuggling drugs into the base and had figured out all the little loopholes.

"After she was discharged, she laid low for a while. I heard she had some hard times. But eventually she got hooked up with a high-level trafficker. Soon enough, Marta was running mules between Mexico and the US. She'd find these Army wives, bored with waiting for their husbands to come back. Marta would offer them money to take a trip to Mexico with a few friends and then carry a bag or two back.

"Marta was real smart about it. She'd make sure these wives would get a chance to party down there, hook up with some handsome beach boy. Then she'd use that to blackmail these dumb bitches. If they got caught or said anything, Marta would make sure their husbands stuck in the middle of the shit somewhere would find out real quick what a cheating whore they were married to. Real piece of work.

"When peace time, or whatever the hell we call it, came around, she had a better idea. Instead of spending three days and a few grand each trip on these bimbos ready to have a breakdown, why not hire the husbands?

"These guys know how to fly remotely operated vehicles a few feet off the ground and avoid radar. For fifty K you can build a half-decent kit if you know what you are doing. There are lots of joystick jockeys looking for something to do that pays better than working retail and trying to rape someone with an extended warranty.

"Marta had the cutting edge advantage on the cartels. They were in the Stone Age with boats and passenger planes. She was making bank quicker. Her mules were electronic. She also started using them for counter-surveillance. That's when she upped the game. If she couldn't recruit you, she would find you and kill you."

"It's a big jump from running drugs to running a cartel," I interject.

"It didn't happen overnight. But she's smart and a fast learner. If life had dealt her a different hand, she'd be running some Fortune 500 company. I don't doubt that for a moment. All this took time. When she got hold of me, she was well on the rise.

"Marta was good at figuring out who was in charge. She could make a deal or cut somebody out of the picture fast. And she got the business. She worked her way up through street suppliers to the people running the fields. She's smart, real smart. In this business, brains are at a premium. Look at where my dumb ass is sitting."

"How would I find her?"

"Find her? You should want to stay away from her. She can smell a narc a mile away."

"They don't pay me to keep away from bad people. Does she have a weakness? A vice?"

"Not a vice. Maybe a weakness," replies Lamont. "Kids. As hard-ass as she is, she's got a soft spot for kids. She has an orphanage down in Mexico."

"Tixato?"

"Yeah. They call her 'Sister Marta' there."

"I've been there. Anywhere else?"

Lamont gives me a surprised look. "You went to Tixato? And made it out alive?"

"There were complications."

"She's got another one in Nicaragua. Coincidentally enough, another high-trafficking zone."

"Where in Nicaragua?" I press.

"I don't remember. The town was called Lexi or something like that. She has a house on the water and a huge dock where she keeps her yacht."

"Yacht?"

"Yeah. She's a very wealthy woman who likes her toys. She's also got friends in high places. People down there don't think of her as a drug dealer. They think she's just some wealthy real estate investor or something."

"What's the name of the yacht?"

"I don't know if I remember. I've never been on it." He sounds like he's telling the truth.

I take a wild guess based on how people choose these kinds of names. "Marty?"

He snaps his fingers. "Yeah, *Marty*, that's it. How'd you know?"

"That's not important. If you can think of anything else, let me know. In the meantime, I'm going to talk to the warden."

Lamont is a first-rate asshole. But he's not a killer. Right now I can see a crosshair on his forehead. US federal prison isn't the same as Mexican lock-up, but it's still not a safe place for a marked man.

"What for?" he asks.

"It's a miracle she hasn't found a way to kill you already. I can only guess that's because her attention has been elsewhere. I'm going to do what I can to see that you're safe now."

I can't let Marta get to him like she did Esteban. Lamont is our only living link between her and X-20.

55

BREYER LEANS ACROSS his desk and stabs a finger in my direction. "Who have you been talking to?"

He's in no mood for anything that sounds like a flippant answer. I play it dumb. "I'm not sure I understand."

"About the pope thing," he replies. "I told you not to take it out of this building."

I have to tread carefully. I can't lie. "I didn't break any regulations."

"I got half a building full of lawyers. I don't need a street cop throwing legal distinctions back in my face."

Being called a "street cop" is a compliment in my book, compared with "showgirl bimbo" or "magic babe." In a strange way, I take it as a sign that Breyer at least takes me seriously. I respect him enough to tell the truth.

"I spoke to my priest in a confessional," I explain matter-of-fact.

He sits back and gives me an odd look. "Your priest?"

"Technically, not my priest. But I did it in a confessional. I wasn't sure how much further than this office my warning was going to go."

"So you went and told the Catholic Church, even though you didn't have any evidence?"

"I had my instincts." I avoid using the word "faith," but I guess that's what it was. While I was talking to the priest downtown, Marta's X-20 goons were parking a truck full of plastic explosive in my basement. If I hadn't said anything and kicked up a fuss, and, I hesitate to admit, if Damian hadn't been watching my back, I'd be dead along with a lot of other people and the plot to kill the pope would be advancing along.

I expect him to yell. Instead, he lets out a sigh. "What am I supposed to do with you? I send you over to Ailes's school for mutant agents, hoping he can channel that energy into something constructive. It turns out he's made you a more resourceful pain in the ass."

"Sir. My goal isn't to subvert you. I'm a cop. I'm just trying to do my job."

"You are also in a chain of command," he replies.

Breyer didn't get his job by sitting still. We both know that sometimes when the person upstairs doesn't get it, you have to push things. The problem is if the results don't justify the action.

"You told me not to leak this to the press. Those were your specific words. My understanding was this wasn't to be made public. I got it. I didn't do that. I didn't go around you within the Bureau. I didn't try to interfere in any of the diplomatic channels, whatever those are supposed to be. I told one priest." I leave out that he's in the most important archdiocese in the country.

"Diplomatic channels," he scoffs. "One priest?"

"Yes."

"Are you sure?"

"Yes."

"Please don't bullshit me. If you have connected friends, just tell me."

That's got to be a sore spot for Breyer, knowing Ailes is rumored to be golfing pals with the president and has Wall Street billionaires on his speed dial.

"Pardon me? The man who met me in Hawkton? I wrote a full report on Mr. Oberst."

"Yeah, him. How'd you find yourself out there? It's not your case."

"I was following a lead on a matter that appeared unrelated at the time."

He scoffs. "Unrelated? Never mind. Do you ever sleep?"

"I can't go back to my apartment. I was just following up on some information about Groom's murder."

Breyer leans back in his chair and puts a hand to his brow. "Have you always been a magnet for trouble?"

"I prefer to think I'm just good at finding it."

He shakes his head. "Too good. Let me tell you what's been going on in my world. Besides this attempted bombing mess that we can't sort out just yet, whether it was some unknown Filipino terrorist group or X-20, I've been getting the State Department yelling in my ear.

"Just so you know, after you left here, I did as I promised. I made calls. An hour later I get someone calling from the Secretary of State's office screaming, I kid you not, *screaming* that we're going to ruin diplomatic relations with the spiritual leader of a billion people if we persist in a line of investigation that not only advances a rather thin notion the pope is going to be assassinated for reasons I can't even understand, but also asks if this same man may be guilty of manslaughter on US soil." He catches his breath and lowers his voice. "All because of your 'instinct,' which so far isn't backed by much physical evidence."

"Well—"

He interrupts me. "Hold on. So . . . Marta Rodriguez watches a room full of people kill her brother in a botched exorcism. Years later she becomes the head of a drug cartel and decides to start getting revenge. She begins by getting the sheriff hopped up on some strange trip where he's seeing demons that drive him to attack others. Then the church blows up from what we can only describe as a 'fat bomb' that makes it look like spontaneous human *whatever*. She then makes another accomplice kill himself on live television using a transmitter and a hidden gun. And . . . and she's watching these events from remotely controlled drones."

"There's more to it—"

His face is red at my interruption. "Let me finish. Her final target is the mysterious man in the room who happens to be the pope. Have I got it? Wait, she tries to kill our intrepid agent, not once, but twice. Am I missing anything?"

It's never easy being the only one to see a pattern and having to explain it to everyone else. The simplest reaction for them is to blame the messenger.

My life would be so much easier if I could ignore things. I wouldn't be all twisted up inside and feel like I was under constant attack. But it's not a choice I'm capable of making. If I get pushed, my instincts are to push back—twice as hard.

I've been bracing for this moment. "Is it too weird? Is that the problem? Ever follow the life story of the guy who shot Kennedy? How about John Wilkes Booth? Did you know his brother was the most famous actor of the day and once saved Lincoln's son from being run over by a train? You tell me, what part of my story don't you believe? Is the C4 that was parked in my basement just some strange coincidence? Is the fact that I've got a witness placing the little girl who was there that night in Hawkton at the head of X-20 not important? The pope? Maybe it wasn't him there that night. My suspect thinks so, which makes him a target regardless if he's on the tape. That's all that matters right now. After that's sorted out, we can figure out if it's true."

"Then what?"

"Same as any other cold case where we find a possible suspect."

"Prosecute the pope?" Breyer massages his temples. "Oh, Lord. What part about him being the pope don't you understand?

Anyhow, that's not the pressing issue right now. I'll let you deal with that later.

"That person at the State Department who was screaming at me—me, the Assistant Director of the FBI, mind you—called while you were gone. Only this time it was in a much more cordial tone. It seems somebody in a very high position of power called her and asked for a favor. A favor only I have the power to grant. I have half a mind to say 'no.' But the other half says 'yes,' because of their previous attitude."

"What kind of favor?" His change in tone catches me off guard.

"He's coming here."

"Who?"

"The pope. He's planning on making a surprise visit at some youth music festival in Miami."

"You're kidding?" Damn. Marta is probably all over this now.

"No. No I'm not. It's in less than two weeks. Now it's our responsibility. We need to know if there's a credible threat to him. We can't have that happen on US soil.

"The Vatican asked for you personally to assist with security arrangements."

"Me? I wouldn't know the first thing about that." I can feel Oberst's machinations behind this.

"Apparently, they have some concern as to whether or not a credible attempt could be made on his life. There's an unanswered question that they believe you can shed some light on."

"I just wanted to bring the threat to your attention. I don't actually want in on this." My plate is too small. My anxiety levels are already at their limit. Having to personally worry about another person's safety makes me even more queasy.

"Too late. You stick your nose in too many places, you're going to get stung." He waits a moment before dismissing me. "You play by your own set of rules, Blackwood. You're clever,

I'll give you that. But right or wrong, I don't forget how you play things. One day you're going to find yourself in a gray area and the people you've walked over on the way might not see it the same way."

This is a threat. Technically, Breyer isn't in a position to reprimand me for going to the priest, maybe . . . But either way, he is letting me know when this is over, I will have to pay a price for going around him.

56

Four hours later, I'm in the heart of the US Secret Service headquarters, three blocks away from the FBI. While some of our mission statements overlap, you can see the cultural differences. The FBI sees itself as protecting the citizens of the United States, while the Secret Service guards the president, our money, and visiting heads of state. The framed pictures of limousine caravans and Secret Service agents standing stoically in exotic locations reflect this.

Dennis Ratner, head of the Secret Service unit assigned to the Pope's visit, appraises me with a look that's one part skeptical and one part leer as I'm escorted into their operation center and introduced around. Dressed in a Brioni suit, hair a little too long and stylish for the Bureau, he looks flashier than the Russian politicians and oil princes he protects.

There's about twenty people here. A mixture of men and women who, thankfully, seem to be a tad less fashion obsessed than Ratner.

He addresses the room full of agents. "This is Agent Blackwood, who I assume you all know of from her many, many interesting past exploits. She's here to keep his holiness from spontaneously exploding or being attacked by flying monkeys."

This is one of those situations where, if I don't respond to his crack in kind I'll look weak, or like I don't have a sense of humor.

NAME OF THE DEVIL

Everything I do or say from now on will be judged in that context. He's baiting me, trying to show how cool and relaxed he is as he asserts his dominance.

"Let's just hope the pope doesn't borrow a government vehicle for a hook-up with a transvestite hooker," I zing back with a smile.

My reply gets a laugh from the room and Ratner blinks.

I spoke to a friend in the capital police for some background before I came here. They knew someone in the Secret Service uniformed division. It never made the news, but a few months ago one of Ratner's foreign assignees managed to cause an embarrassing situation he clearly didn't think made it outside of the office. Guess again.

"Let's hope not," he replies with a cocky grin, trying to keep control of the situation. "So, why does the Vatican think you need to help us dumb saps out?"

"We think the pope may be a target of X-20. We suspect they've been targeting him for some time now. It's rather complicated, but we think they've been using psychological warfare techniques to make him seem unbalanced. He's made erratic speeches, said some unusual things implying he's not in control of his faculties. It has the appearance of a kind of psychological manipulation. The apparent goal is to make the pope think he's possessed."

"Drugs?" asks an agent named Carver. I was told he'd be handling the actual visit, while Ratner was in charge of the advance preparations.

"We don't know," I reply. "They've been testing him to see if he might have been given something. So far all the screenings have come back negative."

"What do you think?" asks Ratner. I can tell he's buying time to process what I just said.

"In the case of Reverend Groom, the television priest who

killed himself, we think we found a form of electronic intrusion where they were threatening him on air and telling him how to act and what to say. Possibly in a manner that made him think he was having some kind of supernatural experience."

"And that's not the case here?" Carver is taking this in without too much observable skepticism. Thank God for small favors.

"Apparently not. But that doesn't rule out other forms of electronic interference."

"Are you saying some kind of magical mind weapon?" Ratner says mockingly. "Maybe we should get a search warrant for Hogwarts."

I set my briefcase down on the table. "We think it's a little more real than that." It's a lot to believe. I get that. I also don't have the time to build the whole case for them brick by brick.

"It's still a theory." Ratner shrugs. "Over here we prefer to work . . . to work . . . to work with *monkey balls*." He's shocked by the words that just shot out of his mouth.

The room is confused by the outburst.

"Monkey balls?" Carver keeps a straight face. "I don't remember that at the Academy."

"What the hell?" Ratner glances around the room, baffled by what just happened.

I point to my briefcase. "I brought this to demonstrate. Thanks for volunteering."

There's a flash of anger on his face, but he's still confused.

I open my briefcase and show them the disc of ultrasonic speakers Gerald cobbled together. "It's just a demonstration device. My coworker borrowed some stuff from an intelligence agency that doesn't want to be named. All we had time for was one phrase."

"Monkey balls?" Ratner shakes his head.

"Gerald's idea. Not mine." I point to the iPod plugged into the device. "It listens for a speaker then synthesizes their voice and aims it back at them with a little delay. What did it feel like?"

"Like an electric toothbrush set to kill." Ratner inspects the device. "This would be great for getting confessions," he admits grudgingly.

"You mean manufacturing them," I correct. "In any event, this is what we think we're looking for."

He looks up. "Normally, as a precaution, we'd sweep the area anyway. No offense to the Swiss Guard, but we take protection protocols pretty seriously."

"I understand that. They do too. The important question is whether X-20 plans to use the oneLove festival as an opportunity." I point to the machine. "I think they're past using that gimmick now. They're in the final stages."

"May I look?" asks a woman named Hamed, who'd watched the demo with a certain amount of detachment.

"Sure."

She begins to inspect the speakers and make notes.

"How would you suggest we figure out X-20's next step?" asks Carver.

I'd sent them my briefs about Marta. Looking at it on the page reveals how many blank spaces there are. Her methods range from the subtle to the extreme, and we still don't understand all of them. "We need to know if they had earlier opportunities. Is the method they used to disrupt him something they could just as easily have adapted to murder him? If the answer is 'yes,' then it seems very likely they've been waiting for a more public situation to kill him in a dramatic fashion. If they haven't had the opportunity yet, then at least we know the degree of protection he has so far has been working."

"We're going to offer him the same level of protection irregardless," replies Ratner.

I bite my tongue at the 'irregardless.' "How many agents will be assigned to this?"

"Probably forty, along with at least a hundred local police

tasked to work with us," Carver points out. "And Dennis, it's 're-gardless,' not 'irregardless.'"

This gets a laugh from the group. I get the impression Ratner is the butt of more than a few jokes here. It seems a friendly enough way to keep him in check.

I suppress my own smile. "We just found out that X-20 is be-lieved to be behind a recent prison break in Oaxaca. They had over two hundred armed men storm the compound. So they're very capable of putting together an army."

"This isn't Mexico," snaps Ratner.

"True. It's not. But before coming over here, I looked up some statistics. Do you know how many X-20 affiliated gang members are currently on parole right now in the United States? At least eight hundred. Those are only the ones documented by gang units as X-20 related or had the X-20 tattoos on their necks visible in arrest photos.

"If they can gather two hundred men for a minor operation, we can only imagine what they'd pull in for something like this.

"I think this is their leader's one single purpose. The existence of X-20 was predicated upon getting her enemies. She's smart. She's rich. She's ruthless. And now she has an army."

The room goes quiet. Assassinations are usually carried out by one or two people. I just outlined the possibility of a full-on military strike.

They're starting to grasp the scope of the situation. I continue. "If she could have killed him before, then we can reasonably assume she has something in mind other than brute force. This is a statement for her."

"How do we settle the pope question?" asks Carver.

"We need to know how they made him act erratic."

"That was all in Europe?"

"Yes. But going to Europe to investigate the locations where he went off-kilter like Groom wouldn't be practical at this point.

What we need is someone there who can be our eyes and ears . . ." My voice trails off as I get an idea. Up until now, I haven't really been able to pursue physical evidence tying the pope into all this. "Can you get a Skype feed on that video wall?"

Hamed brings me a laptop computer wired into their network. "What do you need?"

"One second," I tell her. I pull up the list of speech locations, and pick the pope's second appearance. He was in a reception hall, but the photos I received from Oberst were too inconclusive. I couldn't make out enough details.

I find the number of the building he spoke at on Google. After several rings an exasperated man says, "Hola?" I speak slowly so he'll understand my Spanish. "Excuse me, Señor. I have an unusual favor to ask. I'm calling from the United States and would like to have a look at your building. Do you have a smartphone that can stream live video?"

The young voice responds, "If you're as pretty as your voice then the answer is yes, Señorita."

57

Gustavo, the night security guard in the annex to the Palma Cathedral on the island of Majorca, was very bored when we called. It's probably not the most exciting of jobs. He eagerly took the call from Skype on his personal phone and chatted away as he walked down the long corridor from the security office to the reception hall.

"As you can see, Miss Jessica, this is the room where his holiness paid us a visit," he says as he turns the lens on himself and smiles at the camera.

He's got a broad, friendly grin that would seem better suited for a tour guide than a night watchman.

"Were you there?"

"Sadly, no. I have the night shift and was sleeping. I understood he wasn't feeling well. My brother-in-law said he made a very strange speech." He pans the phone around the room. It looks like any other hotel conference center. "Is this what you wanted to see?"

"Yes, Gustavo. I'd like to get a closer look at the walls and ceiling, if that's possible." I press the mute button on the laptop and turn to the other agents in the room. "In Groom's studio we found a small antenna. Maybe there is something similar here."

Gustavo aims his phone at the ceiling. "Is this where you want to attach the lights for motion picture?"

I couldn't tell him I was with the FBI and Secret Service conducting an investigation. This would raise too many red flags and likely lead us through a lengthy discussion with his superiors. To make things easier, I'd told him I was with a production company doing location scouting. I'm sitting with my back to the wall. The other agents are off to the side, out of range of the camera. "Ideally, we don't want to do anything to hurt the building. We need to see what fixtures are already in place."

"Yes, of course." He holds the phone up as high as he can and walks slowly from one end of the room to the other and back so we can see each section. "Is this helpful?"

"Very much so. Just keep walking like that."

"Poor kid," mutters Carver, covering his mouth with his hand.

"Do you think I might be able to have a role in your movie?" inquires Gustavo eagerly.

I hit the mute button for a moment as the other agents try to suppress their laughter. I don't want to make Gustavo out to be a fool.

"We'll see, Gustavo." I throw the agents leaning in out of the camera range a glance. "See anything?" I can't spot an antenna.

"No," says Carver.

Hamed is making notes on a pad of paper.

The ceiling, except for a few small light fixtures—too small to hide an antenna like the one in Groom's studio—appears clean. However, there's always the possibility something was brought in with a piece of equipment and carried back out.

"Gustavo, could you show us the walls?"

"Certainly. I have nothing else to do. Do you have a boyfriend?"

The question gets me the attention of the room. Hamed glances up from her notepad, and grins. She knows what it's like to be the one girl on the boy's team. "No. Not at the moment."

"Maybe when you come to Majorca I can buy you a drink?" He nervously adds, "That's if you don't have a boyfriend by then."

It's a safe bet I won't be in Majorca anytime soon. And right now, I need to keep our one man on the ground onboard. "How about I buy you coffee?"

"Deal." He scans his phone over the back of the room. At one side there's a large rectangular panel painted the same color as the wall. It looks like a speaker, but it's missing a companion on the opposite side.

This asymmetry stands out to me. "Gustavo, what's that square thing toward the back?"

"It's a, what's the word in English? A speaker. We're having it replaced."

"Why is that?"

"It doesn't work and some delinquents stole the other one. I chased them off myself. They were immigrants. The police arrested them."

"That was quite brave of you."

Carver has an interested look on his face. I mute the feed again and ask, "Can we get a look at police reports for there?"

He nods his head and pulls up the Interpol database on a laptop to my right.

"I have a crazy question, Gustavo. I have two big favors. First, could you put your phone flat against the speaker, looking out? I'd like to see the angle."

"Do the acoustics concern you? Let me get a chair."

A moment later the phone rises and comes to a stop facing out toward the front of the hall. I place my finger in the exact center of the screen. Underneath a restored fresco, it's the same spot where the pope stood when he went off script. Years of working in theaters have taught me good sound design doesn't have the speakers cross in the middle. This is odd.

"Gustavo, do you have a screwdriver?"

"I have a multi-tool on my belt. One moment." He sets the phone down and pulls the unit down from the wall, laying it flat on a table facing up. "I'm beginning to think this is one of those hidden camera shows."

"You said you wanted to be in a movie."

"Yes, but television is different. Oh well." He gives me his broad smile. "If I come in here one night and find you robbing the building, I'm going to be very upset. I won't be able to buy you that drink."

He moves the phone and we watch out of the corner of the screen as his arms take apart the front grill of the unit. I pray for Gustavo's sake there's not some kind of explosive booby trap. I start to think I should have called the Majorcan police.

"Well that is very peculiar," he says.

The other agents lean in to our video screen. I almost shout at Gustavo to show us what he's looking at, but after a long pause, he remembers we're waiting and picks up the phone to give us a better view. Instead of a large speaker element inside, there's a hexagonal arrangement of twenty small silver discs.

This is not any kind of speaker I'm familiar with. I glance across the room.

Hamed types into a computer to the side of me. "Transducer elements," she whispers. "Sonic projection."

"Well, monkey balls," someone murmurs.

I'm too terrified for Gustavo's safety to high-five myself at the moment. "Gustavo, we need you to stay there. We're going to call someone with Interpol to arrange for that to be picked up. Don't touch it, just leave it be."

"I knew it," he replies excitedly into the camera. "You're not movie makers. You're spies. The good kind, right? This thing, will it explode?" He is suddenly nervous.

"I'm pretty sure it won't, but don't touch it just to be safe. And yes, we're the good kind."

Carver tells someone to get on the phone with the local police and arrange for the unit to be taken from the building and inspected. Ratner stands across the table with his arms folded. I can see nods of approval from the other agents. I think I've earned their respect.

"So what exactly does this device do?" asks Carver.

"Let's see if we can find a lonely night watchman in Austria, and then I'll explain."

58

SERGEANT SCHWEIGER HOLDS his phone aloft to give us a clear view of Caravaggio's clear plastic-covered painting *The Crowning with Thorns* while Lieutenant Häupl swings his metal crowbar at the wall across from where the pope made his most recent erratic speech.

Having found the acoustic device in Majorca, we have enough cause to call in all our resources.

Painted plaster fragments go flying, bouncing off the sheets they've hastily arranged to protect the rest of the Kunsthistorisches Museum's exhibits.

There had been a brief debate as to whether or not they should remove the priceless art from the gallery. But waiting for curators to properly move and stow the collection would be too time-consuming. I also got the feeling that if the tactical unit was going to get blown to hell, they'd at least like something nice to look at in the afterlife.

Ratner hides his face behind his hands as the wall begins to crumble. The other agents look equally concerned. I've only been in their unit less than a day and I already have them ordering up the destruction of major European monuments.

To the Austrian authorities, the mere suggestion that there may be some illicit electronic device concealed within the walls has sent the Austrian Special Unit into overdrive.

Häupl has made a fist-sized opening. He reaches up with his thickly armored hand and peels away a sheet of plaster. Men dressed like large beetles stand around with heavy metal shields to form a barrier in the event of a blast. They all look identical in their heavy tactical gear. We can only tell them apart because Häupl appears slightly taller and thinner.

The device Gustavo uncovered in Majorca was one of the technologies I'd been researching. "If you set up series of transducers like that," I'd explained to the Secret Service agents, pointing to the image on my laptop screen. "You can project sound. You can't hear anything at the point of emission, but the small discs form a full sound wave at a distance. I think your tech people use something similar for embassy security to disperse protestors by blasting really annoying sounds.

"Only this can be used for more devious purposes than crowd control. Like my demo with Ratner, if you speak to someone using this it'll sound like your voice is coming from them. No one else will hear it. It'll drive them nuts. You can take it a step further and modulate someone's voice as they speak. Think of auto-tune music. But instead of making a bad singer sound good, you're using their voice to shape different words. You can then make words appear to come out of their mouth, which in some instances triggers people to try to make their speech match. It's like a short-circuit of the speech center."

"And someone is doing this to the pope?" asks Carver, unable to take his eyes off the destruction going on thousands of miles away.

"That's what I think we found in Majorca. It's what I think we'll find here." I hope. But feel guilty for hoping, knowing the deeper implication.

Ratner sits on the edge of a table biting his thumbnail. Our Skype scavenger hunt has quickly spiraled from something that felt like a telephone prank to what could become a major international incident if we end up embarrassing the Austrian police.

He looks at me sharply. The implication is, I better be right. The reality is that this will fall on his head. As much as he'd like to see me proven wrong here, he knows this part of the operation is ultimately under his jurisdiction. He can finger-point all he wants, but it'll just make him look bad. Not that there won't be serious repercussions for me. I really, really don't want to have to explain another failure to Breyer. I've only been here a couple of hours and already I've put millions of dollars of priceless art in jeopardy halfway around the world.

Häupl tears away another piece of drywall. Bare concrete blocks are visible through the gap. He opens up the gash above and below. There's electrical conduit, but nothing else. He steps away from the damage and takes off his gloves to wipe the sweat from under his safety goggles.

Schweiger faces the camera and speaks in accented English. "Should we have found it by now?"

The wall looks just like a ripped-up wall. There's no hexagonal arrangement of discs. "One second." Oh, man. I feel like there's a piano on a thin rope over my head. "Do we have a layout of the exhibit hall?"

A tablet displaying a diagram is handed to me. Diagonal lines connect the pope's position to the points on the wall where the transducers would need to be. It should be right in front of us, except it isn't there.

My skin burns with the feeling of a thousand disappointed eyes watching me, even though there's only two dozen people in the room. Well, I guess there's the people in Austria and all the chiefs watching the live feed.

I can only imagine the reaming that's in store for me.

"Nice going," hisses Ratner, seeing the desperation on my face. "The FBI have the money to pay for this?"

"It was a good call, given what we found in Majorca." Carver tries to reassure me.

"I can't wait to see this one on *Drudge Report* tomorrow." Ratner seems almost gleeful, then has a second worried thought. "I'm not taking the heat for this, Blackwood."

"Is everything okay?" asks Häupl as he steps in front of the video. I can see his reddish hair just under his helmet.

"Yes," I lie, staring down at the image on the tablet. Something seems a little odd. "Lieutenant Häupl, how far is it from wall to wall?"

He motions to a sergeant. The other man comes running over with a tape measure and they unwind it from wall to wall. "Twelve meters," Häupl reads.

Embarrassment completely washes over me. I may have just botched this. It could have been portable equipment that was loaded out. I look down at the tablet again. The number matches. "Hold on," I turn to the Hamed, who made the layout. "Is this in feet?"

"Oh shit!" she replies.

I make the adjustment on the tablet. "Lieutenant Häupl, I got the measurement wrong. Could you try a foot, I mean, um, thirty centimeters, to the left?"

This wouldn't be the first time US-European disaster was caused by a mistake in metric versus US customary units.

He hesitates, then throws up his hands. "Plaster is cheap." He slams the crowbar into the new coordinates, creating a new hole. The plaster falls away. Still no discs.

"How big of a hole do you want to dig yourself, Blackwood?" Ratner chortles.

This is a nightmare I don't get to wake up from. I'm pretty sure I'd rather be giving a speech in my underwear right now.

Häupl pulls away chunks of cinder block, widening the gap. "Would this be inside the wall, perhaps?"

"Maybe," I reply. Anything to give me a chance to think. Where are bomb threats when you need them? Damn it, that's not funny.

"I'm about to call this," Ratner threatens.

"I believe I'm in charge here," Häupl responds over the video stream. "I'll keep going until the lady is satisfied."

"Thank you, Lieutenant Häupl." I gratefully smile and ignore Ratner.

In Häupl's case, it's not that he necessarily believes me, it's that he had better turn over every possible stone. He doesn't have the luxury of pushing this down the line.

Ratner's thumbs type away on his phone. No doubt already trying to cover his ass.

Häupl steps back to survey the fallen plaster. He strips off the heavy protective sleeves on his arms then walks back to the wall. He shoves his bare hands into the space behind the wall, making a face as he strains.

"Please don't electrocute yourself," Carver pleads quietly. Hands steepled under his nose like he's praying, I know exactly how he feels.

"*Ich habe etwas gefunden!*" Häupl shouts.

"What's that mean?" Ratner leaps from the edge of the table.

"He says he found something," translates Schweiger, still holding his phone.

"*Ein metall sechsecks . . .*" Häupl calls out to his team. "A metal hexagon of some kind. Is this what you were looking for?"

"*Ja, ja,*" I reply.

There are smiles all around the room. Hamed claps me on the shoulder.

Häupl and his team bring out their explosive swab kits and a fiber-optic camera to get a better look at the device.

Our reaction is muted while we wait for the results. While we're safe here, our Austrian friends could still be in peril.

Häupl looks up from a handheld monitor. "It doesn't appear to be explosive. But we will proceed cautiously."

"Please do. And thank you," I reply.

"No, thank you." He nods, then turns back to dismantling the device.

Carver sees my grim face. "What's the matter? I've never seen someone proven so right." He steals a glance at Ratner.

Ratner gives me a shrug and pockets his phone. I guess he's decided not to finish covering his ass.

"Do you understand what this means?" I ask.

Ratner replies gravely, "Yeah, I do." He looks over at Carver. "They could have killed the pope anytime they wanted. Instead of some electronic what-not, that could have been a wall full of shape charges and metal bearings. If they just wanted to kill him, they'd have done it already. Blackwood's right. They want to ruin him first by making him look insane or possessed before they do the big number. The real showstopper." He points to the map of Miami on the wall. "There will be one hundred thousand people inside that stadium and another two hundred thousand right outside it. And who knows how many more millions watching around the world." He shakes his head, staring right at me. "Christ. Jesus Christ. This is going to be bad, isn't it?"

Ratner may be an asshole, but he's not an idiot. Even he can see the situation we're in.

I shake my head in return. "It started by turning a sheriff into a homicidal maniac and blowing up a church using human fat. I have no idea how this is going to end."

59

AFTER WE'VE TAKEN this upstairs to our respective superiors, we regroup to assess how circumstances have changed.

One thing is certainly different: I've earned some respect around here. Nobody can deny the threat posed by somebody who was able to smuggle a large electronic warfare device into one of the most heavily protected museums in the world.

"Our adversary has nearly infinite resources," I explain to the task force. "She's wealthy, she has men ready to die for her and she makes it a daily habit to evade the United States government. X-20 has rapidly become one of our biggest security threats because of her. We can't underestimate her."

"Bin Laden tried to kill US presidents, as did Hussein," interjects Ratner.

Seriously? I still have to plead my case to him? "Bin Laden was operating from a cave in the middle of nowhere, in constant hiding. Marta Rodriguez has a two-hundred-foot yacht and walks openly in the streets of Mexico." Or she did, until I ID'd her. But I don't have to point this out. "The financial resources under her control are probably in the billions. If you can imagine it, she can buy it. We've lost wars to countries with less resources."

"Crap. The Atomic Colombian scenario." Carver sighs in frustration. He notices some blank stares and elaborates. "That was one of our fears in the '90s. What would happen if a cartel got hold of a nuclear device? Obviously there'd be no profit in it for them. But if they wanted a bargaining chip in case of capture, a warhead would be hard to argue with. It turned out to be mostly an empty threat, because most of those guys didn't even have high school educations and wouldn't know an isotope from a popsicle. That said, it was a concern." He looks to me. "Is a WMD a potential threat here?"

Oh, fuck.

My mind never even went there.

I think this through out loud. "I don't know. I wouldn't suspect that's the case. Although she was able to arrange for a large amount of C4 to show up in my basement, putting over a hundred civilians in the line of fire. I think this is personal. This will likely be an attack on the pope directly. She has no problem harming bystanders, but they're not her target. As far as I know. But let's not rule anything out. I guess we need to at least make the CIA aware of this."

"Why didn't she take her shot before?" Carver points out.

I'd been trying to put myself inside Marta's head. It's one thing to dissect methods after the fact, like I had to do with the Warlock. This is different. The means aren't as important as the motive. What does she want? "She wants something public. She doesn't just want to kill the man, she wants to take out the entire concept of the papacy. She wants to destroy the idea. She wants to destroy his mind before she destroys his body."

"I think you've lost us there," Ratner interrupts. "Her people are Catholics for the most part. Why would any of them in X-20 support her in this?"

"First of all, I don't think the bulk of X-20 knows what's going on. Second, I imagine they feel a stronger allegiance to their gang than to anything else. Tixato, their biggest recruiting ground, feels very betrayed by the Church and the government. Believe it or not, Marta is one of the biggest benefactors there and in other areas. She's won those people over with orphanages and schools. Not to mention buying off politicians. But third, these people are just as complicated as anyone else. Mexican socialists tried to drive the Catholic Church out of Mexico a hundred years ago. Wherever one group has power, another group resents that power. According to intelligence, many X-20 hardliners practice indigenous beliefs. A lot of them felt abandoned when an earthquake hit the region. X-20 is their religion."

"So what's she going to do?" Carver brings things back to the point at hand.

"I don't know. This all has to be building toward something. Right now she has the pope questioning his own sanity. Inside the Vatican they're actually debating if he's possessed or not. Far-fetched as that seems, even Mother Teresa once subjected herself to an exorcism. Even the Church's most famous members believe they're vulnerable. This is something Marta has worked on for years.

"If I had to take a guess, the method of murder she's devised will be something dramatic, even biblical, in nature. When she can get someone else to do the killing, like Sheriff Jessup, or get Groom to kill himself, she'll do that. But with the Pope, I think it's about striking at his innermost fear. Right now he's doubting himself. When it's time to kill him . . ." I pause for a moment. "She'll want him, and everyone who witnesses it, to believe God has passed judgment on him."

"And not Satan?" Ratner asks half seriously.

I ignore his tone. "The attacks at the church and Groom's suicide all have the overt implication that a demon was involved. The trouble with the Bible is that it's hard to tell the difference between an angel and a demon from their acts alone. Archangel Gabriel is supposed to bring about the destruction of Jerusalem. Sodom and Gomorrah were visited by angels before God destroyed them.

"Rodriguez is toying with people who literally believe this. If she had just killed them outright, she wouldn't have the satisfaction of them thinking in their dying moments that they are bound for hell. In a sense, she's trying to destroy their souls. In the case of the pope, she wants him to think he's finally experiencing God's wrath."

Ratner groans. "Oh, so we're looking for a weapon of wrath."

"Remember, it's not about how we see it. It's about what the pope experiences and what that means. She's been very careful with her methods so far, so she can instill a sense of the supernatural. But, yes, it will be some kind of weapon of wrath."

I look around the room. There are more than a few unconvinced faces. "Think about it this way: You've heard all the horrible ways that drug cartels torture and kill people. Even the extremes the mafia goes to. It's not just for show. The people who run these organizations succeed by thinking of the most horrific and dramatic way to kill their enemies. It's not just advertising. They enjoy this. Marta is very smart, very rich and about the most sadistic person you can imagine.

"We can do the standard security screenings, although I doubt our bomb sniffers or sniper lookouts can spot what she's up to. This is going to be unconventional in the extreme."

Carver shakes his head. "The White House has been very clear they want this visit to proceed. Unless we have a credible reason to think there's going to be an attack at the festival, we can't call off his appearance. Do you think we can find some shred of proof?"

We can't wait for the evidence to be a dead man. "I don't know. We can show that he's been targeted, but there's no clear proof that he's going to be a target here."

"What do we do? If you don't think he's going to be killed in any way we understand, how can we stop that from happening?" Ratner complains.

I've been thinking about this a lot lately. Despite the question of whether or not he was involved in Marty's death thirty years ago, the pope is still a guest of the United States and it's my duty to protect him, even if it means putting my own life on the line. I've had to do perp walks where the people we transferred were some of the most heinous you could imagine: child killers and serial murderers. Still, we'd put them in bulletproof vests because there was a chance someone might take a shot at them. Even for dirtbags like that, we'd form a human shield in open spaces to guard them. Our lives were used to protect theirs.

"I think we only have one choice." I try to find the right way to express what I'm thinking. "We let her succeed."

60

"THE DEAD MAN Walks," I say out loud to the room of Secret Service agents. They're looking at me like they looked at Ratner after his "monkey balls" outburst. "That's what we have to do." I'm speaking more to myself than to them as I frantically work out the details in my mind.

"We have to let Marta think she has a chance of killing the pope. Putting him inside some obvious bulletproof cage will only cause her to change her attempt to some other opportune time. While our lives would be easier if we knew this assassination attempt wasn't going to happen on US soil, that only passes the buck on to some other foreign government who, I'm almost certain, will be even less equipped to stop it from happening.

"Paradoxically, the only way I can see us stopping her is by letting her proceed, but under conditions we carefully control, with safeguards that are invisible to Marta and her people."

"'The Dead Man Walks'?" Carver is still confused.

"My grandfather is a stage magician. He wanted to perform the most dangerous illusion in magic. Not an illusion that *looks* dangerous, like escaping from a straitjacket while dangling from a burning rope, but an illusion that's actually killed more magicians than any other."

"The bullet catch?" Carver asks.

"Yes. Precisely. Grandfather figured out a very dramatic

NAME OF THE DEVIL

presentation that, to this day, no one has replicated or even fully explained. Even the gunman had no idea how it worked. The curtains would go up on Grandfather standing off to the side of the stage, blindfolded, with his back to a post. Like a third-world execution. A paper target would be suspended a few feet in front of his body.

"The marksman he used for this illusion was a celebrated Korean War sniper who had something like two hundred confirmed kills. He would load and secure his own rifle. He brought the bullet himself. He would even sign it in front of the audience.

"Grandfather would stand there in his tuxedo, puffing away on his cigar, and count down from ten. You could see the beads of sweat on the sniper's forehead. The entire theater was silent. Nobody even breathed.

"The marksman would aim and at the count of one, squeeze the trigger. The rifle would fire, the target would puncture, and Grandfather would stagger offstage as if he'd been mortally wounded. He did this every single night of a European tour. Each audience was sure they'd seen the last of him. The curtains would fall to the sound of their stunned gasps. Moments later, the curtain would rise, and he'd come back onstage unharmed. The crowd would leap to their feet, relieved he was alive. To prove the bullet passed through him, he'd hand his shooter a knife and ask him to carve the bullet out of the wooden post.

"Grandfather never touched the gun or the bullet. But somehow the bullet went through the target, and his body, to lodge in the post. It was in a sense, a perfect illusion."

"Sounds dangerous as hell," says Hamed.

"It was. But never for Grandfather. The one thing he counted on was the sniper not missing. Even then, though, Grandfather would have been fine."

"Sounds like a great trick. How does that help our situation?" Ratner protests. He's still fighting with me and unhappy with the attention I'm getting.

"The trick came about after my grandfather got into a discussion with someone about Lincoln's assassination. He declared he could create the perfect bullet-catch illusion, one where even the man pulling the trigger would have no idea how it was pulled off. The rifle, the bullet, they really were all the sniper's. He was more baffled than anyone else. He knew he'd shot my grandfather, yet every night, after the bullet was fired, Grandfather would stumble offstage then walk back on unharmed.

"I think we can adopt the idea behind the Dead Man Walks here. We want the illusion of vulnerability. Certainly we'll need to make it look like we're taking some precautions. If Marta doesn't see some security people in obvious positions, proof that we're treating this like a potential conventional assassination attempt, her suspicions may be raised, causing her to call off the attempt."

"What would be so bad about that?" Trust Ratner to try and pass the buck down the line.

"She can get him anytime she wants. The safest thing is to let her try when we're prepared. Remember, she was willing to kill a hundred people in my building to cover up her plans. If she can't get the pope by himself, she might do something later when people aren't expecting it, involving much more collateral damage."

"So how do we set this up?" replies Carver. I'm glad not all the team leaders are like Ratner.

"We need to bring in the expert himself." I had hoped to come up with a different solution, but there doesn't seem to be any other choice. "I can get my grandfather to come in and help us out. If we show him the staging arrangements, I think he can give us some advice on how to pull this off."

"Hold up," Ratner interrupts. "You're assuming the pope will even go for this?"

I'm sure Oberst will be onboard. "I think they'll go along with this. I've already been contacted by someone affiliated with the Swiss Guard. They'd very much like an expedient end to this situation."

I continue, "But even with this solution, we still have two more problems: protecting the crowd and catching Rodriguez. I have a hunch she's going to want to be here for this. I think she wants to see this firsthand to get the closure she needs.

"We're going to need to evacuate people as quickly as we can if something happens. And if we don't catch her entering the stadium, finding her as she leaves will be a nightmare. Ideally, we find her beforehand."

"We've got almost nothing on her," Carver complains.

"True, but we're working on getting more information from someone who was inside her organization. One thing I think we should track down is the whereabouts of her yacht. It was registered under the name *Marty,* but likely has a different one by now. This could be her base of operations. It's mobile and can go out of jurisdictions quickly. Find the yacht, we might find her."

"I'll get someone on it," offers Ratner. Like it, or not, advance work is his wheelhouse. I just hope he takes it seriously.

"That brings us back to the crowd. We need to protect a quarter-million people from whatever takes place. If we save the pope but lose one life to a stampede we could have prevented, we've failed."

WOLVES

"SOMETIMES THEY'RE NAKED," the odd little girl confided to me as I sat at her play table reading *The Marvelous Land of Oz*, which I found on her shelf. Two years older than me, she was eager to tell me all the things that happened under that roof.

She whispered this to me, revealing the strange world of adults as one child does with another. My house had its own secrets, although nothing as sensational as naked moonlight rituals on the lawn.

Grandfather was in the study with Dad, Devalo, Basso and several other men who'd come for the spiritual session. I was squirreled away in the attic room with the mysterious girl. We both were happy to have someone to talk to who was close to our own age. But we were also equally shy around strangers.

Her hair jet black like my own, she had pale skin and seemed thinner than I was. Her room was immaculate, with each doll and book in its precise location on her shelf. I would find out much later she was Father Devalo's illegitimate daughter, presented as his niece.

"They go into the room and place their hands on the table and hold hands. Even the men," she continued. "They dim the lights and light a candle. That's when it happens."

"What happens?" I wasn't sure if this was play mysterious, like the dancing skeletons in our stage show, or like the spooky stories kids shared at sleepovers.

"Voices. Lots of funny voices."

"What kind of voices?" I asked, in my head conjuring up cartoon voices.

"Dead people. They go in there to talk to dead people."

This was definitely the spooky kind of story, but even at seven I was a hard scare. I focused on the part of the story that was more disturbing to me. "Naked?"

She gave me a knowing look. "Not when it's just the men. That's the other times." She points out of her window. "They form a circle out there in the dark under the stars. They all get naked. And then they do stuff." She smirks at the ridiculousness of adults.

I didn't want to know what kind of stuff. "Have you ever been there when the voices spoke?"

At that age, ghosts were more interesting to me than naked, cavorting adults. Now that I think of it, they still are.

"Lots of times. Sometimes they speak to me when I'm all alone," she replied in a hushed tone. "They often bring me presents. Want to see?" She walked over to a shelf and pulled down a small, colored-glass teddy bear. "You like?"

I took it from her hands and pretended to admire it, but even as a kid I didn't have much patience for silly toys. A bookshelf contained far more treasures for me.

"Do you have one like it?" She watched my face for envy.

"Like what?" I replied as I vanished it from my closed fist. I'd mastered the red sponge ball trick when I was five. I was not expert at seven, but I was good enough to fool a nine-year-old.

The girl's eyes widened and she took several steps back, mouth gaping. "You have the gift," she murmured.

"No, I don't." I thought she meant the bear.

I stepped toward her to complete the trick, but she flung her hands out to protect herself. "Don't touch me!" she hissed.

I reached behind her ear to produce the bear. "It's just a trick."

She jumped back into the corner of her bed, staring down at me like I was a giant spider. I tried to hand her the bear, but she wouldn't take it. I walked over to her shelf and returned it to where it came from. Her eyes followed me all the way, waiting for something else to happen.

"It's just a magic trick," I explained again as I sat down at the small table.

She remained cowering on her bed. "It's black magic. It's evil."

"No, it's not. There's no such thing." I was getting tired of defending myself. I'd seen strange outbursts before and was beginning to think she might be "special."

The girl made a strange hand gesture with her outstretched first finger and pinky in my direction. At that same moment the lights flickered. Someone downstairs let out a loud scream. She pulled herself even more tightly into the corner.

Footsteps came pounding down the hall and the door flung open. "Jessica! We're leaving," shouted Dad as he grabbed my arm.

From outside I heard tires squealing as a car raced away. In the house below there was yelling. Grandfather's voice was loudest, but I couldn't understand what he was saying.

Dad led me down the stairs and into the hallway. Devalo was yelling at Grandfather and pointing to the séance room, his hands contorted into the same frantic gesture the little girl had made.

"You swore to me you wouldn't bring your black magic here!" he roared. "Now! Now! Look what you've done!"

Grandfather swore under his breath and turned toward us. "Let's go."

Inside our car, he gunned the accelerator, tearing down the driveway. I turned to look back, and saw the silhouette of the little girl watching from her attic window.

"Think it worked?" asked Dad.

"The way he tore out of there?" replied Grandfather. "I don't think they'll be fucking with us again."

"I thought you were just going to produce the ring on the table."

"I figured the hand and the dress would get the point across."

"I never saw it coming," Dad admitted.

"Of course you didn't. If you knew what was going to happen, it would have killed the whole thing. The dumb, superstitious bastards." Grandfather lodged a cigar in his mouth, lit it, then cocked his arm across the back of the passenger seat. He tossed me a wink over his shoulder. "Never fuck with wolves."

61

Over two decades later I watch the wolf order a crew around the festival stage in Miami. The gates are about to open and the pope is due to land in an hour. Time is running out.

"Will it work?" Lives are riding on us. Grandfather, to his credit, took this very seriously. Whatever drama there is between us was set aside to pull this off.

"Have I ever disappointed you?" he asks with mock exasperation.

I let out a small cough and fold my arms.

"Yeah, I guess I don't come out looking good on that one. It'll work. Magic, I take seriously."

"It's a little more involved than grave robbing and smuggling a corpse out of Sicily so you can drop its hand on a table in a blackout."

Grandfather looks up from the blueprints on the table in front of him and narrows his eyes at me. "I always said you saw everything." It's more a compliment than a dig for being nosey.

"Did you guys do what I thought you did?"

Grandfather nods. "If it's as bad as you think."

"Why?" I ask as he motions for me to join him offstage.

"Long version or short version?"

"Short version."

"I was broke."

"Okay. Long version," I reply.

"They fucked with us, They threatened you." Grandfather stops and leans against the steps on the side of the stage. "I'm a shitty grandfather. Just telling you that doesn't change things, it only makes them worse; I'm telling you I see the problem, but also saying I ain't going to do anything about it. But understand this, as horrible as I may be at that, you're as dear to me as a daughter. More so than my fuck-up sons. I'd have slit Basso's throat if he hadn't promised to lay off. I'd have cut it right there on the séance table. I would have shoved his dead cunt of a mother's hand down his throat and choked him with the burial gown."

He's an old man now, but his skin still flushes, his eyes filling with rage at the memory.

"These were mobsters, who kill people and make threats all day long," I point out, trying to understand why he went to such great lengths to not just get Basso to lay off, but to scare him.

"They were superstitious, Jessica. They were stupid. I exploited that." He waves his hands, which are now weathered but still possess their dramatic elegance, around the stage. "Sometimes we can use our powers for good. Sometimes we use them for good to protect bastards too, I guess."

I stare at the stage as he gestures and pray that our plan will work. Then I glance across the empty field, hoping we've done everything we can to protect the people that are soon going to be filling the stadium.

Grandfather sees where I'm looking. He puts a light hand on my shoulder. "The only reason these people stand a chance is because of you."

"I just wish there was another way to draw her out," I persist. "There will be so many people here."

"You said it yourself. If she doesn't think she got him here, next time there'll be a lot more collateral damage. We have the advantage now. Next time it will be too late."

"I hope you're right."

"Me too. I don't need the death of the pope and all these people on my conscience. If you need me, I'll be back at the hotel getting drunk." He gives my shoulder a squeeze.

"I wish I could join you."

"No you don't." Grandfather takes a deep breath. "You belong out here. This is what you were meant to do, I guess. I wish it paid more."

There's no mention of our discussion at the airport. In my family, life is a freight train that keeps moving forward. You simply acknowledge that it's moving and charge ahead.

I give him a kiss on his cheek, trying to dodge the thin mustache that always tickled me as a child. And failing.

"You're the man I always wanted to be," he jokes.

62

A HUNDRED THOUSAND HEADS turn to the blue sky and see it . . . a hell-bound meteor spewing curls of smoke, red flames licking its surface as it streaks toward the stadium.

First it was a speck, pointed out by the crowd in the highest seats, and as it moves it grows larger, an angry plume arcing through the air from the sun.

First we could see it. Now we can hear it.

The sound is so loud that I feel its echo in my chest.

People are stunned and confused. Some shriek in fright. Others think this is some kind of pyrotechnic display. The pope, standing onstage at the far end of the stadium, pauses his speech to look up. Calmly, he cavalierly remarks, "I guess they started a little early."

His comment reassures the audience that this is all part of the show.

They begin to cheer.

I run to my assigned position and ask myself what if this is how the world will end, with a stadium wave?

The black ball of fire and ash closes in, flying low over the heads of the audience. Opening his arms wide, the pope is engulfed in flames.

The roof of the stage collapses in a massive inferno. Flaming debris falls into the buffer between the crowd and the stage.

Fire-retardant foam shoots out from a specially placed sprinkler system. People begin to panic.

Over the loudspeakers, a prerecorded message from the pontiff politely instructs spectators to leave in an orderly manner. Orchestral music plays in the background, as if this is a routine announcement.

"Is he alive?" a woman near me shouts.

"Crazy show," replies her boyfriend.

I'll say.

Uniformed police officers line the aisles, guiding the crowd with illuminated batons as they make a somewhat orderly rush for the exits. Disabled and elderly audience members, culled from the vulnerable exits before the event began, are ushered out through the stadium's back corridors. No one is getting trampled or hurt, at least that I can see. But it's still chaos.

I look back at the collapsed stage. The whole structure was designed to contain whatever came at the pope. Underneath its floor is a deep vat filled with water, designed as a scaled-up version of the explosion buckets used by bomb squads to suppress an explosion. There's no earthshaking tremor or spray of steam.

The pope-killer missile is dead.

But there's still no word over the radio about him, or about his would-be assassin.

I know Marta is here somewhere.

This was supposed to be her moment. This is what she's been waiting for ever since the night her brother was killed.

"Unit five, are the exits covered?" I anxiously call into my radio headset.

The only response is an ear-splitting warble. I switch to the open channel. It's filled with the strange noise as well.

I run to the nearest uniformed officer, who is still steering people out of the stadium. "Does your radio work?" I call out.

She shakes her head and mouths, "No."

I wind my way through the stadium and put on the orange vest I'd been concealing in my backpack. I'm disguised as another festival-goer in T-shirt, a light track jacket and jeans, with the aim of flushing Marta out from her hiding spot—so far to no avail.

"Bentler!" I yell at an FBI field agent keeping a careful watch on the tunnel leading to the parking lot. "Your radio work?"

"No! We're being jammed!"

Christ. This was something we hadn't accounted for. I've got no way to contact any of the other people working with me. I don't even know if the pope survived our stunt.

The goal was to use Grandfather's Dead Man Walks illusion to create the effect of vulnerability. The problem is that it's too effective from where I'm standing. I have no way of knowing if it worked. All I can do is count on everyone else doing their jobs. The papal protection detail has their assignment. The crowd-control units are effectively shepherding the confused people out of the stadium and into the overflow area we've made in the parking lot.

I only had one job: to find Marta Rodriguez. And I failed.

Our plan—my mission—was to arrest her before this all began. For the last five hours I've been combing through the stands, section by section, and walking the floor. I must have looked at a hundred thousand faces. More than a few resembled hers. I even had our security team discreetly approach a half-dozen women that could have been her. None of them panned out. When the fireball roared out of the sky, I knew my best chance had passed.

I push my way through a corridor leading toward the exit, keeping close to the walls so I don't cause a fight. Of all the options for a quick and anonymous getaway, this would be an ideal one. Thousands of cars are parked just a few yards away, and the street beyond leads to US 1, which goes all the way to New York. If Marta wanted to make a covert exit, she could have a driver pick her up here and transfer her to a spot near the gate, from where she could make it to the outside streets without waiting hours for all the cars to leave. And this is just one of a hundred different scenarios. She could just keep walking on foot. She could get into a vehicle and stay hidden for hours. Maybe she never even came here at all.

I'm counting on her being motivated by her desire for personal satisfaction. She *needed* to be here. I also think she'll do anything to avoid being apprehended. She's not a risk taker who would chance getting caught in the open or during a random vehicle search. Those are the kinds of odds you pay underlings to take for you.

To the left of the main vehicle exit is a roped-off area where the media village is located. A dozen news trucks are parked in a semicircle, their frustrated crews trying to figure out why they can't speak to their headquarters. The jammer has affected everything.

The only purpose of disrupting our communications would be to enable her exit. She's got to be here.

Somewhere.

I search the sea of thousands of faces.

I look for the unusual.

Across the parking lot I notice five tall Hispanic men walking quickly in a tight pack. Evenly spaced apart from each other, they're moving in a cluster pattern—the way you would move to protect someone in the middle.

I run after them. A cop on a Segway yells at me to slow down, but I flash my badge and tell him to follow me.

The bodyguards are almost halfway across the parking lot. Somehow I have to fight my way through the throngs of people without letting Marta or her security detail know that I've spotted her.

I'm just a hundred feet away when one of the men sees me. He pulls a gun from his belt and aims it in my direction.

"Get down!" I shout at the top of my lungs.

63

GLASS SHARDS SPRAY my chest as Marta's bodyguard fires through the windows of the GM Yukon standing between us. I dive to the ground and return two rounds into his ankles underneath the chassis. Blood spurts onto the pavement and he crumples with a scream.

"Get back!" I yell to a group of college kids walking toward their cars. They look at me, confused, then see the pistol in my hand and run the other way. I spring to my feet and bolt around the truck to see my shooter still writhing on the ground. Dressed in cargo shorts, sandals and a T-shirt, he looks like any other concertgoer—with the exception of the Glock he's gripping in his right hand as he tries to stem the flow of blood with his left. I stomp down hard on his arm, pinning the gun to the asphalt and probably breaking his wrist.

The cop on the Segway comes to a stop behind me. I rip the gun from the wounded man's fingers and hand it to the officer. "Take this! Hold him!"

Marta and her entourage, now one short, are almost at the far end of the parking lot. Two of her men peel off and take defensive positions behind parked vehicles, ready to shoot if I continue my pursuit. There are thousands of people swirling around us. A stray bullet stands a better chance of hitting someone than not, and I can't keep up this chase without expecting an innocent person to get hurt.

I holler into my radio, "This is Blackwood! I have the target in sight! Anybody read this?" The continued garble of the jammer is the only reply.

Damn!

In none of our scenarios did we think about losing the ability to talk to each other. We can't even call an ambulance! We need roadblocks. I need backup. But I can't reach anyone!

Marta will be on US 1, headed toward I-95, in just a few minutes. The arena is far enough from civilization that we could trap her between here and the Everglades, but we're running out of time. Damn it. The jammers are a clever idea, I have to give it to her. She knew pandemonium would erupt when the pope was killed, and to assure her escape she blocked our radios, effectively shutting down our entire ability to respond. Military units have practical contingencies for this. Civilian agencies do not. The last thing anyone expects is a bad guy who drops a half-million dollars on a black-market Russian jamming system.

Everything about Marta is unconventional. I shouldn't be surprised. If I can't speak to the other agencies soon, she could disappear forever.

A wind kicks up as a news helicopter flies into position overhead. A cameraman, buckled to the door, leans out to aim his high-power lens at the wounded shooter and the cop standing over him.

He's got a better point of view than I do.

I shout and wave my gun and badge at the Channel 8 copter. The pilot swings it around so his camera operator can get a better view. I furiously gesture to an empty patch of grass at the edge of the parking lot. He gets it and gives me a thumbs-up.

Landing here probably violates a million different FAA rules, but the pilot doesn't seem too bothered as he brings the craft down with the passenger-side door opened toward me. My long black hair tumbles wildly in the downwash as I charge across the grass to hop inside. The chopper climbs up fifty feet as soon as I close the door. I don't think the pilot has to be told we're a danger to the swarming crowd on the ground.

"You call an Uber?!" he shouts over the roar of the rotors. He has the rugged good looks and cocky grin of a test pilot or a race-car driver. I can see why he went ahead with the risky landing.

I pull on a closed-circuit headset to talk to him. "Do you have radio?"

"Negative!" he replies. "We can't receive or transmit."

"Put an empty channel on the intercom."

He flips through a row of switches and my earphones are filled with the annoying warbling. Even out here at the edge of the parking lot, we're still blocked. A military-grade jammer can blanket several miles. As long as Marta's machine is operating, we're out of the game.

For a fleeting moment I entertain the notion of telling the pilot to chase after Marta. Without ground support to make an apprehension or any means of communication, however, this could prove stupid, possibly deadly. Even if we do spot her, we could quickly escalate into a hostage situation with no units nearby. At the moment, public safety is my priority.

"Fly a loop around the stadium!" I shout to him. "Look for anything antenna-like!"

"Affirmative!" I can tell he's had combat experience, and realizes what's going on with the jammer. I'm pretty sure he also knows what I intend to do.

The helicopter banks to the side as he twists the stick, taking us on a circular path around the structure. I put my gun back in my holster and listen closely to the noise coming through the radio. As we change direction, the pitch alters slightly. I swear it's getting louder. I scan the ground below us for the jammer. It could be disguised in anything: a box truck, a large SUV. We'd screened the parking lot vehicles for explosives with dogs

and radiation detectors, but there was nothing stopping someone from driving a work van into the lot with a hollowed-out
industrial-sized air conditioner strapped inside.

The warbling changes in pitch again and starts to recede. "Go
back!" I yell over the noise.

The pilot turns us around, and I continue to search among
the cars and trucks for something that could contain a jammer.
Hundreds of faces below stare up to watch us circle the area.

"What about that?" calls out the cameraman from the back.
He points toward a tall light stand attached to a portable generator. A suspicious cable stretches from the metal casing to the top
of the mast without connecting to any of the lights.

This might be it. I can't call it in. I have to take care of it myself.
"Drop me as close to the ground as you can!"

The pilot lowers the skids a few feet above the roof of an Escalade. I yank off the headset and open the door. It's still a long way
to the top of the truck.

I jump anyway.

64

I HIT THE ROOF, skid down the windshield and hit the ground, barely managing to land without diving face-first into the pavement. The crowd gives me confused looks. I catch my balance and my breath and run toward the suspicious piece of equipment without the foggiest notion of how I'm supposed to deactivate it. I ignore the screaming pain in my ankles. I don't even know how to tell if this is the jammer, or just a piece of construction gear.

Up close, the generator looks like any other. A keyed switch is in the on position and a green light is glowing. The control panel is locked behind a metal door. There's no way for me to know if I've found it, so I have to make an educated guess that, because the motor is running and the lights aren't on, this is the jammer. I circle the machine, looking for a vulnerable spot. At its rear there's a punched metal grill where the exhaust is located. I stand back and shoot three rounds into the engine compartment.

Defiantly, the motor keeps humming. Two muscle-bound men in cut-off shorts and tank tops flip-flop over to check out the crazy bitch with the gun. I flash them my badge, about to tell them to step back, and get an idea.

"Help me turn this over," I command as I holster my weapon. "Grab the trailer hitch."

"Whatever you say, darling. You're the one with the gun," replies the tanner of the two.

Together we lift the metal hitch and tilt the entire generator backwards. The weight from the light mast, thirty feet in the air, begins to work in our favor. With one last shove, the entire tower topples, crashing into the trunk of a blue Hyundai.

"Stand back!" I yell. I don't know if the thing will explode into flames from the spilled fuel. I grab the cable that runs along the mast and yank it free from its connection inside the housing, realizing too late the smart thing would have been to use my jacket as an insulator to avoid electrocution. Thankfully, I'm not shocked.

"This is Blackwood. Copy?" I call into my radio. The warbling sound is gone.

"Blackwood, this is Knoll. We were having a comm problem."

Thank God it worked. I give a thumbs-up to my muscular helpers, who probably have no idea what our act of vandalism accomplished.

"I think I fixed it. I spotted Rodriguez. She was heading east on 122nd Street with four Hispanic males. I think she's headed toward a vehicle. Copy?"

"Affirmative."

The news helicopter still hovers overhead. "I'm going to try to make visual contact. Copy?"

"Roger that."

I run back toward the Escalade and flag down the pilot, who had clearly been watching the whole thing. He swings the door open and once more brings the chopper down as close to the top of the vehicle as he can. I grip the inside handle and place a foot on the skid, then pull myself inside.

"Head due east!" I tell him. "We're to pursue at a safe distance until Miami-Dade can get a copter here. Understood?"

"Affirmative," replies the pilot as he guns the craft in the direction I'd last seen Marta heading.

A sea of people below us floods through the parking lot and

into the auxiliary lots. The lines of departing vehicles stretch half a mile into the stadium parking area. I can't see Marta letting herself get stuck in that.

"Head toward there!" I point toward a residential area on the other side of the highway. One of my working theories is that she has a car waiting there so she can avoid the packed onramp and get on the freeway somewhere else.

We fly over the highway, above the hordes filtering through the traffic jams toward the neighborhoods where they parked.

"Keep a lookout for anyone driving across medians or going the wrong way to get out of here," I say over the intercom to the cameraman and pilot.

Row after row of houses roll past underneath us. I search the streets for some sign of Marta and her protectors. If they made it to a car already, she'll be almost impossible to find.

"There!" shouts the pilot. He's clearly been involved in enough high-speed pursuits to know what we're looking for.

A black BMW has just blown through a stop sign and is now racing down the opposite side of the street to get past a line of cars waiting their turn at an exit. It could be some random asshole, but it's the only lead I've got.

"Black BMW heading east toward Hyacinth," I report into the radio.

"Roger. What is your position?" asks Knoll.

"In pursuit in the Channel 8 chopper."

"Of course." I can imagine Knoll shaking his head on the other end.

"BMW just made a left turn onto 42nd Avenue. Heading north now," I update.

"North?"

"Affirmative." The nearest turnpike onramp is in the other direction. So are the main arterial roads that will take her into Miami. Where the hell is she headed?

"We've got ground units in pursuit," Knoll explains.

I look below, but don't see any police cars on the road. "Keep following. Not too close," I tell the pilot.

"Roger."

The BMW turns into an industrial area. I flip through my pocket map, trying to see where she might be going. I'd circled down a number of contingent situations.

One pops out. "This is Blackwood. Set up a roadblock at Exeter Executive Airport. I think that's her destination."

"Roger that."

"Can you get a phone line here?" I ask the pilot.

He points to an iPhone connected to the console. "Just dial in there."

I pull up the FAA direct number for the airport control tower on my phone, then dial it in on his.

"Exeter operations."

"This is Agent Blackwood with the FBI. What craft do you presently have cleared for takeoff?"

"We have a Cessna trainer taxiing and a private jet prepping now."

"Is the hatch still open on the jet?"

"Affirmative. They radioed in and said they're waiting for a crew member before departing."

"Tower, do not let them leave! Ground all craft. We're going to be making a landing."

"Who is this again?"

"I'll tell you in person," I respond, and end the call. Then I turn to the pilot. "You mind going the extra mile?"

He flashes me an adventurous grin. "What do you need?"

65

Marta's car continues toward the airport. Police units appear in the distance, but are at least a mile back. I tell myself that at least they have her retreat blocked, for what it's worth. But I know this will not go down without bloodshed.

In the air we've been tailing her from a distance, trying not to alert her, but the whoop of the sirens has probably spoiled that.

I make a gut decision. I can't just be a passive observer. Out here, at least, we're away from the crowds at the stadium. I point out the airfield to the pilot. "We need to keep her jet from taking off. I need you to land me as close as you feel is safe."

There's a nod and another flash of that grin. "We'll put you on top of the wing if you like." I get the sense he's down for anything. It's not a joke that pilots have the highest testosterone levels of any professionals. Right now, that's a good thing.

The engine roars and we shoot forward. I glance back at the cameraman. He's shooting through the closed window, to reduce our drag, but not missing a thing.

The runway comes into view as we pass over a line of warehouses, a long gray stripe of concrete that stands out from the surrounding dull green grass and shiny black plastic rooftops. The pilot aims us down the center and we race toward the cluster of hangars at its far end.

A gleaming white G5 jet sits at the edge of the tarmac, waiting for its last passenger. Two SUVs are parked on the hatch side. This isn't good. She could have armed men waiting to protect her escape.

"Come down near the cockpit!"

He banks the chopper to the side then lines us up nose-to-nose with the jet. Our skids are just a few inches off the ground.

"Check that out," urgently shouts the cameraman from the back.

I look to where he's pointing. Marta's BMW slams through a chain-link fence between hangars and skids onto the tarmac. The driver spins the car into a drift, then pulls up between the two SUVs so they flank her exit. It's a precision move, the kind of thing they teach you in the Academy. Damn it, we're dealing with professionals.

I pull my gun free. Seconds are going to matter.

"Closer?" I don't want to push the pilot more than I have to.

Without hesitating, he brings us a hundred feet from the front of the plane. I can see the pilot flipping switches in its cockpit. There's a man standing behind him with a gun tucked into his belt.

The jet lurches forward to begin a high-stakes game of chicken.

This is no time to screw around.

I kick my door open and fire into the spinning turbine of the right-side tail-mounted engine. There's an awful sound, like the tines of a giant fork catching in the blades of a blender, then billowing black smoke.

"There's a two-million-dollar rebuild," the awestruck helicopter pilot remarks.

I get a sick feeling in my stomach.

A fleet of squad cars pour onto the airfield. We pull up and away so they can surround the plane. "Get some distance," I warn him. "This could get ugly."

Drawing their weapons, uniformed officers leap out of their vehicles, pistols and shotguns cover the SUV windows and the open hatch of the jet.

Two of Marta's bodyguards pop up from behind the hood of an SUV and open fire with AR-15s. Bullets punch through the cars in front of the jet, the officers barely able to duck down in time.

"Where the hell do they think they're going to go?" My pilot nods to the tall cloud of smoke still spewing from the plane's right engine.

"I don't know." The whole situation seems a little odd. I can see bank robbers ending up in a full-blown shoot-out. I expected a smarter escape route from Marta.

She certainly slipped through our fingers at the stadium. And she almost made it this far without us realizing she'd evaded our airport screening.

She's several steps ahead.

Shit! This is her fucking plan!

"Pull back!" I shout to the pilot. I get on my radio. "Tell the units to pull back!" I scream.

"They're already under fire."

"I know. Tell them to clear the area! Now!"

Boom!

Ripping apart in the middle, the jet buckles into the air before a ball of fire consumes it. The shockwave sends us spinning. We dive to the side and almost wedge the rotors into the ground. At the last second our pilot gains control and drops us hard onto the tarmac.

A second fireball erupts when the jet's fuel tanks ignite. Two men, probably Marta's bodyguards, come running from the inferno, clothes ablaze. The police officers, fortunately shielded by their own vehicles, look shell-shocked as they retreat from the fuel fire. A twisted column of oily smoke rises into the air.

More squad cars come racing into the airport to provide backup. Somewhere, a fire engine siren wails as emergency crews hurtle down the highway toward the small airport.

I watch the jet disintegrate before my eyes. Stunned, I have to push my own reaction away and focus on the present.

No. It's not ending like this.

No fucking chance in hell.

I call into the radio. "Suspect may still be at large. Keep coverage of other critical points. I repeat, suspect may still be at large."

"What was that sound?" someone asks.

"Her plane. She must have had a bomb ready," I reply as I leap out of our helicopter to assist the men on the ground.

A police officer, bleeding from his soot-covered cheek, is kneeled over by the edge of the conflagration. I run over to drag him clear of the smoke.

He struggles to his feet and coughs. "What the hell happened?"

"I don't know. I don't know." I set him down gently by the bumper of a backup patrol car. Other responders have cleared the men closest to the explosion. I survey the wreckage and try to wrap my head around what just happened. "Ratner, are you there? Over."

"Ratner, here. What the fuck is going on over there?"

I ignore his question. "We didn't have any marked cars here. What happened to the security point we requested at all airports?"

There's a guilty pause. "I'll check on that. Is she dead?"

Damn it! I want to rip into him on the radio for everyone to hear, but now is not the time so I fight back my raging urge to cuss him out. "We don't know. What about the harbors? Did we track down her vessel?"

"Negative."

His one word answer hardly explains anything. "What do you

ANDREW MAYNE

mean? Did we do a search of area harbors for any vessels that matched the description of her craft?"

"There are a lot of boats in Miami," replies Ratner defensively.

Jesus Christ. My chest is seizing up. I need to gasp for air and scream at him at the same time. Instead, I try to respond as calmly as possible. "Lock down all the harbors."

"What?"

Calm time over. "I said lock them down! Call the harbor masters and the Coast Guard!"

"Why? Didn't she just blow herself up?"

"No!" My eyes water from the stinging smoke. "No, she didn't. She found the hole in our net and may be getting through it right now." *Thanks to you,* although I use every ounce of willpower to avoid saying this over the open radio.

66

THE OCEAN SONG, a two-hundred-foot yacht made in southern Italy, has a curious title history. First purchased by a Dubai real estate mogul before completion, the vessel was bought at a discount by a Chinese billionaire when the man from Dubai saw his property values evaporate overnight. The Chinese billionaire in turn sold the yacht to a newly minted Russian petrol magnate when he decided to go with something larger and Chinese-built.

Sergei Olanoff, current title owner of the *Ocean Song*, hasn't been seen since one of his business partners accused him of embezzling company funds. After it was discovered the Dubai mogul's final payment hadn't been made within the terms of the contract, the *Ocean Song* itself, only ever taken out for one voyage after delivery, idles in a harbor in Greece while a legal battle over ownership wrangles its way through the courtrooms of four different countries. All of this means the one-hundred-and-ninety-foot yacht named *Ocean Song*, currently sitting in the harbor of Biscayne Bay, is an impostor.

Twenty minutes of background-checking all the boats that met the *Marty*'s description would have revealed that no boat of that size titled *Ocean Song* ever left Nassau, or sailed from any of the other ports in her logs.

This revelation took just one phone call to the right person at the Coast Guard.

Ratner blew this one big time. He's been trying to compensate for his screwup by getting on the phone with every contact we have that's so much as looked at an ocean. I sit shotgun in an FBI car racing toward the hotel harbor where the *Ocean Song* is docked while he pieces together the puzzle for me over the phone.

"We got a Coast Guard vessel into the harbor," he says. "They're making the boat return now."

"Do we have ground units waiting?" I ask.

"I'll check on it."

I don't have to point out the pile of shit that's about to fall on him. If he thinks a list of phone calls is going to save his ass, he's mistaken.

I glance anxiously at the field agent driving the car. George Aguilera, a bald, mustachioed Miami native, can't go any faster. He nods to let me know he understands my frustration. We're already full throttle with a Miami-Dade marked car leading the way at one hundred miles per hour.

Knoll calls me from another car. "What's the latest?"

I'd requested him and his team down as support for the festival operation. It felt like overkill at first. Now I realize it wasn't enough. "The jet is still too hot to search. They've visually ID'd several bodies. Potentially a female that could be Marta."

"What do you think?"

I don't know Marta, but I get her scent, if that's any way to explain it. "I think any woman that would put a bomb in a crowded apartment complex wouldn't think twice about killing her own double if it covered her tracks. The bomb was remotely triggered, I'm sure. We're tracking down cell phone-tower data. Most likely someone told her they were under fire and she detonated remotely."

"That's evil. Is this your own guess?"

"Yeah. It's what I'd probably do."

"You've got to stop saying that. You have no idea how much it scares people."

The uncomfortable truth is that I find myself thinking more and more how evil minds work. "Then don't forget me at Christmas."

Aguilera squeals into the harbor parking lot, already full with squad cars and federal agents. I work my way through the blocked-off area toward the long pier where the fake *Ocean Song* is moored. Seventeen pissed-off-looking crew members are sitting on the dock with their hands zip-tied behind their backs. The captain is the only one not bound, and he's in a heated exchange with a Coast Guard lieutenant.

The lieutenant, an African American in his early thirties, turns to me. "You Blackwood?"

"Yes." I scan the crew on the dock. "Is this everyone?"

The captain shakes his head, realizing the severity of the situation. "We had some crew take a launch out."

"After you were told to return to harbor?" I snap.

He's not sure who I am, but can tell by the tone of my voice that I must belong here. "I didn't see it happening."

"Are you the usual captain?"

He shakes his head. "I came on in the Bahamas."

"Was it still the *Ocean Song* then?"

He gives a nervous glance at the Coast Guard lieutenant then stares at the planks of the dock. "I just drive the boat," he says weakly. The records are his responsibility. Signing off on forgeries is a crime. It doesn't matter what he does and doesn't know. He'll lose his captain's license at the very least.

The lieutenant turns to me. "His logs are a mess. We can hold him on that."

I flash my badge and come face-to-face with the captain. "Who was your passenger?"

The captain hesitates, then comes to the conclusion that

cooperation is in his best interest. "The wife of some Venezuelan businessman."

That sounds like an alias if I ever heard one. "Did she board the boat?"

"No. We were going to meet up with her in Palm Beach."

That's a good story to tell if you don't want the captain to know your full plans. I doubt any of the people here really know who Marta is. They could think she's just the wife of the absentee owner, not realizing they're working for her.

"Who left the boat?" I ask.

"Just some cleaning crew."

"Cleaning crew?" This sounds suspicious. "Was one of them a Hispanic female, mid-forties, about this high?"

"Yes."

A cleaning woman. She might as well have been invisible. I never noticed Marta at first. My own bias was used against me. I turn to the lieutenant. "How long ago did you stop the vessel?"

"Thirty minutes ago."

Damn. She could be anywhere in Miami. Once she saw the Coast Guard ship, she bailed as quickly as possible. Besides the airport diversion, she had a backup plan.

I walk out of earshot of the captain and crew to call Ratner. "We need to tell the media that we're stopping cars on all the highways and doing random spot checks."

"We can't do that," he protests in an exasperated whine. "It's almost impossible."

"I know." I'm past the point of explaining things to him. "Give out the advisory, throw up a bogus Amber Alert. Just say we're doing this. Right now, all that matters is that she thinks it's possible. The last thing she wants to do is chance getting caught in a random car inspection."

"So we bullshit."

Asshole, you haven't left us with many other options. "It's all

NAME OF THE DEVIL

we got right now. We want her to stay put. Put out the alert." It's security theater, for an audience with something to hide. This woman just blew up a forty-million-dollar jet as a diversion. She's not going to take any chances. She'd rather hide here and wait things out than find herself caught in a roadblock.

Even if we could do that kind of search, our odds of catching her would be one in a thousand. But as long as we create the impression that we're being comprehensive, far more comprehensive than we can be, she'll be extra cautious.

Knoll strides down the pier. "I take it she wasn't onboard?"

"No. But this is her boat. It's off to plan B for her."

"What's that?"

"I don't know. And we only have a limited time to find out."

67

K NOLL SPREADS A map across the trunk of a car. We all stand around—FBI, Secret Service, DEA, local police and even the Coast Guard—trying to figure out what Marta's next step is going to be. Miami cops are already locking down intersections, but there's no point in trying to stop everyone who matches Marta's general description in this part of town. Absent a photo, I'm the only one who can identify her on sight. Which is, of course, why she wanted me killed.

The computer reconstruction of what I remember, combined with her old Air Force photograph, is good. But I could see that she'd had plastic surgery done since that photo was taken. Our portrait reflects a lot of guesswork about a woman I met for maybe three minutes.

Even still, Marta knows that as the fugitive, she has everything to lose. She can't take chances by counting too much on the idea that she'll blend in. I'm sure she always keeps someone near her who is armed and capable of protecting her. She'll also want to be in constant contact with someone who will help her. If she's like other heads of cartels, Marta already has safe houses, extra bodyguards and crooked lawyers on retainer in Miami.

The map is daunting and also misleading. It gives you the idea that the problem is contained within two-dimensional boundaries, which conveniently fold up and fit in your pocket. But as my

FBI Academy instructor constantly reminded us, the map is not the territory.

There are millions of homes in these square inches. Tens of thousands of warehouses. In South Florida alone, there are several hundred known members of X-20 willing to help her. I assume she'll want to keep her distance from the street-level thugs. They are about as reliable as they are honest. While the core members may be willing to lay down their lives for her, there's no telling how her attempted assassination of the pope is going to go over among the extended members. She's smart. She's going to keep this among her captains at most. I suspect any support she calls upon is going to be most likely from outside the X-20 criminal network.

What she doesn't want to do is hole up in some crack house used by X-20 and find out that the place is already under surveillance by local law enforcement and DEA. At this point, anything directly related to X-20 is a red flag. That said, we've sent unmarked cars and plainclothes detectives to all the spots where X-20 activity has been observed in the remote chance she didn't actually have a plan B.

The Coast Guard lieutenant taps me on the shoulder. "We just got a call from the Navy. They spotted a small submarine about ten miles off the coast."

Are you fucking kidding me? "Seriously? Does she have a damn white cat and sharks with lasers?"

He gives me a sympathetic nod. "Welcome to my world."

"What happened?"

"They chased it until it surfaced. Looks to be a narco sub."

"That would have been her exit plan if you'd stopped her out at sea. She'd have gone onboard."

"Good thing we prevented her from leaving port," he replies. They could search the ship at sea and never find her if she was sitting at the bottom of the ocean in a submarine.

"Yeah." I avoid glaring at Ratner. If he'd done his homework like he said, we'd have staked out the *Ocean Song* and been able to catch her before she set foot on the pier.

Of course, there are a lot of things I could have done. I could have double-checked his homework. Hell, I could have asked about Sister Marta back in Tixato.

Enough regret. I can still get her.

Marta thought the *Ocean Song* ruse was safe because she didn't know how much we got out of Lamont. The little fact that her yacht is really called *Marty* was enough to tell us something might be at play on that front.

"The bodyguard you shot in the foot is at the hospital. He's on painkillers and talking," Knoll informs me.

"Anything helpful?" All we need is an address. One call to the SWAT team and this nightmare could be over.

"He says he's done protection for Mrs. Verdez in the past when she visited Miami."

"Verdez?"

"He thinks she's the wife of a cartel lawyer. He had no idea who she was or what was in store for him at the airport if he made it all the way there."

Interesting. Even people who work that closely with her don't know who she really is. The bodyguard knew he was protecting someone important, who was involved in something shady, but never suspected she was at the center of everything.

"We got his cell phone?"

"Yeah. We're tracking all the inbound and outbound calls." God bless Knoll and his thoroughness.

I doubt there will be anything of use to us. He was, at best, a disposable person for Marta. His purpose was to divert our attention, and to get caught if that helped her escape.

"We get anywhere with the control-tower records?"

"Still looking."

I stare at the map and get an uncomfortable thought. "That jammer?"

"Yeah?" Knoll looks at my finger on the stadium.

"That was some heavy-duty military hardware. And we still don't know where she got what she tried to use to get the pope."

"We got some military people on the wreckage. They think it was a turbine-powered drone. A Chinese knock-off."

This keeps getting worse. "She's dealing in illegal arms. Heavy-duty stuff. The kind of gear half our enemies would want to have."

"Seriously," Knoll says gravely.

"We need to get the CIA and NSA fully on this too. We keep thinking of this in the context of a rich drug dealer's behavior. She's obviously got a whole other level of connections going on."

"I agree."

The Coast Guard lieutenant speaks up, "We just pulled the harbor reports for anything that might match the vessel. About a week ago, we think the *Ocean Song* was harbored in Newport News, Virginia."

"Virginia? That's when the church exploded," replies Knoll. That's not all that far from Hawkton.

"She was there for that too . . ." My voice trails off as I spot the top of the conn tower for the *Ocean Song* sticking out above the marina. "I need to get a look onboard her yacht. This is her home away from home."

68

Molly, a bomb squad black Labrador retriever with a serious demeanor, gives me a suspicious glance before going up the gangplank to do a cursory search of the *Ocean Song* for explosives with her human partner. At almost two hundred feet long, there's a lot to cover.

While we wait for Molly and her bomb squad partners to clear the boat, we compare notes on Marta and try to get a better understanding of this woman.

Our DEA liaison, John Noriega, checks a message on his phone then speaks up. "We've had a person of interest for several years by the name of Marta Diego. Suspected money laundering. She sounds like the description the shooter you caught in the parking lot provided. Very wealthy, she's supposed to be married to an attorney with a practice out of Caracas. The interesting part is her husband is in his eighties."

"Is it a cover?" asks Knoll.

"It makes sense," replies Noriega. "When you have that amount of cash you need clever ways to launder it. The law firm could be an entire front and the marriage just a certificate to give her an identity. Operating out of Venezuela also offers a certain amount of protection from our scrutiny. When Chavez was in power, he was notorious for looking the other way when drug cartels wanted to park assets there."

Marta's ingenuity frightens me. "What do we know about this Diego?"

"She may be the actual owner of several properties around Latin America. Her law firm has created several different organizations that control the real estate." He points to the yacht. "The *Marty* is owned by a company called Vesta Norte. The board members are spread out through different countries."

"Let me guess, all lawyers?" It's a common tactic, and it makes building a case a challenge.

"Yep."

"Do we know of any properties in the United States?" If we can tie her to something here, that would help us trace her connections.

"Not tied to that firm. She's smart and likely to set up firewalls. We're looking into a European connection. Anything she has here would probably be controlled by some firm with an office in Brussels."

Noriega continues, "Your suspect, Lamont, he was caught with about one hundred thousand dollars in cocaine. When we did the seizure we found an ultraviolet barcode on the bags. According to the numbers on them, that was just part of a much larger shipment. Lab tests indicate that batch was all produced on the same day. We're looking at a quarter-billion-dollars-a-year business, just from that channel alone. Who knows how many other separate lines she has running."

There's no reason to think "Marta Diego" is her only alternate identity either. "Can we pull some credit card records?" I think for a moment, remembering the woman I met in Tixato. She had expensive tastes. "Take her photo down to the high-end shops in South Beach. Women's watches, you know the kind. See if anyone recognizes her. She's got good taste. High end but not flashy. Think more on the Hermès side than Dolce."

The men try to interpret what I just said.

"Ask your wives. Think rich, but conservative. Better yet, have some people canvass the Palm Beach stores too. We need names. She'll probably stick to the same cover story—wife of a wealthy attorney, maybe real estate money. Those are boring answers. That's her cover, anything that doesn't bring attention to herself."

"Molly didn't pick anything up," announces the detective with the bomb dog, who have both returned to the dock. "I'd like to do a more thorough search."

"Go ahead. But we're going onboard. We're going to have to risk it." I head up the gangplank and resist the urge to pat the animal on the head.

I start at the bow of the vessel where Marta's stateroom should be located. "Check out the crew quarters," I tell Knoll. "I'll bet she keeps a spare room in case they get boarded and she doesn't want to look like the owner."

Part of Marta's success is her invisibility. She exploits our own biases. If I'd knocked on the door of one of her mansions, she could have answered as the maid and I'd never have thought twice.

The main stateroom, presumably Marta's, is like a large hotel suite. A king-sized bed sits in the middle with a wall separating it from the bathroom area and a walk-in closet. I have to give her credit, the design is tasteful. Lots of wood inlay and natural materials. Nothing overtly flashy that screams drug dealer. I've been on busts where the houses look like they were designed by a cokehead flipping between *Scarface* and the Home Shopping Channel, compulsively buying whatever they see.

Even Marta's bathroom resembles something out of *Architectural Digest*. Everything is picture-perfect. Hairbrushes, makeup and perfume are stored away neatly. I touch one of the towels. It's softer than anything I've ever felt. There's a walk-in shower and a bathtub with high walls. Back in the dressing area, I search through her closets. The brands are all what an affluent woman would wear if she didn't want her outfits to scream "wealthy." They're the kind of clothes a politician's wife would own.

In the bedroom, I find a hidden door that opens to a small office. There's an empty spot for a laptop computer, which gives me an idea. Although the logbooks may be unreliable, we have other means to track where she's been. I call into my radio. "Can we get someone to check IP logs with whoever is their satellite provider? If we can't see who she was talking to, we can at least create a map of where they've been . . ." I stop mid-sentence as my eye catches something.

Behind the desk is a wall filled with photographs. Hundreds of images of young faces smiling at the camera. These are the children in the orphanages she runs. Unlike Groom's show photos, these are personal.

This is her work desk.

She likes to see their smiling faces as she controls a billion-dollar narco empire, killing people, bribing judges and trying to level my entire apartment building.

Damn, she's a complex woman.

I study the photos and see parts of the orphanage in Tixato. The Tixato photos seem to be grouped into one area. The other photos show children in what appear to be different locations.

"Who do we have that's a Latin American expert?" I ask over the radio channel.

"I've been to most places there. What do you need?" responds Noriega.

"Can you come to the stateroom? I want to figure out where all her orphanages are located."

Noriega and I sort through the photographs and put them into three piles. One is for all the Tixato photos. The second is the children whose photographs were taken in a much more rural environment. The third is for children who have features that appear similar to those of people living in the southern part of South America, like Uruguay.

Noriega holds a photo up and stares at something in the background. He snaps an image on his phone and makes a call. "Hey hon, can you do me a favor and tell me what kind of flower that is?" There's a pause. "Got it? Ah, that's it. Thank you." He puts away his phone. "What did you say they called her in Tixato?"

"Sister Marta."

"But she's not really a nun?"

"Hardly."

"I think she may have a nun fixation." He shows me the photograph of a young girl next to a white orchid with three petals.

"What am I looking at?"

Noriega points to the orchid. "That flower is the White Nun Orchid. We know the things she really wants to hide she makes sure there aren't any record of, right?"

"When she can."

"On the DEA's end, this photo helps put things together for us. We don't have any evidence of Marta Diego ever being in Guatemala. It's a black hole for her in Central America. If she goes there, it's under a different name." He points to the flower. "See that? It's the national flower of Guatemala. I think all of these children are from an orphanage there."

"So we know she's been there, but doesn't want any part of her drug empire to lead there?"

"Exactly."

Ratner knocks on the door of the stateroom. "I think you want to see this. I found it stashed in a locker." He walks over with a digital camera. "I was going through the photos, looking for one of her."

Ratner is doing anything and everything to try to make up for his screwups.

"Any luck?"

"No. But I heard you guys mention Guatemala." He shows us a picture a man with a thick mustache trying to pull a fish into the boat. Ratner points to him. "See that jerk-off catching the marlin off the stern of this boat?"

"Yeah?"

He smirks, feeling he's saved a little face. "That's Atilio Baqueró. He's the resident minister for Guatemala in Miami. The time stamp on the photo was taken a week ago. You wonder what he was he doing on this ship?"

69

ATILIO BAQUERÓ IS inside the T Lounge sipping mid-shelf vodka as he talks to a secretary for a car dealership in Hialeah. She's impressed by his diplomatic status and how connected he is to the Miami community. She doesn't mention that she's a former call girl turned DEA informant. He leaves out the part about his wife and kids in Miami Lakes.

While I'm sitting in a car outside, Noriega gives me the play-by-play over the radio as Atilio gets progressively drunker and imagines his powers of charm are only getting more potent. "He just put a hand on her knee."

"Is she going to play along?" That kind of thing would last for a millisecond with me before I'd find an excuse to break his arm.

"I think she's motivated enough."

I'm not sure what that means and I'm afraid to ask. This operation is off the books. Atilio has diplomatic immunity. We don't have anything on him other than a photograph and a hunch. We can't take him in for questioning or even stop him without causing a minor crisis that could get back to Marta.

"He's taken the bait," says Noriega. "They're going outside."

His car, a silver Mercedes Cabriolet, is parked near me in a fenced lot. I wait a few minutes for him to come stumbling along. He drops his remote as he unlocks the car. This becomes the most hilarious event in human history to him and Val as he fumbles trying to pick it up.

He never notices me getting out of my car and approaching them.

Gallantly, Atilio opens the door for her, then makes a crude joke of trying to climb over her as she fastens the seat belt. He laughs hoarsely as he walks over to the driver's side and climbs in.

On cue, Val leans over and plants a kiss on his lips. Atilio returns the gesture and grabs the back of her neck, pulling her to his side of the car. His other hand cups her breast.

He doesn't see the camera flash the first three times I take a picture—even though I made sure the flash was much larger than needed. I step closer to his window and take another shot. Val reacts in a dramatic gesture.

Atilio finally notices me. He looks confused for a moment then gets out of the car. "What are you doing, bitch?" he shouts at me in barely accented English.

I snap another photograph. "I'll bet your wife will love to see these."

He takes a step forward. "This is private business!" He flashes his diplomatic ID. "That is my wife!"

"Sure. Whatever." I take one more photo.

He swats at the camera. I pull it away and shield it with my body. Frustrated, he grabs my free wrist with one hand and raises his other to slap me.

I let the blow land on my cheek then smash the camera into the side of his head. Atilio goes to the ground cold.

Noriega comes running from around the corner and gives me an approving smile.

WHEN ATILIO COMES to, we're in a motel room a half-mile away. He gazes up from the edge of the bed at Knoll and me. "What the hell?"

"We'd like to ask you some questions," says Knoll.

"I don't have to tell you anything." He gets up and heads for the door, a little wobbly.

I stand in his way. "Mr. Baqueró, you step one foot outside that door and this is going live on every television station in Miami. It'll be front-page news tomorrow in Guatemala City."

He waves me off and replies, "Wouldn't be the first time I've been caught."

"We're not talking about the girl. Have a look." I point to the television.

Atilio turns around and sees the image on the screen. It's him grabbing my wrist and slapping me. At that point the camera is behind my back and out of view. The video was shot from an angle over a car. All you see is him argue with me then hit me.

I could have blocked the blow easily. But that wouldn't help me get Marta.

Knoll puts a hand on Atilio's shoulder and pushes him back onto the bed. "Agent Blackwood is a federal agent. We can request to have you prosecuted in Guatemala for that. At the very least, you'll be recalled within twenty-four hours."

"This is a setup," he protests.

"Yes. Yes it is," I admit. "But we're not here for you. We want her."

"Who?"

"You know who. Marta."

Atilio shakes his head. He glances at the television screen and thinks it over for a moment. "Fuck no. I don't want any part of this."

"We just want to know where she is."

"Let me call my attorney."

"No. You touch your phone and that video goes out. You'll never work in government again. Plus we'll push for criminal charges."

He sobers up pretty quickly. "You don't understand. This woman is very powerful. She is also a very good woman. I don't believe the things you've said about her on television."

"Then you shouldn't be afraid of her," Knoll points out.

Atilio ignores him.

"Where is she?" I demand.

His situation is dawning on him. He's afraid of her, but even more terrified of getting fired and sent back home in disgrace. "It wasn't my choice. She has many friends in our Congress. The vice president has been to her orphanages."

"Damn." I suddenly get it.

"What?" Knoll turns to me surprised.

"Where she is. She's on Guatemalan soil. Isn't she?"

"Yes," says Atilio. "You cannot touch her. Without evidence, my government won't release her. Not now, not ever. She has too many friends."

"She's in Guatemala?" asks Knoll.

Atilio stares at the floor.

"No," I turn to Knoll. "She's in Miami. She's hiding in the one place we can't get to her. The one place she's legally safe, the Guatemalan consulate. Isn't that right?"

Atilio gives us a weak smile. "She is our guest." He points to the television. "This is beyond my control. But as I said, I don't think this woman would do the outrageous things you say. To try to kill the pope? This woman is a saint. Only a monster would do that."

70

THE GUATEMALAN CONSULATE is a twenty-thousand-square-foot mansion in Miami that was bequeathed to the country by a wealthy produce importer. Protected by a ten-foot-high fence, a US security firm keeps watch over the grounds while a staff of ten people work inside the building. The day-to-day business of handling passports and visas is managed in a more formal office space downtown. The Miami consulate is more of a showplace for entertaining influential guests and US politicians.

Our hopes of applying pressure on the consulate through political channels were dashed when Latin American newspapers started running stories about how we've wrongly ID'd Elena Lopez, a lowly widow of a Guatemalan physician who ran to the embassy when she was targeted by the largest manhunt in South Florida history.

The real Marta Rodriguez, the newspapers explained, was killed in the airplane explosion that may or may not have been caused when an unidentified federal agent fired into the engine and struck the fuel tank.

My bad.

"This is bullshit," replies Knoll as he reads another headline in the Spanish press.

In our command post, a slightly smaller building a block away, we've been keeping watch and waiting for her to make a move for several days. Right now, it's a test of patience. The news crews still show up to see if there's been any change. We still man barricades and search every car that comes and goes from the building.

By now, even the American press is entertaining the idea that this may be just some big FBI screwup and that we're trying to cover our tracks and create a scapegoat out of poor old Mrs. Lopez.

The fact that the Attorney General has said she's free to leave the US if she'll submit to a fingerprint test doesn't seem to sway those that would rather be stirred by conspiracy theories than logic.

The silver lining is this brought a tremendous amount of attention on X-20. The longer she's inside the compound, the harder it is for her to maintain her empire. It's only been two days, but we're hearing reports of assassination attempts by rival captains on her people. That's an indication they don't think she's going to get out anytime soon.

"How long is this going to keep up?" Knoll asks rhetorically. "The neighbors are bitching up a storm and filing lawsuits. I know we're going to get pressure to take down the barricades. Then what?"

"I don't know. The Guatemalan Congress has called three emergency sessions. Each time they seem to be bolstering more support for Rodriguez."

It's frustrating to know you've caught your suspect, only to be hampered by red tape, politics and a sensationalist press.

"And no fingerprint test?" He groans.

"They're convinced that would be faked." I push one of the newspapers toward him. The front page shows two side-by-side photos. One is Marta's Air Force picture. The other is the woman I saw in Tixato, but with slightly altered features, and shot in such a way to make her appear like a different person. She has much darker skin and different color eyes as well.

Her people are working hard to push the mistaken identity claim. Frankly, it's the smartest option. We've heard she's secretly using the same PR firm as Hamas.

Knoll and I have been kvetching about the situation for hours. He points to the consulate. "So what happens if we don't let her go?"

"That's my biggest fear. Right now she's using the diplomatic crisis to buy time. I'm certain she's just not sitting there idly. She could be planning an escape."

He nods. "If it were anybody else I'd brush that off. But her, she could hire a small military."

"Yeah. If we let down our guard or the Guatemalan government indicates they're losing interest, we're in trouble. It might get messy."

"Can't you do something magical?"

"Not without violating the laws of two countries."

"My biggest fear isn't that she tries to break out. It's that she buys off some judge here to give her enough time to get away."

"Want to go throw rocks?" I ask.

"Yeah. Sure."

It's our way of describing standing on the perimeter. We take a walk down the sidewalk and through the protective blockade. The house is invisible behind the tall metal gates. A CNN reporter doing a stand-up, pans the camera in our direction. I quietly move to the other side of Knoll so I'll be out of the shot.

"Thanks for using me," he mutters, noticing my tactic. "Get your fill from the helicopter-chase footage?"

"I forgot he was rolling," I protest.

"That's what they do. The funny thing on their shoulders? It's called a camera."

"Oh . . ."

"You talk to Ailes?"

"Briefly. His wife wasn't doing so good. But he says she's improving." Once we knew Marta was pinned down here, I gave him a call. He made me feel better about taking so long, telling me he wanted me to focus on the case.

Knoll nods. "He's a good man."

"He's a great man."

"Yeah. Yeah. You know, Blackwood, you don't do too bad when you don't have adult supervision."

I point to the hidden mansion and shake my head. "She's still not in custody. And now we're worried she might buy a WMD or worse to threaten her way out. The monster isn't dead."

"The pope is still alive. Nobody got killed at the stadium. I call that a good day. I can't say as much for the assholes she had working for her that got blown up. But I think you did pretty good."

"I don't know . . ."

"Shut up and take a compliment." His voice gets serious. "Want to know why I'm the only one of a select few that can put up with you? It's because you make everyone else feel bad."

"That's stupid. You're a great cop."

"I'm a good cop. I'm also a good father. I don't think I'm great at both. Maybe a better dad than others. My point is, other people would have pat themselves on the back a while ago and let things carry on. You didn't. Don't go saying that's because you're a cop. We're all cops. You keep at it for whatever tortured Bruce Wayne reason and don't stop. It's that drive that makes us all feel bad about ourselves."

I let his words sink in for a moment. Out of nowhere I speak up, surprising myself. "Did I ever mention my mother to you?"

"No. I met your grandfather and your dad when you were in the hospital. Never your mother. Why?"

"I . . . I just think sometimes that if I don't keep pushing myself, trying to do good things . . . I'd . . ."

"What?"

"I'd do bad things instead of good ones." I rarely talk about my mother. There's a lot to unpack.

Knoll has become a bit of an older brother figure to me. I feel okay telling him certain things. It's a different relationship than the one I have with Ailes.

"Bad? Now you're scaring me." He looks concerned.

I'd been thinking this over and over. "Take a look at Marta. If her life had been slightly different, would she have been a killer?"

"I think these things are born into us."

"Maybe. When she isn't running a cartel that kills and tortures rivals and innocents over territory, she's off saving orphaned kids."

"Capone liked to give out turkeys. Pablo Escobar threw money around. Hitler loved a parade."

"Yeah . . . but they did it out in the open. They did it to prove what good guys they were supposed to be. Marta does all this in secret. Noriega says they even found a trust designed to support those orphanages in case she dies. Does a bad person do that?"

"My dad liked to say character is who we are when nobody is looking."

"She's done plenty of awful things. She's complex. People are complex," Knoll points out.

"I guess that's what I'm saying. I'm complex."

"Not as much as you think. You always do the right thing."

I think about how little I did to reach out to Ailes when his wife was sick. "Not always."

Knoll nods to the police and FBI agents watching the perimeter. "There are a lot of good Catholic men and women here. I don't think they're going to let her get anywhere. Time to go home."

71

I'M LYING IN bed staring at the ceiling of my hotel room in Quantico. I still can't bring myself to go back to my apartment. My biggest fear isn't for my own safety, it's for that of everyone in my building. At least here in the hotel, I'm surrounded by visiting agents that have all taken the same pledge to protect life as I have.

I toyed with the idea of inviting the field agent from Wyoming I met in the bar back up to my room. He was cute, polite and capable of carrying on a conversation without making any kind of innuendo or reminding me that I was an attractive woman.

As weird of a place as I am in, it just didn't feel right. I've never been that type of girl. In the end we exchanged phone numbers and I decided to stick to old habits, rather than pick up new ones under stress.

I didn't pursue the agent for the same reason I never took up the pediatrician's offer of a date. Like Max, they all seem like nice men, the kind of guys you eat with at some restaurant you found on Yelp and maybe, if things work out, one day end up discussing pet names while strolling through Ikea.

I can't image describing to them the decapitated bodies in Tixato, or what went through my mind when I thought the Warlock or his people were going to kill me—or when I think at night about what he still might try to do to me. These are dark things. Sharing them with

men like that, nice men, that doesn't unburden me, it weighs down
on other people's souls. I'm afraid they won't understand, or worse,
they'll see me as an object of pity.

Normally I'd put my nose in a case file. But Breyer has me in
a holding pattern doing basic case cleanup, writing down all the
reports, cataloging evidence. I wasn't sure what the punishment
would be for going around him. Right now it seems to be obliv-
ion. I hope this is it, and not just a time-out while he thinks of
something more severe. I could find myself railroaded out of the
FBI if he really wanted, that or relegated to FBI liaison in the god-
forsaken hellhole of a foreign country's secret rendition center.

Maybe this anxiety is his real punishment. He's letting me
know how much power he has.

Damn him and his ego.

I thumb through the numbers on my phone and dial one.

Not just any number.

His number.

I've been thinking about him a lot. I feel like I'm on the edge of
a knife. I've tried to do what's right and I find myself ostracized
while my target is free.

I never knew being the good girl was going to be this . . . this
painful.

Nobody picks up.

Maybe that's for the better.

But as soon as I set my phone down, it rings.

"Can't sleep?" asks Damian.

"No."

"You might find it a little easier now."

"Why?"

"She's dead."

"What?" I bolt upright.

"There was a fire at the consulate. Marta died an hour ago.
They're waiting for confirmation. But it's her."

She's dead? That's it? I'm relieved and confused.

I get an uneasy feeling. "Damian?"

He knows what I'm thinking. "No. It wasn't me. Trust me. Seriously."

"What happened?"

"I'm sure your colleagues will have some more details in a few hours. I'm hearing on secure channels that people on the ground saw the fire spread from her room. She tried to climb out a window but it was barricaded."

"Who did it?" I can't imagine a rival gang risking the FBI perimeter to do this.

"Who do you think?"

"What do you mean?"

"You don't try to kill the pope and get away with it."

"You can't be serious?" I try to process all of this.

"What? The Church has never ordered anyone killed? Have you missed the last two thousand years? It may not have been the Vatican, but someone with close ties. These people have even killed popes that were a threat to the order of things."

Oberst immediately comes to mind. Would I put this past him? No. But the Catholic Church? "So this was revenge?"

"Maybe. Maybe they just don't want her taking a second shot."

"Damn . . ."

"There's another reason too . . ."

"What?"

"Think about it, Jessica; who did they just kill tonight?"

"Marta. What do you mean?"

"Why did all this start?"

I think back to the root of this case. "Because of Marty. Because they killed her brother. Because she blamed him."

"Because she saw him stand by as they killed her brother. In her hiding space, she watched the pope help kill her brother. It may have been an accident. It may not have even been him. But she believed it was."

"What are you trying to say?" I sense where this is going, but I want Damian to say it.

"I heard a whisper she may have been talking to an attorney about a deal," he explains.

"Her? A deal?" Is that her final option? Threaten to take down the papacy?

"She's got one hell of a bargaining chip with what she knows."

"I didn't hear anything about this." To be honest, I'm not surprised anymore by Damian's contacts. He's brilliant and doesn't have to play by the same rules I do . . . or try to at least.

"This is one of those lawyers you go to when you're a dictator who gets overthrown. High level. Just a rumor. Now it's nothing.

"My point is, Jessica, other than the pope, there was only one witness left to what happened that night. And now she's dead. As rich and powerful as she was, someone with a longer reach got to her."

Marta's death sinks into me. Despite my hatred of her, I wanted to see her brother get his justice for what was done to him. That meant seeing the pope investigated. I stood little chance of getting Breyer to let me look into that. With Marta dead, the only other witness to that night, there's zero chance in hell. "And a potentially guilty man goes unpunished."

"I think the fact that they went to great lengths to have Marta killed shows you how guilty he was. Speaking of which, have you heard from your mysterious friend at the Vatican?"

I don't ask how he knows about Oberst. "No."

"Ever wonder what he was doing in Hawkton that night?"

I had, and couldn't come up with anything that made sense.

"He knew what the pope feared. He wasn't there to see where Marty died. He was there to see if this was where the pope's biggest nemesis was born."

"You think he knew all along who was behind the Hawkton killings and Groom's murder?"

"It's the rational explanation."

"Nothing about this is rational."

"Finally, you're seeing things from my point of view."

Maybe. "Damian . . ."

"Yes?"

"Where are you?"

"Wherever you want me to be."

"I'll leave the door unlocked."

ACKNOWLEDGMENTS

S PECIAL THANKS TO my father, a federal agent, whose cases and incredible experiences inspired me and whose unwavering support encouraged me. Thanks to my brother, an FBI agent, for providing me with helpful information and forgiveness for the dramatic license I took. My literary agents Erica Silverman and Robert Gottlieb. My editor Hannah Wood, for her dedication to this book. Justin Robert Young, for his essential help on every stage of this book. Ken Montgomery, Mary Jaras, Brian Brushwood, Crow Garret, the Weird Things podcast listeners, Diamond Club <> , and the Mayniacs.

ABOUT THE AUTHOR

ANDREW MAYNE is the star of A&E's magic reality show *Don't Trust Andrew Mayne,* and has worked with David Copperfield, Penn & Teller, and David Blaine. He lives in Los Angeles. He can be found on Twitter and Instagram via: @AndrewMayne.

BOOKS BY ANDREW MAYNE

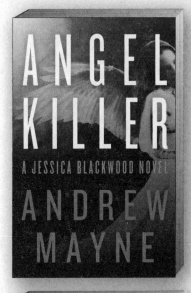

ANGEL KILLER
A Jessica Blackwood Novel
Available in Paperback and eBook

FBI agent Jessica Blackwood believes she has successfully left her complicated life as a gifted magician behind her . . . until a killer with seemingly supernatural powers puts her talents to the ultimate test. A mysterious hacker, who identifies himself only as "Warlock," brings down the FBI's website and posts a code in its place. It hides the GPS coordinates of a Michigan cemetery, where a dead girl is discovered rising from the ground . . . as if she tried to crawl out of her own grave. Born into a dynasty of illusionists, Jessica Blackwood is destined to become its next star—until she turns her back on her troubled family, and her legacy, to begin a new life in law enforcement. But FBI consultant Dr. Jeffrey Ailes's discovery of an old copy of Magician Magazine will turn Jessica's carefully constructed world upside down.

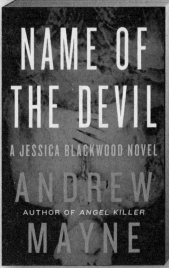

NAME OF THE DEVIL
A Jessica Blackwood Novel
Available in Paperback and eBook

After playing a pivotal role in the capture of the Warlock, a seemingly supernatural serial killer, agent Jessica Blackwood can no longer ignore the world she left behind. Formerly a prodigy in a family dynasty of illusionists, her talent and experience endow her with a unique understanding of the power and potential of deception. When a church congregation vanishes under mysterious circumstances, the bizarre trail of carnage indicates the Devil's hand at work. But Satan can't be the suspect, so Dr. Ailes and Agent Knoll, turn to the ace up their sleeve: Jessica. She's convinced that an old cassette tape holds the key to the mystery, and unraveling the recorded events reveals a troubling act with far-reaching implications. The evil at work is human, and Jessica must follow the trail from West Virginia to Mexico, Miami, and even the hallowed halls of the Vatican.

BOURBON STREET BOOKS